Love Before Covid

by Greg Scorzo

2nd Edition
First printing 2021

Edited by Lizzie Soden
Typeset by David J V Reeves
Cover illustration by Melania Fraser-Hay
Cover design Antonia Attwood

Matador
Unit E2 Airfield Business Park,
Harrison Road, Market Harborough,
Leicestershire. LE16 7UL
Tel: 0116 2792299
Email: books@troubador.co.uk
Web: www.troubador.co.uk/matador
Twitter: @matadorbooks

ISBN 978 1805140 030

British Library Cataloguing in Publication Data.
A catalogue record for this book is available from the British Library.

Printed and bound in Great Britain by 4edge Limited
Typeset in 10.5pt Garramond by Troubador Publishing Ltd, Leicester, UK

Matador is an imprint of Troubador Publishing Ltd

Dedicated to:

Frank Zappa,
Rainer Werner Fassbinder,
Jordan Peterson,
and The Beatles

CONTENTS

FORWARD

This book comprises a set of dialogues in the form of real-time conversations, and it is written by a philosopher. This is important because in a sense this is a contemporary re-visiting of the dialogue form of philosophical fiction.

The reader will encounter exchanges in some ways reminiscent of the style of Plato's Socratic dialogues. Those dialogues were a genre of Greek Philosophy developed during the Classical Period, three-hundred years before the birth of Christ.

As the 'wise' philosopher Socrates wandered around the marketplace, he stopped and had in-depth dialogues with various people. Each word was transcribed by his greatest pupil Plato.

In this book however we have no Socrates character telling the reader what to think. We are on our own. Scorzo lets us think for ourselves.

Incidentally, Socrates unfortunately was later executed on charges of heresy and the corruption of young minds. In fact, he was both a powerful inspiration as well as an irritant to the Athenians of his day. I have my suspicions that Greg Scorzo may well both inspire and irritate in much the same way today.

Unlike in Plato's transcript, the dialogues and the characters you will be meeting are purely fictional. Unlike traditional fiction, however, you could argue that the characters still partake in detailed and dense philosophical exchanges – sometimes without mercy.

The exchanges between the main characters, just like in real-life conversations, can be puzzling, repetitive, passionate, nonchalant, frustrating, occasionally erotic, and sometimes violent or deeply disturbing. Therefore, they are also inevitably laced with paradoxes and contradictions. This is because the characters, much like all human beings, are imperfect.

Humans have always grappled with, but never been able to come up with any answers to the philosophical questions related to love, whether they be regarding adult or child relationships, conditional or unconditional love.

Since the times of those early Greek philosophers, academic philosophy has in a number of ways, been obsessed with knowledge about abstract topics and the ability to turn that knowledge into precise, often technical sounding theories that read like engineering manuals.

Yet with deeply human topics like love, what makes these topics philosophical is their inability to be completely converted into precise knowledge. We can't, without a huge amount of arrogance, create highly detailed theories of love which attempt to convert love into the sort of knowledge one expects to see in theories about macromolecules.

Scorzo's book accepts that there are no simple answers to these problems. However, I'm not sure his book believes in that premise dogmatically. It seems to be saying that the answers to these questions are too complicated to act like we can solve them by doing regular theory. Perhaps we must grapple with them by doing things that are a bit more experimental, because we don't know anywhere near as much as we think we do regarding love's expression in romance, procreation or sex. But even there, I'm only guessing.

This is why *Love Before Covid* is certainly not a happy gallop through a fictional romcom. It's also why it's not a philosophy book, even though it kind of is.

The ingredient that always seems to be omitted from the mix, when we are pondering human relationships, is that these relations involve imperfect and unpredictable human beings interacting with each other. Because people are so flawed, it's sometimes difficult to draw a hard line between abuse and non-abuse, healthy and unhealthy love, or the difference between bullying and someone standing up for themselves. We can all slip into becoming self-centered and inconsiderate. In our intimate relationships we are often so overcome with emotions we cannot always think clearly or make rational judgements.

Love, after all, resides in the mystical, unconscious, and divine realms – in our wildest dreams and worst nightmares. The narratives herein also pose the question of whether we can really understand love unless we are faced with the most disturbing aspects of own minds, often fed by our own life experiences. Do we need to confront our darkest secrets? Do we need to face our shadow side in the Jungian sense – the side of our personality that contains all the parts of ourselves that we do not want to admit to having? The paradox is that only through the effort to become self-aware can we begin to acknowledge our dark side, where any semblance of love can be perverted and made monstrous. Can we only understand what love could be when we face what it shouldn't be? And do we need to be truly loved in order to find the courage to do that?

This book takes the reader on that journey through those conscious and unconscious worlds in the form of the experiences and psyche of one man and his complicated relationships with his past and present; his relationship with his mother, his ensuing struggle about whether to be a father, and his sexuality set against changing gender expectations and contemporary gender politics.

Although we may believe that love is the force that binds us together, we all have different viewpoints regarding what form it should take and how it feeds our major relationships and decision making. There are even some people who don't believe love is the force that binds us all together, as it is merely a manifestation of our minds and therefore not real. This book resides in those opposing conceptions.

The book is also loaded with both psychological and ideological paradoxes. It often pushes the convictions of the reader to their limits.

The plot is essentially centered around a particularly imperfect individual involved in the game of love in the early 21st century. He is not only on a path to learn to love others, but also to learn to love himself. This book forensically scrutinises and teases out particular arguments and moral judgements within the boundaries of his psychology, as well as the society in which he lives.

Moral imperatives around romance, procreation and sex are always changing and this book explores (among other things) how they have been impacted by the politics of the early 21st Century.

The interactions of the characters mirror the paradoxical attitudes, hypocrisies, beliefs, and emerging ideologies that have evolved in this time. The book's plots are also a journey through our contemporary moral maze, regarding how love is becoming impacted by ideology in these polarised political times.

The romantic relationships in this book happen in a way where they are not only embedded in a particular personal history, but in the context of a rapidly changing landscape – a landscape that includes the tearing down of traditional male and female relationships, as well as changing notions of gender expectations and definitions.

Whether the reader decides these developments are 'much needed' or 'needless' is totally up to them. The most important thing is not to reach agreement, but to grapple with understanding why other good human beings may see things differently and not necessarily be evil people.

But, on the other hand, it may be necessary to deal with the fact that bad people with bad ideas do exist. It may be important not to deny that they exist, in the name of affirming how complex and ambiguous the world is. Much like abuse, evil is real. And so is the mistreatment of people in the name of love. Sometimes things aren't that complicated, and it can be cruel (and enabling) to say that they are. Even in today's morally complex culture wars, one side may clearly be in the wrong.

The Wider Context

This period of unprecedented social change has occurred in every dimension of human interaction. In the digital age, with the demise of organised religion and the pace of technological advances in the areas of communication and health, humanity is being hurled forward at breakneck speed, with arguably far less of an overarching, shared moral roadmap.

The moral roadmap has been ripped up into tiny pieces and people are running around chasing and trying to catch all those little bits of paper blowing about in the wind.

We are a deranged eclectic bunch, scrabbling around, fighting over those confetti like pieces and desperately trying to fit them together again, even though essential bits have fluttered off into the air and into the hands of our enemies. Elsewhere other people are also trying to piece them together to make some kind of sense, but with essential bits missing.

Very few are curious enough to see how, if they worked together and combined their particular pieces of paper, they could again create the big moral roadmap picture of shared, consensual viewpoints for the greater good. When we have no shared routes for the forces of love, in which the most essential elements can find their way, this inevitably leads to trouble.

Meanwhile, the tech companies, media, big business and global financial industries are selling us their high-tech GPS moral mapping systems.

Their maps are created by compiling only the landmarks that they chose to include. These are unapologetically programmable systems which can be very seductive in that they give simple answers. Many of us seem to be buying into them, albeit on a subconscious level, uncomfortably and against our better nature.

Certainty and inflexibility about our particular moral view of the world does not bode well for any relationships that involve love. Neither does inflexibility about uncertainty. The reader will have to find where the balance lies.

The future 21st century briefly depicted in this book will most certainly not be the future we find ourselves living in. However, aspects of that future may certainly become part of our actual future. On the other hand, we may nullify these aspects, if we recognise, rather than feverishly deny, that they already exist in the attitudes of the present.

The 21st century has tended to see a fair amount of hatred and intolerance emerge in the rhetoric concerning gender politics. Therefore, this book focusses on romance, procreation and sex. Our best selves depend on love in order to thrive. Yet one can't understand the nature of contemporary romance, procreation and sex, without also presupposing a certain gender politics. At the same time, one can't understand which gender politics are best, without also having an implicit understanding of romance, procreation and sex. This paradox is easier to grapple with, when the zeitgeist makes a good faith attempt to acknowledge it.

In the early 21st century, western culture has been in the grips of a mood, where for the first time in many decades, human relationships have been held hostage to ideology. Sometimes this ideology is explicitly political. Other times it appears deceptively apolitical, because the demands it makes on human relationships are about things as ubiquitous as etiquette and the promotion of mental health.

This book's central narrative pre-empts the COVID 19 pandemic. It also pre-empts the zeitgeist ruptures of both Brexit and the election of Donald Trump, in 2016. It is in many ways charting and reflecting the fear filled attitudes, uncertainties and beliefs that got us there. In the digital age of 'woke', are we now in an age increasingly devoid of love and purely led by hate and outrage?

Bullying on social media, informed by computer algorithms, is becoming synonymous with activism. Each range of beliefs are being sold to us as the ultimate truth. Many people do not want to be contradicted and defend their positions. In some extreme cases, they choose to drown out dissenting voices. This has sadly divided us, causing ruptures amongst lovers, family, and friends. Love and compromise can too readily be replaced by entitlement and war.

We encourage the dark and painful side of love when we abandon the things which make love safe, fair, and capable of sustaining trust and mutually agreed upon goals. Love becomes destructive when bereft of kindness, respect, compassion, understanding, empathy or forgiveness. When we only focus on ourselves and are blindly led by the constructed narratives of the establishment elite, we drift away from loving our fellow humans. The understanding we are all part of a much bigger picture, and a shared spiritual realm, is forgotten at our peril.

Today, we can see the perversion of love by tribal ideology, where love is only love, if it's for someone within our tribe and abuse is only abuse, if it's done by someone in a 'position of power'.

Like love, this book does not follow the easiest and most direct route. This is because our love relationships never follow the easiest and most direct route. It seems that individuals that learn to manage both good and bad experiences with equanimity have the most fulfilling and meaningful lives and relationships.

Maybe there will never be an overriding agreed moral map; maybe there never was. But can we at least begin to have new conversations when our previous battlefields of love have been blown apart and fragmented into hundreds of potentially lethal pieces?

The Future

I have infinite hope for a future after this seismic cultural shift. The global handling of the pandemic has shone a light on the need for human connection and compassion. Unlike many of the uncharitable assumptions about fellow human beings made by those who benefit from those narratives, we have seen, over and over again, that people are on the whole, patient, kind and wanting to support those who are suffering in their communities. We have all been reminded of how precious our loved ones are. We can arguably learn to see more clearly where we were heading, simply by slowing down, reflecting on and acknowledging the wrong turns we seemed to have been making. We can move forward in a more connected, caring and kind-hearted manner. After all, moral wisdom is connected to a love of humankind. Our own intimate relationships are informed by that moral wisdom, (or lack of it.)

However, like this book, that learning experience will be a head-fuck. *Love Before Covid* brilliantly starts some much-needed conversations. It is ridiculously thought provoking and you will obviously have your thinking provoked in a different way to me. It can resonate with you and disgust you in equal measure.

I am still ruminating.

And for that reason, I strongly recommend that *Love Before Covid* be read in tandem with other people, in much the same way as any perplexing and bewildering film should be watched with others and consequently discussed. This is important because the fiction elements of this book are very much influenced by cinema, particularly the films of directors like Rainer Werner Fassbinder, Lars Von Trier and David Lynch.

Great cinema affects us powerfully because the combined effects of images, music, dialogue, lighting and sound can illicit deep feelings and emotional responses which cause us to reflect on our own lives. We are often left bemused and needing to discuss how we interpret the film, with fellow ponderers and mind wanderers.

Unlike shared cinematic experiences, books create our own unique mental feature films. Hence, the look of the characters and scenery, facial expressions, body language, accent, tones and intentions of the dialogue, can never be shared experiences as we read. They are always unique to our own imagination because we all interpret fictional narratives through the direction of our own inner filmmaker – the one who resides in our subconscious.

However, this book offers the possibility of a convergence of sorts. Although each reader will imagine their own mental movie of the book's dialogues; each chapter raises questions and provokes responses in readers that can be shared and discussed, well before the book is finished. Each chapter is arguably a short film unto itself. The films always look and sound different, depending on the mind from which they are created.

Love resists knowledge about love, because we master love by doing it, rather than theorising about it. Yet there is a paradox: bad ideas about love can make us do it much worse.

In the domain of love, ideas are relevant, even if comprehensive knowledge is still impossible.

– Lizzie Soden (COTO – Culture on the Offensive.)

INTRODUCTION

Dear Reader,

This book is both a novel and a collection of dialogues.

The dialogues in this book are moving thought experiments. They portray elaborate, unfolding situations which, at every turn, force the reader to examine his or her philosophical intuitions about a range of topics, situations and people.

These dialogues are not merely fiction told in dialogue form. Fiction is drama that may (incidentally) comment upon or examine philosophical issues. Drama normally involves scenes in which dialogue is used to set up and advance a plot. In this book, plots are used to set up and advance the dialogues of the characters.

The dialogues in this book are something like philosophy, because the dramatic elements are merely a pretext to examine the philosophical issues raised by the situations in which the characters talk to each other. The dialogues happen in real time and are often deeply frustrating, as dialogues are in real life. Reading this book, you may feel as though you are listening in on a series of intensely private conversations.

If you heard any of these conversations in real life, you might feel as though you were being privy to a rather juicy bit of gossip. Or you might call the police. You might shed a tear. You might even masturbate (and then read some more traditional philosophy).

Like any piece of philosophy, the writing in this book is sometimes laborious. However, unlike traditional philosophy, the aim of this book is to explore, rather than resolve, a set of philosophical concerns. There are even issues raised in this book that many well-regarded philosophers find quite silly – too silly to take seriously as philosophy.

Love Before Covid is thus an attempt to invoke the gadfly spirit of Socrates in the 21st century, largely by abandoning the academic tradition he inspired. This book is expected to irritate both lovers of philosophy, as well as lovers of fiction. It may even irritate people from both sides of the 21st century's culture wars.

The plot concerns the love life of a man called Joe Pastorious. However, this book does not tell you what to think of Joe, nor does it sing his praises by showing how much he conforms to the most cherished values of our time. Like many non-fictional people, Joe Pastorious is a complex human being. You may love him or hate him. To call him imperfect would be an understatement, but the degree to which he is likeable or loathsome is thoroughly up to you.

There are other fictional people in this book who also dialogue, but they only make appearances because of our protagonist. In some ways, they explain Joe, much more than Joe explains himself.

Joe Pastorious met his wife Janet Waverley in the autumn of 1999. Joe and Janet fell in love in a place called Leicester, which is a small city in the middle of England. Many things have been said of Leicester, but one thing that is not said enough is it is a fantastic place to fall in love. It was the perfect place for Joe and Janet to fall in love. This is true, despite the fact that Joe and Janet's love is anything but perfect.

To truly understand the imperfect nature of this love, we must go back, not to the beginning, but to an imaginary autumn of 2002. It's not enough to merely remember this autumn, from the vantage point of an imaginary present. We instead must adopt this moment's perspective, seeing its events as though they were happening now.

When in the present, one can't predict the future. Hence, the present is the best place to understand imperfect people. When people are dead and we know absolutely everything they have ever done, this creates an illusion of certainty the present thankfully wipes away. You can't trust a corpse, because there is nothing about a corpse's decisions that may hurt or disappoint you.

A living, breathing person is not like this. They are only capable of being truly understood, when they can be trusted. They can only be fully trusted when their future is uncertain.

Love's power resides in the romance of this uncertainty.

PART ONE: ROMANCE

"The common prejudice that love is as common as "romance" may be due to the fact that we all learned about it first through poetry. But the poets fool us; they are the only ones to whom love is not only a crucial, but an indispensable experience, which entitles them to mistake it for a universal one."

- Hannah Arendt

"Everyone must decide for himself whether it is better to have a brief but more intensely felt existence or to live a long and ordinary life."

- Rainer Werner Fassbinder

"You're going to pay a price for every bloody thing you do and everything you don't do. You don't get to choose to not pay a price. You get to choose which poison you're going to take."

- Jordan Peterson

1. ROMANCE: In the Beginning

Joe is attracted to Janet because she is beautiful, charming, interesting, intelligent, creative, courageous, funny and a great flirt. Janet is crazy about Joe for similar reasons. They have great conversations together.

Joe thinks Janet is an amazing lover and has had more fun with her than he has had with any other person in his entire life. Janet shares all of Joe's important religious and political views. She has similar tastes and shares his hobbies. Joe can spend long periods of time with Janet without either of them getting on each other's nerves.

Janet helps Joe improve some of his weaknesses. Joe and Janet like most of the same people for the same reasons. Janet always considers Joe's advice and very much respects his opinion. She often gives Joe good advice and shares a perspective with him that helps him see things he is sometimes blind to on his own.

Joe and Janet take their commitment to one another very seriously. Both of them will only leave the relationship if they think it isn't working. Joe and Janet only say things to each other that are true. They do this while frequently combining their honesty with tact, so as to not hurt the other's feelings. Joe is always there for Janet when she needs him and vice versa.

Janet has recently started going to therapy to work on problems she has with impulse control. Although Janet doesn't believe that her problems have recently put her in any serious danger, she still worries they could get out of control in the future. After several months of therapy, Doctor Gillian Adams diagnoses Janet as a psychopath. After listening to Doctor Adams explain the reasons for this diagnosis, Janet agrees that she is indeed a psychopath.

Janet is a thrill seeker with completely self-interested motivations. On the inside, Janet cares about people she likes only because of what those people can give her (whether it's good company, loyalty, practical help, fun experiences, stimulating conversation, good sex, advice, or money). She doesn't care at all about people she dislikes who give her nothing. Janet can cry on cue to get what she wants.

Nevertheless, she believes that she is a benevolent psychopath. She believes she is a benevolent psychopath because she never tries to harm anyone. She also tries never to treat anyone unfairly. This is because she understands that harming those she dislikes and treating them unfairly would give her less of what she wants in life. It's not because she cares about the suffering or unfair treatment of people she dislikes.

Janet cares about Joe more than anyone because Joe gives her what she wants from a boyfriend. Most of the time, Joe is good company, fun, sexy, a good conversationalist and someone who is very supportive of her.

Janet also cuts Joe a lot of slack.

She allows him days when he is grumpy and isn't good company because she understands that realistically, you can't have a committed relationship unless you cut your partner some slack. However, if Joe were to permanently stop giving Janet the things that make her happy in their relationship, she would not hesitate to end it.

Janet knows that behaving selfishly and using people makes people she cares about dislike her. She knows behaving this way would especially make Joe dislike her. Because of this fact, she mostly behaves in a way where she doesn't appear selfish or like she is using people.

Sometimes she slips up.

On a few occasions, Janet does show Joe behaviours he finds quite selfish. However, the amount of selfish behaviour she shows Joe is comparable to the amount of selfish behaviour he shows her. He isn't a psychopath.

Nonetheless, when Joe finds out about Janet's diagnosis, he feels frightened, overwhelmed and confused. He's also feeling impulsive.

2. ROMANCE: Self-Interested Love

On the evening of November 5th, 2002, Joe decides to share his feelings with Janet, shortly after both of them have eaten a poorly cooked Mexican takeaway.

It is 7:48pm.

Joe: I don't really know how to say this… you know I love you. You know I think you're the most amazing person I've ever known. But you being amazing isn't going to solve this problem.

Janet: What problem?

Joe: It's difficult for me to say this, but I think our relationship is unhealthy.

Janet: (confused) What?

Joe: It's not coming from the right place. It's twisted.

Janet: I don't understand. We enjoy each other's company; we rarely fight; we help each other grow; we like and dislike most of the same people; we have the same values; we have great sex; we make each other laugh. It's a great relationship, Joe. It's the relationship most people wish they had!

Joe: Janet, you're just listing things that benefit you.

Janet: Of course they benefit me.

Joe: Yeah and if they all stopped, what would you do? You'd fucking leave.

Janet: That's so not fair. If I had a brain injury and became a horrible person that made you miserable, you'd leave as well. You'd have every right to.

Joe: But I'd be leaving because you became a different person. You'd leave for far less than that. What if I couldn't have sex with you anymore? I dunno, if I got prostate cancer and couldn't get erections or something?

Janet: You know I'd be devastated if you got cancer!

Joe: You'd be devastated because of what it would mean for YOU. Then you'd be gone.

Janet: I wouldn't be gone because I love too many other things… your companionship, your sense of humour, your kindness and sensitivity. Honestly, we could work around the sex, Joe. That's not a problem. There are always ways to get each other off. You don't need erections for everything.

Joe: But what if I suffered a depressive episode? What if I couldn't be terribly good company to you for a number of years?

Janet: I'd help you through that the best I could. What else could I do?

Joe: You'd help me through it because you'd be waiting.

Janet: Waiting for what?

Joe: You'd be waiting for me to come out of the depression and be charming again. If you thought I wouldn't, you'd throw me away, like so many other things you toss in the bin.

Janet: If you were miserable for the rest of your life, what kind of relationship would this be? I'd be your bloody carer! You'd hardly ever talk to me. That wouldn't make either of us happy.

Joe: Janet, that's what a good relationship sometimes is. You know, 'through richer, through poorer, in sickness and in health' and all of that.

Janet: You're talking shit. That's one person looking after someone else – someone they were in a relationship with.

Joe: Janet, that's what you do for the person you love if they get ill. Love isn't about being entertained. It's about learning to love the person you're with, no matter what they do or become.

Janet: Joe, nobody wants to love a person who can't communicate with them. Nobody wants to love a person who's become so damaged that they can't be nice to anybody.

Joe: That's where you're wrong, Janet. You're so wrong it's disturbing.

Janet: Don't be silly. If you had a depressive episode, I couldn't know for certain you'd never come back to me, so it's very very unlikely I'd leave you. I'd endure at least a few years of unpleasant behaviour, so you don't have anything to worry about. If you ever get depressed again, we'll work through it. I love you and I'll do whatever it takes to make sure you get better.

Joe: But why is it in your self-interest to spend years of your life with someone so unpleasant? Why not just leave and find someone who isn't depressed?

Janet: Because you're so cool and interesting and sexy and sweet and lovely and wonderful and deep and just… amazing to me. You're everything I've ever wanted in another human being, Joe. I love being with you, whether you're depressed or not. Your company is the best thing in my life. There's nothing in it that's better.

Joe: But you only love me because of my company! What about loving me for me?

Janet: (loudly) I do love you for you! You make me feel happy. Why is that so terrible?

Joe: You should love me even if I don't make you happy, Janet.

Janet: Okay, let me understand this… you think people should stay in relationships even if those relationships make them miserable. You think people should suffer for love. If people are happy and no one's suffering, something's wrong. Is that what you're trying to say to me?

Joe: All good relationships have rough periods – times where partners don't make each other feel good. That's life, Janet. You can't just leave a partner during a rough patch because it's in your self-interest!

Janet: But in a situation like that, it wouldn't be in my self-interest to leave! I'd lose the chance to fix things. I'd rather put up with a few shit years than blow up everything that we've created together. Do you honestly think I would risk ending us that easily? You are my fucking soulmate!

Joe: I can't be your soulmate, Janet.

Janet: What?

Joe: No one can be your soulmate because you don't understand love. You only value me because of what you get from me. You don't love me unconditionally. I don't even feel like you love me anymore. I feel like someone… you've hired to be your boyfriend.

Janet: I haven't hired you. I chose to be your girlfriend because I love you. It's always been like that.

Joe: How can you love as a psychopath? How can you really love me if all you love about me is what I give to you?

Janet: I can't love you unless you give me things I love. You do give me them, for the most part. That's why I love you, Joe. That's why I've always loved you. It's very simple.

Joe: That's the problem, Janet.

Janet: (frustrated) I don't understand why that's a problem! I really don't.

Joe: That's another problem. You're digging your own grave here, Janet.

Janet: I don't know what you want me to say.

Joe: It's not about what you say or how you behave. It's about your motivations. You're scared of us ending… because you're scared of having to find someone else. You're scared of not having someone to talk to every night. You're scared of not having someone who makes you happy. That's not real love, Janet. That's shallow.

Janet: This is ridiculous.

Joe: What's ridiculous?

Janet: You're breaking up with me… because of what amounts to a philosophical difference in the ways each of us interpret love.

Joe: (loudly) It's not a fucking philosophical difference! I'm telling you how I feel!

Janet: I'm sorry, I didn't mean to–

Joe: (interrupting) I don't care if you're sorry… I can't do this! I do love you but I can't be in a relationship with a fucking… someone who's not right in the head! I wish my love for you could overcome this, but it can't! You can't do a healthy relationship! It's sad and horrible but it's the truth, Janet. You don't love. You take.

Janet: Well, I don't agree with you. The fact that I'm "not right in the head" has nothing to do with you not wanting to be with me. We get along great! This is just about a difference in how we interpret love and it's a difference that doesn't even matter, Joe. Think about it: think about all the conversations and the cuddles; think of all the fun and the joy, the help, trust, admiration, respect and support that happens every single day! Think about all the deep fucking love in those things. Doesn't that mean anything to you?

Joe: It's not proper love if one of us can't really love.

Janet: (agitated) That's not fair! How am I supposed to prove that I can love you? Isn't the last three years proof enough of that?

Joe: The more I watch you fight me, the more I can see how this relationship really works.

Janet: What are you on about?

Joe: You're trying to fucking manipulate me! That's what people like you do!

Janet: (loudly) Why is it wrong for me to fight to keep you? You're the one thing in my day that makes everything else work. Being with you makes me feel like my life means something! You're the one who's off your head if you think I'll let you ruin that without a fight!

Joe: It's hardly a fight that shows you actually care how I feel.

Janet: (shouting) Of course I care how you feel! If you were miserable, you wouldn't be with me!

Joe: Exactly. With you, it's all just a self-interested calculation. Where's the love in that?

Janet: Joe, from the bottom of my heart, I love you in the only way I know how to love anyone. This is how I love. I know I'm not perfect and the way I love isn't perfect. But I can only be what I am.

Joe: I know and appreciate that, Janet.

Janet: Do you? Do you really?

Joe: Yes, but that's why it's not good enough. I need real love from a woman. Not what you give me. What you give me is wonderful but it's not real. I wish I could be happy with it… but I just can't.

Janet: (looking very sad) All I've ever wanted was for you to be happy with me. I don't want you to be with me if I don't make you happy. I'm only with you… because I thought we made each other happy.

Joe: We did make each other happy before I found out who you really are.

Janet: (distressed) My God, Joe.

Joe: What?

Janet: (beginning to cry) Hearing you say these things to me… it hurts. I don't normally feel things like this. I can't even describe it. I don't even know how to handle emotions like this because–

Joe: (interrupting) We are finished, Janet! Don't waste your time trying to change my mind. We are over and there is nothing you can do about it!

Janet: (tears streaming down her face) What are you doing? Why are you saying these things to me? I thought I could trust you. You said I could trust you not to hurt me like this!

Joe: (angrily) You don't fucking know what hurt is! You're only upset because I'm inconveniencing you! You'll get someone else tomorrow and act like you never met me! You're only sad because I'm depriving you of something that amuses you, something you like to depend on. You're losing one of your favourite wind-up toys! That's all that I am!

Janet: (crying) It's not like losing one of my favourite wind-up toys! It's like losing my favourite toy that I've ever known, the toy that makes me feel like I'm capable of being a happy person!

Joe: (yelling) I'm not a FUCKING toy, Janet! I'm a person! I'm not here just to keep you happy!

Janet: (crying) But I thought I made you happy!

Joe: You did make me happy… but your happiness and your hurt have nothing to do with me.

Janet: (crying) Anybody in my position would be hurt right now!

Joe: Anyone who has empathy would be hurt if they were in your position. I don't even know whether you actually have empathy. That's one of the reasons I can't be with you.

Janet: (crying) All I have is what I give you.

Joe: (shouting) It's not good enough!

Janet: (wiping away tears) I still can't understand why.

Joe: Because you're just using me! You're totally selfish!

Janet: (passionately) But I try so hard to never make you feel like that! I work so hard not to come across like I'm acting selfishly or being insensitive or using you or anyone else! I have to try way harder than you to adequately project that. It's incredibly exhausting but I do it because I love you!

Joe: (adamantly) That's the problem! It's a projection. It's not real. You're acting out all this behaviour just to keep me from leaving you! I understand the effort you put into it but that effort doesn't change a thing. You're not a giver. You're nice to our friends but it's only because of what they give you. If they ever pissed you off, you'd hate them!

Janet: That is not true. I love our friends for the same reasons you do. Do you mean to tell me that if they all turned into obnoxious dickheads, you'd still meet them for coffee?

Joe: I'm not talking about them turning into dicks! I'm talking about them just doing something that really made you angry. If any of our friends really upset you, you'd hate them. You wouldn't want them in your life anymore. They wouldn't get any second chances. That's the kind of person you are.

Janet: No, I'd be nice to them and have them in my life if I knew it meant a lot to you. I'm not a fucking twat.

Joe: That doesn't matter. You still wouldn't care about them and that's how we're different. If they made me angry, I wouldn't automatically reject them. I could be patient.

Janet: Haven't I been patient with you?

Joe: That's different! You're patient with me because I'm your boyfriend.

Janet: I've been very very patient with you, Joe. In fact, I'm being patient with you right now.

Joe: That's because when you're patient with me… you get serious fucking rewards. Your friends only get to stick around if they don't upset you. All you care about is whether or not they're pleasant company, whether you can have interesting conversations with them. You don't value them because of who they are.

Janet: (defensively) I value my friends because they're the people I like, Joe. I can't be a good friend to someone if I don't like them. And it's hard to like someone if you don't have much in common or have totally different values. That's normal.

Joe: (loudly) No, it's not! You yourself said you don't care about what happens to people you don't like!

Janet: (frustrated) But I only dislike all the same people you dislike!

Joe: But I could feel bad if someone I didn't like got cancer. You couldn't!

Janet: Why the fuck does that matter?

Joe: It matters because it means you can't empathise with people who wind you up! You can only feel affection for people when they give you things on your terms! That's why you can't understand friendship any more than you can understand love. You're a psychopath! You can behave like a nice person but it's all an act! On the inside, you're rotten.

Janet: (crying again) Jesus, you're being cruel…! How can you say that to me?

Joe: Those tears of yours are a good example of what I'm talking about. You could just be acting now. How do I know?

Janet: (crying) You don't trust me.

Joe: Nope.

Janet: (crying) Even after everything we've been through together, you still don't fucking trust me. Nothing I did was good enough.

Joe: You don't have a mind anyone can trust.

Janet: So it's my mind you can't trust. You love my behaviour but hate the way my mind works. Is that it?

Joe: I can only know your behaviour. I can't know you. I can't know whether I'm ever being manipulated or whether I'm in danger. Suppose you suddenly get upset and can't help doing something impulsive. I can't even imagine the crazy shit you're capable of!

Janet: Joe, what have I been like throughout our time together?

Joe: You 'behaved' really well. You 'behaved' like my soul mate.

Janet: Are you honestly saying you think I tricked you into believing you love me?

Joe: Yes, I do. I know you'd prefer it if I hid that from you, but I can't.

Janet: I wouldn't prefer that. I wouldn't want you to hide anything you were feeling about me that's important for me to know. You can tell me what I need to hear without being cruel about it, though. You don't have to hurt me like this.

Joe: I'm not trying to hurt you, Janet. I'm just being honest with you.

Janet: It feels like you're trying to punish me.

Joe: I couldn't punish you even if I tried! You have the thickest skin of anyone I've ever met. You have resilience a normal person doesn't. You won't be hurt by this experience. You'll learn from it like you always do. Nothing fazes you.

Janet: (with a look of despair in her eyes) Tell me what I'm supposed to learn.

Joe: (beginning to cry) Learn that normal people, people who aren't like you… we are incredibly imperfect. I'm not better than you just because you're a psychopath. I'm horrible on the inside too. It's not as if I'm a wonderful person and you're a monster. I'm not a good boyfriend for anyone. When you realise that, you'll move on and be happy. I'm too damaged.

Janet: (still crying) Then why can't you try and be better? Why can't you try to love me? Why can't you just accept and love my behaviour towards you?

Joe: You are lovely in your behaviour, but I don't just want lovely behaviour in a girlfriend. I want a lovely person. You can't be that because your brain's deformed. You were one of nature's mistakes. You're like poison fucking candy. Your mum should have aborted you.

Janet: (crying) Oh God, that's such a nasty thing to say to someone! I don't understand why you have to–

Joe: (interrupting) I'm sorry but I can't help being honest–

Janet: (interrupting) Have I ever said anything cruel like that to you?

Joe: No, you haven't…

Janet: (angrily) I don't say mean things like that to you because I love you! You're my favourite person and I would never want to hurt you if I could help it!

Joe: You're not my favourite person anymore, Janet.

Janet: (wiping away tears) I suppose I'm not.

Joe: Yesterday you were my favourite person. You were my favourite person because you acted like my best friend. You behaved in a way that made you seem exciting and amazing, like someone completely unlike anyone else on this planet. It was a great performance. That performance is the reason we lasted this long. But I can't keep giving you what you want from me. It's doing my head in. I can't put up with you being nice to me… so you can get me to do things for you.

Janet: (wiping away tears) I'm not nice to you so I can get you to do things for me! Being nice to you gives me pleasure. I get pleasure from being with you! I enjoy watching you be happy. I always have, Joe.

Joe: Yeah, you either manipulate me or give yourself pleasure. Do you think I want to waste my life in a relationship with someone like that?

Janet: (loudly) I can't do anything other than that! I can't do anything other than be me!

Joe: That's why you need to stay the fuck away from me.

Joe breaks up with Janet.

3. ROMANCE: Forgiveness

After breaking up with Janet, Joe is devastated. He spends the next six months in a depression. During that depression, he tries to contact Janet in order to salvage something like a friendship with her. She ignores his calls and emails. By the winter of 2003, Joe has gained three stone. He is ashamed of his new body but can't motivate himself to lose weight. Joe is beginning to wonder if he made the right decision when he broke up with Janet.

At the start of the following year, Joe's mother Jodie Green is diagnosed with bladder cancer. In the span of a few months, Jodie transforms from a feisty and acerbic woman into a mournful and despondent victim of a torrid terminal illness, frequently delirious because of the constant painkillers she requires in order to get through each day. By June of 2004, Jodie has made peace with the fact that she doesn't have long to live.

During the final week of July, a weak and ailing Jodie requests to see all the people in her life that meant something to her. She wants to wish them well, to thank them for being a part of her life and to apologise for any pain she has caused them in the past. Jodie even requests to see Janet, despite the fact that Janet is no longer in a relationship with her son. Joe sends Janet an email explaining the situation. Janet does not respond. Joe sends Janet a second, more histrionic email pleading with Janet to meet him for lunch to discuss a potential visit with Jodie, at Glenfield Hospital.

After this second email, Janet reluctantly agrees to meet Joe for coffee (but not lunch) at 1pm, on August 7th, 2004. Janet is in a particularly foul mood that day. She's not only deeply irritated by the hot weather of this particular August afternoon; she has also just found out that a graphic novel she wrote has been rejected by the publisher she most wanted to accept it.

Shortly after 1pm, Joe and Janet are the only customers sitting at a table, smoking cigarettes outside a trendy sandwich shop called 'Stones'. Stones is in St Martin's Square, a small courtyard in Leicester's City Centre. Despite the heat, Joe and Janet are sitting at this outdoor table because it's still cooler outside than inside. Joe and Janet's table is also the only outdoor table bathed in the shade of a nearby tree.

Stones is virtually empty today, despite its popularity. There are only three customers inside the building, all with their backs to the window. Joe and

Janet are the only customers who happen to be sitting outside, facing St Martin's Square. St Martin's Square seems generally deserted, as most people are watching the Caribbean Carnival procession snaking through the middle of the City Centre. Even in Stones, one can hear deep reggae baselines drowning out the sounds of a cheering crowd of everyday people, accompanied by their enthusiastic children. There's going to be a firework display later this evening.

Unlike the families at the Caribbean Carnival procession, Joe and Janet are not everyday people. They are fairly unique among the citizens of Leicester, as both of them can't stand being around fireworks, children, or community festivals. Any public event that attracts everyday people is normally an event they stay far away from. This is why Joe and Janet hate the Caribbean Carnival. They also hate townie pubs. They can't stand the house and cheesy pop music tracks, typically played in Leicester night clubs. They even dislike dancing in public.

Joe and Janet do, however, like Gay Pride. This is because they approve of Gay Pride, politically. But just because they approve of the politics of Gay Pride, this does not mean they would ever go to Gay Pride. Gay Pride, after all, normally contains lots of cheesy pop music, as well as dancing in public.

If Joe and Janet ever go out to hear live music in town, they will either attend jazz, electronic, or experimental music concerts. Their musical tastes have remained this way, even though they no longer talk about music together. Since they broke up, they no longer have conversations.

August 7th, 2004, is the first day since November 5th, 2002, that Joe and Janet are having a conversation.

It is 1:16pm.

Joe: Thank you for meeting me here. I know it's awkward, but I really appreciate it.

Janet: I know you do.

Joe: Look, before we go any further, I just wanted to say how sorry I am. I hated saying all those things to you.

Janet: That didn't stop you from saying them.

Joe: (speaking slowly) I know and I'm just... so sorry so much of it was insensitive and horrible. I just freaked out, really – I couldn't handle the diagnosis. I started worrying about not understanding you. I couldn't make sense of my feelings. It was stupid, I was stupid and said some unbelievably awful shit.

Janet: (looking down) I can't even tell you how much you hurt me.

Joe: (emphatically) And that was the last thing I ever wanted! I never ever wanted to hurt you, Janet.

Janet: Then why'd you do it?

Joe: (sadly) When I said you were just… pretending to be a good person, I think I was almost… verbalising my fears about the diagnosis. I was mad. I was worried my experience of you being so wonderful was just this… big illusion.

Janet: That's ridiculous, Joe.

Joe: I know it is. I know I should have trusted my experience of knowing you. That fucking diagnosis made me feel like I couldn't trust or understand anyone! I was in free fall. I couldn't make heads or tails of the world!

Janet: (abruptly) Then you should have waited until your head calmed down before you made any major decisions!

Joe: Yeah, ideally. But the reality was you suddenly told me you were a fucking nutter, Janet. Psychopaths aren't nice people. They're cold conniving bastards. That's what people think… when they know you've been diagnosed that way. You're a movie villain, basically.

Janet: (loudly) But you shouldn't have thought that! You knew me intimately, Joe. You saw me nearly every day. We lived together for two years!

Joe: I know this, Janet. I know I made a huge mistake.

Janet: Nearly every day, I had fun with you, brainstormed with you, went for walks with you, gave you advice, asked for your advice, wrote with you, listened to music with you, watched films with you, talked to your friends, made you laugh, made you orgasm. I even bathed you when you were depressed, for fuck's sake!

Joe: You did do all that… and it was incredible.

Janet: (indignantly) I was incredible! I held you when there were tears in your eyes, always. I calmed you down when you were anxious! I was even patient when you were behaving like a child. I was fucking loyal to you when I didn't have to be!

Joe: I know you were.

Janet: I put up with shit most people wouldn't have even understood.

Joe: (with deep regret) You were amazing, Janet. There's no two ways about that.

Janet: So your fear of me was bigotry.

Joe: (looking down) Maybe it was. I don't know what it was, really. All I know is it was wrong. I hate knowing what I did.

Janet: Does that mean you want me to feel sorry for you?

Joe: No, I just want you to know how sorry I am.

Janet: You emotionally destroyed me, Joe. You happily tossed me aside 'cause I have patterns of behaviour that deviate from the socially accepted habits of normal people. And you don't even like normal people!

Joe: I'm not asking for sympathy. I just wanted to explain to you why I reacted the way I did.

Janet: (adamantly) You reacted the way you did because you lacked the decency to see what was right in front of your face for three years!

Joe: Maybe I wasn't strong enough… but it's hard finding out your partner is a psycho without it making you doubt shit. I mean–

Janet: (interrupting abruptly) Hearing about my diagnosis didn't 'make' you do anything! You chose to reject me because you couldn't do the decent and humane thing of trusting your actual experience of me!

Joe: Well, yeah, but anyone would doubt their experience of a partner if they got a psycho diagnosis. Come on, Janet. Think about how you'd feel if you were me.

Janet: (sarcastically) I can't do that, remember. I'm a psychopath.

Joe: (sighing) Janet, I was scared of you. I was fucking frightened and I only did what anyone would do.

Janet: Yeah, anyone who let fear cloud their judgement, anyone who let cowardice push them into bigotry.

Joe: (frustrated) You don't have to keep saying it! I know it was horrible! It was bigoted and it was nasty and I still hate myself for it, okay? I hate breaking up with you more than anything I've ever done, Janet. It's torn me up inside! I can't even describe how much pain I'm in because I lost you, but how I reacted is how anyone would react!

Janet: It isn't, Joe. It's not normal to turn into a horrible bastard when you're afraid of something you don't understand.

Joe: Unfortunately, it is. And it's normal to think you might not be able to cope in a relationship with a psychopath! It was a horrible mistake, I was a complete twat, but it was still understandable, under the circumstances.

Janet: (emphatically) No it wasn't! You were fucking sadistic! You said I was a shitty partner for you, that I didn't understand love and friendship and that I was only 'behaving' like a nice person!

Joe: I've said worse to other people, Janet. It wasn't even that bad. With my dad, I once said–

Janet: (interrupting loudly) You said I was rotten on the inside and that my mum should have aborted me! You said my brain was deformed!

Joe: You have to translate me sometimes, I–

Janet: (interrupting again) I've never been hurt like that by anyone in my whole fucking life, Joe. I loved you and trusted you and you made me feel like I should fucking do myself in! I would never do that to you and I'm the one who's supposed to be dangerous!

Joe: (sighing) I know that. I totally misjudged everything and made the worst choices – the worst choices I've ever made about anything. I wish I could take back everything I said that night. It was like a different person came over me.

Janet: That's an excuse. It wasn't a different person. It was you.

Joe: (softly) It was the side of me I'm ashamed of.

Janet: Well, no side of me would ever say those things to you, no matter what diagnosis any therapist gave you. I went out of my way all the time to express my feelings to you tactfully. I always made a huge effort to treat you with kindness!

Joe: I know you did. You were wonderful and I regret what happened every day, Janet. I've had to go to therapy about this. I'm on anti-depressants. I've been in bed for weeks on end.

Janet: (shaking her head) You got off easy peasy compared to me.

Joe: (irritated) Look, I understand you're cross, but you don't realise or even understand what I've had to go through without you even bothering to return my calls or emails. You don't know how hard I've worked with my therapist to even be sitting here with you!

Janet: You should have worked harder to stop yourself from turning into a lump of lard.

Joe: (frustrated) I know that. I know I look like shit, but this is the best I can do right now.

Janet: The best you can do?

Joe: (defensively) I've been suffering from a depression! I struggle to get out of bed, let alone do anything. The only thing I can manage is comfort eating and that's obviously not good for me. I totally lost my sense of portion control. It's emotional eating that's doing me in, so that's what I have to work on. I'm trying to break out of these habits so I can slim down!

Janet: (sarcastically) Nice one! I never knew chocolate cake for lunch was soooo healthy.

Joe: (irritated) Losing weight doesn't mean you can't have a piece of cake! It's the calories you eat throughout the day that matter!

Janet: Whatever.

Joe: (sighing) Look, I can only do what I can to try and get my life back together at a pace that works for me. I'm trying my best to just get back to normal! I can't do it all at once. I'm trying to learn how to cope with daily routines. I haven't been able to write for the past year and a half!

Janet: I can see where this is going. You want me to feel sorry for you.

Joe: You're not hearing me, Janet.

Janet: You want me to see how unattractive you've made yourself. You're going to say that the reason I should feel sorry for you is that you're riddled with guilt about what you did to me. The guilt has made you feel lazy and useless and so you have become lazy and useless. But I can rescue you. You need my love to make you whole again. Is that where this is going?

Joe: I'm obviously not explaining myself well. I'm not looking for sympathy.

Janet: If you don't want sympathy, then why explain yourself to me at all?

Joe: (with deep sadness) I guess it's part of the closure we never had. It's something like healing.

Janet: Well, of course. You can feel healed if you think I might pity you.

Joe: (frustrated) No, it's not like that!

Janet: Then tell me how it is, Joe.

Joe: (with tears in his eyes) I don't care whether you accept my apology! I have to apologise for me. If I can apologise, I know that I've done everything I can to atone for my mistakes. I'm sorry, Janet. You can take or leave my sorry. I still have to say it.

Janet: You always play the victim. It's pathetic how manipulative you are.

Joe: (sarcastically) Thanks for all your understanding and empathy.

Janet: (angrily) You don't get any empathy! You can't bear the pain of knowing you betrayed me. So you want forgiveness when you deserve fucking hate!

Joe: Fair enough, Janet. I do want your forgiveness.

Janet: (with contempt) And then when you figure out that an apology isn't going to give you your precious forgiveness, you apologise anyway. Why? Because it makes YOU feel better, you fucking hypocrite!

Joe: Why am I a hypocrite?

Janet: (loudly) Because you're apologising for YOU! Not for me!

Joe: I'm apologising because I hate knowing I hurt you, Janet.

Janet: (loudly) You being sorry has nothing to do with you asking for my forgiveness!

Joe: (loudly) Of course it does!

Janet: Did it ever occur to you that it might make me feel good not forgiving you? Did you ever think that perhaps forgiving you might be harder and more painful than simply forgetting you?

Joe: (indignantly) You forgave me for plenty of other things I apologised to you about before. I don't see why you can't forgive me now.

Janet: I forgave you because I loved you then! I knew I had to put up with some of your idiotic behaviour because that was the price I had to pay for your good side. I was happy to pay that price before you betrayed me.

Joe: (ardently) I didn't betray you! I got scared and was unfair to you. But I never wanted you to be in any pain! I love you, Janet. I'm still in love with you!

Janet: Why should I believe you?

Joe: (pleading with Janet) I don't know… All I can tell you is how much I hate everything I did. The things I said to you when we broke up… they were the worst mistakes of my life! I didn't mean any of them and I wish with all my heart that I could take them back! Every single one of them!

Janet: (loudly) You can't take them back! You said them! You're going to have to live with what you've done. Take some responsibility!

Joe: I am responsible! I was in the wrong, but I've definitely paid the price for that. I've suffered so much since then, Janet. I just don't want to keep on suffering. I wanted you to come here so we could put this behind us.

Janet: (abruptly) Don't fucking lie to me! You wanted me to come here so I would visit your porn star mum.

Joe: So are you gonna be permanently angry with me now?

Janet: (irritated) I'm angry because I'm here and can see you! Not having you around is best for me 'cause then I don't have to deal with the anger. I'm not normally an angry person and I find anger unpleasant.

Joe: Then why does me wanting to come to a truce make you so angry?

Janet: (rolling her eyes) Because you betrayed me! How many times do I need to keep saying that? If someone betrays another person who loved them and they feel bad, they deserve it! You're not even taking that on board. You think you deserve a truce with me and you don't!

Joe: I never said I deserved a truce with you.

Janet: Then why do you want one?

Joe: (sighing) I don't know… I thought it could be the best thing for both of us. I know there isn't a chance of us getting back together, but I thought maybe we could still be friends. I thought holding a grudge would just… make everything more difficult.

Janet: There's absolutely nothing wrong with my grudge, Joe. It's deserved.

Joe: That doesn't matter. Holding a grudge eats you up inside. For me, anger's a destructive emotion. I would think it is for most people.

Janet: (with disdain) That just means holding a grudge eats YOU up inside. But you're not the one with the grudge, it's me. And my grudge suits me fine, thank you.

Joe: So you think you can be happy hating me and writing off how important a part of your life I was?

Janet: (sarcastically) How kind of you to pretend to appeal to my self-interest, Joe. I'm sorry to inform you that unlike you, I can be very happy hating you.

Joe: Well, that's not healthy. Hate isn't a healthy emotion.

Janet: (loudly) It's not a healthy emotion for people like you! I'm a psychopath, remember. I don't need to forgive people because I'm too weak to carry a grudge!

Joe: It's not a sign of weakness to forgive people, Janet. It's a sign that you love people.

Janet: Forgiveness is a necessary evil. In this case, it's not necessary. I don't love you anymore. You saw to that.

Joe: (frustrated) But forgiveness isn't evil! Forgiveness is love. That's what love is!

Janet: Everyone you love makes mistakes. You cut them slack or else you can't love them. But if they betray you and the love is no longer there, you no longer have to forgive their transgressions. In fact, there's nothing that feels nicer than hating someone when they bloody deserve it. That's justice.

Joe: You sound like you enjoy hating me as much as you liked loving me.

Janet: It's not even comparable, Joe. On most days I don't even experience the hate I'm feeling now. I don't waste my time thinking about you.

Joe: I think you're confusing hatred with hurt.

Janet: (loudly) I can tell the difference between hate and hurt, you fucking bellend!

Joe: Janet, come on, you know you don't really hate me. You know you wouldn't be here if–

Janet: (interrupting) You don't know anything about me! You assume that because of the time we shared together that I'll always have a fondness for you. I don't succumb to sentimentality that easily, Joe. I have dignity and self-respect that you don't. You can't make me love you if I choose not to!

Joe: (incredulous) How much more suffering do I need to go through before you think I got what I deserved? Do you want me to be debilitated for the rest of my life? Would that make you happy?

Janet: No, that wouldn't be proportionate to what you have done.

Joe: What would be then?

Janet: You gave up and betrayed me. You deserve no love, no forgiveness and no sympathy from me. Ever. If that makes you miserable for the rest of your life, good. You deserve to suffer. If you're in any pain because of me, that's your problem. As far as I'm concerned, you brought it on yourself.

Joe: (disgusted with Janet) So you see yourself on some righteous crusade to see if you can be happy at my misery?

Janet: I don't need to be on a crusade to do that! I'm a psychopath, Joe. It's very easy for me to be happy your mum's got bladder cancer. If it was up to me, she'd also have breast cancer. That woman is nothing but a violent and emotionally abusive cunt. I would say I'm glad she's dying, but now I'm not so keen on you being relieved of that burden. You deserve a few more years of that nasty overbearing bitch.

Joe: (shocked) What the fuck, I can't believe I'm hearing this from you! I've never seen you like this before.

Janet: It's about time you did. It's about time you actually listened to me.

Joe: (shaking his head) You're being so cruel, it's unbelievable.

Janet: (angrily) You think I'm the one who's being cruel? You're the one who made excuses for her while she terrorised your dad every day! She nearly beat your sister to death, and you never told the authorities! You never told your stepdad about any of that when he decided to have a baby with her! You think that's not cruel?

Joe: (loudly) She's my mum and she's dying!

Janet: (loudly) And she's having the luxury of dying! She's only forty-eight. She deserves to live at least another thirty years in unbearable pain! That would be fair, given how she's treated the people in her life. She deserves all the fear and anguish and suffering that cancer can give a person!

Joe: If you feel that way, why did you come here today?

Janet: Because I thought it would be fun to tell you to your fucking face that I'm happy we'll all be rid of her. That woman is nothing but a nasty piece of shit. If I could get away with it, I'd have killed her years ago.

Joe: (taken aback) Wow…

Janet: (smiling sadistically) You're not the only one who can be cruel when they want to be, Joe.

Joe: I guess not. But if this is the real you, I'm glad I'm finally seeing it.

Janet: (yelling loudly) The real me chose to be a good partner for you! And the effort I made to be benevolent and kind was an effort you will never understand!

Joe: You were manipulating me, Janet.

Janet: (shouting) I changed my fucking personality for you!

Joe: (loudly) I didn't want that!

Janet: (yelling angrily) Yes you did, you prick! I gave you everything you ever wanted from a woman!

Joe: (loudly) I didn't want you to have to work so hard to be a decent human being! I wanted that to be natural! I didn't want to be with someone whose kindness was totally at odds with their nature. That was terrifying!

Janet: (loudly) You're lying! I never scared you before I told you about my diagnosis! I know when you're scared and when you're not. I could make anyone frightened for their life in two seconds! You know I don't fucking do that! I work hard to be kind.

Joe: (emphatically) That's fake! It's not kindness if you have to work at it!

Janet: (loudly) It absolutely is! You made me work to be kind every fucking day!

Joe: (shaking his head) It wasn't genuine. You forced yourself to be kind, but I didn't want to be with someone who has to force it.

Janet: (angrily) I forced myself to be kind because I loved you! I never lied to you about anything you needed to know! I never hurt your feelings; I listened; I was patient; I was forgiving. It nearly killed me, but I did it all because I wanted to be good for you! You made me feel things I didn't understand! I never loved anything that hard! I hurt myself for you, Joe. I fucking hurt myself!

Joe: If it hurt so much, why didn't you split up with me?

Janet: Because I would have died for you, Joe. I loved you more than anything! You were my soulmate.

Joe: I obviously wasn't if you hate me now.

Janet: (with disgust) No, you were and then you ruined it. That's why I'll never be able to love you again. That's why I can't stand you now. You're a fucking traitor.

Joe: (definitively) We were never soul mates, Janet. My soul mate is a person who can forgive weaknesses in other people. You aren't that person.

Janet: (loudly) I forgave you for all the days you were grumpy and sulky! I forgave you for that horrible fucking family you made me be nice to because it was your family and I loved you!

Joe: I don't think you ever really did forgive me. You pretended to forgive me so I would be more fun and amusing for you later. You tried to manipulate me into being whatever you wanted. That's not a soul mate, Janet. That's a dog trainer.

Janet: (boiling with anger) You lying fat piece of shit! I can't believe what a sad fucking excuse for a human being–

Joe: (interrupting) I was right about you! I was right about you not knowing what love is! Love is about forgiving people who hurt you. Love is about even being able to forgive people you hate!

Janet: (shouting) Fuck off! That's abuse! That's the love you have for your mother! She spent most of your childhood beating and humiliating you and you won't stop loving her! You're pathetic!

Joe: Would you lower your voice please?

Janet: (loudly) Make me, you fucking coward!

Joe: So I'm a coward because I choose to forgive my dying mother for her faults?

Janet: (angrily) You're a coward because you eat shit from the women that are supposed to love you! You think love means tolerating abuse. That's why you're pathetic! That's why you weren't good enough for me.

Joe: (indignantly) No, that's why I'm better than you, Janet. I'm not a psycho. I can be human in ways you can't. I can love people unconditionally. I can give love to somebody like my mother. I can love her even after all the things she's done to me!

Janet: That's 'cause you have no dignity. It's sick what you let her do to you.

Joe: (passionately) It's not sick! I'm loving the woman who brought me into the world! And I'm forgiving her because she needs to be at peace with herself.

Janet: You're forgiving a woman who tried to rape you. She only stopped when you met me.

Joe: (defensively) My mother never hurt me as much as she was hurt by her own parents! That was all she knew when she raised me, but her illness is changing her, Janet. I can see her differently now that she's dying. I can see her good side for the first time. She's very vulnerable. I can see vulnerability in her for the first time!

Janet: (rolling her eyes) She doesn't have vulnerability. She nearly killed you when you were a kid, sexually abused you when she got tired of kicking your face in and now wants you to forgive it all because she's dying. She's a nasty piece of work.

Joe: (loudly) But she wasn't always like that! She could be fun sometimes.

Janet: You were only pretending to have fun to placate her because you were scared and you wanted to shove down how much you hated her. That's your coping mechanism.

Joe: (frustrated) I know it is... I know she made a state of her life... but she tried her best to be a good mother, Janet. She wanted to love me, even though she couldn't do it very well.

Janet: She should have been sterilised, Joe.

Joe: (looking down) I don't care. I can't hate her. I can't hate the woman who gave me my love of books. She introduced me to jazz and Bergman films. She taught me how complicated people can be!

Janet: She's not complicated. She's an evil bitch. Evil people do evil shit because everyone always forgives them.

Joe: (loudly) That's bollocks! Everyone needs the chance to be forgiven when they leave this earth, Janet. It doesn't matter who they are or what they've done! My mother's a human being!

Janet: (loudly) Your mother's a fucking cunt! You're delusional if you think you should forgive her for anything! She deserves to die knowing you and everyone else who had the misfortune of knowing her hates her! It's not fair to forgive someone when they deserve to be despised. It's not fair to all the people who deserve to be loved!

Joe: Janet, she's my mum! She doesn't have to apologise to me for anything. I don't think she necessarily deserves to be forgiven for all the things that she's done to me, okay? I can't deny how much she hurt me and my sister. But I don't have much time with her and I love her... I love her and so I want to forgive her.

Janet: Yes, and reward her for her life of hurting people. That's unjust and insane.

Joe: You can't apply justice to human relationships.

Janet: (categorically) Nothing is more important to me than justice.

Joe: (angrily) That's because you're fucking arrogant! No one can be perfect all the time! If you can only forgive people when they deserve it, people can't ever grow and change!

Janet: (loudly) Rewarding bad behaviour doesn't make people change! It enables them! If the only reason people change is they get a reward, they haven't changed! They've just blackmailed you!

Joe: (shouting) But that's what most people are like!

Janet: (angrily) It doesn't matter! If people can only be nice by getting rewarded for being horrible, they don't deserve rewards. They deserve contempt! You reap what you sow!

Joe: Janet, if what you're saying is true, no parent should ever love a child.

Janet: (even more disgusted with Joe) God, I expected so much better from you. But hey, maybe we were never soul mates. I need to be with a man with enough self-respect to avoid becoming such a slimy fucking coward. You were such a waste of my time, Joe. I'm so glad I can see that now. I'm so glad I can see that I made the mistake of loving a man who thinks abuse is love.

Joe: (even more disgusted with Janet) You don't understand people!

Janet: (loudly) You don't understand abuse!

Joe: (loudly) Ordinary people can't live up to your high standards! You can't love people if you can't cut them slack for not being perfect!

Janet: (shouting) Your mother abuses you and that's what you think love is! You won't stand up to her! You won't tell her to stop punishing your father! You make the people she hurts feel like you're against them too! That's the kind of person you are!

Joe: (loudly) I'm a person who loves people!

Janet: No, you're a spineless piece of shit, just like she always said you were. That's why you can't hate her. You like being abused. That's what this is! You probably would have stayed with me if I was more like her.

Joe: (deeply hurt) Jesus, you're making me feel horrible, Janet.

Janet: (loudly) Good! I wish you felt worse!

Joe: But I can still love you. I can. That's the difference between my mind and yours, Janet. I can forgive you for everything you just said about Mum.

Janet: (sarcastically) Yes, you can forgive me for telling you Jodie Green is trying to take advantage of you. How kind of you, Joe.

Joe: (contemptuously) I can forgive you even though I think you're a selfish, nasty, pompous and unforgiving little bitch. And you know what else? I can still love you. I can still love you even though I never want to see you again!

Janet: (with disdain) I don't fucking care! You don't love people for the right reasons.

Joe: I don't love people because of reasons. No one has to earn my love.

Janet: And that's why you love your evil fucking mother. That's why you won't listen to me.

Joe: (sarcastically) Maybe I find it hard to put faith in the wisdom of psychopaths.

Janet: Well, you invited me here, so you're going to hear that wisdom anyway. You're an enabler, Joe. You're deluded. You're easy to manipulate. If anyone loves you in a way that's healthy, it freaks you out. That's why you left me. You didn't leave me because I'm a psycho. You left me because I was good to you! I was nice to you and you had to punish me for it.

Joe: (angrily) You weren't nice to me! None of your kindness was real! If it was real, you wouldn't hate me now! You could forgive me the way that I can forgive you!

Janet: (shouting) You didn't fucking forgive me! You said you didn't want to see me again!

Joe: (fed up and exhausted) Janet, go back home and leave me the fuck alone! Meeting you here wasn't a good idea. I can't talk to someone with a heart of stone.

Janet: I'm not leaving and neither are you.

Joe: What?

Janet: I'm not letting you out of this chair until I've said my piece.

Joe: (confused) What do you mean you're not letting me out of my chair?

Janet: (suddenly cold and steely) Just try and get up and see what happens, Joe. Go on.

Joe: Are you threatening me?

Janet: (with hatred in her eyes) Yes and I'm forcing you to hear me! You're not leaving this table until you've heard me! You're not getting up and going home until you've fucking heard me!

Joe: (rolling his eyes) I guess I don't have a choice then. I'll do my best to pretend I'm interested.

Janet: (angrily) Just shut up and listen to me, Joe! My brain is weird. I can't communicate, properly. The words are stuck!

Joe: What?

Janet: (sighing) …God is cancelling me out. It's giving me a false persona. It's backwards… I'm thinking in reverse.

Joe: What is that supposed to mean?

Janet: (suddenly tearing up) I can hate you… and enjoy the thought of you suffering… but at the same time, I can also love and forgive you… I can switch… I can love and be compassionate… if you just give me a minute…

Joe: (rolling his eyes) Oh fuck off, Janet…

Janet: (crying) I came here to tell you… about love and forgiveness… and my mouth won't open…

Joe: (loudly) I hate this shit!

Janet: (crying) I hate you but that's not why I came here… I needed to tell you something… about love…

Joe: (angrily) You can't love other people!

Janet: (crying loudly) My life meant something when I loved you… and you fucking took that away from me! I needed you!

Joe: You can't love anyone but yourself.

Janet: (crying hysterically) I gave you everything I had…! I gave you my life…

Joe: You're going to live alone and you're going to die alone.

Janet: (shouting like a crazy person) I MADE YOU FEEL LIKE YOU WEREN'T ALONE!

Joe: (calmly) My mother deserves to be loved more than you, Janet. She may have abused me for most of my life, but when she's nice, it's real. You're a fucking fake and don't deserve shit.

Janet: (screaming and banging her fist) I'M NOT FAKE!!! I JUST NEEDED YOU TO LOVE ME! I'M A GOOD PERSON!

Joe: (calmly while Janet sobs) Do you remember what you told me the day we moved in together? You said you didn't have empathy and that you'd never be remembered as anything other than an evil little cunt. You said you hurt people every day you don't do the right thing and kill yourself. I convinced myself you were wrong, but then I realised you actually told me the truth, Janet. That's why I broke up with you.

You're arrogant and intolerant and manipulative and you have no compassion for people who don't think like you. You don't even care about me or my mum! You care about justice and don't give a toss who you have to hurt in order to make it happen. You're sadistic about it – far more so than me. And that's why you're going to die alone, my love. You're going to die alone with justice while rest of the world lives with love. You're broken…

Janet: (crying desperately) I know I'm broken... but I love you so much, I–

Joe: (interrupting sternly) I know what you are now, Janet. You finally showed me what you are. I understand. The glasses are off. I can see the person sitting in front of me.

Janet: (sobbing and shaking her head) You hurt me… because of her… I should have killed that fucking bitch…!

Joe: (interrupting) No, Janet. I hurt you because I decided not to love you anymore. You're bad for me. I don't even like you now.

Upon hearing these words, Janet springs up from her chair in a rage, grabs Joe's cake fork and quickly shoves the fork into Joe's right eye. Joe screams as his burst cornea pops out of his eye socket and blood streams down his face.

As Janet looks at the fork protruding from Joe's face and realises what she's done, she starts to panic and run down the street as Joe's piercing screams merge with the sound of the deep base of the Caribbean Carnival's reggae beats. Janet runs away from St Martin's Square crying, muttering under her breath, "I shouldn't have done that. I love him. I still love him…"

Joe himself is rushed to hospital, shrieking and shaking. This is by far, the most physically painful and frightening experience of his twenty-seven years of life. But it's also more complicated than that. It changes Joe's mindset. On the one hand, he is both traumatised and terrified by Janet's act of violence. But on the other hand, Joe also feels it's incredibly important to get through the experience. The impending death of Joe's mother Jodie motivates him to be brave and live to the best of his ability, despite having a now permanent disfigurement.

Throughout the remainder of 2004, Joe suffers from post-traumatic stress disorder while having to get used to seeing with only his left eye. But he also motivates himself to resume his normal routines and manage his stress. By the beginning of 2005, Joe is regularly writing poems and short stories again.

Despite the terror of Janet's violence, it relieves him of the guilt and sadness he felt over having broken up with her. Joe feels his final conversation with Janet unequivocally verified that his worst fears about her were correct. For the first time, Joe starts to believe Janet has never been anything other than an evil person. He begins to believe she never really loved him. He starts believing she only manipulated him in ways that gave him the illusion he was happy with her.

It is ironically because of Janet's violence that Joe feels like he can move on with his life. He cannot, however, motivate himself to lose the three stone he has put on. Joe jokes about having an eye patch and tries unsuccessfully to become comfortable being a chubby man with a nice smile. He tries in vain to accept that he is no longer the gorgeous young man he was in 2002, a man Janet regularly bragged was "like a more chiselled version of Marlon Brando in a fifties Kazan film."

The day Janet managed to shove a cake fork into Joe's eye, Joe also managed to convince both the police and the doctors that the entire incident was a random attack by a stranger high on drugs. Joe felt ashamed of his decision to protect Janet, as it was unjust and possibly dangerous. But much like Joe's new eating habits, he felt it was not in his control.

Fortunately for Janet, there were no witnesses.

4. ROMANCE: Fantasy

By the beginning of 2006, Joe has become an excellent English teacher for adults with special needs. He not only teaches effectively but also inspires many of his students to become better people. He is proud of his work, which he finds much more fulfilling than his personal relationships.

After the weight gain and eye patch, Joe finds it much more difficult to find romantic partners he is attracted to. He is no longer confident about how he looks. Nonetheless, he still dates, hoping his good conversation and charming smile will compensate for his new appearance he jokingly refers to as "the tubby pirate look."

Being single and looking like a tubby pirate, Joe feels thoroughly unsexy. Yet this feeling is itself, quite familiar to Joe. Even as a gorgeous hunk in his youth, Joe felt thoroughly unsexy. He felt as though his dazzling looks were an ornate mask, a mask that could temporarily hide the loathsome personality underneath the fit exterior. Trying to live without this mask is incredibly difficult for Joe. Being single is even more difficult.

Between 2006 and 2015, Joe has two relationships. The first is with Pamela Cassard, an extremely intelligent university lecturer. Joe thinks Pamela is very plain looking. He is only slightly attracted to her. But because of his weight and eye patch, Joe thinks he should force himself to be attracted to Pamela much more than he actually is. Joe thinks a plain looking woman like Pamela is the best he can do.

Although Joe and Pamela have much in common, Pamela spends most of her time arguing with Joe. Within a few weeks of their relationship, it dawns on Joe that Pamela actually enjoys this. She likes constant debate for its own sake, saying things she doesn't believe because she finds debating so much fun. She'd much rather argue with Joe than give him a hug. Joe finds this incredibly frustrating and it makes forcing himself to be attracted to Pamela much more difficult. Yet Joe stays with Pamela for three years.

On November 1st, 2009, on the evening of their third anniversary, Pamela confesses to Joe that she has had three affairs throughout their relationship. The reason she gives for having had these affairs is that she was never physically attracted to Joe and needed to have sex with men who could satisfy her. When Joe hears this, he feels shocked, confused, angry, hurt and finally humiliated.

During that same evening, Pamela tells Joe she is leaving him for a French businessman called Roland. When Joe asks why she is choosing Roland over him, Pamela responds that Roland is more self-confident, industrious, intelligent and handsome. She also mentions that Roland has a much bigger penis. Joe is grateful Pamela doesn't say anything about his weight.

In the three years after Joe's relationship with Pamela, he gains another two stone. By the end of 2012, Joe is officially a fat man. He decides to stop dating altogether. By the early months of 2013, Joe is descending into another more severe depression where he suffers from constant intrusive thoughts: inner voices which scream that he is both a terrible failure and someone leading a thoroughly inconsequential life. Joe finds it increasingly difficult to fight these voices, feeling both thoroughly unlovable and like the idea of suicide is strangely comforting. Joe can't shake the deep suspicion that he isn't good at anything and that the world would be a better place if he were dead.

What eventually allows Joe's depression to lift is a chance encounter with a dance instructor named Loraine Klein on April 1st, 2013. Joe meets Loraine in Tesco Express, when she is yelling at some teenagers for purposefully tripping Joe and laughing as his groceries fly out of his hands. Loraine helps Joe to his feet, puts his groceries into a basket and even pays for the bottle of red wine that broke and splashed its contents across the white floor. Joe thanks Loraine profusely for her help and then offers to buy her a drink at a nearby pub called Firebug. Much to his surprise, Loraine says 'yes' and the two of them spend the rest of the night drinking and talking about how much they hate bad parents. Before Loraine goes back to her flat, she gives Joe a long hug that ends with a sensuous kiss on the side of his mouth.

By the next morning, Joe has developed an intense infatuation with Loraine. A mere two days later, Loraine confesses to Joe that she is falling in love with him. A day after that, Joe and Loraine begin a relationship together. Joe is elated.

However, Joe won't tell Loraine about either his struggles with depression, or his intrusive thoughts. He's afraid that if he's honest about his mental health problems, Loraine will suddenly see Joe as a tiresome burden, causing their blossoming romance to come to an end. Joe will do anything not to ruin this new relationship, especially since he feels both physically unattractive and like someone who doesn't possess most of the qualities women find desirable in men. A relationship with a woman like Loraine feels as if it's a miraculous accident, like something Joe doesn't really deserve.

Hence, it wouldn't be an exaggeration to say that for Joe, meeting Loraine was a cosmic event. Meeting Loraine felt like God's way of encouraging Joe to embrace his life with passion and enthusiasm.

In the first twelve weeks of his new relationship, Joe is happier than he has been in many years. However, by the middle of July 2013, Joe's happiness begins to fade considerably. Joe becomes acutely aware that Loraine is very different to him and can be very demanding.

However, Loraine is gorgeous. She is the most physically attractive woman Joe has ever been in a relationship with. In fact, Loraine is one of the most physically attractive women Joe has ever seen. Loraine is a tall brunette with fair skin and absolutely stunning features; she has an athletic, perfectly sculpted yet utterly voluptuous body. Loraine is more beautiful than most of the actresses, models and porn stars Joe has had the good fortune to gaze at. When she walks into a room, most of the men in that room feel nervous, while the women feel insecure.

Joe loves this almost as much as Loraine does.

Joe also appreciates the fact that Loraine is a very honest and straight forward person. He can always depend on Loraine to do whatever she says she's going to do. Joe never feels like he has to guess how Loraine is feeling. With Loraine, what you see is what you get; Joe always knows where he stands and this makes him feel safe.

Feeling so safe allows Joe to cope with the fact that he and Loraine are so different.

Loraine likes to spend most of their time together doing housework or running errands. She is intelligent but mostly talks about things that need doing. Joe finds most of their day-to-day activities together very boring. He finds the lack of intellectual conversation tedious. The frequent sex soon feels like a chore. By March of 2014, Joe is enjoying the company of his friends much more than he enjoys Loraine's company. Yet the relationship continues.

Simultaneously, Janet Waverley's career is skyrocketing. By 2013, she is not only a best-selling author of politically motivated graphic novels. She is also becoming quite a charismatic public intellectual.

Janet is regularly wheeled out by the BBC to make television appearances on current events programmes. She also does eloquent and heavily viewed vlogs in addition to making quite mesmerising speeches at rallies and university campus halls. Janet champions causes like universal basic income, the plight of the Palestinian people against Israeli aggression, feminism and green energy. She also does TED Talks on subjects like the benefits of globalisation, new revenge porn laws and body positivity.

Ten years after their last conversation, Joe still does everything he can to avoid Janet and is frightened by the prospect of coming into contact with her. No human being throughout his entire life made him more frightened than Janet did on the day she stabbed his eye with a cake fork.

On the night of April 3rd, 2014, Joe sees Janet on the panel of one of his favourite political discussion programmes, BBC's Question Time. Joe's first thought upon seeing Janet's image is just how little she has changed since he last saw her. Throughout the episode, Janet passionately defends the poor, exposes the ways immigrants are unfairly demonised and makes an impressive impromptu speech at the end of the programme about the importance of treating people as individuals. Joe agrees with everything she says and is amazed at how she uses rhetoric to make the other members of the panel look ridiculous when they try to argue against her. She does this without coming off as condescending or belittling. Janet even jokes with her opponents and compliments them about the few things they do say that she agrees with. The audience is enraptured by her.

By the end of the discussion, at least two of her panel opponents are, to the amazement of the host, beginning to question their own party lines and agree with Janet. As the closing credits roll, everyone on the panel is either smiling or has a look of astonishment on their faces. It seems as if two of the male panellists have quickly developed a crush on Janet; there's a subtle (but noticeable) air of flirtatiousness throughout the entire discussion. Janet's social charisma is like a lightning rod. This is the Janet that Joe remembers falling in love with. However, she is now even more articulate, witty and persuasive. If Joe didn't know Janet, she would be his dream woman. This scares the shit out of him.

This is the woman who, throughout their relationship, was able to hide a homicidal streak that shocked Joe when he finally saw it. This is the woman who stopped him in mid-conversation to disfigure him by casually blinding him in one eye. Joe's last memory of Janet is of her walking towards him with a cake fork in her hand, looking like she had a very deliberate desire to kill him. Joe thinks murder was her true intention and the fact that he merely lost an eye was a fortunate accident of circumstance. Now Janet is on his television: a terrifying and violent person who appears likeable… ridiculously likeable!

Joe hasn't been this frightened by something on the TV since he was a child watching The Exorcist. Yet he is transfixed and can't help but watch the show to completion. After witnessing Janet's appearance on Question Time, Joe still tries to ignore her, even though he sees her numerous graphic novels and essay collections popping up in his favourite book shops. He notices she is on several of his favourite TV programmes. Whenever he sees Janet in something he is watching, Joe switches to another channel or turns off the TV.

By the summer of 2015, as much as Joe doesn't want to admit it, his relationship with Loraine is incredibly difficult for him. Yet he stays with Loraine because he loves her and wants to honour the commitment he has made. Despite its difficulties, Joe can see himself benefiting from having Loraine Klein as a girlfriend. Loraine makes Joe a more punctual, disciplined person. Because of Loraine, Joe lives in a big house that is always clean, his finances are always in order, he has become an excellent cook and he is getting regular sex for the first time in years.

When Joe thinks about Loraine, he feels relief. He feels like he understands who she is. He never has to worry about what she is thinking because she tells him straight away when she is unhappy. Her bluntness can make Joe angry, but he never feels manipulated by Loraine. More importantly, Joe loves thinking about how many millions of men would be jealous of him every time they fuck.

Thinking about jealous men is the part of sex with Loraine that Joe enjoys most.

5. ROMANCE: Consideration

On the evening of July 28th, 2015, at exactly 8:23pm, Loraine Klein sits Joe Pastorious on their settee for a conversation about their relationship that Joe isn't expecting.

Loraine: Look Joe, I love you. You're a good man and a total sweetheart. I appreciate everything you do for us in this relationship. Do you understand?

Joe: I understand.

Loraine: But something feels wrong to me. It's hard to explain it.

Joe: Now I don't understand.

Loraine: It feels like something is… missing.

Joe: What's missing? We're with each other all the time; we support each other; we have a great sex life; we've created a beautiful home together; we love each other unconditionally. Isn't that what a relationship is supposed to be?

Loraine: I don't know. I'm not complaining about you. I'm not saying anything you've done is bad. I appreciate you and love you to bits.

Joe: Then what's the problem?

Loraine: (looking down) I worry that you only love me because you're supposed to love me.

Joe: (confused) What?

Loraine: I feel like you aren't getting your needs met in this relationship.

Joe: (adamantly) Of course I'm getting my needs met in this relationship or else I wouldn't still be with you.

Loraine: It doesn't feel like that Joe. You're always more excited to spend time with your friends.

Joe: Well, Loraine, I see you every day. I don't see them every day. Everyone in my life gives me something different that I value in different ways. But you should know that you're the person I love most. That's why I see you every day while I only see them two or three times a week.

Loraine: (sighing) I don't know, Joe. I'm confused.

Joe: Are you saying you don't feel loved by me?

Loraine: No, not at all. I feel very loved.

Joe: Then what's the problem?

Loraine: It's hard to pin down. Something just doesn't feel right.

Joe: (getting frustrated) What is it? What doesn't feel right?

Loraine: I feel like everything we do together isn't something you actually enjoy doing. It never feels like you're having fun. It feels like you're only doing what I want because you love me, like it's a duty.

Joe: Well, in life, no one excites you every day. But when you love someone, that doesn't matter. You make an effort to push on. You accept the limitations in the other person. You accept the limitations in yourself.

Loraine: I don't know. In theory, I agree.

Joe: What do you mean, 'in theory'?

Loraine: Joe, I like feeling like my boyfriend wants to be with me. I like feeling like my boyfriend's actually excited to spend time with me. It's not fun feeling tolerated just because somebody loves you.

Joe: (definitively) But I'm not just tolerating you because I love you! I enjoy you like mad.

Loraine: What do you enjoy, Joe?

Joe: Everything about you.

Loraine: I have a hard time believing that.

Joe: Well, I accept everything about you because I love you. I enjoy being with you, even with all of your flaws and all the ways that you're different to me. I wouldn't want you to change a single thing about you! That's how much I love you, Loraine.

Loraine: But why do you love me that much?

Joe: Because I just do! I chose to love you that much.

Loraine: But why did you choose to love me that much?

Joe: (thinking hard) It's hard to describe what makes you fall in love with someone. I was attracted to you; I felt good being around you; I loved how you stood up for yourself and didn't take any shit from anyone; I noticed how giving you are; I was impressed by what a hard worker you are. There are a million reasons why I fell in love with you.

Loraine: I know all of that. I'm not saying you're in the wrong or that I'm angry with you for any of it.

Joe: Then what feels wrong?

Loraine: It just feels like… you decided to love me when we got in this relationship.

Joe: That's what happens in any relationship.

Loraine: It doesn't feel like I've done much since then to make you want to love me.

Joe: That doesn't matter. I love you unconditionally, Loraine. That's the only way any relationship can last.

Loraine: Joe, do you feel happy in this relationship?

Joe: (emphatically) Of course I do! I'm loving the person I chose to love! I love you for you. I love you in all of your imperfections. I love you because of all the ways we're alike and all the ways that we're different.

Loraine: Joe, I get bored by the long-winded conversations you like to have. I can't stand most of the movies you like. I'd rather listen to cats wailing than hear most of your free jazz records. I don't understand your weird poetry; I'm not interested in the galleries you like to visit; I don't eat meat; I don't smoke. I'm not even a Leicester City fan… I hate football!

Joe: But I don't make you do any of those things, Loraine! It's fine. I don't eat meat when you're in the house; I smoke outside; I only read my poetry aloud with my friends. I don't expect you to come along to watch me read my poems at spoken word gigs because I know you'd be bored. I don't get offended, honestly. I don't need us to be alike in every aspect of our lives.

Loraine: Even in bed, I don't like any of that kinky BDSM shit you go for. I like to be penetrated and then I like to have a clitoral orgasm where you use your hands or your mouth to finish me off. I don't like role play games; I don't need to wear a costume to get off. A massage and a bath before we start will do me fine!

Joe: (reassuringly) I know all of that and I'm fine with it! You know I love having sex with you. You're beautiful. You're only focusing on the negatives. You're forgetting all the things we have in common.

Loraine: I know all the things we have in common, Joe. We both want kids; we like to cook Indian food together; we don't like loud parties or gambling; we quite like rainy days; we hate roller coasters. I like your big heart and you like it when I wear skimpy shorts and other men stare at my legs. We both like our cinnamon rolls every Saturday morning.

Joe: (sighing) You're describing all of that in a way where you're making it sound like trivial bullshit.

Loraine: Well, the way you act makes it seem trivial.

Joe: What do you mean?

Loraine: You make me feel like I'm your fucking daughter half the time.

Joe: (frustrated) What are you on about?

Loraine: On most days, regardless of what we're doing, I feel like you're doing it because it's good for us. I feel like you're doing it because you want to prove that you love me.

Joe: How does that translate into me treating you like a father?

Loraine: (pausing for a bit)...When I was a kid, my dad used to watch cartoons with me every day when I came home from school for an hour. I could tell he hated the cartoons and would much rather be doing something fun with my mother. I'd say, "Why aren't you with Mum? Wouldn't you enjoy that more?" He'd say, "I'm spending time with my daughter, Loraine. I love you."

Joe: Why do you hold a grudge against him for that? Of course he loved you.

Loraine: He loved my mum as well but there was a difference.

Joe: Of course there was a difference. You were his daughter and your mother was his wife.

Loraine: No, you don't get it.

Joe: Explain it to me then.

Loraine: He loved my mother because... he enjoyed her. Every time he was around her, he seemed like he was having fun. He never seemed bored. He never seemed... like he was doing something every day to make her happy. He always seemed like he was making himself happy just by being with her.

Joe: Well, if he never put himself out to make her happy, maybe he wasn't the best husband for her.

Loraine: No, he was a great husband for her. When he died, she was distraught because she lost the love of her life, Joe.

Joe: Well then, he must have put himself out for her at some point.

Loraine: Whether or not he did isn't the point! The point is, with me, he was bored. I was a kid. Children bored him. I couldn't talk to him the way my mother could. I didn't like any of the things he loved, but he loved me anyway. He sat patiently in the audience during my dance shows I knew he couldn't give a toss about. He was just proud because I was his daughter.

Joe: But that's what a good father does. Good parents sacrifice.

Loraine: I hated it.

Joe: Why?

Loraine: I didn't want to be tolerated out of love. I wanted to him to like me.

Joe: But he was your father. He wasn't supposed to be your friend.

Loraine: He spent so much effort trying to pretend he was enjoying my company. The fakeness of it made me feel physically sick. I tried to get away from him most of the time. I couldn't bear his pretending.

Joe: Loraine, most adults aren't interested in the stuff that excites their children. That's why parents take an interest in their children and love them unconditionally. You don't watch cartoons with your daughter because you like the cartoons.

Loraine: My dad's love for me didn't feel nice.

Joe: Your dad was there for you, even when he could have done the easy thing and ignored you. That's a good parent, Loraine.

Loraine: I wish Dad would have said to me, "Loraine, I love you because I am obligated to even though you bore the fuck out of me." Instead, he'd say things like, "I love you but I can't compare you with your mother. I love you both equally and differently."

Joe: Of course it was an equal but different kind of love. You were his daughter.

Loraine: Yes, one love was about duty. The other was about happiness.

Joe: I think you're being very hard on your dad. He seems like he isn't so different to most parents. Look at how you turned out. I think it's pretty obvious he did a good job with his daughter.

Loraine: (irritated) I don't care how much he loved me or how good of a job he did with me. I don't want to be loved like that by my own fucking boyfriend! I want to be liked! I want my boyfriend to be mad about me the way my dad was crazy about my mum! I don't want to feel I'm being fucking tolerated.

Joe: Don't you think you have some unrealistic expectations about what a relationship is supposed to be like every day?

Loraine: (sighing) I don't know. All I know is I don't like how this feels.

Joe: Loraine, no relationship can thrill both partners every day until death do you part. I think you have some kind of romcom fantasy of what a relationship is like. All romance is a work in progress and it's a struggle. All couples have days where they bore and frustrate each other. There's always periods where one of them isn't fun to be around.

Loraine: I know that, Joe.

Joe: The only way a relationship can succeed is if you're not just looking after number one. It's hard work and you have to fight for your relationship. Otherwise, you just become selfish. You piss your partner off and become inconsiderate. Forget monogamy; forget mutual support. When someone in a relationship just becomes 'me me me,' it's fucked. Self-centred people can't have relationships that last.

Loraine: (rolling her eyes) I know all of this, Joe.

Joe: Then listen to me: if love is conditional, it just won't work. Your partner loves you until you bore or annoy them and then they leave. If you want any kind of relationship at all, you have to learn to love your partner for all their strengths and weaknesses. You have to love them no matter how much they change over the years. You have to grow with them, wherever it is they grow to. That takes work.

Loraine: I know this as well, Joe. You're not saying anything I don't already know.

Joe: If you had a stroke and we couldn't have sex or talk and I had to spend all day feeding you while you shook like an infant, I'd do it. I'd spend the next forty years of my life doing that because I love you.

Loraine: But what kind of relationship would that be?

Joe: A committed relationship that lasts, in sickness and in health.

Loraine: (annoyed) Hang on a minute, you don't even want to get married.

Joe: That's only because I don't agree with marriage. We don't have to prop up some archaic patriarchal institution to totally commit to each other. You know I'm totally committed to you for the rest of my life. That's why I'm living with you; that's why I'd spend the rest of my life looking after you if you had a stroke and couldn't do anything.

Loraine: Well, I'm not sure I'd be happy about you staying with me if I had a stroke. If you spent all day looking after a grown infant, that's not a healthy relationship for you.

Joe: Why?

Loraine: You'd be missing out on all the good bits of a relationship. I'd be getting all your devotion and care. You'd get nothing from me. The whole relationship would be totally one-sided.

Joe: (passionately) But I'd be happy because I'd be looking after the person I love!

Loraine: But are you sure that would really make you happy?

Joe: Loraine, relationships aren't like bank loans. You don't have to pay back all that you owe. You can't expect to get things from your partner that are always in proportion to what you can give. Sometimes your partner can give way less than you and you still love them anyway. Those things can always switch. You might one day be the one getting more from them than what you can give back.

Loraine: (sighing) I know… you're right. Maybe the problem is… I feel like I haven't been asserting myself enough in this relationship. Maybe I'm not standing up for my needs and I'm assuming it's because you're not happy.

Joe: If that's the case, just tell me what you need! I'm your boyfriend. I'm here to make sure you get those needs met.

Loraine: I know and I appreciate you so much for that. No one's ever loved me as much as you.

Joe: (awkwardly) That's because you're the love of my life. Now tell me what I can do to make you happier in this relationship.

Loraine: Well for starters, I'm really tired of you pressuring me to hang out with your poetry friends. I don't understand what you guys talk about half the time and I'm sitting there bored out of my skull. I'd prefer it if you go have coffee with them somewhere else rather than have them come here all the time. There's a lot of things we could be doing together on those nights. We'll be missing the fireworks for the Caribbean Carnival if they come over this weekend.

Joe: I understand. But what about your friends that we see in Derby?

Loraine: You like my friends.

Joe: Well, I think they're okay.

Loraine: The point is, it doesn't irritate you to spend time with them.

Joe: Jill and Claire irritate you that much?

Loraine: Joe, all they do is speculate about pointless shit, moan about austerity and read aloud pretentious rubbish they've scribbled on those little note pads.

Joe: I like their poems.

Loraine: You are so much better than them, Joe. I don't understand what you're on about, but I can still tell it's more well written and imaginative than their self-righteous bullshit. Every time Jill reads her menstruation slam poems, I want to fucking punch her.

Joe: (rolling his eyes) I'll meet them at Starbucks.

Loraine: The other thing I need from you is more evening meals. I get home at eight and you're home by seven, most days. When I get home from work, you know I'm stressed and need satiation to get a sense of calm. I hate cooking that late after work. It's too stressful.

Joe: Okay, I'll make sure to have something ready.

Loraine: The third thing that irritates me is on weekends when we have the day to spend together, you're often in your room with your headphones on.

Joe: That's really the only time I have to listen to music. I don't put that on in the living room because I know you hate it.

Loraine: Joe, the only time I get to spend the entire day with you is on the weekend. What's more important, a day with your girlfriend or listening to Eric Dolphy for the umpteenth time?

Joe: (reassuringly) Of course you're more important to me! I can't tell you how sorry I am if I ever made you feel like music comes first. That was never intentional on my part.

Loraine: And the last thing I want to talk to you about is something I need to be completely honest with you about.

Joe: Okay.

Loraine: Now I'm not saying this at all because I'm trying to hurt you.

Joe: I know, I know. What is it?

Loraine: Joe, I wouldn't be with you if I didn't think you were a handsome guy.

Joe: I know. And you know how beautiful I think you are.

Loraine: But at the moment, you're a handsome guy who is buried under way too much fat. It's embarrassing.

Joe: I know it is. I'll go online tonight and research a diet plan I can get on. Maybe I can–

Loraine: (interrupting) Take off your shirt.

Joe: What?

Loraine: Take off your shirt. I want to show you something.

Joe: What, right now?

Loraine: Just take off your shirt.

Joe takes off his shirt. Loraine then pulls down Joe's trousers and underpants. Loraine is staring down at Joe's flaccid penis and protruding belly.

Loraine: Now, babes… I know you haven't got the biggest cock in the world. That is not the problem. But look at this.

Loraine puts her hand against Joe's flabby belly.

Loraine: This right here… this is nasty.

Joe: (embarrassed) I know, but I can't really do anything about that right this minute.

Loraine: Your gut hangs out further than your erection, Joe. I can handle the eye patch. I can handle the man boobs. But this is disgusting.

Joe: (uncomfortable) I know, but this isn't the nicest way to talk to me about this, Loraine.

Loraine: I'm being honest with you because I want you to be more self-confident. I don't want to hear you whinging about how you feel unattractive.

Joe: I appreciate that but there are more tactful ways of helping than insulting me.

Loraine: (irritated) I'm not interested in beating about the bush anymore. I want you to become more self-confident and I want you to have a body your beautiful girlfriend is happy with! Confident guys are way more sexy.

Joe: I know that but–

Loraine: (interrupting) You know as well as I do that If I sugar coat what I'm trying to say, you won't take it on board.

Joe: (loudly) Of course I'll take it on board!

Loraine: (yelling) THEN BE A FUCKING MAN AND DO SOMETHING ABOUT IT! You've had enough time to do something about it already and you keep eating the same nasty shit! I'm sick of it, Joe! It doesn't look good when we're walking down the street together and people are staring at me, wondering what the hell I'm doing with you! That's not good for either of us.

Joe: I know.

Loraine: (loudly) I'm going to be pregnant next year! You need to model good habits for our kids. You need to be there for our kids without having a fucking heart attack at forty!

Joe: I know, I know.

Loraine: Now tonight you're going to get a diet plan and we'll order the food in for the week. I also want you to start working out on the Wii again doing those press ups. You'll feel so much better once those boobs start shrinking. Who knows? I might feel like I'm having sex with a man.

Joe: You don't have to put it in such a crude–

Loraine: (interrupting) You're the one person I can say whatever I'm thinking to Joe. Whatever I'm feeling about you I can say to your face! I can't do that with anyone else.

Joe: I know but… sometimes you can be rather blunt.

Loraine: My honesty is how I show my love. Don't talk about that like it's a bad thing.

Joe: I'm sorry.

Loraine: Now I'm famished. If you start cooking now, it'll be too long before tea is ready and I'll have a headache. Nip to the shop and get me a small pizza with a green salad. You're having just a green salad. And don't buy any pop or anything. You can have a glass of water with lemon when you get back.

Joe: Okay, I should be back in about fifteen minutes.

Joe proceeds to walk out the door.

Loraine: Joe…

Joe: Yes?

Loraine: Thank you for being so sweet to me today. I knew everything would be okay if we talked this out.

Joe: I love you, Loraine.

Loraine: (smiling) I love you too, Joe. I've never had a boyfriend as giving as you.

Joe: That's the kind of boyfriend I try to be.

Joe and Loraine smile at each other as Joe leaves.

But Joe is not happy. He is disturbed because he has just seen a side of Loraine he has never seen before. Loraine has been demanding and insensitive in the past. However, she has never been cruel to Joe about his body. This cruelty makes Joe feel very hurt.

Joe thinks about how hard he tried to calm Loraine's fears about his needs not being met in the relationship. This is how she repays him? There is no way, after what she said to him, that Joe is going to feel like having sex with her tonight. Walking home with dinner, he can't bear to look at any windows or mirrors. The reflection of his own body is making him feel physically repulsed.

When Joe brings the dinner home, he and Loraine sit together eating. Loraine tucks into her pizza and salad while Joe eats his salad without much enthusiasm. He's not terribly hungry. Loraine can sense something isn't right.

Loraine: Joe, I'm sorry if I was a little harsh about your eating habits earlier. I just want you to be happy.

Joe: I know you just want me to be happy.

Loraine: I worry about you. I worry about your health. And I know how you feel about yourself because of your weight and your eye. So I just want you to remember how fit you were and know that you can look like that again, baby. We can get you fanciable again over the next year. It's not impossible.

Joe: Like I said, I'll sort a diet plan tonight and we'll plan it out into our shopping list.

Loraine: I just want you to feel confident and happy. I want you to feel like you belong in this relationship.

Joe: I thought I already did belong in this relationship.

Loraine: You know what I mean.

Joe: (looking down) You mean only hot people belong in this relationship.

Loraine: Joe, how many times have you talked to me about how you don't like how you look anymore?

Joe: Yeah, but I thought how I looked didn't matter to you.

Loraine: It obviously matters to me! I'm your girlfriend and it's my job to have sex with you. You're not going to be happy fucking me if you know I'm not happy with how you look. And I want you to have a good time in bed with me. I don't want you to feel like you're ugly.

Joe: I thought you'd love me enough to enjoy lovemaking, regardless of what I look like.

Loraine: Would you enjoy sex with me if I gained seven stone?

Joe: Of course I would.

Loraine: Stop lying, Joe.

Joe: Why do you think I'm lying?

Loraine: (emphatically) Because I couldn't give you a fucking stiffy if you weren't attracted to my body! I'm slim and toned!

Joe: Your beauty isn't just about how you look.

Loraine: (rolling her eyes) Oh, please. Come on Joe.

Joe: (passionately) There's more to you than just how you look!

Loraine: I know that! But how I look is a big fucking part of why I'm beautiful and it's a big part of why we're together. Your girlfriend is gorgeous, babes.

Joe: I know you're gorgeous, but I'm going to be with you when you're old and wrinkly. I'll still be making love to you.

Loraine: You'll have to work a lot harder then to shag me. And it would be nice if we could have a few decades before we're old and wrinkly where neither of us has to work that hard to find the other one attractive.

Joe: Well, if you love someone, you want to make love. It doesn't matter what the other person looks like.

Loraine: Do you want to fuck Jill and Claire?

Joe: Of course not.

Loraine: Exactly!

Joe: (rolling his eyes) That's different. We're mates.

Loraine: Yeah and I'm not threatened by those mates of yours 'cause I know that even if I wasn't in your life, they would always be just mates.

Joe: Why do you say that?

Loraine: Jill's a right minger and Claire's twice as big as you!

Joe: Well, I don't agree with you. Claire's pretty. Being a big woman doesn't mean you can't be attractive.

Loraine: She's not fucking pretty, Joe. She looks like a stuffed white bin bag. And when she wears her black sandals, her feet look like fucking loaves of bread. I look at Claire's face 'cause I can't even bear to look at her feet and looking at her face isn't that pleasant.

Joe: (sighing) I don't understand why you hate Claire so much.

Loraine: I don't hate her. I just think she needs to sort herself out.

Joe: You know, she asked me yesterday to tell you how much she appreciated you fixing her shower last week. You saved her three hundred quid.

Loraine: Well, I'm glad but she still needs learn to fix herself. She's disgusting.

Joe: Loraine, if she feels happy with how she looks, it's none of your business. You have no right to judge her.

Loraine: I'm not judging her. I know she can get her kit off. I know she's had boyfriends before. I'm not saying she should be banned from sex.

Joe: Then what are you saying?

Loraine: I just think… she's a bit of a saddo. The next time she's fucking some unlucky sod, she'll have to be on the bottom, so she doesn't crush the poor bloke.

Joe: That doesn't mean he won't enjoy it. There's still the missionary position.

Loraine: Yeah, and it'll be like trying to find the wet hole in a giant blob. It'll be a miracle if he doesn't have to think about somebody else in order to get a fucking hard on. I do not envy that poor bastard.

Joe: (shaking his head) Loraine… that's really mean.

Loraine: (annoyed) Claire doesn't respect herself. If she doesn't respect herself, why should I? Why should anyone respect her?

Joe: Because she's a great person. I know you don't see that, but I do. And whoever winds up being her next boyfriend will see that.

Loraine: (loudly) WHY SHOULD A MAN RESPECT A GIRLFRIEND WHO TREATS HER BODY THAT WAY? Why should he have to put up with that? Why should he have to lie and pretend a big blob of shit is beautiful? That's like slavery!

Joe: If a guy can see the things in Claire that I can, there's no reason why he wouldn't want her. If and when a guy sees those things, Claire will be beautiful to him.

Loraine: (sarcastically) Oh yes. If you were single, I'm sure you'd be aching to stick your cock in her.

Joe: Of course I wouldn't, but that doesn't have anything to do with Claire. That has to do with me. I'm not into big girls. But there are plenty of guys who are.

Loraine: You mean there's plenty of guys who think they couldn't do better; guys most women wouldn't touch with a ten-foot pole, guys who are scraping the bottom.

Joe: (sighing) I know it's a small pool of blokes, but there's someone for everyone, Loraine. Claire's too lovely a person to have to be alone. I know it won't be easy to find her next boyfriend, but I'm positive someone out there somewhere will see how kind and interesting and funny Claire is. If he gives her a chance and really gets to know her, he'll start to see those things. He'll start to want her.

Loraine: He might in the beginning 'cause he enjoys spending time with her and the romance is new, but that'll soon wear off. He'll start to notice what she looks like and then he won't want her anymore. She'll either lose him or she'll have to stop eating herself to death.

Joe: Or maybe he'll love her because he can see how beautiful she is on the inside.

Loraine: (adamantly) She's not beautiful on the inside. She's a selfish fucking pig.

Joe: No, she isn't Loraine. Not at all. She's one of the most giving people I know.

Loraine: (incredulous) How can you say that? She wrecks her body with junk food and expects everyone to fancy her!

Joe: (sighing in frustration) That's not selfish. That's having an eating disorder and wanting to be treated the same as everyone else.

Loraine: (annoyed) No, that's like expecting people to fuck you even though you don't brush your teeth and you stink! If you love someone, you take a shower and brush your fucking teeth before you expect them to get naked and cum with you! It's called consideration.

Joe: (quietly) Weight loss is a lot harder than taking a shower or brushing your teeth.

Loraine: (emphatically) Anything that's worth having you have to work hard for! Not making an effort to look nice means you're not working to make yourself attractive. Not making an effort and expecting to get fucked anyway is dickhead behaviour, especially if the person you expect to bang actually makes an effort to be sexy.

Joe: So is this a roundabout way of saying I'm a dickhead?

Loraine: It's not a roundabout way of saying it. You need to fucking lose weight, Joe. You're a fat bloke with wobbly bits who's fucking a 10. You're not even a 4. Doesn't that bother you?

Joe: (rolls eyes) Of course it bothers me!

Loraine: Well, it should bother you more! You're useless without me nagging you. All your friends lick your arse and fill your head with lies.

Joe: Well, so do you Loraine. All this time, I was under the impression my girlfriend actually thought I was handsome.

Loraine: I never lied to you about that, Joe. I know there's a handsome guy in there. I've seen the photos. I'm just tired of him hiding in blubber.

Joe: (defensively) Well, so am I, but losing weight is going to take a lot of time. It's not an easy thing!

Loraine: It's not easy becoming a fat lump of lard either but you certainly worked hard at that.

Joe: (sarcastically) Well, if me being fat bothers you so much, you're free to break up with me until I'm fit enough to deserve you… You can tell your friends we'll get back together when I look as hot as them. And I'm sure they'll tell you to stop wasting your time and leave. There are so many other thinner male fish in the sea just waiting for a crack at the beautiful Loraine Klein! I'm sure that's what Sasha will tell you before he tries to have a go at you himself.

Loraine: (irritated) Oh, shut up! If he says that, he can fuck off! You and I are having a family together and that's why I want us to be on the same page, Joe. I know you don't like your body any more than I do, so let's sort it together for the kids and set an example.

Joe: (softly) Loraine, when I said I didn't like how I looked, I wasn't talking about you. I was talking about my self-confidence in public. I wasn't talking about feeling like I disgusted you.

Loraine: (reassuringly) You don't completely disgust me, Joe. It's just how you look when you're naked. It's your stomach, really. Nothing else.

Joe: (deeply hurt) But how could you have sex with me for all this time if my belly was that repulsive to you?

Loraine: Well, I chose to focus on other things: things like your face or the sensations, things I was thinking.

Joe: (on the verge of tears) Then why couldn't you just keep doing that without making a big speech about how much you hate my wobbly bits?

Loraine: Because you knew our sex life wasn't working for me. That's why you kept asking me all those stupid questions every time we had sex. "Was it good for you when I did this? Should I move a little to the right when I do this?" I knew why you were asking me those questions.

Joe: (softly, trying his hardest to hold back tears) I just wanted to make sure you had a good time, Loraine. I didn't think you were working hard not to be sick every time we made love.

Loraine: Well, then I misread you. I'm sorry for that but you have to be honest with me or I will misread you.

Joe: (frustrated) I thought you just knew why I was asking you those questions.

Loraine: I'm not a mind-reader Joe. You have to tell me how you're feeling.

Joe: (sighing) I know.

Loraine: Look, I love our relationship because we can tell each other anything. But sometimes I feel you aren't comfortable with that. Like right now. I'm expressing my feelings to you and it feels like you're trying to censor me. Can you imagine how you'd feel if I tried to censor you?

Joe: Well, can you understand why you might be hurting my feelings?

Loraine: No, I can't. You asked me to be honest. But if you want honesty, you need thicker skin. If you want me to open up to you about my feelings, I need to trust that you can take it. Being in a relationship with a beautiful woman isn't easy. You need to be strong, darling. Most men aren't strong enough and that's why they don't get what you have. They settle for women they don't fancy.

Joe: Why do you keep making this about men?

Loraine: I'm not in a relationship with a guy because I'm attracted to any person who happens to have a cock, Joe. I want a relationship with a real man.

Joe: What's a 'real man'? A gender typical man?

Loraine: No, it's a man who isn't intimidated or hurt by me when I'm honest about my feelings. You're the first person I've ever met who I thought could be that man.

Joe: I highly doubt that, Loraine.

Loraine: (irritated) Joe, you know I've never broken up with any boyfriend before. I've always been the one who they break up with!

Joe: Don't take that to heart, Loraine. Lots of men are threatened by strong women.

Loraine: Yes and that's why I love you so much! You can handle me. My mouth never gets me in trouble with you. Or at least... that's how I thought things were... until you started getting stroppy.

Joe: (sighing) I haven't been stroppy.

Loraine: (adamantly) You have been lately! You came back with the food with this look on your face. It's driving me round the bend!

Joe: What look on my face?

Loraine: This 'you hurt me but I'm not going to tell you why' look. That pathetic look you do when you're upset about something but you just want to sulk.

Joe: Well, maybe my feelings are a little hurt. I am human.

Loraine: Well, you're not dealing with your feelings like an adult, are you?

Joe: Probably not. I suppose… most of the time, my hurt feelings aren't particularly fair because they're just a product of me not accepting your limitations. So if you do say something that hurts my feelings, I normally do something to process my emotions in a way where… I don't have to burden you with them.

Loraine starts to tenderly stroke Joe's arm.

Loraine: Aww, baby, I appreciate that. It's very humble of you to admit when your feelings are wrong. That's another thing I love about you.

Joe: (passionately) I try very hard to always admit when I'm in the wrong! I've had too many bad experiences when I was younger because I couldn't admit when I was wrong. I don't want to repeat that! Don't you know that about me?

Loraine: Yes, but lately you've been slipping, Joe. Especially today. There's anger and hurt in your face that's directed towards me. I'm sorry but I don't fucking like it.

Joe: (looking down) I know you don't. I'm sorry.

Loraine: I've had enough men in my life look at me that way. I don't need you to start looking at me that way.

Joe: (reassuringly) I get it, Loraine. The last thing I would ever want is for you to feel like I can't handle you. You know I love everything about you! I'm just human. I sometimes get hurt even when it isn't fair. But you're right: sometimes my feelings are wrong.

Loraine: And that is why you need me in your life. You're like a pitiful little baby, without me. You need someone to kick your arse! (laughing)

Joe: (smiling) It's sad but true.

Loraine: You're lucky I'm going to keep you and we're going to work through our problems, whatever they are.

Joe: I know and I appreciate that so much. I don't want to lose you either.

Loraine: Then you have to trust me.

Joe: I do trust you.

Loraine: (loudly) Then don't pull a fucking face when I'm trying to help you better yourself!

Joe: (annoyed) Loraine, I'm not always aware of my facial expressions. They just happen sometimes. Sometimes I look sad and it has nothing to do with anything that's happening in the external world. Sometimes it's just a memory that reminds me of an emotion that creates a mood that's related to sadness but sadness itself comes out in the expression and–

Loraine smiles condescendingly and puts her hand over Joe's mouth, mid-sentence.

Loraine: (interrupting) Joe, do your girlfriend a favour and please shut the fuck up. You're dragging us into another conversation about nothing and it's maddening. We don't need to analyse your fucking facial expressions, okay?

Joe: I was just trying to say that I don't want to be blamed for facial expressions that don't express my feelings. I can't help having certain facial expressions when I'm in certain emotional states because–

Loraine: (interrupting loudly) Finish this deep conversation about your face with one of your friends!

Joe: (quietly) …I was just trying to explain myself.

Loraine: (annoyed) You don't need to explain yourself. Now go upstairs, find and plan out a diet for yourself. Then at midnight, come to bed. I'll be waiting for you.

Joe: (confused) You want to have sex tonight?

Loraine: Of course I do!

Joe: But what about my body?

Loraine: I'll do my best to carry on ignoring it if you make an effort to change your eating.

Joe: (sarcastically) Oh, cheers.

Loraine: (emphatically) Joe, I need sex on my days off to fall asleep! I can ignore your wobbly bits if I know you're not gonna look like this forever. It's not a problem, okay? I'd rather sleep than let myself have insomnia 'cause you've got a weird tummy. I just don't want it to stay like this permanently. I care about your health!

Joe: I know… and I appreciate that.

Loraine: Alright, get your arse upstairs, get cracking and them come to our room at midnight and fuck me. I want to be alone for a bit if that's okay.

Joe: Okay. Before I go up, I'm sorry if I forgot to ask you about this earlier but… how was yesterday at work? Are things becoming less stressful? You know how I worry about some of the accusations the kids have been making and I don't want you to think that I'm being paranoid, but it's only because I love you and…

Loraine: (interrupting loudly) Just shut up and go upstairs! You're giving me a fucking headache!

Joe quickly goes upstairs while Loraine turns on the television, watching reality TV programmes in the living room. Loraine always prefers to watch her favourite television programmes alone.

Meanwhile, in his office, Joe goes online and finds a diet plan he is happy with. He then quickly plans the shopping for the next week. Joe also decides to surprise Loraine and order her an expensive handbag he knows she will absolutely love. It will arrive in three days. Joe expects that the purchasing of this gift will make him feel better; it doesn't. A half hour later, he is still upset.

Joe is annoyed with himself because he doesn't want yet another argument with Loraine. All the issues between him and Loraine should have been resolved during their last conversation. Something still doesn't feel right.

Joe tells himself, "Okay, maybe Loraine is a bit shallow but what's the point of being upset about that? Everyone is flawed. Her flaws are no worse than mine. Remember Joe: you have a beautiful woman who loves you. She's always honest with you; she tolerates your weak points and still wants to be with you; she's committed to working through all the issues you both have in your relationship; she never makes you feel like you're being manipulated. You've created a beautiful home together. She's going to help you lose weight and become more self-confident and she's kind enough to have sex with you anyway until you have a body the two of you are both happy with. Not only that, but she wants to have sex with you all the time! You're going to have beautiful children together!"

Nonetheless, the negative feelings won't go away. Joe is dreading midnight.

Joe knows he won't be able to get hard without extra help. Joe can't get erections for Loraine after she hurts his feelings. Rather than be honest with Loraine about this, Joe decides to use the mental image of another woman in order to stay hard while he penetrates Loraine. Joe does this at least once a week and he knows exactly who tonight's imaginary woman is going to be.

Joe visits Pornhub and browses through clips of Davis McFarlin, his favourite porn star. Davis is an attractive blonde who Joe thinks looks vaguely like a younger Kylie Minogue. Joe doesn't normally fancy blondes (or Kylie Minogue) but thinks Davis is no ordinary porn star.

Joe, being a heterosexual man in his late thirties, has watched hours and hours of porn throughout his life. Yet he has never seen porn so suffused with animal passion, nor has he seen a female porn star look so arrogant while having sex. Joe, of course, isn't so gullible as to trust what he sees with his eyes. He suspects Davis's extreme arrogance is just a well-executed performance. On the other hand, Joe thinks that if it is all just acting, that makes her even sexier.

Joe puts on a pair of headphones and starts playing a twenty-minute minute clip of Davis darting her long tongue in and out of a Korean porn star named Licky Linda. Joe doesn't fancy Licky Linda but doesn't particularly care. This scene is one of the more erotic porn clips Joe has ever watched from beginning to end. Davis herself looks extremely self-satisfied, like she magically knows the impact her porn is having on him. It's as if Davis is seducing Joe, confidently performing for the camera and slowly turning Licky into a blubbering mess, all at once.

After about fifteen minutes, Licky herself no longer appears to be performing. Her eyes are closed and she's breathing heavily, as if her own intense feelings have become too intense to turn into anything sexy for the camera. In the final minutes of the clip, Licky looks less like a porn star than a woman giving birth – as if the pleasures coming from Davis's mouth are ripping her apart. After finishing this clip, Joe presses play to watch it a second time. As Joe stares obsessively at Davis and Licky, he can hear the first waves of unusually large rain drops running down his office windows.

A classic July thunderstorm is unfolding over Leicester. It always starts with rain and then gets progressively louder. As it kicks into high gear with a loud crack of thunder, flickers of white light brighten Joe's office like flashbulbs. Joe takes his headphones off, as Davis and Licky are now frozen on his laptop screen. The house Wi-Fi is no longer working and Joe is generally unnerved by all the noise and violence of the weather. He can hear the sky rumble loudly, punctuated by the percussive droplets of persistent rain. He can see more distant lightning bolts outside his windows, lightening he worries will eventually strike the roof and electrocute the house.

Downstairs, Loraine is absolutely loving the storm…

It makes her horny.

PART 2: PROCREATION

"I find the question of whether gender differences are biologically determined or socially constructed deeply disturbing."

- Carol Gilligan

"We never care to know new people unless we are sure we shall like them."

- Gertrude Atherton

"If man makes himself a worm, he must not complain when he is trodden on."

- Immanuel Kant

6. PROCREATION: In the Beginning

Joe and Loraine live next to a lesbian couple named Eve Fenn and Alice Adler. Both Eve and Alice like Joe and Loraine.

Loraine likes to flirt with Alice, whenever she can. Alice loves flirting with Loraine and thinks Loraine is one of the sexiest women she has ever met. Loraine is pleased by Alice's obvious lust because Loraine enjoys sexually teasing any woman she knows is attracted to her.

Despite her constant teasing, Loraine does not like Alice. Loraine thinks Alice is nothing more than a badly dressed slag who talks rubbish, has too many piercings and stinks of B.O. Loraine also dislikes Alice's partner Eve. Loraine dislikes Eve because she can sense that Eve likes Joe. More damningly, Loraine thinks Eve is intelligent, attractive and successful. Unlike Alice, Eve doesn't smell of B.O.

Eve and Alice are both twenty-nine. They have been in a very loving relationship since they were both fourteen. Alice loves Eve because she thinks Eve is intelligent, deep, sensitive and always looks after the people she loves. Eve loves Alice because she thinks Alice is witty, free spirited, charismatic and incredibly brave. Since their late teens, Eve and Alice have planned on spending the rest of their lives together. Although neither of them believes in marriage, both have been living together in various flats since they were eighteen. Because of Eve's income, they've only just been able to afford a beautiful spacious home in Clarendon Park near Leicester City Centre

Eve works as an Art History lecturer at the University of Leicester. Her research is on important female artists that have been unduly forgotten throughout history.

Alice is a bartender at Firebug, a popular local venue that showcases new bands, stand-up comedians and other events. Although she makes far less money than Eve, Alice loves her job and is very good at it. Both her customers and her colleagues are very much enamoured with her. She recently came third place in a national 'Midlands Bartender of the Year' contest.

Alice is revered for her friendly personality, cheeky sense of humour, extensive knowledge of cocktails and the nearly acrobatic manner in which she can quickly mix a drink. Alice is a great multitasker and even manages to do magic tricks to amuse her customers, all the while chatting to them and taking their orders. She makes it all look effortless.

Another reason Alice is so successful is she aggressively flirts with both her male and female customers. Unlike her co-workers, Alice is shockingly good at flirting. So much so, that she often accidentally seduces men and women who are far more attractive than she is. A few women have complained that Alice was inconsiderate of their feelings, deliberately causing them to experience romantic yearnings she had no intention of reciprocating. However, the overwhelming majority of people Alice flirts with simply find her great fun.

Eve doesn't like Alice's flirting, but understands it's an important part of Alice's job. So Eve reluctantly tolerates Alice's flirting, as long as she doesn't have to hear about it when Alice comes home. Eve also doesn't like the fact that Alice posts weekly YouTube videos of her playing sexy drinking games. She especially doesn't like it when these videos involve Alice kissing minor celebrities. But like the flirting, Eve accepts this is part of what has made Alice so successful in her bartending career.

When Alice isn't bartending, she enjoys rock climbing, cooking vegan food, kick boxing, listening to jazz, smoking weed, repeatedly watching David Lynch films and writing poetry.

Alice often reads her poems at a local café called 'The Crumblin' Cookie'. Most of her poems are about the spiritual experiences of yogis and religious gurus. Alice also likes to research academic literature on Eastern religious mysticism in her free time, using Eve's university card to access the university's library books and journals. Whenever Eve sees Alice researching and reading, Eve always feels very proud of her.

One of the difficulties in Eve and Alice's relationship is the fact that Alice works every night in an environment where she is surrounded by alcohol. Throughout their relationship, Alice has had periods where she displayed erratic and self-destructive behaviour because of binge drinking. The reason these periods have not destroyed Alice's life is because of the emotional support she receives from Eve.

Eve often stops Alice from doing things she would otherwise regret. Eve sometimes worries she is overbearing and controlling. However, Alice always reassures Eve that she is doing exactly what Alice wants her to do.

Eve has been the reason Alice can thrive and be successful in her career. Alice constantly reminds Eve that she needs someone in her life to give her boundaries. In fact, Alice wishes Eve would give her more boundaries.

Although Eve is typically the partner in the relationship that does the guiding and protecting, Alice sometimes has to support and look after Eve. This is particularly true when Eve experiences her own periodic bouts of depression. Eve is deeply ashamed of her mental health difficulties, so Alice is the only one who is in a position to support Eve when she is feeling vulnerable. The first bout of depression Eve experienced was when she told her family she was both a lesbian and in love with Alice.

Eve grew up in a large religious family where, as a child, she was very close to her mother Cara, as well as her extended family of aunts, uncles and cousins. Because she was a very shy and introverted child, Eve's family were also her only friends. After coming out as gay at the age of fourteen, everyone in her family (other than her father) decided they no longer wanted anything to do with Eve. A few of them wrote her long hand-written letters explaining, in great detail, how she was a bad person that deserved to burn in hell. One of these letters was written by her mother.

Receiving Cara's letter was the biggest shock of Eve's life. Eve was always much closer to her mother than she had ever been with her father. As a child, she considered her mother her closest confidante. As an eccentric and quiet adolescent, Cara Fenn was the only person who made Eve feel understood, accepted and utterly adored, not in spite of, but because of her unique eccentricities. Hence, Cara was the last person Eve ever expected to write this kind of letter.

The experience of reading it felt like dying.

Eve practically fainted when she reached the bottom of her mother's hateful barrage of distinctly theological insults. She spent the next three days weeping in spasms of uncontrolled hysteria. Cara had also penned a hateful and rage filled letter to Eve's father Shayne, demanding a quick divorce. Cara was shocked that Shayne wanted to defy God, accepting and encouraging his daughter's sexual deviancy. Shayne was shocked that a religious woman like Cara could suddenly be such a hypocrite on the subject of divorce.

Three days after receiving her family's letters, once the constant sobbing had subsided, Eve went mute. She couldn't speak for the following two months and even found it hard to ingest food without vomiting. Eve couldn't go to school, let alone bathe herself and spent the next year riddled with crippling bouts of chest pain. Throughout all of this, Shayne was useless, not knowing how to handle his daughter's unexpected breakdown. It was Alice who was much more useful, quickly replacing Cara as Eve's nurse, life coach and best friend.

If it hadn't been for Alice's fiercely supportive love, Eve would have eventually committed suicide. Although this powerful nurturing enabled Eve to passionately embrace her life again, it never removed the terrifying and traumatic impact of being rejected by her family. To this day, Eve still has a deep-seated fear of being rejected by the people she loves. She often feels like no matter what she does, she can never be good enough for people.

Eve does, however, always feel good enough for Alice, but it's not because they are in a relationship. It's not even because they love each other. It's because throughout the last decade, Alice has had much more difficulty being a stable and responsible adult. Alice's drinking has been far more crippling to her than Eve's sporadic bouts of depression.

Nonetheless, throughout the past year, Alice has been able to maintain some sobriety without a lot of nagging from Eve. This is largely because of Alice's therapy sessions with Doctor Gillian Adams. These therapy sessions have been quite useful for Eve and Alice's relationship. It's changed the dynamic whereby Eve is normally the one who looks after Alice. Because of Alice's newfound stability, she has been able to support Eve throughout an emotionally difficult year. However, this support has been nowhere near what Alice gave Eve when they were teenagers.

Eve resents this.

She also resents many other things about her life, particularly her job.

Although Eve loves researching and writing about unduly forgotten female artists, she can't stand the aggressive environment that is academia. She feels like she lacks the cut-throat competitiveness that enables one to rise to the top in institutions of higher education. Eve even dislikes most of her colleagues, suspecting that they look down on her. Most of the time, she's right about this.

Neither her colleagues nor her students particularly respect Eve. But it's not because of her politics. It's not because she's a woman, nor is it because of her young age. It's certainly not because of the high quality of Eve's research or her competency as a communicator.

It's because both her colleagues and her students see Eve as someone easy to take advantage of.

Eve is also stressed and angry because she works under a female head of department called Roey White. Roey has a habit of making snide comments about Eve: subtly inappropriate remarks that are sarcastic, belittling and mean. Because Roey is so sly in her bullying, she can humiliate Eve in front of her colleagues without being called out on it. Humiliating Eve is one of Roey's favourite pastimes, making Roey feel both powerful and someone who men in the department will respect and admire.

In staff meetings, Eve is routinely ganged up on by the rest of the department. Regardless of whether Eve's colleagues are male or female, nearly all of them are quick to dismiss her ideas, treating her as though she is an idiot who doesn't deserve to work alongside them.

Even her students constantly interrupt Eve during her seminar discussions with them. Some of them try to antagonise her, asking her questions which presuppose she is either a bad communicator, or someone who has the audacity to come to her seminars unprepared. Occasionally, Eve's students accuse her of being a misogynist and a transphobe.

But Eve doesn't feel like she can just quit her post at the University of Leicester. She feels too unconfident in her ability to get another job. Eve desperately wishes Alice would help her gain some confidence, but Alice seems distant and obsessed with her own career as an amazing (if impulsive) bartender.

7. PROCREATION: The Maternal Instinct

On the evening of July 28th, 2015, at exactly 11:20pm, Alice texts Eve with the following message:

> We need to talk after I'm done with work. This is important. There's something I can't hide from you anymore. I'll be home at 3. I'll wake you up if you're asleep.

Eve is immediately worried. She's terrified that Alice has been secretly drinking.

Eve texts back:

> Just tell me what it is! Don't do this to me. I'm all alone tonight.

Eve spends the next four hours in a panic. There's a storm outside. Thunder is booming. Eve can see lightening through the windows.

Alice does not text back until 3:48am. She writes:

> I'll be home in 5 minutes. Put the kettle on.

This is their conversation, after Alice arrives back home.

Eve: So what is it? What did you need to talk to me about? Why did you text me like that?

Alice: Before I tell you this, I just want you to remember how much I love you. There's nothing I'm going to say that will change any of that. You know that, right?

Eve: Of course.

Alice: (pausing) I've been exploring some things with Doctor Adams. Feelings.

Eve: Feelings?

Alice: Yeah, things I haven't been admitting to myself. Things I need to let out, really. I've been thinking about them all night on my shift. I haven't really been able to concentrate.

Eve: You mean about alcohol?

Alice: Well, that and some other more traumatic things that are really difficult for me to understand, let alone verbalise. My therapy has been a healing process for me, Eve. Doctor Adams has been fab, honestly. Very empathetic, very perceptive. I've never had a therapist this good.

Eve: Well, that's wonderful. I mean, it's wonderful that you can confront so many of your demons in these sessions. That's what I always hoped would happen.

Alice: I can manage them because of her. It's like my mind is a tangled ball of string she helps me unravel.

Eve: Everyone has things in their head they need to untangle. And it's not often you find the right therapist for that. They're all so different.

Alice: I think everyone would probably benefit from some therapy. You just need to find a good therapist and they are fucking rare.

Eve: You're more right than you know.

Alice: Of course I am. You could do with some therapy as well, really.

Eve: You don't have to remind me. I've been struggling really bad lately.

Alice: Eve, there are so many ways you could totally blossom if you were less driven by fear and self-loathing. It breaks my heart watching you the way you are. It's like you hate yourself.

Eve: It breaks my heart too!

Alice: It's like you're leading half a life. You're your own worst enemy. It's not other people, Eve. It's you.

Eve: Maybe, but it's late and I really need to get to sleep. Can you please tell me what it is you needed to talk about?

Alice: You stop yourself from being free. You stifle yourself and then you blame everybody else.

Eve: That's what you wanted to talk about?

Alice: It's part of it.

Eve: I don't understand.

Alice: You're not well and that's part of why I'm having problems. You do need to get help and stop putting things off.

Eve: I haven't had therapy in ages.

Alice: My therapy has been the best thing I've done all year, Eve. Maybe five years.

Eve: Well, I can believe that. It's amazing what a change I've seen in you.

Alice: I think part of the reason I've struggled so much is I've been in denial. I've been shoving down parts of who I am. That's what I talk about in my sessions.

Eve: I thought you talk about drinking.

Alice: Well, we obviously talk about that as well. It's all related. You can't separate any of these issues from each other.

Eve: Well, I'm glad you're getting help but I've never wanted you to feel like you have to shove anything down. That's awful. I've never wanted you to shove down who you are for me or anyone else.

Alice: Eve, you know I love you more than the world. I can't stand the idea of confusing you. I just want you comfortable around me.

Eve: I know you do.

Alice: That's why I sometimes have to hide things.

Eve: Have you been drinking?

Alice: I know I'm not helping you right now. But that's not because of you. None of this is your fault. In some ways, this is more about me than it is about you. I know that doesn't make much sense. But you know… I don't always make sense.

Eve: Alice, if that bothered me, I wouldn't still be here.

Alice: That's why I'm still here too. I trust you. I've always trusted you.

Eve: Then I need you to trust me enough to be honest with me. It's late and I'm tired but I'm listening to you now.

Alice: I know that, but I'm frightened, Eve.

Eve: Alice, I need to know whatever's going on in your head. I need to know how I can help.

Alice: I'm always so worried about disappointing you. It's part of why I have so much trouble sleeping.

Eve: You've never really disappointed me, Alice.

Alice: I feel guilty because of all the things you do for me, all the time you've given up making sure I got the help I needed. You didn't have to do any of that and I embarrassed you so much.

Eve: Honey, you're my bezzie, remember. Of course I try my hardest to make sure you're okay, but that's not a reason for you to feel guilty about anything. If I wasn't happy looking after you, I wouldn't do it.

Alice: I still can't believe all the things you did for me when I was a wreck. I feel like I owe you so much; like in our relationship, you're the mum and I'm the kid.

Eve: That's not how I see it. There's plenty of things you do to help me. There's plenty of times when I'm the one who needs looking after. In fact, now might be one of those times. It's not one-sided, Alice.

Alice: I know, I know… but I can't help but feel like it would be unfair of me to share certain sides of myself with you, like you deserve better. Does that make any sense?

Eve: I only deserve the truth. It would only be unfair of you to hide shit from me. We're a team, remember.

Alice: I know that. I know that rationally.

Eve: We're not in a relationship where one of us is sorted and the other person's a mess. We're both beautiful messes.

Alice: That's true, isn't it?

Eve: Absolutely. There's absolutely no reason to feel guilty about anything. This is a relationship.

Alice: You're right, really. I know I shouldn't be scared.

Eve: I've seen you at your worst, Alice. I've seen you lying on the pavement covered in piss and puke. I still picked you up and took you home and I've never regretted that or anything else I've ever done for you.

Alice: You don't regret any of it. It's amazing to me that you don't.

Eve: It's not amazing. It's what you would expect. There's nobody who gets me more than you, no one who teaches me more, nobody that's more inspirational to me, no one more patient when I'm making a tit of myself.

Alice: You don't make a tit of yourself, Eve.

Eve: I do sometimes.

Alice: (giggling) Maybe once every five years.

Eve: Well, even if that's true, I still feel like I'm the one that mostly learns from you. Not the other way around.

Alice: Really?

Eve: You're so brave and courageous and funny and confident all the time, I always feel way less interesting. Even the way you face your demons just knocks me for six. You push and push and push until you get what you need from people. Even with utter twats, it's like you can move mountains. I've still never met anyone like you. No one I've ever known can get people to do things like you do.

Alice: That's how I've had to be throughout my life. That's why I'm so good at my job.

Eve: You're bloody relentless.

Alice: I know I am.

Eve: And that's why I can always trust you, no matter what happens. I know you're fighting in my corner. You're always protecting me.

Alice: You give me the strength to do that, though.

Eve: I know I do, but remember: you help me grow and change, no matter how stubborn I can be sometimes. You always get me to think in new ways.

Alice: I do help you grow and change though, don't I?

Eve: (slightly embarrassed) If I'm honest, you're the reason I'm a vegetarian.

Alice: (giggling) I'm still working on getting you to become a vegan.

Eve: (laughing) Well, even you have limitations, mate.

Alice: (smiling) I'll get you when you least expect it.

Eve: As always, I appreciate your dedication. But don't hold your breath.

Alice: Don't underestimate me babes.

Eve: (giggling) Don't underestimate my love for cheese.

Alice: (looking at Eve affectionately) You can be such a stubborn bitch, Eve. But you're my stubborn bitch.

Eve: I can't help but love being your bitch. Always have.

Alice: Of course you do. It's good for you in the end. It's just not easy getting you to try new things. I don't know why I'm so persistent all the time. I must really believe in you.

Eve: I know you do because you get me: you understand how I work and what makes me smile. I trust your ideas, even when they seem a bit crackers. I know there's always a good reason behind what you have to say, even if you can't always articulate it.

Alice: Well, you need someone to stand up to you sometimes. That's why I row with you so much.

Eve: I thought it was the makeup sex, afterwards?

Alice: (smiling flirtatiously) Well, that too.

Eve: You know, if I'm honest, with most of our rows, you normally get me round in the end. Even when the end is after four in the morning!

Alice: And you persuade me to do a lot of things I wouldn't even think about otherwise. If it weren't for you, I wouldn't be sober right now. I would have done an MA and wasted time and money.

Eve: Well, I know what you're like, Alice. I know it wouldn't be your thing.

Alice: You keep my life on track. It's like a roller coaster, but you always keep it on the rails. I always feel pointed in the right direction.

Eve: That's what we do for each other, isn't it?

Alice: I want you to know I never take it for granted. I know how lucky I am to have had you in my life all these years. I know I'm a handful.

Eve: (smiling) You think I'm not a handful?

Alice: I just worry sometimes. I overcomplicate things in my head. I worry you'll hate me if I surprise you with something. I know how you hate surprises.

Eve: Alice, there's nothing you need to hide from me. Anything you need to say can become part of our lives in some way. Even if it upsets me, even if it surprises me, I'll figure it out and we'll deal with it.

Alice: Will we?

Eve: Of course we will! We always deal with shit. We don't give up on each other.

Alice: I know we don't. I've never given up on you and I never will. Everything in my life revolves around you. It's been like that since I was a kid.

Eve: Can you believe it'll be fifteen years next week?

Alice: It's crazy, but it's an amazing crazy. I never thought when I met you that we'd still be together at this age. I never thought I'd still be with my first love.

Eve: Me neither. It's actually one of the things I'm most proud of.

Alice: It's amazing it worked out, with everything being so difficult. Not to mention all the bloody homophobia!

Eve: (sighing) Yeah. All of that was a total nightmare. Do you remember how bad it got?

Alice: Of course I do. You stayed with me even though coming out made you lose most of the people you love.

Eve: That should show you just how much I love you.

Alice: It does.

Eve: And I don't regret any day that I've loved you. Not even that day you hit me. No matter how tough things got, it's always been worth it, because you've always been there with me. I can die knowing I loved my favourite person. The world told me I shouldn't, but I did.

Alice: It's bizarre how lucky we are, really.

Eve: (smiling) Words can never do it justice.

Alice: I sometimes take it for granted because life feels so ordinary and mundane. But when I stop and think about what I have, our love is maybe the most precious and mysterious thing I've been blessed to live through, even with all its problems. It's not perfect, but nothing wonderful ever is.

Eve: Good. Now I'm struggling to remain conscious my love, so let's please deal with the imperfect truth. Tell me what's so difficult to get out of your head so we can talk it out and go to sleep.

Alice: This is so fucking hard…

Eve: Alice, this is me.

Eve takes Alice's head in her hands.

Eve: Look at me… think about who you're talking to.

Alice: Right now, I feel like I did when I came out to my parents.

Eve: But I'm not like them! I'm not judgemental. I'll always accept you.

Alice: I'm still worried. I'm worried you'll think I'm being stupid.

Eve: Do I ever tell you how you should feel?

Alice: No, you don't. You're pretty tolerant of me, actually. You always try and understand.

Eve: Then tell me. Just tell me what this is.

Alice: I don't know why saying this is so difficult. I should trust you. I know this should be easy. It just isn't.

Eve: Why isn't it easy?

Alice: I don't know if you'll cope.

Eve: That actually hurts me, Alice.

Alice: I'm not getting at you. I'm really not.

Eve: Then why can't you tell me whatever it is you think I can't handle?

Alice: It's not that I don't trust that you'll understand, really. I just know you always need time to digest things and I don't want to hurt you. And it's never been the right time to do this.

Eve: (chuckles) Well apparently, 4am is the right time.

Alice: When I need to talk, I need to talk.

Eve: Then tell me what it is.

Alice: These feelings didn't happen because I think you're bad for me. You've been nothing but lovely in every way I can understand the loveliness of another person.

Eve: Then be lovely and tell me what this is about.

Alice: This isn't something I've chosen, Eve. This is something that's been with me for a while now. I've tried to make it go away; I've tried to conquer it. I've been ashamed of myself for it, but I wake up with it every day, staring me in the face, telling me I'm deceiving myself by not letting you see it.

Eve: Then let me see it.

Alice: There's nothing that hurts me worse than the idea of losing you, Eve.

Eve: You won't lose me. I just need to know what I'm being kept from seeing.

Alice: You've been my everything and I know this is crazy, Eve. I know you know me inside and out. You know me deeply in every way, every way except this way.

Eve: You're not transgender, are you?

Alice: This is so hard to talk about…

Eve: (nervously) I won't stop loving you, if that's what it is you're hiding. I'd never reject you because of who you are! It might be hard getting used to a man's body, but that won't stop me from eventually doing it. I'll work at it until it happens. Even if the sex doesn't work, I won't reject you. I'd never reject you, Alice. I just need you to feel like you can be yourself with me. That's what's important.

Alice: I know it is.

Eve: You would never lose my love over who you are! My love for you transcends anything about your body, anything about how you self-identify, anything about how you want to live. You've got me, no matter what.

Alice: Eve, I appreciate that. But I'm not transgender. (laughs)

Eve: (irritated) Then what is it? What the fuck is it?

Alice: I'm worried you'll panic.

Eve: Have you been taking speed again?

Alice: Of course not!

Eve: Do you still want plastic surgery?

Alice: No, not anymore. It's not that.

Eve: Is it something about work? Are you nicking money from the tills? Did you fuck another guy without a condom?

Alice: No, I've been good.

Eve: (irritated) Then just tell me what it is! Just spit it out! Please.

Alice: I want to be a mum.

Eve: (shocked) …What?

Alice: Actually, it's not just that. I want each of us to have a baby. I want us to be pregnant together at the same time.

Eve: But… why?

Alice: I'm really broody now. Like, really, really broody. I'd do anything to make this happen, Eve. It's intense.

Eve: (confused) …What?

Alice: It's totally instinctual, like my body's telling me that I MUST do this. It won't let me not do it. It's beautiful.

Eve: But you can't stand being around children. I like children more than you do.

Alice: I know. That bit's confusing for me as well.

Eve: You even hate babysitting your nieces. I'm the one who plays with them while you go upstairs and do your workouts. Whenever any of our friends has a baby, you complain endlessly about how all they talk about is nappies and breastfeeding. You rarely see them once they have a kid!

Alice: I know I need to work on this, Eve. Doctor Adams is helping me.

Eve: But you don't even like to hold babies. You can't stand working with kids. Every time a teenager sits next to us at Starbucks, you move to another seat – even if they're quiet!

Alice: Eve, I know all of this is unhealthy and we're working through it. Doctor Adams thinks I've been blocking children out of my life for some reason.

Eve: Well, working on being more tolerant of kids is fine. But that's different to wanting to be a mum.

Alice: I know it's different, but the tolerance would help. I need to handle being around kids if I'm going to be raising my own children.

Eve: Are you absolutely sure you want to raise children?

Alice: I'm more certain of this than I've been of anything in my entire life.

Eve: Really?

Alice: Eve, the idea of not having kids makes me want to die.

Eve: You know I don't want you to be in any pain, but don't you think that's a bit dramatic?

Alice: Not at all! This is what most women feel like when they get broody. Doctor Adams says these feelings are natural.

Eve: (confused) I understand.

Alice: I'm not sure you do.

Eve: Well, maybe it's hard for me to understand.

Alice: Why?

Eve: How can you want to be a mum if you find being around children so bloody difficult?

Alice: I just want us to have kids together, like everyone else does.

Eve: Okay, but Alice, I'm not getting pregnant. I don't want that. You know I've never wanted that.

Alice: It's not so difficult these days with all the good sperm donors.

Eve: That doesn't matter. I don't want to hurt some innocent children because of a daddy who doesn't want anything to do with them.

Alice: Eve, what's wrong with two parents being female? I thought you supported LGBT rights.

Eve: I didn't say there was anything wrong with two women raising children. It's just that... Well, kids could end up with abandonment issues when they know they have a father who doesn't want to actually be their dad. I know all about that.

Alice: But that's only because of wider society, Eve. It's a social convention. We're supposed to get rid of things like that.

Eve: Maybe, but you can still cause pain when you try and socialise a kid out of something that... feels so instinctive. You're basically telling them to suppress their feelings.

Alice: What's wrong with that? If nobody forced dickheads and bigots to suppress their feelings, you and I would be in prison today.

Eve: So you want to just bully society into doing the right thing? You don't think social change ever happens because people are persuaded over time to think differently?

Alice: I think we can persuade our daughters that for all practical purposes, we are Mummy and Mummy. There's no need for Daddy. Daddy's a stranger.

Eve: Well, I don't want to have to convince a child they have no need for a daddy. In fact, I don't want to deal with any of this. I have no desire to get pregnant or be a mummy.

Alice: (irritated) But what about me? What about what I want?

Eve: Well, do what you want. If you truly want to be a mum, I'm the last person who would ever get in your way. If this is serious, if you're not just confused about something, then by all means, do what feels right. Be a good mum, if that's what you want to be.

Alice: But don't you want to have a baby as well?

Eve: No… I'm happy with my life the way it is. I don't want you to be unhappy in your choices, but I'm happy in mine.

Alice: But if I have a kid that means you're going to have to raise it with me. You might as well have one too. Kids often need a sibling to be socialised properly. Two parents can't do it on their own.

Eve: I know that, but I just don't want to raise children. I've never wanted to be a parent, Alice. I'll stay with you, but I don't want to raise your kids. That's your job.

Alice: Well, this isn't exactly fair. What if I don't want to be a single parent?

Eve: Don't be one then. You don't have to be a parent. It's not written in stone.

Alice: So this is how it is: I'm either forced to become a single parent, or I lose you. This is exactly what I thought would happen. I'm sorry I kept you awake, Eve. I thought you actually cared about me.

Eve: (adamantly) Don't say that! I care about you more than anything! And I want you to do whatever it is that makes you happy. If you want a kid, we'll figure out a way to make it happen! I promise.

Alice: (irritated) You're so fucking patronising!

Eve: What?

Alice: You're acting like this isn't serious, like I'm going through a phase, or something.

Eve: Well, I'm sorry if that's how I'm making you feel. I know this is serious. I can't imagine how you must be feeling right now. I just don't want you to make a daft mistake because you're feeling broody. You need to really think about this.

Alice: (indignantly) What right do you have to tell me I'm making a mistake?

Eve: It's not about what I'm telling you. It's about what you've told me repeatedly for years and years: You can't stand children.

Alice: I don't need to love other people's children. I just need to love ours.

Eve: Alice, darling, I know you better than anyone else on this earth. You're almost afraid of children. Be honest with yourself.

Alice: (loudly) I'm not afraid of them! I just don't enjoy most of the kids I've ever talked to! We didn't connect. You connect with them more than I do!

Eve: That means you don't want kids.

Alice: No, it means I'm still immature. I'm trying to grow up.

Eve: Alice, not wanting kids doesn't make you immature.

Alice: Doctor Adams didn't think she wanted kids. She hated kids, just like me. But when she accidentally got pregnant with twins, a switch flipped in her head. Her perspective, her personality even, just completely and totally changed. She knew for the first time that she could love children and she knew she would love her own children more than she ever loved anything else. Everything else pales in comparison to the love she has for her baby girls now. The decision she made to keep them was the best thing she ever did!

Eve: But don't you worry she put her girls at risk?

Alice: (loudly) She didn't put them at risk! She made the best decision of her life!

Eve: I know that, but I mean… she chose to have kids, knowing full well the odds were she'd hate being a parent. She's lucky that didn't happen, but the odds were not in her favour. That's not so nice a thing to do to your potential offspring.

Alice: You don't know what the fuck you're talking about. When a woman has a baby, the hormones in her body produce oxytocin. Her brain chemistry changes when her body releases oxytocin and that's what generates a life-long bond with a child. That's how parent-child love happens!

Eve: That's different to being a good parent. Being a good parent is a day-to-day process that extends over time. It's a serious commitment; it's boring and frustrating a lot of the time. Some days it makes you want to pull your hair out.

Alice: All the best things in life are like that. A good job is like that. Relationships are like that.

Eve: But motherhood isn't something you're well suited to just because you've given birth. It's about facilitating a person's growth from infancy to adulthood. It's stressful and it drives you mad. Initially, it involves not getting a lot of sleep, trying to breastfeed, changing nappies and trying to guess why your baby's been screaming for hours. Then a few years on, it's about cooking and cleaning, taking the kids to school, re-arranging the house so it's kid friendly, stopping them from being naughty, telling them off, putting up boundaries, having a bed-time routine. If we had kids, you, my darling, would have to get much better at domestic chores and routines. You couldn't be spontaneous the way you are now; you couldn't be out every night until 4am; you'd have to do mornings and you'd have to put all this effort into a person who might, at the end of the day, be really fucking hard to get on with. You could have a kid that doesn't gel with you. It could be a kid that's not someone you would even be friends with, if they weren't your kid.

Alice: None of that matters, Eve. All mums get through that shit. Love for your children is more primal than anything. It pushes you through the tough bits. It's not like loving a friend. It's not conditional.

Eve: But it's incredibly difficult and a good parent is in it for the long haul. It's not just about feeling broody.

Alice: Any mum is already in it for the long haul once she's bonded with her baby. That love happens because of hormones. If you feel the maternal instinct, alongside that instinct is an unbearably powerful and immense love for your child, once it's born. That's just human biology.

Eve: But a lot of parents find it hard to like children that are quite different to them, or children with behavioural problems. Maternal instincts don't change that.

Alice: They do if we're talking about decent parents.

Eve: My mother didn't find it easy to love me when she found out who I really was and it went against her whole perception of what I should be.

Alice: That's because of how selfish your mum is. Cara isn't a normal person.

Eve: (sighing) I know she isn't.

Alice: Most people are good parents, Eve. People are built for that, especially women.

Eve: Well, I don't know if that's actually true. I don't know how well most women cope with motherhood.

Alice: Don't you think you're being a bit judgemental?

Eve: I don't know. It's just–

Alice: (interrupting) Good mums always do a good job of loving their kids. They love their children more than they love themselves, their parents, their partners, their friends, or anything else. That happens naturally. Personality clashes don't matter.

Eve: But it's not like that for everyone.

Alice: Well, if there's nothing wrong with you, it just happens. Everything turns out fine.

Eve: Alice, be realistic. All of that may be true if you naturally love children. But as I keep saying, you find it painful to be in the presence of a child.

Alice: Enjoying other people's children has nothing to do with whether or not I should become a mother. Women who find children hard always love being parents once they do it.

Eve: And what makes you so sure they always love it? What makes you so sure they love it on the days it's painful and exhausting?

Alice: The fact that they love it is the reason they carry on. Women love being mums when they get to be mums. It's only beforehand that they sometimes get nervous.

Eve: So, you think even women who hate children love being mums when it happens to them.

Alice: Of course I do! It's different when it's your kid. Everybody knows that.

Eve: It sounds like you think nobody in their right mind would choose not to have children.

Alice: Well, I know it still happens. People sometimes make mistakes they regret.

Eve: You make it sound like motherhood isn't a choice.

Alice: It's not a choice, really. It's like being gay or being trans. This is part of being a woman. We're built to breed; we're baby making ovens. You can feel it in your heart.

Eve: Well, I don't feel this thing you're describing and I never have. Does that mean I'm less of a woman?

Alice: It means it probably hasn't happened to you yet! It means maybe you should be more patient. Don't make a judgement about it until it does.

Eve: Well, what if I don't want it to happen? What if I like our life the way it is? What if I'm happy not having to clean up nappies and calm down tantrums? What if I don't want to live with a stroppy teenager? What if I like only living with you?

Alice: None of that has anything to do with whether or not you want to be a mum.

Eve: (loudly) But it does! Why should you be a mum if you don't want those things?

Alice: Eve, listen to me: being a mum isn't like choosing a career. It's not something you do because the job description sounds appealing. Everybody knows parenthood can drive you batty some days. Women do it because they know they can't be truly happy unless it happens. It's like being around other people. Humans are social creatures; we need the company of other people. It doesn't matter who they are. Women need to have children, just like women need to love and communicate with others. It's just what women are like.

Eve: (irritated) But every woman is different!

Alice: People are far more alike than we like to believe. We're all human.

Eve: But we know not all women need to have kids in order to be happy. Not all women are heterosexual; not all women want to get married; not all women need to wear makeup. Not all women need to have boxes of expensive jewellery or bake chocolate biscuits or be posh or live in the bloody suburbs, Alice. Humanity is diverse!

Alice: You're putting words in my mouth.

Eve: I'm not. I'm just trying explain how–

Alice: (interrupting) You're not listening. You always do this.

Eve: I am listening, but you also need to think about what I'm saying! We live in a democracy, Alice. Women have rights. Being a mother is a choice today. That's why society allows women to terminate a pregnancy. That's why supporting that right is called being 'pro-choice.'

Alice: But I'm not against anyone having an abortion. You know I'm pro-choice.

Eve: Then why do you keep saying having a child isn't a choice?

Alice: Women can't control when they're broody and the World Health Organisation considers infertility a disease. Everyone knows it causes depression. I thought you knew that. I thought you were educated, Eve. Your students look up to you.

Eve: (loudly) That doesn't have anything to do with motherhood not being a choice!

Alice: Eve, calm down.

Eve: (loudly) I am calm!

Alice: Then listen to me. I need you to really listen.

Eve: (distraught) I am listening.

Alice: If you're a normal woman with a natural hormone cycle, you will NOT enjoy life without children. If you're psychologically healthy, if your body isn't seriously off in some way, you'll most likely regret not doing whatever you can to conceive while the option is still available. That's what it says in any fertility blog.

Eve: Alice, there are plenty of women who blog about how happy they are not having children.

Alice: They're in denial, like I was. When you're in denial, you go out of your way to convince other people you're happy. When you're happy with your choices, you don't write a fucking blog about it. You don't need to.

Eve: And what makes you so sure none of those women are happy?

Alice: Your body punishes you for not having children. It makes you unhappy.

Eve: That's not true, Alice.

Alice: That's what all the infertility literature says! That's why infertility is considered a disease. The recommended treatment isn't therapy; it's conception. Why do you think IVF exists?

Eve: Well, my body hasn't 'punished' me for living the life I want.

Alice: You can delude yourself into thinking you're different. But trust me, babes. Statistically speaking, you will most likely get broody at some point in the next few years. If you ignore it, you won't be pleased with yourself. You'll make yourself miserable. You don't want to be miserable, Eve. You've already struggled with depression. You don't need more of that.

Eve: And why are you so certain that having a child won't make me miserable? Why are you so sure accepting something I don't want would make me so unbelievably happy?

Alice: Because at this point in your life, you can't know whether or not you want to be a mum. You haven't experienced the urge yet.

Eve: Well, what if I get it and I still prefer my life the way it is?

Alice: You won't. That's not what human beings are like.

Eve: (rolling eyes) So once again, it's not a choice. Every woman loves being a mummy, once it happens.

Alice: Any woman who's normal.

Eve: Well, then you're with one abnormal fucking woman, Alice. Not only am I gay, I can't imagine motherhood making me happy. I never could.

Alice: You couldn't imagine liking sex when you were nine either.

Eve: (confused) What are you on about?

Alice: When you're a kid and you first find out what sex is, you can't imagine why anybody in their right mind would want to do something so strange. It seems mad people would enjoy something so icky. Right?

Eve: I suppose.

Alice: During adolescence, when you become sexual, all that ickiness goes away. Sex becomes hot and passionate and beautiful. It makes you cum and when you look back on your childish feelings, you laugh at them. They become absurd, crazy even… unless there's something very wrong with you. Maternal instincts are like that.

Eve: Maybe, but I don't look at urges that way. I don't have sex whenever I feel the urge to have sex.

Alice: Eve, you should have sex more! I've never discouraged you from exploring people outside of us.

Eve: I know you haven't.

Alice: You know I'd love to see you go down on another woman. That's always been one of my fantasies, but you never want to go there!

Eve: Well, maybe it's not one of my fantasies.

Alice: Maybe you're afraid.

Eve: Afraid of what?

Alice: Afraid you'd actually like it. Afraid you'd actually enjoy going down on Loraine.

Eve: Well, maybe I understand that just because I feel an urge to do something, that doesn't mean I should throw caution to the wind and act like an idiot. I have urges to eat too much. I have urges to sleep when I should be awake. I have all sorts of stupid urges.

Alice: I just think you should just do whatever it is that makes you happy. I'm not someone that would ever stop you from being happy, Eve.

Eve: I know that, lovely. I just want you to hear me now.

Alice: The problem though is you're not hearing me. You're the one that stops you from being happy. That's what I'm trying to tell you.

Eve: Alice, I'm self-reflective enough to know that I make myself unhappy. I can listen to you when you say that. I know I'm not perfect.

Alice: You're so repressed and fearful, I honestly think you're at a point where you don't even know what makes you happy. That's how damaged you've become.

Eve: So, I'm damaged because I'm happy not being a mum?

Alice: Eve, you can't fool me. I can see through your bullshit.

Eve: Alice, how could you possibly know what–

Alice: (interrupting) Happiness is fucking chemical, Eve. It's neurological. Depression is neurological. I'm only trying to help you make the best of your life. That's what we do for each other in this relationship, like you said. We're a team.

Eve: I know that. But what's best for me has to do with what I KNOW I WANT in my life.

Alice: Nobody completely knows everything they want in their life. You can't lead a meaningful life if you never take any chances.

Eve: Well, one thing I absolutely know is I don't want the day-to-day minutia of being a parent. I don't want to commit myself to cleaning up nappies and fighting tantrums every day. I want to enjoy children and I can do that by seeing them in small doses. I can enjoy kids if I see them as much as I see my friends. If I had to live with any of my friends, we'd fall out. The only person I can live with is you. That's why my life is set up this way. Now can we go to bed?

Alice: Eve, before I got broody, I felt the same way as you. But you have to trust me. You'll change. Everyone does.

Eve: But I don't want to change. I don't even want to feel broody, Alice.

Alice: Why be so closed minded about that? Why not let just let your instincts just emerge, the way they do in most women?

Eve: Because I just don't want them. I don't want to even want to be a mum. I like the desires I already have.

Alice: (adamantly) But you're missing out on what every woman says is the most wonderful experience in the world! Why deprive yourself of that?

Eve: Because I like grownup conversations. I like being able to swear and talk about sex. I like to watch Davis McFarlin porn in my living room. I like being able to walk around my home naked, as long as I shut the curtains. I like being with someone it's not my job to control, someone I don't always have to cook and clean for, someone who knows how to share and have a conversation without interrupting, screaming or throwing shit around.

Alice: But do you think that's healthy, though? Do you think it's healthy to be so rigid?

Eve: (irritated) You think I'm unhealthy because I don't want to live with daily nappies and puke? You think I'm unhealthy because I don't want to live with a mardy teen I have to control?

Alice: You've cleaned up my puke. You controlled me when I needed it.

Eve: (loudly) That's different!

Alice: I don't see how it is. I bathed you and drove you to hospital when you couldn't get out of bed, when things were really bad five years ago. Don't you remember?

Eve: It's not the same! We're grownups and those incidences were complete one-offs. We're normally independent people who can do basic shit a child can't.

Alice: (loudly) But that's not their fault, Eve!

Eve: (loudly) I know it's not!

Alice: Then why punish them for that?

Eve: (loudly) I'm not punishing anyone!

Alice: Yes, you are. You're angry because a child can't behave like an adult. It's like you're punishing them for boring you. That's what's going on here.

Eve: No, Alice. I'm choosing not to create a child that would ever bore me.

Alice: (incredulous) But why? That child needs you to love it!

Eve: (yelling angrily) Because I don't fucking want to love a child!! I don't have the patience for raising a child and neither do you!!

Alice: (loudly) But I'm trying to change! I'm tired of being this way!

Eve: Well, maybe I don't want to change. Maybe I don't want to give up my life for someone that hasn't even been born. Maybe I don't want to have the patience to love someone who doesn't understand me, someone that might be the sort of person I don't even enjoy spending time with.

Alice: You sound like you're proud of that.

Eve: I'm not proud of it; it's just something about me that's never going to change. I can be patient, but not for things I fundamentally don't want to do. I'm not someone that wants to be a mum. I never have been. I have love for you and my friends and I can babysit for them, but that's it! I'm childfree, Alice. That means I'm voluntarily childless. I don't ever want to have children. Even if I could have kids and sacrifice very little, I still wouldn't want them.

Alice: But why can't you learn to love in new ways? Why don't you want to grow and experience love in ways you never thought possible?

Eve: I don't know why I'm this way… I just am. This is who you've been in a relationship with for fifteen years.

Alice: I think you sell yourself short.

Eve: I do what's right for me, Alice. That's why I chose you over my own family.

Alice: But how you can know motherhood isn't right for you? You've never done it!

Eve: I don't know. I just do. I feel it very, very strongly.

Alice: Eve, why do doctors always refuse to sterilise young women that haven't had children?

Eve: Because the doctors are worried they'll regret it. I know that. I'm not thick.

Alice: Exactly. That means you *can't* know how you want to live the rest of your life until you've actually been broody. Experiencing broodiness changes you. You ignore that urge at your peril. Ask any doctor.

Eve: (sighing)…I hate doctors.

8. PROCREATION: Oppression

Eve is quite frustrated with Alice. She's not only frustrated with Alice for engaging her in a heated argument at four in the morning. She's also frustrated with Alice for being so dogmatic about something she should be more open-minded about. Alice is supposed to be a progressive, but the way she is talking to Eve doesn't seem progressive at all.

Alice is also bisexual and bohemian. She has an openness to alternative lifestyles that seems completely at odds with the things she is now saying about motherhood. It feels to Eve like Alice is acting as though being a woman without children is a terrible predicament, rather than simply one of many possible lifestyle choices that can bring happiness and fulfilment. This isn't how queer women are supposed to think. Queer women are supposed to be tolerant and flexible in their family choices. Or at least, that's how Eve thinks queer women are supposed to be.

Eve: I really don't understand why you're behaving like this. It's like you're a different person.

Alice: Don't gaslight me, Eve. I'm tired of you trying to manipulate everything.

Eve: (loudly) I'm not manipulating anything!

Alice: Then please do me a favour and stop the bullshit, okay? I'm not your enemy. I'm just trying to help you.

Eve: I know that, but you need to understand that I really am childfree, Alice. I'm not lying or manipulating you when I say that. I really don't want to raise children, I really don't want to get pregnant and I really don't want to give birth.

Alice: But again… why, Eve? How can you be so sure about something you've never even experienced?

Eve: Because I know what I'm like when a kid throws a tantrum. I hate it; it deeply upsets me. So, having the responsibility of dealing with tantrums isn't a permanent job I would ever voluntarily take on. Love wouldn't compensate for how horrible it would make me feel. I'd wind up resenting my kid.

Alice: Kids don't spend their whole lives in tantrum mode. That's such a stupid argument.

Eve: I don't care. I don't want to deal with any tantrums, ever.

Alice: Maybe we should end this conversation.

Eve: (confused) Why?...I thought you wanted to talk about this…

Alice: You're not listening. You're shutting me down. I hate it when you do this.

Eve: (angrily) I'm not shutting you down!

Alice: You always lecture me about how it's important to think through things carefully. You should practice what you preach.

Eve: (loudly) I have thought about this carefully!

Alice: I at least thought you wouldn't talk down to me.

Eve: (exasperated) I'm not talking down to you! I just never knew you'd suddenly feel this way! I'm trying to understand! This has come out of NOWHERE and it's nearly five in the morning!

Alice: It's come out for a reason. You say you love me, but you've never asked me how I felt about having a baby.

Eve: (passionately) That's because we always planned our lives together without kids being a part of them!

Alice: (angrily) But why haven't we discussed this for ages? Things change. Why didn't you check with me??

Eve: (loudly) Because you hate children and I put up with them because I have to!

Alice: (loudly) But I'm trying to change! I'm trying to be a better person!

Eve: Well, I didn't know that before tonight.

Alice: Why did you just assume you knew what I wanted?

Eve: (with sadness) …Because I didn't think you were 'normal' Alice. I thought you loved our life together. I thought you felt comfortable planning a life around us being a family of two. I thought you were happy living with just me, that I would never bore you, or make you feel like a big part of you needs to be suppressed.

Alice: (angrily) You have never asked me though!

Eve: (looking down and shaking her head) Fine, that was my mistake. We should have talked about this earlier. That's one thing I was careless about. I admit that. We should have talked about our family plans again.

Alice: You're the reason we're up at this hour, having this fucking conversation. It's not me. You're the problem.

Eve: (trying desperately to reason with Alice) Alice, when we first got together, the only lesbian parents we knew were people who had kids from other relationships with straight people... Having kids as a lesbian couple wasn't an issue then. People didn't really think it was possible. We're only having this conversation now because we have choices we didn't have before!

Alice: But this isn't a choice, Eve. I'll kill myself if I can't get pregnant.

Eve: (sighing) That's not going to happen, Alice. I would never let that happen to you.

Alice: It feels like I don't have your support. I feel like you don't care about me.

Eve: (irritated) You know I support you, but this isn't just about whether YOU can have children. This is about whether I get forced to become a mum! What about my feelings?

Alice: You know what this is like? It's like I'm transgender and I am trying to be brave and come out. But instead of supporting me, you're acting like my feelings are silly.

Eve: That's because your feelings aren't just affecting you. Your feelings have fucking consequences for me and my life.

Alice: (passionately) That's what transphobic parents always say to their kids!

Eve: (loudly) I'm not a transphobe and you're not trans!

Alice: (angrily) Eve, you're worse than a fucking transphobe! You're acting like a self-hating trans person. Like someone who can't even admit who they are, because they're obsessed with suppressing any feelings that don't conform to society's norms.

Eve: (angrily) Fucking hell, you're the one who's trying to get me to conform!

Alice: (loudly) No, I'm not! I'm just sick of you kidding yourself!

Eve: Alice, I can only tell you the truth; the truth as I see it; the truth as I know it and the truth as I feel it in the deepest parts of my soul. I'm a cis woman, I'm a lesbian and I'm childfree. This is my truth. This is who I am and this is who I've always been.

Alice: (shaking her head) You're just describing what society wants you to be.

Eve: (incredulous) You think society wants me to be a childfree lesbian?

Alice: Society is totally homophobic. Society would prefer only straight people raise children.

Eve: So, you want me to go against society by turning off my feelings? You want me to repress who I am, so you can 'smash the patriarchy?'

Alice: No, but I don't want you to give up on us and break us up. Breaking up is the one thing I would hate more than anything.

Eve: (angrily) And you think I wouldn't hate that?

Alice: If you hate it, then why can't you give us a chance? Why can't we raise a family and stay together?

Eve: (yelling) Because I'd hate it and you won't fucking hear me! You're not listening!

Alice: You don't have to keep shouting at me.

Eve: (feeling exhausted by Alice) I'm sorry… it's just, I feel like I can't defend myself. I can't explain or justify why I don't want kids. It's like… no reason's good enough for you.

Alice: But you don't need to defend yourself, Eve. I'm not attacking you.

Eve: I know, I know… I'm sorry. I just can't explain how this feels.

Alice: You don't need to explain your feelings to me. I just need you to not belittle my feelings.

Eve: I'm not belittling you, Alice.

Alice: Then why won't you listen to me?

Eve: I am listening, I just disagree with you.

Alice: It feels like you're pushing me away. Like you know what I'm saying is true and you don't want to hear it, so you're trying to make it look like I'm attacking you. This is so immature, Eve. You're better than this.

Eve: I don't think you're attacking me, but I do think you're trying to fundamentally change how I feel. My feelings about this aren't being acknowledged or valued.

Alice: (loudly) You don't even know what your feelings are! You're only feeling what society wants you to feel!

Eve: (angrily) And you think you know my feelings better than I do?

Alice: (emphatically) No woman knows what they want until they become broody! It can make EVERYTHING you've ever felt flip right on its head!

Eve: Well, some of us don't want our personalities to completely change. Some of us like who we are.

Alice: (giggling) Babes, I love you to bits, but you can be a stubborn cow sometimes. You always resist me when I show you something new and positive. It takes you time to get there, I guess.

Eve: (irritated) That's so condescending!

Alice: (passionately) You're the one who's being condescending! You think you know more about queer politics than I do!

Eve: This isn't about queer politics. This is about what I want to do with my life.

Alice: No, it's not. It's about homophobia, Eve. You're preventing queer people from being taken seriously as parents. You're reinforcing a stigma.

At this point, Alice is very confident that she will soon get what she wants from Eve.

Alice feels like she is skilfully defeating an opponent during a kick boxing match, an opponent who lacks Alice's stamina and coordination and who is also woefully underprepared.

This is why it doesn't matter how hard Eve tries to explain herself. Alice will always have a comeback. Alice is quite adept at mixing her comebacks with belittling insults and expressing anger that she's not actually feeling. Alice has been practicing all of this in her head for nearly two weeks.

However, achieving victory is still quite painful for Alice. She finds it very difficult to hurt Eve, given that Eve is the love of her life. But Alice also feels like she needs to stay focused on winning, because she's trying to do something that will greatly benefit Eve. Because Alice is trying to help Eve, Alice thinks winning is more important than whether or not Eve is in pain.

In order to stay focused, Alice keeps reminding herself, "I'm only doing what straight women do all the time. In fact, this is probably why we exist as a species. This is what women have been doing to men for thousands of years."

Eve, on the other hand, is still confident that if she fully explains herself, Alice will finally understand that their relationship is more important than procreation. Eve thinks that if you love a childfree person, your love should ultimately be more important than whether or not you want to have a child. In a similar way, Eve thinks that if you have a child, your love for that child should ultimately be more important than whether or not that child makes you a grandparent. Eve thinks that if she can demonstrate that her childfree status is an expression of her authentic self, Alice will realise she is being silly and the two of them will finally be able to go to bed. Eve is tired and frustrated, but still working hard to quickly resolve this dispute.

This is partly because Eve can't sleep if she knows Alice is cross with her.

Eve: (trying to stay awake) I'm just being myself, Alice. I know I'm a very flawed, fucked up and imperfect gal. I know I'm not a paragon of virtue. But the fact that I don't want kids isn't something terrible about me. It doesn't make me a broken human being, even if it's not good for queer people. And it certainly doesn't invalidate how much we love each other.

Alice: Oh, shush. You know you'll love it when you're holding them in your arms. You'll remember tonight and laugh. You'll laugh at how ridiculous you were being.

Eve: (exhausted) Just give it a rest, Alice. We can talk more about this tomorrow. Let's be friends and go to bed.

Alice: It doesn't matter if we talk about this tomorrow. Once you see our children… once you see their faces, you'll change. You'll have all the patience you need.

Eve: But that's not a patience I want to develop. I don't want to love being a mum. I'm happy not liking children. I'm happy preferring the company of adults.

Alice: (angrily) But that's fucking bigoted!

Eve: Bigoted or not, I like my life the way it is. I don't want to love children.

Alice: (loudly) That's like saying you don't want to learn to be kind to strangers! Or get along with people that are different to you!

Eve: I know it sounds awful…

Alice: (disgusted with Eve) It's narcissistic, like you can only love people like you.

Eve: (frustrated) I don't like how it sounds either, alright? But I can't do anything about it!

Alice: I feel like I don't know you… like the person I thought I loved all these years is just a narcissistic bigot who thinks all kids need a daddy.

Eve: That's not what I am and that's not what I think, Alice. I'm just–

Alice: (interrupting) You're propping up the myth that gay couples are selfish party arseholes who can't stop shagging! That's what straight people think when they look at us! They think we're freaks!

Eve: Well, I'm not a freak, but I am an eccentric and I'm fine with that. I don't mind being different to other people.

Alice: (adamantly) But we're not living in a time where queer people can be outsiders anymore!

Eve: I thought we were living in a time where it was okay to be an individual.

Alice: That's capitalist bullshit, Eve. We're living in a time where we have to fight for all queer people to finally have the opportunity to be included in society.

Eve: But isn't it more important that queer people are free to make their own choices?

Alice: (irritated) That's a load of Ayn Rand rubbish. Every choice is political. You know the personal is political. You fucking teach it!

Eve: (sighing) …I just want to be myself, Alice. I don't want to live in a world where I can't be myself.

Alice: (with disdain) Everything is always about you, isn't it?

Eve: Maybe it is narcissistic, but I'm not bringing a child into the world if it doesn't feel right.

Alice: Do you really think the feelings of one individual are more important than the stigmas queer couples face when they try and start families?

Eve: (softly) …They might not be, but I still don't want to have unwanted children, just to remove somebody else's stigma. I know that's not helpful for promoting justice. I know it's not progressive. I know it's selfish, but–

Alice: (interrupting) I had no idea your family damaged you this badly. It's so sad.

Eve: (sighing) It could have been my family; it could have been my mum; it could have been all the years I was bullied by other kids. It could have been a million things.

Alice: You really do need some therapy. I'm concerned about you.

Eve: All I know is I'm not hurting anyone.

Alice: (rolling her eyes) Um, you're hurting queer parents, for starters.

Eve: I mean in my day-to-day life… I'm not hurting any child. It doesn't hurt anyone that I have the family I've always wanted. It doesn't hurt anyone in my day-to-day life that I'm not a mum and have no desire to be one.

Alice: (loudly) But you are hurting people! You're hurting me!

Eve: Well, I'm not exactly getting your compassion or understanding either.

Alice: Oh, yes you are. You're also getting my love.

Eve: This doesn't feel like love, Alice. It feels like you're putting pressure on me. That's honestly how it feels.

Alice: (passionately) That's because you're confused and you need time to think about this! I know how you are.

Eve: (feeling even more exhausted) ...I feel like I'm trying to communicate something important about who I am.

Alice: (dismissively) You're not communicating anything.

Eve: I feel like you're dismissing everything I'm saying, like you're trying to silence my voice.

Alice: (shaking her head). You don't even know what your voice is doing. If you could hear yourself now and hear how crazy you sound, you'd wonder why I'm even talking to you. The shit coming out of your mouth is fucking demented. It's almost like you're on crack, Eve.

Eve: (shaking her head) I feel like… you're trying to medicalise me… like you're trying to convince me I'm ill or something, for not wanting to breed my way into a suburban family. That's how this feels.

Alice: Well, then you're reading the situation wrong. I just want you to stop talking bollocks.

Eve: It's not bollocks to be childfree, Alice.

Alice: You're in denial, babes. You need a wake-up call. You do that for me when I need it.

Eve: (angrily) Well, I don't feel like I'm getting a fucking wake-up call! I haven't been to sleep yet!

Alice: (loudly) That's because you're pushing it away! You're not listening!

Eve: (getting more and more angry) I am listening! And what I'm hearing is you trying to push me into having children! And not only that, you're making me feel crazy for thinking I should have a say in the matter!

Alice: But I'm giving you your say. You can say anything you want!

Eve: Then why won't you believe me when I tell you I'm happy being childfree?

Alice: (disgusted) God, do you have to be so rigid in how you define yourself? Does that actually make you happy?

Eve: (exasperated) Yes! It makes me happy!

Alice: (shaking her head disapprovingly) I don't understand you. I can't figure you out anymore

Eve: Well, this is who I am.

Alice: It's so sad… I'm with an unbalanced nutter who thinks children need a father. That's why you don't want to be a mum, isn't it?

Eve: (getting fed up with Alice) Maybe it is! Or maybe I don't like having to clean up after children! Or maybe I like not having the patience to teach another person how to wipe their bum!

Alice: You know what you are? You're a snob. You're a middle-class snob.

Eve: (sarcastically) Yes, I'm so snobby… to think a woman might not want to stick her hand in shit!

Alice: (looking very sad) Eve, it's not just snobby. It's cold and uncaring.

It means you're not who I thought you were.

Eve: Who did the hell did you think I was?

Alice: Eve, we're going to get old someday. All the things you're happy not having the patience to do… you'd have to do all those things for me, if anything bad happened.

Eve: (loudly) Of course I would! This isn't about that!

Alice: What if I got early-onset Alzheimer's, like your dad? You made yourself have the patience you needed to care for him. Why do that for him and not for me? You made me wipe his arse with you!

Eve: (loudly) You know I'd wipe your arse if I had to! This isn't about the distant future! This is about choosing to wipe a kid's bum every day right now!

Alice: (sighing) …You just said you were well chuffed with yourself for not having the patience to wipe someone else's bum.

Eve: (in frustration) It's different with you. You're my equal! You're an adult! You're autonomous!

Alice: So was your dad.

Eve: I know that, but he stopped being all of those things, Alice. He stopped being my equal. He became someone who couldn't make decisions, someone I had to treat like a toddler. That's why it was painful. I don't want to look after someone like that again if I have a choice about it. If it happened to you, that would be different. It wouldn't be a choice!

Alice: (incredulous) But you're choosing not to do that for your babies. Why don't you want to look after your own babies?

Eve: (loudly) Because I don't want to have any fucking babies! I just want to live with my life with you! What's so fucking terrible about that!!?? What's so terrible about the last fifteen years!!?

Alice: Nothing really, but we're getting older now.

Eve: What does that have to do with anything?

Alice: We need to grow up.

Eve: I already have grown up.

Alice: (indignantly) No, you haven't. You can't just be selfish and hate people that are different to you. The fact that you don't know that really fucking disturbs me, Eve. I never thought you could be so intolerant!

Eve: (exasperated) …What the fuck?

Alice: (angrily) If you carry on like this, I'll miss out on the most wonderful experience that comes with being a woman! I'll be deprived of what I need, with this big hole in my heart. You'll break my heart, Eve. You'll kill me if I can't have children with you.

Eve: (trying to remain calm) Alice, have you actually thought about me? Have you thought about what would break my heart?

Alice: I think about it every day and it saddens me more than anything.

Eve: (passionately) It would break my heart having people in my home I have to look after, people completely dependent on me, people who can't make decisions or do basic things, people I have to control, people I might not even like. It would break my heart if my life was ten times harder than it actually is! It would break my mental health!

Alice: That is pure unadulterated bullshit, Eve. Infertility is what's bad for your mental health. Children are what make life meaningful.

Eve: I'm sorry but they can't be, Alice. Not for someone like me.

Alice: (yelling) WHY NOT? WHAT MAKES YOU SO DIFFERENT?

Eve: (sighing) I don't know, Alice… The things that make most women happy don't make me happy. I'm not like a normal woman, maybe. Maybe I'm more like a man. I don't know if that's what's–

Alice: (interrupting disapprovingly) You're looking at it in such a selfish way. You're so spiteful and arrogant, it's disgusting.

Eve: (loudly) Tell me how what I said is spiteful!

Alice: (adamantly) You should know why it's spiteful! Feminist men love children. It's you that hates them.

Eve: (passionately) But I don't hate children!

Alice: It's like you're forgetting that your children will actually grow up. They'll become adults who love you. They'll be your legacy and they'll love you more than anyone!

Eve: (loudly) Yes and we might not fucking like each other!

Alice: That's conditional love, Eve. That's worse than bigotry. It's damaging.

Eve: It is what it is, Alice.

Alice: (with disgust) I hope you don't love me that way!

Eve: (loudly) It's the reason I can love you! I love you because of how much I like you! That's why I want you in my home every day.

Alice: (definitively) Well, thankfully, once we have kids, you'll change. You'll think about our home in a completely different way.

Eve: (adamantly) Alice, you can have as many babies as you want, but I AM NOT becoming their second mummy. If I devote my life to people in my home, I want them to be people that have already been raised. I want the people I love most to be people that are already my equals, not dependents.

Alice: (angrily) So it's true! You won't raise a child because you think it's inferior to you!

Eve: It's not that it's inferior to me. It's that–

Alice: (interrupting) You talk about kids like someone who abuses them!

Eve: (frustrated) No, I don't! I would never harm a child!

Alice: Then how can you hate the idea of raising your own child? How is something so magical for women so painful for you?

Eve: I don't know Alice… I don't know why I'm the way I am. I'm just me. I've always felt this way.

Alice: Then do the right thing; do the humane thing. Face your demons head on. Don't give in to them and be stupid. You do that enough as it is.

At this point, Eve is beginning to feel something she has never felt before: Eve's feelings are being hurt by Alice.

In the past, Alice has disappointed and frustrated Eve. Alice has made Eve deeply angry. She has even been physically violent with Eve. But Alice has never hurt Eve, emotionally. This feeling of being hurt reminds Eve of how her family made her feel, when they rejected her for being a lesbian.

Reading their hand-written letters, Eve felt like she was being blackmailed. There was nothing Eve could say, no argument she could give and no compromise she could offer, that would induce her family to give her even the slightest bit of acceptance. It was as if Eve was forced at gunpoint to either pretend to be completely straight or lose the love of all the people she felt closest to.

Eve: (with sadness) You know, I always thought I'd be rejected by people for wanting to love a woman. I thought people would think I'm disgusting for that. I lived all my life with that pain.

Alice: Where did this come from?

Eve: (sighing) I never thought I'd have to worry about children…. this is mental.

Alice: You thought women in lesbian relationships hate children?

Eve: No… I just thought you would never act like a straight girl. I didn't expect to be treated like this for not wanting kids, Alice. I thought I'd get more acceptance from you.

Alice: (loudly) You're the one who can't accept what people need! You think you're enough to make a woman happy! You think you're better than a son or a daughter! What a fucking ego you have!

Eve: (softly) Maybe it's my ego. Or maybe I was crazy enough to think loving JUST me wouldn't be so horrendous and unbearable to someone…

Alice: It doesn't have to be unbearable, Eve. It's unbearable if I can't have kids with you.

Eve: (feeling like a disposable commodity) I actually thought that if you fell in love with me, that if you stayed with me for this long… that maybe you could be happy loving me and me alone. I didn't think that happiness was impossible…

Alice: Well, I'm sorry but it is impossible. My body now needs us to raise a family together. I'm broody.

Eve: (looking down) Yes and your broodiness makes you hate me for being myself.

Alice: I don't hate you. I just don't like it when you reinforce social norms.

Eve: (sighing) I'm not reinforcing anything, Alice. I'm just trying not to have my life destroyed before I go to sleep.

Alice: (defensively) Babes, I'm only doing for you what you've always done for me! You always tell me when I'm being selfish, when I'm behaving irresponsibly, when I'm not practicing self-care.

Eve: I know I do.

Alice: When I fuck up, you pull me up on it. I need that and so do you.

Eve: But I haven't fucked up.

Alice: You're trying to take the piss and I'm setting limits. I'm giving you boundaries.

Eve: (suddenly feeling angry) So are you my mother? Is that how this works?

Alice: I won't let you get away with bigotry and narrow-mindedness, especially about things that are so important for our community. Do you honestly think that I would let you get away with saying that kids need a father?

Eve: (angrily) I feel like you don't respect me anymore, like you're happy to walk all over me because you think I'll just sit there and take it!

Alice: (like a stern parent) Eve, I'm trying to set a good example for you. I'm trying to love you and show you how to be happy!

Eve: (loudly) This doesn't feel like love! This feels like my family all over again.

Alice: Why?

Eve: (yelling) Because you're acting like your beliefs are more important than me!

Alice: (loudly) Just go to bed! I can't talk to you about this anymore.

Eve: (surprised) …Why?

Alice: (contemptuously) I can't believe what a cold fucking bitch you are! You make me sick if I'm honest. I regret ever having met you.

Eve: (shocked and hurt) …What?

Alice: Sometimes I wish you did kill yourself. You know that? I give you so many chances and you let me down, over and over again.

Eve: (taken aback) …Just because I'm childfree?

Alice: How can I trust that you love me? How do I know you can love anyone? How can I trust that you're even a good person?

Eve: (confused and hurt) …I don't understand.

Alice: (like a disappointed parent) You're rejecting motherhood! You're rejecting the deepest love that there is, the love that teaches humans how to love, the most primal love a queer woman could ever experience for another person! When you belittle the sacredness of that love without ever having experienced it, that makes it hard for me to love you, Eve. I'm being honest with you, here. I'll always love you but I'm just saying… it's not easy right now.

Eve: (feeling very sad) You don't find it easy to love me?

Alice: (disapprovingly) Not always. The way you talk about our future sometimes… It's shocking how callous you are.

Eve: (shaking her head) You know, I never thought such a big part of who I am…could make me lose everything… twice. I didn't think my life would wind up like this. Never in a million years.

Alice: (abruptly) Oh, get over yourself! Women can't choose to settle for relationships where their partners hate children. I love you but you have to face reality!

Eve: You're not happy with me, are you? That's what this is about. It's not about babies or queer politics. You're upset at me.

Alice: I am upset at you. Telling me you won't have kids is like forcing me to be straight. It's that bad.

Eve: (incredulous) Blimey, Alice! You're making it sound like I'm oppressing you because I'm not–

Alice: (interrupting loudly) You are! You're fucking destroying our lives! And you're destroying any chance you'll ever have of making a woman happy! Not just me.

Eve: (looking very sad) I feel like you don't love me anymore.

Alice: Well, I feel like you've lost me, at this point. It's like you've lost yourself.

Eve: (feeling hopeless) I feel lost, Alice… I never thought I'd lose the love of my life… Not over kids…

Alice: (suddenly reassuring) But you don't have to lose the love of your life over kids! Don't give up on our relationship so easily!

Eve suddenly thinks about what it would be like to break up with Alice at this moment in her life. Eve knows that she's not psychologically strong enough to handle a break-up. She knows she couldn't cope with being all alone, especially during a time when she's battling a depressive episode. The idea of suddenly destroying the relationship that helped Eve survive her own adolescence seems utterly terrifying.

Eve: (anxiously) I'm not giving up on you, Alice! I'd never give up on you! I need you…

Alice: I need you too! You're the person I need more than anyone!

Eve: (in fearful desperation) But I'm just so scared right now… I'm so frightened of losing everything… I don't know how I could cope with things the way that my brain is–

Alice: (interrupting) There's no reason to be scared, Eve. Just take a deep breath and stay calm.

Eve: (sighing in a panic) I don't want to be rejected again… I couldn't handle that… Not by you… not now…

Alice hugs Eve and holds her face in her hands.

Alice: You're not getting rejected, Eve. Don't worry about that, okay? That's the last thing I would ever want. All the best things in my life are there because of you.

Alice kisses Eve to comfort her.

Alice: I couldn't be happy without you anymore than I could be happy without a child.

Eve: (still scared) You've been my life for fifteen years! I can't just end that all like it's nothing! I'm not well enough. It's like I'm going under again. I can feel it. I can't even keep track of time…

Alice: (smiling tenderly) You think I don't know that? You're too transparent for your own fucking good!

Eve: Last week when you were in Hull, I didn't get out of bed for two days. I didn't tell you that because I didn't want you to worry about me.

Alice: (with love in her eyes) Why do you think I'm not in Hull now? I know you need me to be here, silly.

Eve: (like a frightened child) …Will you promise to look after me then? Or do I have to worry about going through this alone?

Alice: (softly with a warm smile) You've got me, Eve. You've got me. I'm not going anywhere, you donkey. I love you to bits.

Eve: I know… I know that… This is just so crazy… I feel like such a horrible person…

Alice: (affectionately) Don't worry about how you feel! You're feeling whatever you need to feel right now.

Eve: (suddenly feeling guilty) I don't know why I am the way I am, Alice… The things I'm saying about children sound so horrible…

Alice: You're just confused. Your feelings will sort themselves out. They always do.

Eve: That's what's so horrible. I'm not confused, Alice.

Alice: If I were you, I'd take a diazepam and get a good night's rest. We can talk about this more tomorrow. I'll make you a nice lunch. We can watch Mulholland Drive in bed. Then we can have afternoon tea at Mrs Bridges.

Eve would love to go to bed and be held by Alice, in this moment. She'd love to just end this conversation, as there is now an opportunity for her and Alice to go to sleep without being angry at each other. But Eve still can't bring herself to go to bed until she knows that Alice accepts that she is childfree.

Eve: Alice, I need to know something.

Alice: …What?

Eve: I need to know that our life the way it is… that it's not awful for you. I need to know I'm good enough, the way that I am.

Alice: I won't leave you, but you can't be so pig headed! I need you to hear me!

Eve: (in sad desperation) I'm trying to hear you… I'm really, really trying to listen and think about what you're saying Alice… I'm just so scared…

Alice: It's obvious you're scared. You're scared of not being perfect. You don't believe in your capabilities sometimes. I know that about you.

Eve: I know you do.

Alice: (with love in her eyes) But you always come through, my beauty. You always excel and impress the shit out of me.

Eve: (feeling momentarily reassured) Thanks love. I can do that because you're the one I have supporting me.

Alice: I'll never go away, Eve. I'll always love you to bits, but you have to trust me. You know that I know what's best for you. I'm the only one who can look after you.

Eve: (nodding her head) I know you love me.

Alice: But you need to listen to me right now. You're not well.

Eve: (sighing) I know I'm not.

Alice: Then why do you keep arguing with me?

Eve: (trying to think clearly) I guess… I just need your help when I'm doubting myself sometimes… It doesn't happen very often, but sometimes I just need you to remind me I'm not a terrible person.

Alice: You're the furthest thing from a terrible person! You think you'd be a bad mother but that's complete toss. You're already like an amazing mother, the way you look after your friends. You always give such good advice. You protect people in your life when they need you – not just me. You do that for everyone you care about. You're like the mum I wish I had!

Eve: I'm scared of being pressured into being a mum… I'm scared of you leaving me… I'm scared of everything…

Alice: I'd never leave you. We're having kids and there's nothing scary about that.

Eve: (fearfully) I'm scared of giving a kid a mum that would rather live the life I'm leading now… I'm scared of resenting my son or daughter… I'm scared of resenting you and regretting this choice.

Alice: How many times do I have to repeat this? Women regret NOT having children. They don't regret having them. Even the ones who are ambivalent about it, when they get pregnant, always say it was the greatest thing that ever happened to them. Every mother knows nothing else in her life is more important than her children. Nothing is more satisfying than loving and raising a child. Not friends, not sex, not even a career.

Eve: But I'm not normal, Alice… I don't even feel like a woman now...

Alice: Everyone is unique, honey. But we're all human.

Eve: Can't some humans be happy without having children? Isn't that even possible?

Alice: You're not that kind of human, Eve. I've seen you with my nieces. I can see your maternal streak – and not just with them, I can feel it even when you look after me. It's there; you can't tell me it isn't. And I've honestly never felt anything like it – not even with my mum. I feel completely and totally nurtured by you, like you instinctively love and protect me – every cell in my body. It's unreal how good you are at it.

Eve: Alice, I appreciate what you're saying about me, but that's not the same thing as wanting to be a mother. I'm a childfree woman with a maternal streak, not a woman who wants to be a mum. If I had a kid, it would be because I love you, not because I want it. I'm childfree, Alice.

Alice: (irritated) Don't define yourself with stupid terms like that! When you're dogmatic, you don't do yourself any favours! You limit your opportunities. You miss out on the things that could be the very things you've always needed. Life is always a surprise, Eve. But you have to be open to the best surprises. You can't shut yourself off from them.

Eve: But having a kid isn't a happiness-guaranteed surprise. And it's permanent. It's not like trying out a new job to see whether or not you like it.

Alice: I know it's not. That's not what I'm saying!

Eve: With motherhood, if you don't like it, it's not like you can quit and do something else. You can't change course without ruining someone else's life – the person it's your job to love more than anyone.

Alice: Would you, of all people, willfully choose to ruin a person's life? Would you choose to ruin the life of someone you love?

Eve: (sighing) No… I wouldn't.

Alice: You're not a bad person, Eve. I've never seen you choose to hurt another person and I don't believe you ever would, even if you hated them.

You never let people down. That's not part of your character.

Eve: I know it isn't.

Alice: (smiling) I mean, don't get me wrong, you're a stubborn cow sometimes.

Eve: That's how you see me…

Alice: And yeah, when you're stubborn, you sometimes say nasty things that are cruel. But I know that's not who you are. You're a good person.

Eve: I'm a good person because I care about people, Alice. But not the way a mum loves her children. I'm maternal but not motherly.

Alice: (rolling eyes) There you go again, using labels. Why can't you just be yourself? Why is that so hard for you?

Eve: I'm not labelling myself. I'm just trying to tell you what I am. I don't know how else to tell you if you can't hear me.

Alice: You don't have to tell me anything. I already know you're not childfree.

Eve: (exasperated) Fuck, I don't know how to convince you that this is me! It's like you're trying to make me something I'm not! It's like you're beating me down!

Alice: (giggling) Whatever, babes.

Eve: (angrily) It's like you're trying to give your kids a mum who doesn't want to be their mum! Like you're trying to punish them!

Alice: (calmly) Eve, have you ever met a single woman in your entire life who told you she regretted being a mum?

Eve: (loudly) No woman would ever feel comfortable sharing that with me! Or anybody!

Alice: (emphatically) That's because women who regret it are a tiny, tiny, statistically insignificant minority! You're being paranoid if you think you'll be that sort of person, honestly! That's like worrying you'll become a paedophile!

Eve: (shaking her head) We have no way of knowing what the percentage is of women who regret having children… If half the mums in the world regretted it, we'd still never know.

Alice: Of course we would!

Eve: It's not something straight women can admit in polite society; admitting it makes people hate them. If a straight woman ever says she regrets being a mum, the world treats her like she's a piece of shit who should fucking kill herself.

Alice: That's because hetero mums who regret their babies normally have personality disorders. Any woman with a kind heart would never regret the experience of raising a child.

Eve: (sighing in exasperation) So it's all quite black and white… All good women want to be mums, eventually. Only bad women are discontented with motherhood.

Alice: I wouldn't necessarily put it that way.

Eve: But that's what you're saying, Alice.

Alice: Not necessarily. I just think it's important for people not to delude themselves.

Eve: Well, apparently you think I'm an unbalanced nutter.

Alice: (defensively) I don't think that! That's not what I said!

Eve: Then what are you saying, Alice?

Alice: I just think people shouldn't suppress their natural instincts. People shouldn't have to hide who they are, Eve. Conservatives want people to hide. Those are the people in this world that are fucking evil. You should be angry at them, not me.

Eve: (quietly) …I know that.

Alice: (adamantly) You know it's important for gay people to come out of the closet! You know how important it is for transgender kids to be brave and change their bodies. None of us choose who we are. The idea that we can choose our identities is totally right wing. You can't choose not to feel like a woman any more than you can choose to be straight.

Eve: But people know what they are because they feel it very strongly.

Alice: (nodding her head) Sometimes.

Eve: Alice, I feel very strongly that I don't want to have children. I feel very strongly that it would *not* make me happy. The idea of having a child makes me feel very sad. It makes me as sad as the idea of losing you. Does that count for anything?

Alice: Of course it doesn't, babes.

Eve: (incredulous) …But I don't understand… Why don't my feelings matter?

Alice: (loudly) Because they're not yours! You have internalised homophobia! Don't you get it? The world wants you to think you should be childfree!

9. PROCREATION: Misogyny

Eve feels like she is being pummelled in a kick-boxing match by a much stronger, quicker and energetic opponent. She is physically tired, emotionally exhausted and would love to crawl into bed and weep herself to sleep. But something inside Eve won't let her go down. Something inside her needs to fight for something. Eve doesn't even feel like she's fighting Alice. She feels like she's fighting something much bigger than Alice.

This inner need to fight feels particularly masculine to Eve. It feels male. It feels like something Eve would disapprove of, intellectually. Eve doesn't like conflict. Nor does she like masculinity and its historical impact on the world.

Eve's own masculinity feels toxic to her. It feels toxic, even though it's making Eve be much more candid with Alice than she's been in years.

Eve: Okay, I admit it: I'm what you think is a cold fucking bitch. I'm childfree and I love it, Alice. I don't love it because I'm busy, or because I need to travel 'round the world like a fucking rock star. I love it because I don't like children. I've always known I don't like them and I've always felt uncomfortable in their presence. I fucking hated even being a child! I wanted so badly to be an adult, so I could finally be around adults instead of children. I hated being forced to play with other kids. I never had any friends. I never even felt like I was a child. It was like being trapped in the wrong body. I felt grownup inside even back then and now that I am a grownup, I don't want to share my home with children. I don't even want to share my life with them. I'd honestly prefer they stay the hell away from me. I know that's not going to happen, but it's what I wish would happen. I can't stand the company of children, Alice. I can't stand most kids I've ever had a conversation with and I definitely can't stand your nieces. I fucking despise them. I despise them even more than you do. I'd rather live with men than live with children.

Alice: Why haven't you ever told me this?

Eve: (sighing) I don't know… I guess I didn't want you to think I was that horrible…

Alice: Well, that was stupid. Children bother me far more than you.

Eve: (loudly) Stop calling me stupid!

Alice: Eve, listen to me: you were a kid that got badly bullied and now you're projecting all that behaviour onto children, as a whole. That's why you need therapy.

Eve: (frustrated) I'm not saying I think children are bullies! I'm saying I feel comfortable with adults in a way that's always felt natural. I never felt that way with children, whether I was an adult, or a child. Childhood was something I waited to grow out of. I'm happy I did.

Alice: (shaking her head) You need to revisit your childhood. You need to sort this shit out. You're an adult now.

Eve: I am sorting it, Alice. I'm choosing not to live with people I don't like. I'm choosing not to live with people I don't enjoy.

Alice: That's not healthy though, Eve.

Eve: (emphatically) But it is healthy! As long as you're a good person, being an auntie who babysits is healthy enough!

Alice: That's rubbish! Women who don't want kids are damaged, psychologically! They suppress their natural urges because they can't give unconditional love! That's what Doctor Adams says!

Eve: Then she's a daft cow. Cold and arrogant women have kids because they feel all the stupid urges you're describing. Those are the neurotic mummies from London no one can stand. Good mothers have kids because they like them, not because they feel fucking broody.

Alice: (giggling at Eve) Sorry love, but broodiness is what motivates women to take on the responsibilities of motherhood. Without those stupid urges, women would be selfish, like you are now.

Eve: Then why are you with me? Why are you with someone you think is so selfish?

Alice: Because we live in a capitalist society where everyone is encouraged to be selfish and materialistic. The urge to breed is one of the few things that push against that.

Eve: But we're living in a time of austerity, Alice. It's like your therapist has brainwashed you or something.

Alice: (dismissively) Oh, fuck off. If people thought like you did, the human race would die out. Not only would no one look after children, nobody would look after anyone who got sick...

Eve: That's still better than the world you're describing.

Alice: I'm describing a world where women aren't fucked up like you.

Eve: No, you're describing a world where motherhood is like fascism, where birth will erase my feelings about children, make my personality disappear and turn me into this happy, baby-worshipping robot.

Alice: (loudly) That's only what it looks like from the outside! That's what it looks like when you don't have the urge!

Eve: I can't imagine why anybody would want that urge. It sounds like the experiences people have when they join a religious cult.

Alice: (angrily) Broodiness is the most wonderful urge in the world! Ask any woman what it's like to give birth! If you think women shouldn't conceive, you're the misanthrope! You're the fascist!

Eve: I'm just trying to understand what–

Alice: (interrupting) You live in fear! You hate what you don't understand!

Eve: What am I not understanding?

Alice: Motherhood teaches you how to really love a person. You can't truly love a person if the reason you love them is you have a lot in common. That's just friendship and friendships end. True love is love with or without common interests. It's love because the beloved needs it, not because it's a doddle.

Eve: But not all women can do that sort of love. Some of us only want to love people with personalities that mesh with ours.

Alice: (loudly) No, some women are fucking stubborn! You know you don't love me for my personality! Your love for me is deeper than that!

Eve: Yeah. But the love is there because I like you. It's not there because you need it.

Alice: (angrily) Yes, it fucking is! You stayed with me when I was abusive, when I alienated most of your friends. You lost your fucking family because of me! You stayed with me even though I fell in love with a man for a year! I even beat the shit out of you the day you got your Masters! I could have killed you that night and you're still here with me!

Eve: I did all of that because I love you. Not because you needed my love. There's a difference, Alice.

Alice: If you love me so much, why do you hate the thing that's most important to me? Why can't you love a child?

Eve: (speaking hesitantly) The reason I can't love a child is… motherhood disturbs me, if I'm honest. The idea of some urge in me changing my personality and making me love things I hate is disturbing to me. In fact, I can't think of anything more horrifying than loving a creature that can't do anything and treating it like it's more wonderful than everyone else. It's like getting a virus that would make me give up research so I could pursue a career at McDonalds.

Whenever someone says they're going to have a child, I lie when I tell them congratulations. All I can think about is the fact that they're pushing a stranger into my world and I'm going to have to accommodate that stranger, regardless of whether I like it – regardless of whether she is lovely or some gobby lad with ADHD...

And it never matters to mums whether their babies are intelligent and interesting. Sometimes it feels like when babies turn into wonderful people, that's when mothers are truly disappointed. That's why when I hear mums talk about how much they love their babies, I actually feel sad for them. Babies can't do anything and they get more love and devotion than the kindest, wisest adults. That may be necessary for the survival of our species, but to me…it's just tragic. It's a flagrant injustice. And instead of treating it like that, people worship it like it's some sort of tear-inducing miracle. That's disgusting to me… in fact, it's not even disgusting. It's de-humanising and degrading and I hate it. I hate it with all my heart.

Alice: (incredulous) Are you fucking mental?

Eve: Maybe I am… I don't know.

Alice: (shocked) This is all because of your childhood! It's because you actually hate all children! This is coming from such a wounded place of pain in you, I can feel it.

Eve: I'm sorry but this is just how I feel. I know motherhood is necessary and I know it can be done in a healthy way. I don't condemn anyone for doing it. I just think it should be done for the right reasons.

Alice: Then why do you hate it so much?

Eve: Because it's not just. It's not based on what people deserve. Love for babies is your body pulling love in all the directions it doesn't naturally go.

Alice: But Eve, for most women, it does naturally go in those directions. You're the one that isn't natural. I love you but technically, you're the one who's more like a freak of nature. It's not women who love being mums.

Eve: (sighing) Some women are like me. Some women don't want to be mums, but very few have the courage not to cave in and be like everyone else. That causes a lot of guilt and pain in the world.

Alice: Women don't cave in, silly girl. They realise there's no alternative. Women can't choose their identities any more than you can choose not to be gay.

Eve: (definitely) That's nothing but extremist bullshit, Alice. Motherhood needs to be a choice! For it to be a choice, you have to be able to say no. It's not healthy if you can't say no! It's coercive.

Alice: Then why are women always encouraging each other to have children? Especially women like you who have doubts?

Eve: Because we live in a patriarchal society where women are socialised to think of motherhood as some kind of obligation, something that makes you decent and feminine. It's backward and reactionary.

Alice: But if what you're describing is patriarchy, wouldn't it be men who think of motherhood as an obligation?

Eve: (thinking hard) …I don't know, maybe it's like a twisted dance between men and women. Women are expected to be hot and put out and subordinate themselves to men in most areas of life. In exchange for that, women act like pushy little bitches when it comes to procreation.

Alice: (giggling) You think men benefit from letting women act like pushy little bitches?

Eve: I don't know. Maybe women put up with being bullied as long as they're allowed to bully someone else.

Alice: But in this case, isn't it normally men who women bully? Men who are hesitant about becoming fathers? Men who wait too long before the eggs dry up? Men who won't commit?

Eve: Maybe it is. Maybe men allow themselves to be bullied.

Alice: (trying hard not to laugh) So, you're saying men allow themselves to be bullied by women in order to keep the reins of power? Like, women allow men to control society in exchange for being able to push men around at home?

Eve: (sighing) …I can't think of any other reason women are such bitches about babies. I've never met a man who gave a fuck about whether or not I got pregnant. It's always been women. It's women who won't shut up about it, not just you...

Alice: Well, that could be because women are naturally more compassionate than men. We don't want other women to suffer, especially if some charming stranger convinces them they could be happy living in a "family of two."(mocking Eve).

Eve: (with disgust) God, I hate that shit! I just wish women had kids because they wanted to be parents. I wish it wasn't some fucking purification ritual, where new mummies have to give impassioned speeches renouncing the emptiness of childfree life.

Alice: But that's how women feel, Eve. After their babies are born, they feel like not having children is a form of self-harm.

Eve: (with contempt) Yeah and those twats never stop telling me how much I'm hurting myself by putting off pregnancy. I wish I could smack them sometimes. I hate having to explain myself to those fucking bitches. I'd love to just–

Alice: (interrupting) Those bitches are the reason you're here! That's why your mum tricked your dad: so you could be here with me! That's a good thing!

Eve: It's not a good thing, Alice. I hate the fact that I'm here because a man who never wanted to be my father was tricked by my mother. Sometimes I think about killing myself just to punish her for that.

Alice: (reassuringly) But you can change! You don't have to hate yourself! You don't even have to hate your mother, Eve. You can forgive Cara for what she did to you. Forgiveness helps you become a much better parent.

Eve: You're making me hate her right now. You're making me hate most women.

Alice: Well, maybe your students are right when they call you a misogynist. Have you thought about that?

Eve: I don't give a fuck if those spoiled little pricks hate me.

Alice: Well, if you don't want to get sacked, you might ask yourself why they hate you.

Eve: (with contempt) I know why they hate me. They think like you.

Alice: Eve, you're projecting yourself onto me. I don't hate anyone. I don't believe in hate.

Eve: (angrily) Well, I do. I hate this conversation we're having. I hate the way the left thinks about identity. I hate your right-wing therapist and I hate her kitchen wisdom about how childfree women are twats!

Alice: Doctor Adams is a sex positive feminist, Eve.

Eve: (passionately) Well, whatever she is, she thinks that my choices are delusions, that I'm making myself unhappy by doing all the things that make me feel like I'm just being myself.

Alice: (smiling mischievously) …I suppose she does think that.

Eve: (indignantly) She thinks that I don't have reproductive choice in any sense that I understand the concept, that my value as a human is nothing independently of my competency as a breeder. She's telling you that our relationship means nothing if I'm not a mother, that any love I have with any woman should get annihilated if she wants to join the mummy brigade and I feel the slightest hesitation!

Alice: Well, if you want to be negative, you can think of it that way. Or you can think of it like most doctors and psychiatrists do.

Eve: (sarcastically) And how is that?

Alice: The experts understand that human females aren't happy with partners that don't want to give them babies. They understand that infertility is painful and dangerous, that being a parent is a sign of maturity, a sign that you're at peace with your humanity.

Eve: (angrily) Yeah and who I am doesn't matter! It doesn't matter how kind I am. It doesn't matter if I'm funny or sexy. My accomplishments don't matter; my creativity doesn't matter; my uniqueness doesn't matter; my compassion and love don't matter. My pain doesn't even matter. If I choose not to raise a child, I don't deserve to be loved by a woman. That's what you think!

Alice: It's not that I think you don't deserve to be loved by a woman. I'm just stating a scientific fact. You're not attractive to women when you refuse to raise a child. If you don't like babies, that cancels out everything that's attractive about you. It makes you ugly. It makes you an acquaintance, not a life partner. That's how it is for most women.

Eve: I know that, Alice. It just tears me up inside.

Alice: (shaking head) Don't be such a diva! Nobody would ever tell a woman who wanted children to stay with a man who didn't. Everyone would encourage her to drop his arse.

Eve: (passionately) Yeah and I don't fucking agree with that either! It's cruel to end a relationship with an existing person to devote your life to someone who could be anyone, someone that hasn't even been born. It's mean-spirited. It's treating perfectly nice people like disposable commodities.

Alice: But Eve, men are disposable commodities.

Eve: (incredulous) What?

Alice: Think about the reality. If a straight woman wanted children and stayed with her childfree husband, would things work out? Would there be anything other than resentment?

Eve: (sighing) …Probably not.

Alice: She'd eventually hate that guy, wouldn't she? You know she would.

Eve: Maybe. I can't say whether or not–

Alice: (interrupting) Even your granny left your grandad because she wanted more than six children. That's why two of your uncles are mixed race!

Eve: I know that, too.

Alice: And what about my family? Dad was with Mum for fifteen years. Was he a bastard? Did he cheat on her?

Eve: I know he was a good feminist, Alice. You don't have to keep reminding me.

Alice: He wasn't just a great dad to me and my sister, he looked after Granny when she got cancer, he paid for our big house and gave Mum more love and devotion than she'd ever had from any man in her entire life! But all of that meant nothing when she wanted to have Callum and Dad told her 'no.' She dropped him without thinking twice and he fucking accepted it. He didn't complain!

Eve: I understand all of this, Alice. But I don't have to be happy about it. Just like I don't have to be happy with the fact that I find motherhood disturbing.

Alice: You tie yourself in knots with these weird attitudes of yours. Life is so much happier when you just accept what the queer community needs from you.

Eve: I know it probably is. I just wish things were different. I wish we were less like straight women.

Alice: Why?

Eve: (sighing) …I wouldn't get attacked or threatened because I didn't want a third person in my relationship.

Alice: Well, I'm sorry Eve, but we are like straight people in many ways. The things that make women happy are universal. Sexual orientation has nothing to do with it.

Eve: Possibly. I couldn't say one way or the other.

Alice: (sighing in frustration) You know, you make me so angry with you. It drives me mad, Eve. You drive me fucking mad.

Eve: I know I do.

Alice: But not because of the babies.

Eve: Oh?

Alice: Look, I'm not very lovable, compared to you. But you are one of the most amazing and kind people that lives in Leicester. But you don't believe it. You act like people shouldn't care about you, like you're not even kind enough to raise a family.

Eve: (looking down with sadness) I'm not perfect, Alice. I don't just have amazing qualities. If I did, I'd have more of the things I want from the people in my life. I'd have more of what I want from you.

Alice: Eve, look at me…

Alice puts her hand on Eve's shoulders, looking into her eyes.

Alice: (smiling warmly) You have all the qualities of a great mother: you're intelligent, broad minded, patient, compassionate, trustworthy, able to put other people before yourself. You're also fun, open, beautiful, incredibly sweet and an amazingly effective teacher. Those are the qualities everyone wishes they had in a mum. Those are the qualities that make a mother great, Eve. You'd be wasting them if you didn't have kids.

Eve: But those qualities got cancelled out by my lack of broodiness, remember.

Alice: No, they didn't. You're not giving into that shit. You're fighting it with me. We're fighting it together.

Eve: (exhausted) I'm not fighting anything, Alice. I'm done fighting.

Eve pulls Alice's hands off her shoulders and walks away. But Eve's energy is now dwindling. Her emotions are starting to crowd her thoughts. Her masculine side feels like it's fading away from her. It's as if Alice has somehow struck a hard uppercut against it. Eve's masculinity is now on the ropes, one or two blows away from crashing into the canvas.

If Eve's masculinity gets counted out, Eve will find herself agreeing to get pregnant. Or at least not disagreeing when Alice repeatedly tells Eve she is going to get pregnant.

Alice: (following Eve) Eve, you're fighting your delusions with me! You're ending marginalisation in our community and getting pregnant! That's the most kind and compassionate thing you will ever do in your lifetime. And for you, it's a real achievement!

Eve: You keep saying I'm going to have babies.

Alice: You are and sooner or later you'll accept it. We're not going to bed until you accept it.

Eve: (confused and exhausted) Why am I being forced to accept something I don't want? Why is my partner doing this to me…? You're supposed to be nice to me, Alice.

Alice: (abruptly) I am being nice to you! I'm looking after your mental health. I wouldn't let you be childfree any more than I would let you commit suicide.

Eve: (sighing) … I think I'm actually feeling suicidal now.

Alice: That's why I'm making sure you get pregnant. You need to get pregnant before your brain gets bad again.

Eve: (too tired to argue) I feel like my brain is bad... Like it's deformed… Like I'm… sub-human or something…

Alice: You'd only be that if you didn't have children.

Eve: (softly) Then why do I feel like it anyway?

Alice: Because you're hurting, Eve. You feel like even though we're having babies together, I'm still rejecting you. You feel like I'm rejecting who you are.

Eve: (feeling deeply sad) I think you're right.

Alice: I know you more than you know yourself, Eve. You're hurting badly. It's in your eyes. Look at you.

Eve: (softly) I haven't been this hurt in ages.

Alice: But pain is a chance for growth, honey. Be positive.

Eve: (with a look of despair in her face) ...It's like you've plunged a knife into my heart. I can't even cry.

Alice: I know and I'm so sorry it hurts like that. When you're hurting, I hurt as well. I wish I didn't have to say any of this to you. I wish I could tell you things were fine. It would be so much easier.

Eve: (tearing up) I know it would. But you're hurting me… so badly right now… I'm in so much pain…

Alice: (softly) But it's ultimately more important that I tell you the truth, Eve. It's like when you told me I needed to quit drinking. The truth always hurts.

Eve: (tears streaming down face) I'm not even hurting… It's worse than that…It's worse than anything…

Alice: I know it's bad, honey. But it'll get better. Just trust me. I won't let you go under.

Eve: (crying) …I'm already under.

Alice: No, you're not. Not yet. You're just feeling sorry for yourself.

Eve: (sobbing) I feel like... I'm dying inside… I feel like I shouldn't be here…

Alice: You're not dying. You're strong and compassionate, Eve. You've just forgotten something.

Eve: …What?

Alice: I'm going to make you happier than you've ever been in your entire life! You'll get to experience being a mum!

Eve: (crying) …I wish it didn't hurt so much.

Alice: I know you're in pain but trust me: You'll thank me in the future. You'll thank me with joyful tears in your eyes. It'll be the most awe-inspiring and transformative experience you've ever had!

Eve: (crying) I'm sorry… I can't–

Alice: (interrupting) Our kids will make me seem insignificant, in comparison! You'll do things for the kids you'd never dream of doing for me! You'd go to prison for them!

Eve: (sobbing loudly) That's fucking terrifying…!

Alice: Shh… don't make yourself upset, honey. It's not terrifying. You're just not ready yet…

Eve: (crying and pulling away from Alice) I'll never be ready for that…

Alice: (impatiently) Eve, unconditional love is what life's all about! And sooner or later, it will make you happy! Your body will literally push you. You just need time, like you gave me time to quit drinking. I know you hate all this now and it's totally understandable, given where you are in your life. You're in a dark place. Life is dark before you're broody, but I know how you feel. I've been there!

Eve: (crying) That's not why I'm in a dark place… But I love you… I still love you Alice…

Alice: I love you too.

Eve: (crying) I love you… and I want you to be happy… even if it's without me…

Alice: (smiling tenderly) I don't regret a single day I've ever spent with you, Eve. You're my co-pilot in life. That's why I'm choosing you. We're going to be mummies together, yummy mummies.

Eve: (wiping away tears) I feel like I don't have any choices… You have choices… and I don't…

Alice: No, there are some choices you do have. You can choose for me to completely cut you out of my life. You can even choose to end your life, if that's what you really want.

Eve: (sniffing) I'm not going to kill myself, Alice. You know I would never–

Alice: (interrupting) Then you need to think about how valuable your life is. Everything in your life is precious, but you can ruin it all by being stubborn and refusing to see what's right in front of you.

Eve: (in frustrated sobs) I don't want to ruin our lives… You mean more to me than anything, Alice… This is just so hard… I feel so fucking confused…

Alice: Of course you do. You don't want to die without children…

Eve: (in deep pain) …I don't want to die.

Alice takes Eve's hand and strokes it tenderly. Alice's behaviour is enraging Eve, but she feels too emotionally drained to do anything other than seek comfort from Alice. Eve is in so much pain, she no longer wants to fight for what she wants in her life. She just wants to go to bed and be held like a child. So she relaxes and lets herself enjoy the feeling of Alice stroking her hand.

Alice is close to victory.

Alice: (speaking gently) Honey, when those babies pop out, you'll look at everything, even me, in an entirely different way. You'll be a different person, a better person.

Eve: (sighing) I want to be a better person.

Alice: We all do. That's another reason motherhood is so good for women.

Eve: (like a wounded animal) I couldn't cope, losing you right now… I wouldn't be able to get out of bed every day… I don't have any support, apart from you… You're all I've got, Alice.

Alice: You won't lose me, baby. Let's go to bed together. I feel like we need to hold each other. We're both tired.

Alice starts rubbing Eve's neck.

Eve: (tired and exhausted) I need to be held now… I'm not thinking straight, anymore.

Alice: (whispering calmly) Which is why it's a good idea that we go to bed now… You always cheer up when I hold you…

Eve: When I'm in your arms… it's like I don't have to worry about anything…

Alice: (smiling tenderly) You don't have to worry about anything, Eve. Everything will be ace.

Eve: (rubbing her own forehead) I know it will, love. It's all just so crazy. I can't make sense of the shit that's happening in my brain. I feel like I'm losing the plot.

Alice: (speaking softly in Eve's ear) You're not going mad… Just trust me… Let me take control on this one. I know what I'm doing… I know what'll make you happy…

Eve: (sighing) I do trust you… You know I trust you…

Alice: Millions of men go through what you're going through every day… They think they don't want children… They feel like their girlfriends are pressuring them. And you know what happens?

Eve: What?

Alice: (reassuringly) The baby arrives… and those men can't imagine ever feeling upset again. Male feminists get that.

Eve: (nodding her head) …I know they do.

Alice: Even when girls trick blokes into using a broken condom, the men are always happy when they meet their beautiful babies. They're not like your dad, Eve. They're not psychos.

Eve suddenly steps away from Alice, once again.

Her masculinity is bruised and beaten, but still managing to rise from the canvas and continue the fight.

Eve: (distrustfully) Are you saying it's alright to trick blokes into becoming dads?

Alice: No, I'm saying fatherhood is a great gift.

Eve: Well, it is if you *want* to be a father.

Alice: No, honey. Being a parent makes you want to be a parent. That's why any man who isn't a psycho can't help loving his children.

Eve: But not all men–

Alice: (interrupting) Yes, not all men. There are some absolute dickheads who won't man up and be responsible, but most men do the right thing.

Eve: I meant most men wouldn't want to be tricked into having children.

Alice: Do you have any empirical evidence to back that up?

Eve: (sighing) ...No.

Alice: And do you have any stats to show that most loving and happy fathers were never tricked or pressured into having children?

Eve: No. I can't even imagine how you'd collect–

Alice: (interrupting) There's a reason you can't. It's because men fall in love with their babies, Eve. When they see their children, unless they're hard-hearted bastards, men want their kids to be safe and looked after. That's what good men do.

Eve: But they can still resent the woman who tricked them.

Alice: That kind of resentment only damages children, Eve. It's not healthy or loving. Imagine how a kid would feel if they knew Daddy had been tricked by Mummy? They'd feel unwanted. They'd feel unwanted and that would be a nasty situation.

Eve: Alice, you know I was in that nasty situation. You know what it did to me.

Alice: Exactly. And imagine how much better you'd feel if your dad just kept his feelings to himself.

Eve: (softly) I'm not sure I'd want him to keep them to himself…

Alice: Having children makes men happy, Eve. That's why men don't mind being pushed and prodded until they step up and do the right thing. Babies are good for most men. They help men appreciate women and become more subservient.

Eve: (confused) ...Is that what you want? You want men to become subservient to women?

Alice: (matter of factly) We've had thousands of years of patriarchy, Eve.

Eve: (confused) I know that but–

Alice (interrupting) Don't you think it's time for a change?

Eve: (disturbed) …I need to think about this in a different way, Alice. I need to feel… I don't know. This is getting too weird for–

Alice: (interrupting abruptly) Tomorrow I'll make an appointment with the doctor. We'll go together.

Eve: For what?

Alice: (irritated) You know what for! Don't give me any shit about this, Eve. I'm tired now.

Eve: I'm tired too, Alice.

Alice: Then go to bed. You need some rest.

Eve: So I'm having kids then?

Alice: Yep.

Eve: I'm having kids… even though I've never wanted any.

Alice: Yes, you are.

Eve: …I'm not quite sure how that just happened.

Alice: You made the right decision.

Eve: I'm not sure I did.

Alice: Of course you did. You decided to be in a relationship with me.

Eve: So, I'm having children… even though I'm childfree, even though there's nothing wrong with being childfree.

Alice: (loudly) You're not fucking 'childfree!' Stop saying that!

Eve: …So if I choose not to have children, you won't allow me to be happy because you'll reject me. My body won't allow me to be happy because of the depression that happens if I don't conceive. And if that depression doesn't kick in, the rejections from other women I love will keep me from being happy. It's like an elaborate matriarchal system designed to punish me if I try to be happy without babies.

Alice: (nodding her head) It's called 'Mother Nature', Eve. Now let's go to bed.

Eve: I understand why you think motherhood isn't a choice now, Alice. It makes complete sense.

Alice: I'm glad it's finally making sense. There is no choice, really. Look at the world. One gender has to dominate.

Eve: (speaking hesitantly) But Alice… when I look at the world, I don't see a place where one gender has to dominate. I see a democracy that's supposed to contain people like me.

Alice: What?

Eve: It's supposed to contain eccentrics. It's supposed to contain choice and diversity and tolerance and compassion. People are supposed to empathise with–

Alice: (interrupting) People are supposed to empathise with children!

Eve: But I do empathise with children and that's why I'm not getting pregnant, Alice. I can empathise with children, even though I don't like them. I want all children to know they can grow up and be loved by women, even if they don't become parents.

Alice: (angrily) But they won't be loved by women!! They'll be rejected!!

Eve: (passionately) Not if they are truly loved. Not if they are loved by a woman who understands that deep connections with living and breathing human beings are more precious and mysterious than the chance to satisfy any biological urge. The chance to be a parent is never more important than–

Alice: (interrupting loudly) Don't be a stupid cunt! Men need to be parents to know how to love and protect women! They need to be in families! You and I need to have a healthy family, so I can support you!

Eve: Alice, why can't you support a childfree woman?

Alice: (yelling angrily) Because I can't love a fucking freak! I'll fucking hate you and that'll make you suffer!! You'll be tormented! For your sake, you need to get pregnant, Eve! This is important. I'll commit suicide if you don't get pregnant!!

Eve: So you're blackmailing me. I either spawn a kid or you kill yourself. If this is what–

Alice: (interrupting aggressively) Shut the fuck up, Eve! You don't have the strength *not* to have kids! You couldn't cope on your own. You need me to look after you. You said it over and over again.

Eve: I was right earlier. You're forcing me to get pregnant, without even getting my consent.

Alice quickly pushes Eve hard with both hands, nearly knocking her over.

Alice: (screaming violently) I DON'T GIVE A FUCK ABOUT YOUR CONSENT!! YOU'RE GETTING PREGNANT AND YOU'RE GONNA LIKE IT EVEN IF YOU HAVE TO FORCE YOURSELF TO LIKE IT!!

Eve: (flabbergasted) This is like rape, Alice…

Alice: (giggling like a naughty child) Deal with it, babes. You're gonna be happy. You're loving your babies and this is happening. I'm making you happy and you're not fucking stopping me.

Eve: But how can I love you if this is what you're making happen?

Alice: Your body will make you love me.

Eve: And what if I don't want it to?

Alice: You can't control who you love, Eve. That's why you're a fucking dyke. (laughing at Eve).

Eve: (with a sudden resolve) You know Alice… I'm tired of all this.

Alice: We should go to sleep then. I need to be up before noon.

Eve: I need to give you something.

Alice: (rolling her eyes) You can give me a massage. My neck hurts.

Eve: I'm going to give you the one thing you need even more than a baby. Something no one's ever given you.

Alice: Fine. Make it quick. I'm tired.

Eve: I need you to know I'm not responsible for your shitty choices. You can't bully me that way anymore.

Alice: (smiling dismissively) Whatever, babes.

Eve: (boiling with anger) And I will never ever feel responsible for you choosing to end your life. SUICIDE IS SELFISH AND COWARDLY AND YOU WILL NEVER FUCKING BLACKMAIL ME WITH IT AGAIN!

Alice: (smiling mischievously) Oh, yes I will. You can't stand up for yourself. That's why you're having both of our babies, Eve. I'm not even getting pregnant.

Eve grabs Alice's cup of tea and throws it at Alice, as hard as she can. Alice quickly moves out of the way, as the cup smashes into the wall behind her, breaking into a million pieces. The tea and broken glass bounce back off the wall and hit Alice's neck and the back of her head.

Eve: (screaming at the top of her lungs) GO FUCK YOURSELF YOU FUCKING SLAG!!!

Alice: (yelling) BLOODY HELL, EVE… WHAT ARE YOU DOING...?

Eve grabs a chair and holds it over her head, walking towards Alice. She looks as though she intends to break it over Alice's head.

Alice: (screaming): PUT THAT DOWN…! PLEASE, EVE… OH GOD…

Eve: (screaming menacingly) FUCK YOUR BABIES… FUCK WOMEN… AND FUCK QUEER PEOPLE!!

Eve throws the chair at Alice, as hard she can. Alice barely manages to leap out of the way, as the chair smashes onto the floor, breaking and scattering across the room. With her adrenaline pumping, Alice attempts to run to the kitchen, but trips on one of the broken pieces of wood and falls down. Eve stands over Alice, as Alice quickly covers her face with her hands. Eve repeatedly kicks Alice in the stomach, while Alice curls into a foetal position. Eve kicks her hard, over and over again.

Eve: (shouting and kicking): I WON'T GIVE IN TO YOU!!...YOU WON'T EVER FUCKING BLACKMAIL ME…EVER!! I'LL NEVER GIVE YOU WANT YOU WANT… EVER!!

Alice: (smiling behind her hands) That's my girl…

Eve: (screaming and kicking) I'LL KILL YOU!! I'LL FUCKING KILL YOU!! YOU FUCKING CUNT!! YOU FUCKING RAPIST!! I'LL GO TO PRISON… AND I WON'T EVEN FEEL GUILTY!!

For Eve, this is very strange behaviour.

Eve has never been violent with Alice. In fact, Eve has never been violent with anyone. Nor has she spoken to anyone this way.

Alice, however, feels relieved. Although Alice does not enjoy being repeatedly kicked, she has a newfound respect for Eve. This, after all, was the response Alice was attempting to elicit from Eve throughout the entire evening. It thankfully confirmed to Alice some things about Eve she had recently begun to doubt. Things like:

1. Eve is still a childfree woman, just like Alice is. Neither woman has any urge to pro-create.
2. Eve could never love a child as much as she loves Alice.
3. Eve will always (eventually) give Alice consequences for her bad behaviour.
4. Eve loves Alice enough to end their relationship, in the event the relationship maintains itself on the condition that one partner suppresses something important about who they are.

In order to find out 1–4, Alice chose to lie to Eve. Alice told Eve she needed Eve to have children. She did this to test Eve. Alice made it look as though broodiness was the centrepiece of her therapy sessions with Doctor Adams. In actual fact, the centrepiece of Alice's therapy was Alice's drinking. However, Alice did confide her worries about Eve to Doctor Adams.

Alice told Doctor Adams how much better Eve is with children than she is. She told Doctor Adams that she worries Eve secretly wants to be a mum and is repressing this fact so as to stay with Alice. Alice also told Doctor Adams that she feels guilty in the relationship, that she can walk all over Eve because Eve doesn't have the strength to stand up to her. Doctor Adams responded that it was important to make sure Eve was strong enough to give Alice boundaries. She also said it was important for Alice to make sure that Eve had the same life goals as Alice.

Alice agreed with Doctor Adams.

It was important to Alice that her relationship with Eve wouldn't reach a point where a certain conversation would happen. This is a conversation Alice has noticed occurring over and over again, in different variations, amongst both her customers and friends. It typically happens among couples that are in their early thirties.

Partner A will announce to Partner B that Partner A wants children.

Then, a discussion will commence, a discussion where there is a shared presumption that a negotiation is occurring, a negotiation where the couple may decide to have or not have children. However, this appearance of negotiation is an illusion.

Much like in politics, Partner A controls the conversation to strong arm Partner B into doing what Partner A wants.

If Partner B shows any hesitations about parenthood, these hesitations will be treated by Partner A as irrational fears.

If Partner B expresses an emotional resistance to their role as parent, Partner A will frame this emotional resistance as a personal weakness on the part of Partner B.

As the discussion proceeds, it will become apparent that none of Partner B's reasons for avoiding parenthood will ever be treated as legitimate reasons.

If Partner B does not enjoy the company of children, Partner A will respond that this is irrelevant and that Partner B is destined to enjoy the company of their own children.

Even if Partner B has had a lifelong desire to love only adults in their home, Partner A will respond that this is not a valid reason to avoid parenthood, only a reason to get rid of this lifelong desire (so that Partner B can become a good parent).

If Partner B still refuses to cave in at this point, Partner A will resort to emotional blackmail.

Partner A will reveal to Partner B that their relationship will be destroyed if Partner B does not become a parent.

If Partner B is still steadfast in their refusal to become a parent, Partner B will endure an emotionally devastating break up that Partner A will then blame them for.

Partner A will attempt to convince Partner B that their love for Partner A was inept – the reason being that Partner B ONLY wanted to love Partner

A. Partner B will be labelled cold, self-centred, and immature for the crime of wanting to love only one person in their relationship – the person they fell in love with.

Having endured the typical conversation about ensuing parenthood, Partner B normally does the easy thing, caves in and embraces parenthood. This is why Alice needed to test Eve. She needed to know that her life partner was strong enough to remain steadfast in a discussion where her childfree desires would be ridiculed, mocked, dismissed and demonised.

Eve came through in the end, refusing the relationship, refusing to become a parent and refusing to concede that her childfree desires were simply weaknesses and pathologies. Eve also refused the conventional wisdom that anyone can be a good parent, even those adults who hate children.

Moreover, Eve did something that went much farther than even Alice was hoping. It made Alice incredibly proud of her. That evening, Eve didn't merely defend her childfree status by talking about her lack of maternal instincts. She refused to accept that maternal instincts were good reasons to have children. Eve instead hinted at something Alice had learned from her own mother: good parents mostly go against their natural instincts, when learning to understand and accept their children.

When parents rely on their natural instincts, they find it easiest to love people like themselves. Children are rarely such people.

Throughout Alice's procreation test, she did her best to oppose Eve's rebuttals in a way that was relentlessly condescending and insensitive – the way she's watched so many women talk to their blokes at work. This was not easy, as Alice often found it hard not to cry. As the dawn turned into a beautiful sunny morning, Eve was acting like a deranged psychotic. But she stood up for herself in a way that impressed the shit out of Alice, who was rooting for her the whole time.

Alice was impressed, despite also finding much of what Eve said politically reactionary.

Alice did not agree with Eve's comments about women and queer people.

10. PROCREATION: Moving On

Alice predicted that Eve would break up with her, once she revealed the elaborate procreation test she had given Eve. Alice had no problem being subsequently rejected. For some time, Alice has been wanting a temporary break from the relationship. Alice has been in love with Eve since she was fourteen. That means Alice never had a period in her youth where she could enjoy going on adventures or having illicit sexual encounters with married men.

What also interests Alice is being single and having the time to pursue some lifelong dreams: climbing Mount Kinabalu, spending a month at a Tibetan Monastery and getting bumfucked.

Alice would like to pursue these dreams without inconveniencing Eve. She feels like she needs some time to grow, so that she can become a more mature and disciplined person who practices self-care. Alice wants to be her best self for Eve, since she has seen first-hand just how hard Eve tries to be a good partner for her.

Alice knows she will eventually get back with Eve. She knows neither of them will ever stop having feelings for each other. She also knows they can't be friends with each other for very long without falling in love again. Hence, Alice is choosing not to remain in contact with Eve for about a year. However, she tells another lie to Eve: that the only way they can both be happy is to stop communicating permanently. Eve reluctantly agrees to this, so she can effectively move on with her life. Little does she know that Alice plans on resuming their relationship in a little over a year.

Alice moves into a small flat near Narborough Road, a much grimier area of Leicester. It makes Alice feel like a student again, which she enjoys very much. She loves both the Turkish restaurants and the used bookshop in this area. Alice also enjoys walking down Narborough Road itself, in the early hours of the morning. She's exhilarated, rather than frightened, by her new neighbourhood's reputation for street crime.

In the more middle-class part of town, Eve begins to create much more satisfying relationships with people at Leicester University. She works hard to gain the respect of her colleagues and students. For the first time, Eve gives them boundaries, standing up for herself anytime she senses they are trying to belittle her. When any of her colleagues act as though she is inferior to them, she becomes pushy and bosses them around, treating them as though they are inferior to her. As a result of this, they treat her as their equal.

Eve has also learned a way to make friends with Roey White, the head of department who had a habit of making snide comments about her. Eve now openly makes witty and self-deprecating remarks about herself, before Roey has a chance to. This new confidence, humour and self-awareness makes Roey quite fond of Eve. Eve also flirts with Roey, primarily by gently mocking her. Sometimes Eve makes jokes about how clumsy Roey is. Other times she draws attention to her lisp.

Roey now has a crush on Eve. Eve plans to do nothing about this crush.

Eve has an even better relationship with her students. She now understands that many of her students are deliberately trying to test her patience. In those situations, Eve knows the best response is to show how unafraid she is of making them feel horrible.

If any student interrupts Eve during her lectures, she angrily pulls them up on it, in front of the entire group. She no longer waits until the seminar is over to politely ask them to raise their hand and wait for her to call on them. Eve understands that the threat of public humiliation is a far more effective tool for generating their compliance and respect. Another tool Eve uses to control her students is to act like she's vaguely disgusted by them, without ever specifying a reason why.

Whenever a cheeky student insinuates Eve is either unprepared for a seminar or a uniquely bad communicator, Eve curtly demands that the student immediately leave the room, after which Eve lectures the other students about the consequences of aggressive and defamatory behaviour. Eve does something similar to any cheeky student accusing her of being a misogynist or a transphobe. Eve always finds a way to twist the student's words so that she can then accuse that student of being a misogynist or a transphobe. Eve is quite skilful at twisting people's words. She now thinks this skill is a necessity for anyone wishing to work in higher education.

Because of Alice's procreation test, Eve's entire outlook on life has changed. She now thinks it is a mistake to be nice to people trying to cause pain. Eve is instead a strong believer in the principle that people trying to cause pain should suffer greater pain, regardless of whether they are her students, or her colleagues. Hence, both her colleagues and students no longer try to upset Eve. They know better than to make her angry; when Eve is angry, she's frightening.

As it happens, there is no one Eve is angrier with than Alice. She's angry at Alice for deceiving her, for causing her to experience emotional turmoil on par with the worst experiences of her teenage years. Eve is also enraged at how Alice deliberately toyed with her feelings, seemingly enjoying the thrill of seeing how far she could push Eve, how guilty and self-doubting she could make her, even how much she could psychologically torment her.

This anger, however, is tinged with some ambivalence. Although Eve doesn't approve of Alice's procreation test, she can't help but admire the brazenness, courage, and tenacity of it. Eve also can't help finding it incredibly sexy – the way Alice was so adept at making her feel such extreme emotional anguish.

Eve thinks about Alice's cruelty, nearly every night. Afterwards, she sleeps like a baby.

Thirteen months after Alice moves out of Eve's house, Eve does something that seems almost out of character. She sends Alice a direct message on Facebook, asking if she'd like to meet up for drinks at 'Mrs Bridges', a local Leicester tea and cakes shop. The two meet and it becomes apparent within minutes just how much they both have missed talking to each other.

Alice tells Eve about her spiritual and sexual adventures, making Eve laugh so hard that she spits tea on her croissant. Eve winds up having the most enjoyable afternoon she's had in, well, thirteen months.

This enjoyment disturbs Eve; she knows it shouldn't actually be there. After Eve broke up with Alice, her perception of Alice changed. She stopped seeing Alice as an eccentric and sweet woman, plagued with the vices of erratic and self-destructive behaviour. She started to see Alice as an extremely selfish and cold bitch; someone dishonest, impulsive, and manipulative – a woman capable of harming Eve. Alice is no longer a person Eve can trust as a friend, let alone a romantic partner.

Strangely, none of these beliefs seem to have any connection with Eve's subsequent feelings and decisions. Eve finds herself forgiving Alice very quickly for everything she did to her. Shortly after that act of forgiveness, Eve finds herself falling in love with Alice again, for the first time since she was fourteen. All of this is completely baffling to Eve, given everything she now believes about Alice.

Like her violence towards Alice, her new found love feels unreasonable, irrational, like something that doesn't flow out of either her character or her values. In fact, it doesn't really feel like it's her decision.

Alice's love for Eve feels decidedly different: it feels quite comfortable and familiar, like it's almost mundane. Loving Eve has always felt instinctual for Alice, like something Alice has no say in, whatsoever. It's a thoroughly unconditional love, a love Eve could never make disappear, no matter how much she ever hurt or betrayed Alice.

Alice will always love Eve. She'll always love Eve, even if Eve would prefer never to see Alice again.

In the autumn of 2016, Eve and Alice re-unite as a couple, beginning a much more exciting and passionate romance. Both Eve and Alice maintain this chaotic and explosive love through a combination of forgiveness and humour. Despite great difficulties, Eve and Alice never consider the possibility of splitting up.

Yes, they often row. They often fail to understand each other. They even regularly drive each other mad. Yet both women love each other more than anyone else they know. In fact, there's no one they like or enjoy more than each other. It's as if they're soulmates caught in a violent whirlwind of explosive passion – a passion that brings them joy as much as it brings them hate, tears, and unexpected adrenaline rushes.

This second much more explosive relationship contains an element that was lacking in their first: regular physical violence. Every three months or so, Eve finds herself bruised and bloodied at the hands of Alice. Eve reluctantly accepts this violence, in part, because it is never unprovoked. During their biggest rows, Eve always throws the first punches. Alice only hits back in self-defence.

Because of Alice's kickboxing skills, Eve's blows never connect, while Alice's hard kicks and swift uppercuts sometimes send Eve to hospital. During these hospital visits, Alice is normally beside Eve, holding her hand and stroking her hair, telling her how much she loves her. Eve feels quite close to Alice in these intimate moments. They effectively calm Eve's explosive anger, despite the severe pain Eve suffers as a result of attempting to beat up an amateur kick boxer.

The pain of Alice's blows often makes it hard for Eve to walk. She has to lean on Alice's shoulder like a crutch, especially after the rows where Alice has kicked her vagina.

On October 7th, 2018, Alice nearly blinded Eve, brutally shoving both her fingers into Eve's unprotected eyes. This was in response to Eve lunging at Alice in a hysterical rage, shortly after Alice confessed that she had been regularly sleeping with two of Eve's favourite students.

After this brutal act, Alice unfortunately couldn't accompany Eve to Leicester Royal Infirmary, as she was already late for work. Alice instead called an ambulance for Eve and then rang her neighbour Joe Pastorious, asking him to spend the night comforting Eve in hospital while Alice completed her shift at Firebug.

Alice asked Joe to comfort Eve in hospital, partly because of what had happened to his own eye and partly because Alice could sense Joe would make a great friend for Eve. The three of them had been acquaintances for years, but Alice felt they should all get closer.

Joe followed Alice's instructions, spending the night reassuring Eve that her vision would return, while simultaneously making Eve feel both physically safe and emotionally nurtured. Joe eventually drove Eve home after the doctors examined her eyes, eyes which were quite swollen and hurt badly whenever Eve looked to her left. With her hand in his, Joe gently led Eve from his car back into her well-furnished two-story home in Clarendon Park. His hands felt strong and gentle, even though they were smaller and softer than Eve's own hands.

Joe slowly walked Eve from her front door to her beautiful kitchen, where he first put the kettle on and then sat across from Eve at an expensive marble table Alice recently purchased using Eve's credit card. Joe and Eve spent the next few hours eating biscuits and green tea at this marble table, engrossed in a rambling conversation about Patti Smith and Eve's favourite Frida Kahlo paintings. Joe was shocked at how much Eve seemed to be enjoying their conversation, given that she was both in pain and high on painkillers.

Joe chatted to Eve until Alice arrived back home from her shift. Alice was relieved Eve seemed to be having such a pleasant evening with Joe, particularly since Eve had spent the earlier parts of the day in such emotional and physical agony. Alice also felt incredibly lucky to have a nice neighbour like Joe Pastorious.

If it hadn't been for Joe, Alice would have been sacked from the most amazing job of her life. Alice would literally do anything to be able to keep bartending at Firebug. That night, Alice was so happy she didn't get sacked for being late, that she didn't even mind that Joe had eaten most of her chocolate biscuits. Joe mistakenly thought Alice was happy Eve would not be spending the rest of her life as a blind woman.

In reality, Alice wasn't particularly bothered by the prospect of Eve losing her eyesight.

From Alice's point of view, if Eve had gone blind, it was entirely Eve's fault. Alice, after all, was only defending herself from Eve's brutal violence, violence Eve was initiating more frequently, as time went on.

That night, a part of Alice was disappointed she didn't successfully blind Eve. This is because Alice knew, more than anyone, that if Eve had suddenly lost her eyesight, she would finally learn the harsh lesson that violence only leads to heartache and suffering. Being blind might also get Eve to start examining her more controlling behaviours, particularly her insistence that Alice must not have spontaneous sexual encounters with Eve's students and friends.

While Eve was in hospital and Alice was bartending, Alice wondered if a blind Eve was more likely to act like a civilised human being when Alice confessed she was regularly having sex with Eve's nephew Conor and was now pregnant with his child. But since permanent blindness was probably not on the cards, Alice knew Joe Pastorious was the next best thing.

In the spring of 2018, Joe self-published his first novel, a quasi-autobiographical suspense thriller detailing a violent young man's quest to find his birth mother.

Some of Alice's lovers adored Joe's book, as it was both a completely unpredictable page turner and a surprisingly wise treatise on ways damaged young men process anger and self-loathing. Alice enjoyed flirting with Joe at work, but after hearing about his first book, she decided that Joe needed to be in Eve's life, somehow. There was something about the way Joe expressed himself Alice was certain would help Eve develop the tools she needed to practice tolerance and manage her anger.

After Joe left Eve and Alice's flat with a full belly and a smile on his face, he didn't consider the possibility that Eve was in hospital because Alice had shoved both of her fingers into Eve's eyes. However, Joe still doubted what happened was the bizarre and improbable accident both women emphatically told him it was.

Yet despite this secret doubting, Joe thoroughly enjoyed his night with Eve Fenn. Both in hospital and in her kitchen, he found Eve's conversation delightful and fascinating. She had a way of thinking about life and art that felt quite familiar to Joe, like she was a kindred spirit of sorts.

As Joe walked back to his house thinking he would like to have tea with Eve more often, he also felt slightly unnerved. Joe couldn't articulate exactly how, but a part of him could sense Eve was in some kind of danger.

Before Joe returned to his house, he watched a temporarily blind Eve interact lovingly with Alice after she returned home from work at ten past three in the morning. Joe watched the two women laughing and playing with each other, making him laugh in the process. Their attitude seemed nonchalant, as though nothing of any major significance had happened that night. Joe could also sense a palpable warmth between Eve and Alice; a warmth that seemed both emotional and physical.

Joe left their flat at 4:18am, because Alice announced that she and Eve needed to 'go bird-washing' for the remainder of the evening. Joe didn't know exactly what Alice meant by this, but it gave him an erection anyway.

Once Joe was gone, Alice quickly undressed Eve, laid her down on their big soft bed and expertly performed oral sex on her for a good thirty minutes. Throughout those thirty minutes, Alice thought about her plans to seduce Conor's sister Fiona, Eve's favourite niece. Eve instead thought about Joe Pastorious. Eve needed to cum hard, to distract herself from both the intense anger she felt and the overwhelming pain in her eyes.

After her orgasm, Eve tried in vain to fall asleep.

Eve was deeply disturbed by the feelings Joe had elicited in her that night – feelings that made her doubt she was both a lesbian and in love with Alice. In fact, talking to Joe gave Eve a terrifying glimpse of what life could be like in a heterosexual relationship. Eve always expected to feel oppressed in such a relationship…never aroused and excited and certainly never safe and contented with life. Yet during Eve's traumatic evening being looked after by Joe Pastorious, she was feeling all of these things.

This is why Eve quickly decided she never wanted to speak to Joe again. Alice never understood why Eve suddenly developed such an intense aversion to him. Alice was looking forward to Eve and Joe's friendship, as it would make her own life much easier.

Alice thought Eve needed a close friend who Eve didn't fancy, but who could still give Eve emotional support that was outside of Alice's abilities. Alice thought that if Eve had such a close friend, Eve would be less stressed and more open minded about sex and this in turn, would help Eve control her anger and violence.

Eve disagreed very strongly. She had no desire to be more open minded about sex, nor did she have any desire to control either her anger or her violence. Eve thought they were justified, under the circumstances. The circumstances were that Alice slept with two of Eve's favourite students and then nearly blinded her.

In addition to feeling so angry, Eve was also (ironically) feeling broody for the first time in her life. Alice didn't yet know this in October of 2018, which is why Alice was temporarily keeping her pregnancy with Conor's baby a secret. Like Eve, Alice too had been feeling broody for the first time in her life. Broodiness was the reason Alice decided to stop using condoms after having sex with Conor for a few weeks.

Alice started having unprotected sex with Conor Fenn on the night of his eighteenth birthday, August 6th, 2018. From May of 2018, Alice had also been having protected sex with Conor's father Michael, Eve's older brother. Eve didn't know that Alice and Michael were having sex, nor did she know about Alice and Conor.

On October 7th, 2018, Michael also didn't know that Alice had been having unprotected sex with his son, nor did he know that Alice was now confirmed pregnant with his son's child. Additionally, Michael didn't know that the reason Alice chose to have unprotected sex with Conor, rather than him, is Conor's age made the idea of getting pregnant more exciting. Although Conor had just turned 18, he still looked (and acted) like an acne ridden fourteen-year-old with a severe case of ADHD.

On the morning of November 8th, 2018, Alice finally revealed by text to Conor that he was going to become a daddy. Alice also revealed that she had lied to him about using birth control, trusting that Conor would be happiest finding out about this pregnancy once the baby had been gestating for a few months. After they had sex, Conor often watched Alice swallow a contraception pill. He didn't realise it was actually folic acid. Deceiving Conor in this way made Alice incredibly horny, after which they would have sex again.

Alice, of course, was enraged at Conor when it became apparent that Conor was not happy with the prospect of becoming a father. She then texted him numerous insults and threats, even claiming the pregnancy was mostly his fault. However, Alice had hope that once the baby was born, Conor's feelings would change. Unfortunately, Conor's feelings couldn't change.

Conor told Alice he was 'childfree' before they started having sex. Alice insisted he would someday change his mind, since Alice herself had recently changed her mind.

After Alice gave birth to her baby, she began to believe for the first time in her life that no one was really childfree. Childfree people were simply in denial about their true nature and it was up to wiser people to shake them out of this delusion. Alice now thinks that sexual seduction is an especially potent way that women can shake men out of the delusion that they are childfree.

Eve does not agree with Alice, despite no longer feeling childfree.

Alice first revealed her pregnancy to Eve during the afternoon of November 8th, 2018, shortly after her protracted text row with Conor. After hearing the big news, Eve's first instinct was to pick up a kitchen knife and stab Alice.

Instead of acting on this impulse, Eve did something that surprised Alice. She calmly stated that Alice was a horrible human being who she never wanted to see again.

Alice laughed dismissively at Eve, after which she announced that she was going to name her baby Cara, to punish Eve for her selfish behaviour. As Eve tearfully pleaded with Alice not to give her baby this name, Alice punched Eve as hard as she could, knocking her across the floor and breaking her nose. Alice had never punched Eve this hard before, but she felt strongly that Eve deserved it.

Despite Alice's expectations, Eve didn't fight back. Alice was pregnant, after all and Eve could never harm a child. Nor could she knowingly allow a child to be abused. This is why Eve quickly apologised to Alice, even while she was still on the floor covered in blood. After Alice accepted Eve's apology, Eve decided she was going to work hard to fix the problems in her relationship with Alice. Eve was trying desperately to become Cara's second mummy. This wasn't because of broodiness. Eve was far too frightened for the wellbeing of Cara to allow Alice to raise her as a single mother.

Unfortunately, Eve's presence as Cara's second mummy does nothing to stop Alice from parenting Cara exactly how she wants to.

Although Eve doesn't realise it, she has always been powerless to stop Alice from doing exactly what she wants to do. When Eve isn't being violent towards Alice, she too does exactly what Alice wants her to do. This is why Eve Fenn still loves Alice Adler, despite everything Alice has done to her. Alice wants and even demands that Eve love her unconditionally. Hence, their relationship is still going strong.

Throughout the remainder of Alice's life, she will never worry that she is abusing Eve Fenn, Cara Adler, Conor Fenn, or the many families she is instrumental in breaking apart. Such a worry wouldn't cohere with her political beliefs.

Alice doesn't believe in the concept of 'abuse'. She thinks it's an oppressive social construction, much like monogamy, or the idea that having children is a choice.

PART 3: SEX

"As women, we get the message about how to be a good girl – how to be a good, pretty girl – from such an early age. Then, at the same time, we're told that well-behaved girls won't change the world or ever make a splash."

- Phoebe Waller-Bridge

"The prostitute is not, as feminists claim, the victim of men, but rather their conqueror, an outlaw, who controls the sexual channels between nature and culture."

- Camille Paglia

"And in the end, the love you take is equal to the love you make."

- The Beatles

11. SEX: In the Beginning

During the summer of 2015, Davis McFarlin was both Eve Fenn and Joe Pastorious's favourite porn star. Both Eve and Joe had many orgasms thinking about Davis. However, Eve only thought about Davis while she was masturbating to Davis's porn. Joe also thought about Davis when he wasn't masturbating to her porn.

Joe regularly thought about writing to Davis, just to see what it would be like to interact with such an unbelievably sexy woman. Joe thought Davis was almost as sexy as Janet Waverley.

Joe frequently wondered not only what it would be like to fuck Davis, but also what it would be like to talk with her, have coffee with her and perhaps hold her hand on a park bench. Joe had what you might call a crush on this woman, a crush which gave him a gooey feeling in his stomach, whenever her image popped in his mind. Joe would frequently daydream about seducing her, impressing her, making her laugh and getting her to fall madly in love with him.

Unlike the other women in Joe Pastorious's life, Davis McFarlin lives far far away from Leicester. Hence, Joe doesn't really know Davis McFarlin. But he does know that he isn't really in love with her. Joe only knows that she's American and so sexy it's freakish.

Joe also doesn't know that Davis comes from Los Angeles. And Joe knows virtually nothing about Pasadena. Pasadena is a city in Los Angeles County, a city that happens to be quite important in the life of Davis McFarlin.

Before the explosion of social media, people from neighbouring Los Angeles suburbs would often drive to Pasadena to walk along its quaint and colourful streets. The Pasadena streets are prettier and far more cultured than most of the suburban streets of Los Angeles. Pasadena people are pretty too, but not like normal Los Angelenos are pretty. Pretty people in Pasadena often wear glasses, cardigans, argyle socks and pinstripe jackets. Sometimes they appear like stylish grad students (or glamorous movie stars playing stylish grad students). This is why some have said that Pasadena, more than any other area of Los Angeles County, is like a little European city.

In Los Angeles, areas in Hollywood or The Wilshire District could accurately be described as 'cool'. Pasadena isn't cool. It's 'intelligent person cool'. That means when you walk down its streets, you feel like an intelligent and interesting person, even if you aren't.

Pasadena is brimming with middle class intellectuals, artists, and forward-thinking people who like old jazz, patchouli oil, and the newest South American beers. Perhaps that's why, even though he isn't, Matt Damon seems like he's from Pasadena – so does Ethan Hawke. Many people who seem like they're from Pasadena actually come from other places in Los Angeles. Many of these people are online. Hence, young Los Angelenos don't have as much of a reason to go to Pasadena as they did in the late 20th century.

As recently as the early 00s, nerdy teens from sprawling Los Angeles suburbs would troll the alleyways of Old Town Pasadena, hoping to meet someone older, smarter and willing to have a spontaneous conversation with them about something deep and philosophical.

This rarely happened. And it was kind of tragic, as those same teens were often very lonely, daydreaming about the prospect of finding love near Colorado Blvd. They would daydream of meeting and impressing an attractive, articulate and scholarly looking thirty-something in one of Pasadena's beautiful bookstores.

This too, rarely happened. Attractive, articulate and scholarly looking thirty somethings tended to avoid teenagers. Adults in Los Angeles generally wanted to stay far away from teens who had crushes on them. It didn't matter how beautiful these teens were.

In the 2010s, Colorado Blvd was still one of the more beautiful streets in Old Town Pasadena. On this beautiful street, there was a beautiful bookstore called 'Vroman's'. In that bookstore, there was a coffee shop called 'Jones Coffee Roasters' which made beautiful little cups of coffee.

In the early autumn of 2016, two women are having a conversation with each other in Vroman's during a beautiful Sunday afternoon. It is 2pm. Both women are drinking tasty cappuccinos with butterscotch syrup in them. The woman on the left is quite attractive, according to Los Angeles. She's thirty-four. The woman on the right is thirty-three. It would be unfair to say that the woman on the right isn't attractive. It would be fairer to say that unlike the woman on the left, the woman on the right looks more like someone who isn't from Pasadena. She's not white. It's the woman on the left who is white. In fact, the woman on the left looks like an English movie star who might be found playing a femme fatale in an American indie film. The woman on the right is chubby and Mexican, so she doesn't look like an English movie star who might be found playing a femme fatale in an American indie film.

In the Los Angeles of the early 21st century, white people are often considered more beautiful than Mexicans – even skinny Mexicans who themselves are very beautiful. But the relative beauty of each woman is less important than who they are and why they are talking to each other.

These two women are Davis McFarlin and Lena Rodriguez.

Both have known each other since they were small children. Neither of them found it easy to relate to other kids. During their childhoods, they both dreamed of being friends with adults. Because they were children, adults naturally had no interest in being friends with them. Davis and Lena were never particularly good at talking to other children, because both girls refused to do small talk and thought most of their peers were boring. As adults, they still aren't good at small talk and find most adults quite boring. When Davis and Lena were teenagers in the late 90s and early 00s, their lack of small talk skill was a major social liability. This was because both of them grew up in a Los Angeles suburb called Downey.

Downey was not like Pasadena. It's still not like Pasadena.

Teens from Downey were often willing to drive in over forty-five minutes of slow-moving, smoggy traffic just to spend an evening shopping in Pasadena. Teens from Pasadena, on the other hand, didn't normally drive to Downey to do anything. When Davis got her first car in 1999, she often drove Lena with her to Pasadena. The two of them spent a lot of time walking and shopping on the streets of Old Town. They bought a plethora of strange hats, books, dinners and CDs, during many fun Friday evenings. They also watched quite a few art films at Pasadena's Laemmle theatre: films like 'Existenz', 'Boise Moi', 'Momento', 'Dancer in the Dark', and 'Requiem for a Dream'.

Davis and Lena both dreamed of accidentally meeting a well-dressed, well-spoken man in his thirties who would rescue them from their mundane lives in Downey. They described this idealised man to each other constantly: a funny, self-deprecating, but still buff, clean shaven coffee house intellectual who read Anna Akhmatova, played chess and had a spacious, beautifully designed Pasadena apartment with Renee Magritte paintings hanging all over the walls. In their heads, Davis and Lena could talk to this striking man of letters for hours, never getting bored. The one difference between Davis and Lena's version of this guy was that in Lena's head, he always had a British accent.

Unfortunately, neither of them ever met anyone resembling this perfect person when they were teenagers. Their young lives felt empty without him, like he was the missing ingredient in their eventual happiness. For both girls, it was as if he needed to exist, even if he was nowhere to be found in their immediate surroundings. Unlike Davis, Lena was making a concentrated effort to find him.

During her senior year of high school, Lena applied as an English major to the University of Austin Texas and was accepted. She was confident she could find her perfect boyfriend in Austin, as the city had an impressive reputation for being a bohemian hub. That same year, Davis was dropping out of her first year of junior college, having just given birth to a son.

The father of Davis's baby was a hunky football player named Ben Marquez. Despite being hunky, Ben was far from perfect.

Conception happened a year earlier, while Ben was a sixteen-year-old junior at Warren High School. Lena was also a junior at Warren and was taking notice of Ben. Ben was a jock, but he was also a math nerd and someone who seemed unusually kind. Because of this, Lena had a huge crush on Ben. It was a crush that seemed to be cementing into friendship and a friendship that seemed to lurch towards the beginnings of romance. Lena and Ben were making gaga eyes at each other, or at least that's how Lena saw it. They had once held hands.

Neither had said 'I love you' yet, but Lena was expecting it to happen very soon. Then, one evening, Ben got drunk and had sex with Davis, who was then an eighteen-year-old freshman at Cerritos College. Shortly after Davis told Ben she was keeping their baby, Ben became Davis's boyfriend. Ben told Lena that he still had feelings for her but couldn't ignore his new responsibilities to Davis and his yet unborn child.

Davis had quite different responsibilities to the ones Ben had. Unlike Ben, Davis was legally an adult.

This was in March of 2001, six months before 9/11 and one month before

Ben's seventeenth birthday.

On October 4th, 2002, when their baby was not yet one year old, Davis McFarlin finally married Ben Marquez. Everything felt more legitimate, as Ben was now legally a grownup, just like his hot young wife. When the two of them got married, Davis decided to keep her last name. Ben, being a feminist, was proud of her for this. Ben was also proud of Davis for many other things, one of which was her beautiful, tall, toned (and white) body. These things made Ben especially proud to have started a family with Davis. It made his Mexican parents proud too. Or at least, they were proud by the day of the wedding.

Lena, however, was not proud of Davis, even though she attended the wedding as a bridesmaid. Lena was not proud, even though she pretended to be proud. She did this pretending because Lena thought she should be happy for Davis and Ben. Davis and Ben, surprisingly, seemed like they were good for each other. Both acted very much in love. They were always laughing and giggling, tickling each other on park benches, or getting kicked out of restaurants for making too much noise. Wherever they went and wherever they got asked to leave, they were always with their beautiful baby boy, a boy both parents unanimously decided to name Max.

They thought this name was special, as Davis and Ben both had grandfathers named Max. Davis and Ben's lives were cluttered with little romantic coincidences like this. They both had fun constantly talking about them, regardless of whether Lena wanted to hear any of it.

To Lena, it looked as though Davis and Ben had much more fun being new parents than most married couples. Davis and Ben also seemed like surprisingly competent parents, hardly phased by the stresses that made more responsible thirty-somethings complain of dirty diapers and sleepless nights. Max was like an exciting video game both of them found it hard to stop playing. They made teen parenthood look less like a youthful mistake than an idyllic fantasy come to life. Watching Davis and Ben, you'd think teen parenthood was not only easy, but blissful – like their lives were a montage from a life insurance commercial.

Lena could also observe that Davis turned out to be a far better wife for Ben than she could ever be. Davis was intelligent like Lena, but unlike Lena, she was also fun, sexy and always looking extremely confident at whatever she was doing. Davis was whiter than Lena, skinnier than Lena, more middle class than Lena and even braver than Lena. This made Lena assume Davis must also be a more passionate and adventurous lover. After birthing Max, Davis managed to quickly exercise her post-baby body back to its sleek, bikini ready norm. Davis had athleticism Lena did not. Lena had acne Davis did not.

So Lena tried hard to be happy for Davis and Ben. But as much as she tried, she just couldn't do it. There was another reason for this.

Davis told Lena that when she first fucked the highly intoxicated Ben, he didn't really know where he was. He had just drunk seven cans of beer and downed two tequila shots. Davis herself only drank half of one beer. Afterwards, Davis apologised profusely to Lena for what she had done. She apologised profusely because she knew Lena had feelings for Ben. But knowing Lena had feelings for Ben didn't stop Davis from having unprotected sex with an underaged kid who didn't know he was actually having sex.

Davis was only apologising for fucking a guy her best friend had feelings for. But she wasn't apologising for also taking advantage of that guy and forcing him into teen fatherhood. Lena couldn't believe Davis was capable of something so cold and heartless.

She was in shock.

A part of Lena wondered if technically, Davis had actually raped Ben. But Lena quickly convinced herself that this worry was ridiculous.

Her reasoning went something like this:

It was true that Ben seemed frightened and confused when he first talked about Davis's pregnancy. Yet within a few weeks, he seemed genuinely excited about becoming a dad. Also, Ben was a guy, which meant Ben was responsible for getting drunk and having sex, even if he couldn't exactly remember the sex. And there was also the fact that although Ben was sixteen, he looked like a twenty-five-year-old fitness instructor. So whatever Davis did to Ben, it couldn't have been rape. Ben was far too happy to be a rape victim.

Nonetheless, when Lena found out about Davis's surprise pregnancy, her perception of her best friend completely changed. Lena wasn't angry with Davis for what she did to Ben. Lena thought she would be, but she instead felt something else, something which surprised her. This feeling was far more difficult for Lena to understand, an emotion which seemed both calm and primal at the same time. At first, Lena thought it was seething rage, but it wasn't that.

It was a strong feeling of superiority. Lena felt superior to Davis.

Lena suddenly saw Davis as trash, or at least something approximating a pathetic and pitiful loser. Lena began to see Ben as a loser too, but never quite as big a loser as Davis. Davis, after all, was an intelligent young woman who could have gone to college. She could have had an amazing career doing something where she could make a ton of money. But she gave it all up to become a boring suburban mom, shitting all over her education and destroying her many career prospects. And she did it all because she was a trashy slut, a cum guzzling gutter bitch, a ho so skanky she got pregnant by taking advantage of a drunken high school junior.

Davis didn't exactly rape him, but she took advantage. This was the narrative in Lena's head.

During Lena's first year at UTA, she was secretly happy to get away from Davis and Ben. She knew they wouldn't be moving out of Downey anytime soon. This made Lena feel good. When Lena moved in her new dorm and set up her first AOL instant messenger account, she deliberately did not add Davis and Ben as IM buddies.

However, she still answered the occasional phone call from Davis. She loved hearing how confusing Davis was finding life as a young mother. This contradicted the extreme confidence Lena saw with her own eyes, whenever she watched Davis play with Max. These calls made Davis seem not just trashy, but fake and foolish – like a pathetic piece of shit.

A part of Lena knew her feelings about Davis were petty and unkind and she even tried to suppress them. But she just couldn't do it, as they were too embedded in her personality. Rationally, Lena knew that Davis's situation was complex and that she was more than just a trashy skank who tricked a sixteen-year-old into raising a family with her. But Lena couldn't be rational. She couldn't experience Davis as anything other than a disgusting slut, destined for a sell-out life of sandwich making, bad sitcoms and PTA meetings.

Davis, on the other hand, knew nothing of Lena's true feelings towards her.

From Davis's perspective, Lena had simply moved to Austin and was too busy to spend much time with her. Because of this, Davis often missed Lena; she missed her badly. Although Davis was one year older than Lena, Davis still looked up to her. Talking to Lena always made Davis feel calm, like Lena had a perfect understanding of Davis's confusing and often chaotic thoughts. Talking to Lena didn't feel like talking to even a best friend: it felt like therapy for Davis and the absence of this constant therapy made Davis feel unsettled, like it was much harder to navigate her new life as a young mother. It was much harder than life had ever been before Lena moved away.

Lena, on the other hand, found it very easy to become immersed in university life. She finished her BA with high honours in 2005, completed her Masters in 2007, her PhD in 2010 and she landed a good paying job at her alma matter in the fall of 2011. Lena was impressive to people, especially the sort of thirty somethings who would hang out in Pasadena bookstores back in Los Angeles. Many of these men wanted to date Lena, more because of her mind than how she looked. Lena ignored them, in much the same way that the adults she had crushes on ignored her when she was in high school. Lena was too busy with her burgeoning academic career to have time for a relationship. She also didn't feel terribly horny much of the time.

However, by 2011, Lena still did not have two things Davis did have: a husband and child. Lena wanted those things badly. She didn't want them in her teens or early twenties. But she wanted them now, as she'd already spent most of her adult life traveling the world, writing acclaimed short stories and academic papers.

Life as a suburban mom was suddenly not seeming like the hell on earth Lena had always imagined it would be, especially since she had a thriving career that could co-exist with children and a husband.

Lena was only twenty-eight and had landed an academic job most of her fellow grad students would kill for. Because of her new income, she was quickly able to eat at fancy restaurants and wear expensive, stylish clothes. By the spring of 2012, Lena had a book deal with a prestigious publisher of new, critically acclaimed works of fiction by up-and coming Latina authors. Davis, on the other hand, had never wanted to be an academic. She never had a desire to be unusually well off, financially. Davis didn't even see the point of eating in fancy restaurants.

She did, however, want something Lena had: a life and career outside of Downey. Davis found herself being the primary caretaker of her son Max while Ben supported the three of them by going out to work. Although Davis loved the process of raising her son, she hated life in suburban Downey. She hated the ugliness of Downey's architecture, as well as the absence of anything resembling high culture. Davis also hated her neighbours. She thought they were boring and self-destructive; she even hated how they dressed. Davis found her existence in the town she grew up in, utterly soul crushing. She spent many weekend afternoons in Pasadena with Max, chatting in the Starbucks joined to the Barnes and Noble bookstore on Colorado Blvd.

Occasionally, Davis would take Max to Vroman's and the two of them would read to each other, sharing hot cups of apple tea with honey. These were the happiest moments of Max's childhood. He loved impressing his mother with how well he could memorise, recite and analyse her poems. Davis was shocked to be the mother of such a brilliant child prodigy, while Max was amazed that his mother could write words he could think about so obsessively. Her writing was like a video game he found hard to stop playing.

Davis began writing poetry when Max was just a toddler, in order to cope with the monotony of her suburban existence. Unbeknownst to many scholars and literature fans, Davis became an amazing, if under-appreciated, poet and essayist. In 2007, she set up a website where she posted her large collection of sonnets, poems and experimental writing. Davis got many positive comments and even a few essays about her work, written by a small group of loyal fans.

But Davis could never figure out how to get the kind of online audience she wanted, a community of fans big enough to make her forget that she lived in Downey. There were never any publishers who wanted to take a chance on her unusual manuscripts. By the beginning of 2012, Davis stopped sending out her book proposals, convinced that the best idea was to self-publish some of the pieces that were particularly popular with her online fans.

Nonetheless, there was still something about self-publishing that made Davis feel thoroughly mediocre. In 2012, self-publishing was often described by successful authors as a sign of weakness, an indication you were the only person interested in your own work. Or at least, that's what Davis imagined Lena would say, if Lena still had time for her.

Lena signed on Facebook for the first time in May of 2012. Within two days of creating a Facebook account, she accepted a friend request from Davis. By this point, Lena had become curious about what had happened to Davis McFarlin and her family. So, on July 28th, 2012, during an LA visit where Lena spent time with her parents, she decided to meet Davis, Ben and ten-year-old Max at a Starbucks in Santa Monica. The four of them met at 1pm and wound up chatting until 9pm that evening.

That day, Lena's feelings about Davis's family changed. She no longer saw Ben as a loser; she suddenly saw him as a loyal and kind man who did his best to support his family. She even remembered why she was so attracted to him as a teenager. Lena could also see that baby Max had grown into an incredibly sweet and intelligent child that Lena absolutely adored. Talking to Max was like talking to a grownup, a very polite, well-mannered and interesting little grownup. Max was like the child Lena would have chosen, if she had the luxury of choosing her own offspring.

Lena still saw Davis as foolish and pathetic. However, she no longer felt complete disdain for Davis. She instead felt (slightly) sorry for her. She felt sorry for an old friend who was wasting her life in Downey, writing what was probably very shitty poetry. During this visit with Lena, Davis talked a lot about her poetry website and how much she loved the process of writing. Max talked about it too. Although Lena feigned interest, she had no intention of reading a single one of Davis's poems. If she had, Lena would have discovered that Davis was actually a much better writer than she was. This would have infuriated Lena.

After their day at Starbucks, Lena continued corresponding with Ben, Max and Davis on Facebook. Lena corresponded more with Ben and Max than she did with Davis, during the period between the autumn of 2012 and early 2014. By February of 2014, Davis was rarely on Facebook. Lena didn't notice this much, because she was busy chatting with other Facebook friends: friends that were either not from Downey, or acquaintances who could give her career opportunities. Ben and Max were also on Facebook much less than they had been, prior to February of 2014. But they were still around, occasionally making witty or sweet observations that Lena would like and share, whenever they popped up on her timeline.

By the summer of 2016, Lena had been hired as a professor of literature at UCLA. Upon receiving the news, she quickly announced on Facebook that she was moving back to Los Angeles. Even though Lena didn't like the idea of moving back home, she knew, career wise, it was a huge step forward.

The area near UCLA was worlds apart from Downey. There were lots of gay people in this area. Lena thought she could talk to them about fashion, if nothing else. While Lena was preparing for the move, Ben and Max started suddenly posting a lot on Facebook. It was mostly stuff about how proud they were of Davis and how much they loved her. Davis, however, didn't post hardly anything.

Again, Lena didn't notice Davis's absence. She was too busy planning the move to her new West Hollywood apartment on September 11th, 2016.

Exactly two weeks after Lena moved into that apartment, she drove down to one of her favourite hangouts as a teenager: Old Town Pasadena. She decided to do some reading and shopping at Vroman's bookstore on Colorado Blvd. That day Davis, by coincidence, decided to do that very same thing.

12. SEX: Elitism

Lena Rodriguez hadn't been to Vroman's bookstore in ages and didn't mind the arduous drive from West Hollywood to Pasadena. She was too excited, looking to re-connect once again with her favourite parts of Los Angeles. Regardless of her now low opinion of the City of Angels, Los Angeles was still home for Lena. And that Sunday, she felt happy to be home again.

Traffic was unusually light that afternoon. It had rained during the morning. There were puffy clouds, mixed in with a beautiful blue Californian sky. The trees had droplets of water bouncing off them. It was a weirdly chilly day in Los Angeles – great weather for wearing a cardigan. Lena, as it happened, wore cat-eyeglasses with an expensive cardigan that day. She knew the ensemble fitted the sophisticated city she had such fond adolescent memories of.

When Lena walked in Vroman's, she felt exhilaration. The smell of coffee and books was the same as it had always been. Everyone in the store looked cosmopolitan, worldly and like they enjoyed reading The Economist for fun. They all had very serious expressions on their faces, like they were deep in thought. Some of them had beards they were stroking. Lena smiled, thinking to herself, "I'm so glad I'm here again. These are my people." She didn't mind that, unlike her, none of her people had brown skin.

While in Vroman's, Lena bought two books by Alice Munroe, one of her favourite writers. She decided to have a cappuccino while thumbing through her new paperbacks in Jones Coffee Roasters. The post-book purchase cup of coffee was always the most fun part of buying any book in Pasadena. If you sat next to a window, people on the street could see you reading and pondering. Lena always felt at peace during these moments. She could even hear the faint hum of an outdoor jazz concert. Being in the presence of live jazz always made Lena feel urbane and sophisticated, even though she didn't particularly like jazz.

While waiting for her cappuccino, Lena got a bit of a surprise. Davis, who she hadn't seen for four years, was standing next to her, also waiting for a cappuccino. Davis was carrying two white bags, filled with movie poster themed T-shirts and a few pairs of skimpy shorts. Davis had spent the past few hours walking up and down Colorado Blvd, doing some shopping in some of Pasadena's more colourful indie shops.

After their drinks were made, Davis and Lena grabbed a table and began a more in-depth conversation. Davis was excited to see Lena and both women were more than a little curious what the other had been up to. They had, after all, spent many evenings together in this very bookshop as teenagers.

Davis and Lena were surrounded by adults who mostly looked like attractive and stylish grad students: Pasadena grownups. If the two women had noticed the presence of minors, people like their former selves, their conversation might have been very different. But because they were only in the presence of other adults, they felt they could say whatever they wanted to each other.

So, this is what they said:

Davis: (with a big smile on her face) It's amazing you've come back to LA! I can't believe it. I never thought you'd come back.

Lena: It's amazing UCLA actually hired me.

Davis: And I'm so happy they did! Every time I go on Facebook, it seems like you're at some conference in Boston or Virginia.

Lena: It's just part of my job, Davis.

Davis: Yeah, the photos you post… it always looks like everyone's on some expensive vacation or something.

Lena: Well, conferences are like romantic vacations, but nicer and with smarter people.

Davis: Really?

Lena: Yeah, everyone you talk to has something interesting to say. You get to stay in swanky hotels, eat good food. Everybody wears these really serious, scholarly suits. But you know, no one's really serious afterwards when the alcohol comes out. It's great.

Davis: (smiling) You're making me envious.

Lena: Well, you shouldn't be. You can find cool people anywhere, Davis. You just have to spot the sorta person who can have a good conversation.

That's why it's good to know a few things about fashion.

Davis: Well, if you live in Downey, the cool people are mostly on Facebook. And in the last few years, I've been so busy I haven't even been on Facebook all that much.

Lena: Busy's good. I'm glad that we're both busy.

Davis: Me too. It's better than doing nothing, right?

Lena: When we were kids, we used to get so bored. Do you remember how boring high school was?

Davis: (smiling) No, nothing was ever boring with you around, Lena.

Lena: Really?

Davis: You ALWAYS got me to do the craziest shit. I'm surprised I didn't get expelled, with a friend like you.

Lena: (giggling) Davis, I never made you do anything you wouldn't have chosen to do anyway.

Davis: (proudly) You brought out my inner rebel.

Lena: And what ever happened to that rebel?

Davis: It's taken me many years to rescue her.

Lena: Really?

Davis: Yeah, it's like… I was thinking about something you told me when we were kids the other day.

Lena: What did I say?

Davis: You said we weren't normal people.

Lena: Well, we're not really, are we?

Davis: I was remembering this moment during the last day of tenth grade. Right after we were in detention. You looked at me and said "Davis, you and me girl…we are *not* made for raising families in stupid suburbs." And now that I'm a mom in Downey, that seems more true than ever. Especially when I look at all the fat ass moms pushing strollers around the fucking Downey Landing. Have you been there recently?

Lena: No, not since about… 2008.

Davis: I mostly go there for the vegan food. But it always reminds me of how right you were when you said we were too smart and cool for a life like that.

Lena: I don't remember this, but I'm sure I was on my period.

Davis: You said we deserved better, that we could see through things people we knew couldn't.

Lena: I said that?

Davis: You were pretty profound for a fourteen-year-old.

Lena: (giggling) I'd feel more profound if I remembered saying any of this.

Davis: You said a lot of things that day. I remember all of them.

Lena: Really?

Davis: You also said I should never be ashamed of my talents or how I choose to live my life.

Lena: Were you feeling ashamed that day?

Davis: I don't remember. I just remember that day, you said all the things my mother should have said. That's why I'm so glad I knew somebody like you, growing up.

Lena: (smiling) I'm glad I knew you too.

Davis: You were like my mom! But way nicer.

Lena: Not really, more like your big sister. Even though you're a year older than me.

Davis: It's weird. I don't have people like you in my life anymore.

Lena: But you have Ben and Max. That's a fully-fledged, loving family, Davis. In that respect, I'm the one who's envious of you!

Davis: I do love the both of them, but they are a handful. They're boys.

Lena: Is it hard to deal with Max now that he's going through puberty?

Davis: I wouldn't say that he's hard to deal with. I'd say… he's kinda preoccupied, distant maybe.

Lena: That's totally normal.

Davis: I know but it still pisses me off.

Lena: Teenagers piss everyone off. Remember what we were like?

Davis: Well, it wouldn't piss me off if Max were a normal kid.

Lena: What do you mean?

Davis: We used to do everything together. We liked the same TV shows; we read a lot of the same books, which is amazing, given his age. He got my poems better than the people who wrote me essays about them. He's a fucking brilliant kid, Lena. It's hard for me to even keep up with him.

Lena: Well, there's another reason I'm envious. You've got a wonderful son and an amazing husband.

Davis: I have a thoroughly ordinary husband.

Lena: I wouldn't say that. I'd say you have a practical husband, a husband that's kind, helpful, loyal, makes good money and really puts himself on the line for you and Max.

Davis: (smiling) I'm falling asleep already.

Lena: He's a good guy, Davis. Loads of women would love a guy like Ben. He's been a good guy ever since high school.

Davis: It's funny. I never knew what you saw in him… until he started doing my homework assignments and it suddenly become obvious, he was really fucking gorgeous.

Lena: (playfully) Yeah, you fucking stole him from me, you bitch.

Davis: Sometimes I think I shouldn't have.

Lena: Don't say that, Davis.

Davis: I love him, but he bores the shit out of me, Lena.

Lena: But he really really loves you. Come on! Every week he posts something on Facebook about how much he adores you and Max. I see them on my timeline.

Davis: He doesn't love me enough to lose thirty pounds. He doesn't look like he did when you last saw him, Lena. He's balding now.

Lena: Well, don't you love him anyway?

Davis: It would be easier to if we could have a conversation about something other than budget sheets. He's obsessed with money.

Lena: Well, he's an accountant. That's his job.

Davis: I don't know how he stands it. I'd kill myself if I had to do what he does every day.

Lena: But Davis, everyone is different. Some people enjoy that kinda thing. And we need people like that in the world. Some of them, like your husband, are actually very nice.

Davis: I know we need people like that in the world. But I don't need 'em in my house and especially not in my bed.

Lena: Maybe you guys just need something to, you know, re-awaken that passion I remember so vividly.

Davis: For me, that's like… ancient history.

Lena: Well, I remember it all very clearly. You guys were crazy in love during my senior year. I almost stopped being your friend, I was so pissed off you snagged Ben.

Davis: I know that and I do appreciate that you stayed with me. You got used to us as a couple when you didn't have to.

Lena: I know I did.

Davis: You never tried to split us up, even though you were so jealous. Lots of other girls tried to take Ben away from me. But not you, Lena.

Lena: That's because you were my best friend and I wanted what was best for you! And Ben. I thought you guys were good together.

Davis: You know, it's amazing to me that he chose to be with me. I felt so unconfident at that age. I always felt like, compared to you, I was really inarticulate. Maybe not less pretty, but less eloquent.

Lena: You were smart in your own ways. There weren't too many kids that could make a teacher cry.

Davis: (smiling) I used to love pissing off the teachers that really liked me.

Lena: Do you remember the time you told Mr. Holden we were catholic atheists?

Davis: Yeah, I do. I'm surprised you remembered that. I haven't thought about that for years.

Lena: I still think about it sometimes. I think about how you made those T-shirts for us that said, 'I don't believe in God because I believe in Jesus'. You wore them to Bible club.

Davis: (giggling) Yeah, I think I got that idea from you. You said Jesus rose from the dead so that everyone else can die without having to worry about heaven or hell.

Lena: (giggling) Yes, Jesus died for the biggest human sin: stupidity. I still believe that, even now.

Davis: Yeah, it's all coming back to me. The day after we got kicked out of Bible Club... I wrote that essay about how all Christians were retards. That was the only homework I ever did for Mr Holden.

Lena: And he didn't fail you?

Davis: Nah, I used to flirt with him all the time. A couple of times I could see the bulge in his pants.

Lena: Really? I thought he hated you.

Davis: I think yelling at me used to turn him on.

Lena: (laughing) You were really good at pissing people off.

Davis: There's nothing else to do in Downey, even now.

Lena: You think Downey's that horrible?

Davis: It's the worst!

Lena: But haven't you made peace with it? I mean, you chose to live there. You married a guy who went to Warren High School and works for Kaiser Permanente. You can't get more Downey than that.

Davis: I know, I know. Love makes you do strange things before it goes away.

Lena: But is your life in Downey really that… I don't know, unbearable?

Davis: Max and my career are what make my life worth living. Not Downey. And not Ben.

Lena: Well, then why don't you move out of Downey?

Davis: Ben likes it here and so does Max. His friends live here.

Lena: That make sense. With the internet, I guess it doesn't matter if your town is… not exactly exciting. Every time you open a laptop, you can always surround yourself with people and media that's completely tailored to you. We couldn't do that when we were kids.

Davis: You would think the internet would make Downey more bearable. But in some ways, it makes it worse.

Lena: Why?

Davis: There's more of a contrast between the world inside your house and the world outside your front door. It's depressing walking around my neighbourhood. Everyone's so fucking bland. And fat.

Lena: Yeah, but I'm sure some of those people are nice, once you talk to them.

Davis: (smiling) Lena, you're the one who said you wished 9/11 happened in Downey.

Lena: (laughing) Yeah, that's because I was a dumb kid who was angry at the world!

Davis: You weren't dumb at all!

Lena: I was arrogant as fuck. I was also really intolerant and bitchy, most of the time. I was SO hard on other people, Davis. I couldn't appreciate anything about anyone even remotely different to me.

Davis: What's there to appreciate about Downey? It's fucking suburbia. And the traffic's horrible now – it's worse than it's ever been.

Lena: Well, a lot of the people we grew up with: our neighbours, the other kids, even some of the teachers… they really cared about us.

Davis: I don't remember anybody caring about me.

Lena: Your parents cared about you.

Davis: Yeah, but that made them shitty parents. They were overprotective and paranoid.

Lena: Well, they were nice to you some of the time. I do remember that.

Davis: I don't.

Lena: And I'm sure they've been helpful to you with Max. It's always good to have grandparents for babysitting, right?

Davis: I don't see Mom and Dad anymore.

Lena: (shocked) What??

Davis: My dad's a control freak.

Lena: I know that, but he's still your dad.

Davis: I don't want people like that in my life anymore.

Lena: But he's your father. He's the reason you're here.

Davis: I don't have to tolerate people in my life that are unhealthy. It doesn't matter who they are. Part of being a grownup is learning to put up good boundaries.

Lena: I know that. But there are always things you can do to repair a relationship.

Davis: I don't want to repair anything with Dad.

Lena: What about your mom?

Davis: Anyone who remains loyal to that bastard is no friend of mine.

Lena: Not even the woman who introduced you to Ezra Pound?

Davis: I don't owe her shit for that.

Lena: I know you don't. It's just that she's your mother and–

Davis: (interrupting) You don't owe people friendship just because you fell out of them. Life doesn't work that way.

Lena: I know that. It's just… I guess I have a lot of fond memories of your mom and dad. They were always really sweet, compared to my parents. They used to take us on vacations. Your dad used to build all those train sets for us and play string quartet records while we had tea. Don't you remember?

Davis: That's 'cause he liked you more than me. He'd compare me to any fucking kid I had over the house. He couldn't stand the fact that I didn't give a shit about impressing him or being his perfect little girl.

Lena: That's not how I remember him.

Davis: You didn't have to live with him, Lena. You only got to see his good side.

Lena: Well, you never told me he was that bad. I knew he was controlling, but not to the extent that you would cut him out your life.

Davis: I didn't want to talk about him when I hung out with you. You were like an escape from him.

Lena: What's so horrible about him?

Davis: Loads of things. It's not just that he's a control freak. Every time we had a conversation, I felt like he was judging me, waiting for me to say something stupid. And if I said anything he didn't agree with or didn't want to hear, he'd leave in the middle of the fucking conversation and roll his eyes at me. That's why I used to fantasise about switching his angina medications.

Lena: So he made you feel like you were letting him down?

Davis: He made me feel like shit.

Lena: But I don't remember your mother being like that. She always seemed really proud of you.

Davis: Every time I did something that wasn't what she wanted, she'd humiliate me. If I ever wore something she thought looked sexy, Mom would give me a fucking lecture about getting raped. Can you believe that? Like it was my fault if some douche bag attacked me.

Lena: Yeah, but we're talking about the late '90s here. People weren't aware of things the way they are now.

Davis: Well, it would be nice if Mom understood she was fucking victim blaming me every time I left the house.

Lena: Was this because of the 'EAT ME' shorts you used to wear?

Davis: She couldn't handle it whenever I was just being myself. If I wore tiny shorts, she'd get freaked out if I went out at night. She was that stupid.

Lena: Well, I mean, can't you understand that now, as a parent? Don't you ever tell Max not to do dangerous shit at night because he could get mugged?

Davis: That's different. He's a guy.

Lena: I know it's different but care for a child's wellbeing always comes from a place of love. Even if it doesn't express itself in a way that's… very sophisticated, politically.

Davis: If Max gets the shit beat out of him because he's wandering around Hollywood with a pair of headphones on, it's not 'cause society tells anyone it's okay to hurt him. If Max gets attacked, it's because some asshole outside the norm of humanity decided to fuck up a kid.

Lena: Yeah, but you still tell him not to walk around in Hollywood with headphones on at two in the morning, right?

Davis: Violence is different to rape. We live in a culture where boys are taught they have a right to control women's bodies, that girls exist to give them hard ons. It's like we normalise male ownership and control of women. Rape is just an extension of that.

Lena: Well, I don't see why your mother's a terrible bitch for wanting to do whatever she could to make sure you didn't get raped.

Davis: But she was a bitch, Lena. She made me feel like if anything bad ever happened to me, it was totally my fault. She'd obsess over stupid shit, like the fact that I liked to flirt with older guys. When I turned seventeen, on the morning of my fucking birthday, she told me I had a reputation for being a slut. Can you believe that?

Lena: Why didn't you tell me that at the time? You drove me to Canters that day.

Davis: I didn't want to talk about it.

Lena: (sighing) Well… that I can understand. It's not very nice to hear your mom tell you that on your birthday.

Davis: I'm so happy now that I don't have people like her in my life. I get such a kick out of knowing she'll never know what a cool fucking grandson she has.

Lena: She doesn't see Max?

Davis: Max doesn't want to see her. Not when I told him the things she used to do to me. He doesn't like slut shaming either.

Lena: I honestly had no idea she slut shamed you this badly, Davis. It always seemed like your mom and dad were kind of… liberal. Your mom was always talking about George Carlin. And your dad had long hair.

Davis: They weren't liberal; they lied to people. People thought they were lefty because they were artists and they did a lot of shit for the homeless. But they were just as repressive and just as misogynist as any fucking 4chan meme; they just hid it better.

Lena: Really?

Davis: Everyone thought that because Mom and Dad made weird things that they were weird people. But they weren't, Lena. They were normal: they liked Titanic; my mom used to watch 60 minutes at night; Dad would play Rolling Stones records over and over and over again…and not the good ones from the 60s, the bad ones from the 80s.

Lena: But in a way, don't you think all of that brought you to where you are today? Like, if it hadn't been for them, you wouldn't have created the life for yourself that you did, with all of its uniqueness and all of its little eccentricities?

Davis: Not really. I brought me to where I am today. My parents mostly got in the way.

Lena: Well, the way I look at it, I didn't have the happiest childhood. My parents didn't really understand me. Neither did most teachers or kids I went to school with. But the dissatisfaction that came from that sense of isolation, in a way, propelled me into all the things I do now. That's why I moved to Austin and my first apartment wasn't some crappy shit hole in Whittier. It's why I got my PhD. It's why I published all those papers and my first book before I hit thirty. It's why I've just been hired to teach at UCLA.

Davis: (smiling) You're amazing, girl.

Lena: The point is, everything that happened to me which made me feel like an outsider also helped me create all the things I have now. My life really really suits me; that's something very few people I know actually have. And I don't think I'd have it if I wasn't an angry kid who felt totally misunderstood and breathtakingly out of place in a little city called Downey.

Davis: But if you had parents who understood you, you'd be way farther along than you are now. You'd be living in fucking New York, if you had a family that actually nurtured you. You always wanted to live in New York. Don't you remember?

Lena: I'll still get there… I'll find a way.

Davis: (smiling) Knowing you, you will.

Lena: Of course I will. But the fact that I'm not there yet isn't because my family didn't nurture me. I'm not there because that's not a hurdle in my life I've crossed yet.

Davis: Yeah, but if your parents actually got you, it'd be so much easier.

Lena: Maybe, maybe not. It's true that my parents don't really know me. But that's true of a lot of kids.

Davis: But doesn't that piss you off?

Lena: Well, the only thing that still upsets me is that much of the time, my parents acted like my feelings didn't matter all that much. They still do that now, sometimes.

Davis: That's because they were religious.

Lena: That's part of it. It's also because they just expected to have a kid who didn't mind being poor. My family doesn't aspire to much, so they didn't know what to make of me. Plus, they never read any books and they're still fucking obsessed with soccer.

Davis: I guess growing up means learning you don't need Mom and Dad's approval.

Lena: I suppose. In the end, it's probably best to get validation from people who appreciate what you bring to the table.

Davis: That's why I'm so happy with my career.

Lena: Right, how's the website going?

Davis: Oh man, so much shit's been happening. It's amazing, Lena. I can't even tell you what it's been like. I feel like I'm in the middle of a hurricane.

Lena: People really love your poems, huh?

Davis: Well… they didn't actually. A couple of years ago, it kinda became obvious that people don't go on websites anymore, especially to read longer pieces of writing. For a while, I thought about just giving up. But then I got an idea.

Lena: And what idea was that?

Davis: I could spend all this time trying to make something that only a tiny, fringe audience would ever get excited about. Or I could sell something that could instantly delight huge chunks of men… and allow me to live out one of my wildest fantasies.

Lena: Are you writing erotic stories?

Davis: No, I'm doing something so much more exciting than that.

Lena: …And that would be?

Davis: I've decided to resuscitate a dying breed, to make it seem new and exciting for people again.

Lena: I don't understand.

Davis: I run a porn website now.

Lena: A porn website?

Davis: Yes, but not just any porn website. We're re-inventing 'the porn website' for the social media age, taking things up a notch. It's really exciting.

Lena: (taken aback) Wow!

Davis: It's different to the web porn of the past. I'm a porn star who stars in movies, but I also get to work as a new kind of sex-worker. But in both roles, I get to have total control. I have sex with my clients, but it's set up in a way where I'm more like one of their clients. Isn't that cool?

Lena: I can see why this would appeal to guys. Men love to give women control now. That's the new big turn on for men. Lots of women writers I know are doing books about this. Men giving up control is a big market today.

Davis: That's what I thought when I saw our Google analytics. People fucking love this, Lena. Even Janet Waverley wrote an article about me. She says I'm bringing elitism back into porn. She even says she masturbates to me! Isn't that amazing?

Lena: (not knowing what to say) I guess. Which Janet Waverley are you talking about?

Davis: The writer who did that book on how psychopaths can be normal people.

Lena: Oh, I know her.

Davis: (excited) Really? You know Janet Waverley. *The* Janet Waverley?

Lena: Yeah, we met at a conference on literature and mental health a few years ago. It was really boring, so we spent most of the day just hanging out and ignoring everybody else. It was fun.

Davis: (in awe of Lena) Wow… that is so fucking amazing! I'd absolutely love to come with you to conferences and just hang out, you know? I'd love to be able to just randomly meet celebrities and chit chat, like we're doing now.

Lena: Well, you might meet some celebrities in the future. A lot of musicians want to meet porn stars. Or at least they did when we were growing up.

Davis: Do you have Janet Waverley's email address?

Lena: No, we just hung out that day. We didn't exchange emails, or anything like that. She still lives in London, I think. As far as I know, she's not even on Facebook or Twitter.

Davis: What a bummer! She's someone who's brain I'd love to pick in real life. I love her vlogs. I've read three of her graphic novels.

Lena: I'm sure she'd appreciate hearing you say that.

Davis: Well, knowing that she watches me is a huge honour. When I read her piece about me in Buzzfeed, I almost cried.

Lena: Does it make you proud when you think about who your work might be reaching?

Davis: I don't think I've ever been this proud of anything I've ever done, Lena. I know that may sound weird, but it's true. Porn saved my life.

Lena: (curiously) Really? It saved your life?

Davis: Yep. It helped me overcome a depression, it made me feel good at something for the first time and it really helped with a lot of other negative things that were happening. When we got super successful at such a quick pace, it was literally like being re-born. That's how crazy all this is for me, Lena. I get excited whenever I talk about it, it's so fucking surreal.

Lena: (smiling) I can imagine.

Davis: Not a day goes by when I don't get at least two hundred messages from dudes telling me how much they wanna fuck me.

Lena: Well, that doesn't surprise me. You are very beautiful. You've always been much more beautiful than me.

Davis: That doesn't mean much. Sexiness always trumps beauty and you've got sexy in spades, Lena.

Lena: (flattered) I have my moments.

Davis: (flirtatiously) And don't think I don't pay attention to them.

Lena: I probably should get laid more. I haven't thought about sex in years. I've been so busy.

Davis: Well, if you wanted to, we could–

Lena: (interrupting) No, I don't think that would be good for my career. And besides, if I'm honest, I don't think I'm pretty enough to be in porn.

Davis: Maybe not. You're kinda plain looking.

Lena: (awkwardly) So ...who films you? Who films your scenes?

Davis: I write and direct most of my vids and pick all my co-stars. I even do a lot of the production design and post-production. Everything is specifically tailored to turn on my fans. Weirdly, that brings in people from all over the internet. It's much more exciting than just doing generic porn.

Lena: You know, this, in a way, seems like something you would do. I always knew you were a talented filmmaker. When we were kids, you used to go on and on about wanting to be the female David Cronenberg.

Davis: Well, maybe in the future, once we save more money. Who knows? I could wind up doing features. I'd actually love that.

Lena: And you'd be great at it too. I used to love the little short films you made in your bedroom.

Davis: In a way, this still feels like that. I'm literally making movies in my bedroom a lot of the time.

Lena: (smiling) That's wonderful.

Davis: For me, it really is. It's a beautiful creative outlet.

Lena: So I'm curious: how many people have you had sex with on camera?

Davis: In the past two years, I've had sex with two hundred and eight.

Lena: (surprised) Holy shit!

Davis: Yeah, a hundred and sixty-four of them have been women.

Lena: That's interesting. I would have expected your partners to be male.

Davis: Nah. You gotta smooch the pooch in this industry if you wanna rise to the top.

Lena: I guess that makes sense. I just had no idea you were bisexual. You never checked out any girls when we were in school.

Davis: I thought about girls a lot. I just never said anything.

Lena: Really?

Davis: Yeah, I didn't want to make you uncomfortable. And we both liked guys, so it just seemed safer to talk about that.

Lena: So, do you enjoy gals as much as guys, now?

Davis: It's hard to compare, actually. I was really nervous when I did my first girl/girl scene. I had to get used to the smell. But after that, it started to feel pretty natural. Now, I'm really good at it – probably better than most people.

Lena: (giggling) Well, you would be good at it. You've licked more vaginas than most men!

Davis: (smiling) That's the best part!

Lena: Really?

Davis: Yeah, that's one of the perks of being a female porn star. It's the one thing I think a lot of women in the industry have always been embarrassed to talk about.

Lena: What do you mean?

Davis: You get to have sex with all the hot women every guy wishes they could bang! It's like getting the golden ticket to Willy Wonka's chocolate factory, except the candy's eye candy.

Lena: I can see why some women might feel that way.

Davis: And you're the one who doesn't have to look inside the window, wishing you could have a taste. All the guys are on the outside, looking at you – especially the awkward guys who can't talk to women. You know, the pathetic ones who still live at home and jerk off all over themselves. They'll never have anything like the pussy you get in this industry.

Lena: You like that aspect of it?

Davis: (enthusiastically) Hell yeah!

Lena: (taken aback) You like knowing shy dudes can't have sex with the women you do?

Davis: (enthusiastically) I fucking love it. That's what makes girl/girl scenes so hot, Lena. I get horny just thinking about it.

Lena: So... is this the elitism angle that Janet was talking about?

Davis: (nodding her head) Yeah, but it's not really me that's elitist. It's human nature.

Lena: Do you ever worry that this is… I don't know…

Davis: What?

Lena: Do you ever worry that sometimes… porn makes people feel like they don't deserve to have sex?

Davis: What people?

Lena: People with problems… people that are less attractive.

Davis: (rolling her eyes) No one's saying you don't deserve sex, Lena. I'm talking about guys.

Lena: (sarcastically) Right. I forgot.

Davis: I would never tell a woman she doesn't deserve sex if somebody wants her. I'm sex positive, Lena. I think all women deserve a chance to have sex – even ugly women.

Lena: (trying to be tactful) Davis… when Janet wrote that article about you bringing elitism back into porn, you sure she wasn't criticising you?

Davis: (thinking hard) Well, it was kind of ambiguous… but it doesn't really matter, either way.

Lena: (incredulous) How could it not matter? I thought you said you were a fan?

Davis: (matter of factly) I am a fan and I gave her an orgasm, Lena. Janet Waverley masturbates to me. That's what made me almost cry.

Lena: But what if she masturbates to you, even though she doesn't like you? What if she feels guilty afterwards?

Davis: (with pride) That makes it even hotter.

13. SEX: Social Change

Davis, at this point in the conversation, is happy. She's happy to see Lena; she's happy to tell Lena about her new career in porn and she wants the conversation to last as long as possible. Talking to Lena makes Davis feel like she understands her own mind better. It's like a therapy session she's needed for years.

Davis: I want you to feel free to ask me any questions you might have about my career, Lena. Don't hold anything back. Don't be embarrassed. You're the one person I needed to talk to about my new life.

Lena: Why me?

Davis: I want you to be as excited about it as I am. You understand me better than almost anyone.

Lena: I don't even know what you'd want me to ask you.

Davis: (smiling) Just be yourself. Be Lena for me.

Lena: What does that mean?

Davis: Just ask me anything you're curious about. Ask me the first thing that pops in your head.

Lena: (thinking for a few seconds) Okay… so tell me, Davis, what's the best thing about being a porn star in 2016?

Davis: That's such a stupid question.

Lena: Why?

Davis: (giggling) It fucking turns me on. Hello?

Lena: Well, it doesn't turn on every porn star. For some women, being in the adult industry is more of a job. Some porn stars don't even see what they do as sex. I read a paper about that by Roey White, when I did my Masters.

Davis: Well, good for her but I don't work that way. I don't need to deny reality, Lena. Porn is sex and I fucking love it. I love how I make money. I'm not conflicted about the fact that people want to watch me. I love everything about that.

Lena: Okay, fair enough.

Davis: I'm an exhibitionist. I'm an exhibitionist from deep within my being. I'm not like you, I'm different.

Lena: I can see that, Davis.

Davis: You can't shame me over this, Lena. I won't stop.

Lena: I wasn't trying to shame you.

Davis: I'm talking about the world. The world looks down on women like me.

Lena: I wouldn't say it looks down on you. I'd say for most people, sexual exhibitionism is just weird. It doesn't feel natural.

Davis: Well, it's not normal. You're right. That's part of why it's liberating.

Lena: When you're an exhibitionist, it's pretty random who can see you having sex. It's random who you're getting off, isn't it?

Davis: (smiling) Yeah, that's part of the appeal, honestly. I could be turning on any dirty old man I would never date in a million years, any hot guy with a jealous girlfriend. I love pissing off the girlfriends. That's so much fun.

Lena: Is that because you like making women feel inadequate?

Davis: I don't make women feel inadequate. They already feel that way. I just trigger things that are already there – things they haven't dealt with.

Lena: And you like having that effect on women?

Davis: (smiling) It makes me wetter than anything.

Lena: I guess I don't understand what's so sexy about that, but everyone's different. There are probably things about me you'd never understand.

Davis: Maybe. All I can say is, if there's anything that I really really love, it's making men feel things, very very strongly. That's why I used to write.

Lena: You don't write anymore?

Davis: Nah. What I do today affects the world way more than writing ever could. Porn is visceral; it's orgasms. Orgasms have a universal appeal.

Lena: So... what's your website called?

Davis: www.InsideDavis.com

Lena: Interesting title.

Davis: (proudly) It's to the point. Like me.

Lena: So, is this a site where you put up clips and do private shows for your fans?

Davis: Well, it's a newer, more sophisticated version of that. I don't really do web cam shit. This is modelled on the process of raising a social media profile.

Lena: How does that work?

Davis: If you join my site, you get access to all my unedited porn movies. If you write me an interesting paragraph about yourself with an accompanying pic, you get to interact with me. On Monday and Tuesday nights, the people with interesting paragraphs get to participate in a WhatsApp group. If you stand out in the group chat because you're interesting and hot, you get twenty-five points. If you keep being interesting in the chat and I notice you and enjoy your company, you get more and more points. When you get a hundred, we have a private DM for an hour.

Lena: And what happens during this private DM?

Davis: We have a conversation about something I'm interested in. If you seem genuine and cool and interesting and sexy, you get another fifty points. If we don't hit it off, you go back to zero in the group chat.

Lena: What happens if you get a hundred and fifty points?

Davis: You get a chance to take me out for dinner. If I enjoy your company, you get to take me out again. If I enjoy a second date, at the end of it, you get a hand job. If you can last more than five minutes without cumming, you get a third date. If you do well on that date, you get to attend a party where I have sex with two hot chicks on a big pool table. You get to watch me and film it on your iPhone.

Lena: Wow. iPhones are handy these days, aren't they?

Davis: At the end of the party, I take you into the bathroom and you get some oral. You can choose to film that if you want. Most guys don't because they aren't big enough to feel comfortable being filmed with their dicks hanging out.

Lena: Do women get to compete in the WhatsApp chats?

Davis: Nah. I mean, there aren't many women on the site anyway. But the policy is, if you're a girl and you're hot and local, I'll basically do whatever you want.

Lena: So have loads of women been asking you to have sex with them?

Davis: No, they haven't, weirdly. It's mostly men. Women have sex with me because it's good for their careers. But I have almost no female fans, apart from Janet Waverley.

Lena: That's pretty strange, given how little they would have to do.

Davis: Yeah, the babes don't know what they're missing. Maybe they're just jealous. Who knows? But until I can figure out how to tap into that market, I have to hire my party chicks.

Lena: So where do these sex parties happen?

Davis: Since last year, we've been doing them at the house in Downey. I've also hired a couple of Puerto Rican guys to do the filming: Manolo and Benji. They always do a good job. Both of them are cute, so sometimes I unofficially blow them afterwards in the attic, after everybody else leaves.

Lena: Isn't that dangerous with all the potential STDs?

Davis: Not really. We're tested all the fucking time. I don't do anything with anybody who isn't tested. All my fans have to get regularly tested; that's part of how you get to be a platinum member of 'Inside Davis'. The platinum members are the ones who get to compete in WhatsApp. Manolo and Benji are platinum members, so it all works out fine.

Lena: So who else is there at the sex parties?

Davis: It's normally a bunch of my porn star friends. I mean, they're not really friends. They're the people I have sex with on camera. They're not fans. If you let the fans into those parties, they get fucking aggressive, I swear, Lena. You cannot trust guy fans to behave themselves if there's a group of them, especially if booze is involved.

Lena: How often do you have these parties?

Davis: We have them once every six months.

Lena: And what do Ben and Max do when you have these parties?

Davis: Well, they're allowed to hang out for the first hour or so. Then when I get naked, they go into the garage and play video games.

Lena: Wow, they do that for you?

Davis: They actually do more work for the parties than I do. Ben does all the invitations and Max cleans the house and gets it ready before the guests arrive. Both of them prepare the drinks and food snacks.

Lena: Shit, they must really love you.

Davis: Yeah, this is one area when Ben's quite handy to have around. And of course, he loves counting the money and doing the accounts.

Lena: So, it seems like Ben and Max are, in their own way, a big part of Inside Davis.

Davis: You could say that.

Lena: Well, I mean they're not just okay with you being a porn star. They plan and prepare your sex parties.

Davis: In some ways, they're both good to me. I can admit that.

Lena: I mean think about it, Davis. You make porn and you've got a website where men compete to have sex with you. You talk to these guys on WhatsApp chats. If they're hot and impress you, they win your contest and get a blow job after watching a sex show. That's what Ben and Max are living around and facilitating. It's all happening in their home.

Davis: No, that's not quite right. The guy who gets blown is just a semi-finalist.

Lena: What?

Davis: If you want to get into the finals, you have to last more than seven minutes while I suck you off. During that BJ, I try to get you off as fast as I can. During the last two minutes, I stick my finger up your ass. If you can withstand all that pressure and make it into the finals, you and another finalist have to battle each other for me.

Lena: How does that work?

Davis: The finalists take me out to Porto's and we all have sandwiches and juice. After we eat, we go back to my place. Both guys suck each other off while I watch and masturbate. It's so fucking hot, Lena. They swallow the spunk and everything.

Lena: So... these guys are bisexual?

Davis: No, they aren't! You'd be AMAZED at what you can get straight guys to agree to when they wanna fuck you. It's freaky.

Lena: (uncomfortable) It sounds freaky.

Davis: Yeah, but that's part of what makes it so unique. I get to watch straight dudes perform a gay sex show for me. Then each guy takes turns going down on me. Whoever makes me cum first wins.

Lena: And what does the winner get?

Davis: To be inside Davis.

Lena: So vaginal sex?

Davis: Well, that and I go over to his house and we watch my porn together.

Then I fuck him and sleep in his bed. If I really like the guy, I might do something dirtier like piss in his mouth. That's always fun.

Lena: You mean if he's into that?

Davis: (giggling) If a guy wants to fuck you, you can get him into anything.

Lena: Really?

Davis: Yeah, it's not like with women.

Lena: How so?

Davis: Oh, come on. Men are basically wild dogs. With all that fucking testosterone in them, they don't get hurt by things like women do. At least not the hot guys who work out. And those are the only men I play with anyway.

Lena: So is every hot guy who wins Inside Davis happy with the grand prize?

Davis: Absolutely. After it's over, the winner always tells me I'm better than his wife or girlfriend. Most of the time, she doesn't even know I'm fucking her man. I always do a better job than her anyway. It's crazy.

Lena: (shocked but trying to seem open-minded) …I wouldn't have expected that.

Davis: Yeah, the girlfriends never take any responsibility. They blame me for their shitty relationships.

Lena: Why do you say that?

Davis: If they were better lovers, their guys wouldn't have to hide me. We could all have a threesome and everybody'd be happy. But that'll never happen with a jealous girlfriend. And they always suck in bed, Lena. In fact, most of them won't even suck a guy. That's how bad they are. And they're miserable too – absolute killjoys with saggy tits. They can't even do a hand job right.

Lena: It sounds like you don't like women very much.

Davis: (adamantly) Oh, not at all! I love women, Lena. Women are beautiful.

Lena: Then don't you care about ruining their relationships?

Davis: They ruin their relationships; not me. They're the ones who keep their man on a leash.

Lena: Are you thinking that maybe women are too possessive of men?

Davis: I think all women would be a lot happier if they just accepted that some chicks are exceptionally gifted in bed – like some ladies are really good at music and baking, you know? As a female, you gotta come to grips with the fact that you've lost the competition, sometimes.

Lena: But why do you think women are competing with you?

Davis: No, it's me. I'm the one competing with them. And they're pissed off that I won. They take it personally.

Lena: Okay.

Davis: I mean, be realistic. You can't stop your man from trying to fuck a gal who's better at making him cum than probably 99% of women on planet Earth. You just can't take that personally.

Lena: (with a raised eyebrow) So you're saying you're better at sex than 99% of women?

Davis: (emphatically) Absofuckinglutely! This is my talent.

Lena: What makes you so confident about that?

Davis: Every guy I've ever been with becomes obsessed with me after we have sex. Guys who fuck women for a living will tell you I'm the one chick they wish they had in their bedroom when the cameras are turned off. I can get any co-star of mine rock hard, five or six times in a row. Other women in the industry can't do that. Even Ben got obsessed with me after we first had sex.

Lena: (rolling her eyes) But Davis, you were carrying his child. Of course Ben was fixated on you.

Davis: Well, he didn't know that until I was preggers for about two months. We had loads of sex before he knew he knocked me up, Lena. I convinced him to fuck me without a condom even though he was nervous about getting me pregnant. Then I made him cum so hard he nearly passed out. He didn't have a problem after that. (giggling)

Lena: I thought Ben was drunk when you first had unprotected sex.

Davis: He was, but after that, he wanted to stay sober when we did it. We fucked on coke a few times, but I had to convince him to do that, too. He was always so scared before I got him to loosen up and have fun. I wish he would loosen up more now.

Lena: (surprised and deeply hurt) ...I don't remember you telling me any of this.

Davis: Yeah, we were doin' it like bunnies for the first few weeks: four or five times a day. I miss that so much, Lena. Ben could never get it up like that now. Back then he could cum over and over and over again, all day long. Now I'm lucky if it's three times a week. He can't even last more than ten minutes.

Lena: Is that why you started Inside Davis?

Davis: That's part of it. Ben's horrible in bed now and I need good sex more than three times a week. That's for sure.

Lena: (holding in anger) So is sex with your winners... making them obsessed with you too? The way Ben got obsessed with you?

Davis: Oh, hell yes! I've never had a guy not cook me breakfast the next day. While we eat in bed, I normally do a post-interview that goes up on the website. The guys always talk more than me during that interview. It's weird.

Lena: (trying to remain calm) ...What do they talk about?

Davis: How much they love being with a woman who understands men.

Lena: How do you think you understand men?

Davis: I do for them what most women are afraid of doing.

Lena: Which is?

Davis: (matter of factly) I get them off as hard as I can. I push them to the edge.

Lena: What does that mean?

Davis: I say or do whatever gets them off harder than anything. If they start screaming, I make them scream louder. I push them as hard as they can go, until they either collapse or fall asleep. Nothing is off limits – except anal.

Lena: Are you saving anal for Ben?

Davis: No, I don't do anal. But that doesn't matter 'cause even women who do anal aren't half as good as me. I think most women are scared of male pleasure today. Just like most men are scared of strong women.

Lena: Hmm… you could be right about that. I don't know–

Davis: (interrupting) It's obvious, isn't it, Lena? Men act like assholes. The culture encourages dudes to act like rapists and frat boys. That's why most women are afraid of male pleasure.

Lena: Well, I'm not sure I would agree. But I know many smart women who would say what you just said. And some men.

Davis: Assholes don't get to fuck me; that's one of the things I'm most proud of about Inside Davis. There's never been another porn site which guarantees that only nice guys get laid. And I'm good to them for that. None of my winners ever have to get naked in front of a crew or even a camera, unless they want to. All they have to do to win is be interesting, hot, well groomed, considerate and someone who can keep up with me in a conversation. Those are all the things any nice guy should be to get a woman into bed.

Lena: Do any of these guys become friends with you afterwards?

Davis: Nah, I wouldn't wanna be friends with them.

Lena: Why not?

Davis: Well, it would be awkward…

Lena: Because they're your fans?

Davis: That and they don't really see me as their equal. They treat me like I'm above them or something.

Lena: (like a therapist) Well, is that something you really want? Do you really want to feel superior to men who like you?

Davis: I can't help it! Any woman would look down on them! You'd look down on them!

Lena: I guess for most women, it's not sexy when a man puts you on a huge pedestal.

Davis: It's the opposite of sexy. It's childish.

Lena: So how many contest winners have you had?

Davis: Four so far. I fucked my last winner on Friday.

Lena: And who was he?

Davis: He's called Jered Blaha, or at least that's his stage name. He's a really good bass player in a fusion band I like called Knots. He's got such a great ass, Lena. The winner before Jered was a comic book artist called David Vastupidavuskatse. He's this tall guy from Estonia with a really sexy goatee and these perfect shoulders. Both of them were super hot and super smart and totally considerate of me and my needs. They fucking deserved the orgasms I gave them. That's part of what makes this so much fun; it's like I'm giving men rewards for being the good guys.

Lena: But they're not good enough for you to be friends with.

Davis: No, they aren't. But they're still really attentive and sweet and giving. It's way better than anything that ever happens with Ben.

Lena: So how does Ben feel about all of this?

Davis: Well, in the beginning he wasn't really all that comfortable

Lena: When did he get comfortable?

Davis: When he understood it was something I needed to do.

Lena: Well, Ben's a good guy, Davis. A lot of guys would hate it if their wives were porn stars.

Davis: Well, that's stupid. Being married to a beautiful woman is a privilege. Being married to a porn star is even hotter; it's the ultimate male fantasy. Every man wants that, if he's honest with himself.

Lena: I think for some men it's a little threatening.

Davis: Why would you be threatened if you're secure in yourself?

Lena: Well, it's hard being totally secure in yourself. That's hard for men and women. Being confident and secure in who you are can take years to achieve. A lot of therapy is about that.

Davis: At the end of the day, Ben's married to a woman most of his friends wish they could bang. They'd fuck me in their wildest dreams, Lena. And some of their wives aren't bad looking.

Lena: I'm sure Ben knows that.

Davis: (giggling) Other men get so jealous around him. It's hilarious. It makes him uncomfortable, but I can't help but laugh. They're so cute when they get nervous around me.

Lena: So do you watch your porn vids with Ben?

Davis: I wish!

Lena: What do you mean?

Davis: Ben doesn't like looking at me on film. He's fucked up in the head that way.

Lena: (shaking her head) Davis, that doesn't mean he's fucked up.

Davis: No, he feels inadequate. I tell him there's nothing to be jealous of, but he never listens to me.

Lena: Well, he might be listening to you. It just might be hard for him to feel that this is all okay.

Davis: Well, he should feel it, Lena. I'm his wife and the mother of his child. He knows I don't lie.

Lena: (frustrated with Davis) This isn't about you lying. It's about–

Davis: (interrupting) He's upset 'cause most of the people I fuck on camera are hotter than him. That's what he says.

Lena: And what do you say to him when he tells you that?

Davis: I tell him if he'd spend less time eating fast food and more time at the fucking gym, he might feel less inadequate. Then we might both be able to enjoy 'Inside Davis.'

Lena: Yeah, but he might be overeating because he feels inadequate. Or scared.

Davis: If he stopped feeling sorry for himself, he'd realise how good he has it. He's married to one of the most successful fucking porn stars of this decade. I'm in the top ten lists of at least thirty websites that rank the best porn stars of all time, Lena. And it's only been two years since we started.

Lena: I know that but sometimes a man feels inadequate. Men can feel inadequate when women don't stroke their ego.

Davis: (annoyed) Ben's got himself the most desired woman on the fucking internet! People are sooo envious of him! I get so many emails from guys who say they wish they were him! And a lot of them are hotter and have way bigger dicks! I save all the pics they send me.

Lena: Well, I imagine you would. Maybe Ben is just–

Davis: (interrupting) Ben won't fucking allow himself to enjoy this because he doesn't believe in himself.

Lena: But why does he feel that way?

Davis: (angrily) God, it drives me bonkers! It would be easier if he was just boring. I could handle that, but not this. This is fucking pathetic, it really is.

Lena: Well, insecurity takes patience to handle and eventually overcome – from both you and Ben. You're in a relationship together.

Davis: But I am very very patient, Lena. It's been over fifteen years and I'm still with him. Lord knows how many times I've thought about leaving Ben.

Lena: Before you created Inside Davis, did you guys talk about his feelings? Did you discuss how he felt about you becoming a porn star?

Davis: Of course we did.

Lena: Do you think maybe he lied when he said he was okay with it? Do you think he said he was okay, maybe to not disappoint you?

Davis: No, we've always been very honest and straight forward with each other. He'd never placate me.

Lena: Well, that's good.

Davis: I told him the truth. I said if he wanted to stay with me, my new career was something he'd have to be a man and get used to. I can't stand possessive guys. Ben knows I would never put up with that kind of relationship.

Lena: But when you told him you wanted to be in porn, what exactly did he say? What was his reaction?

Davis: He tried to manipulate me, but I could so see through that shit. He kept saying, "Are you sure this is what you really wanna do? Are you sure, Davis? Have you thought about this?"

Lena: And you told him you were sure?

Davis: Of course I did. I am sure. I'm more sure about this than anything I've ever done.

Lena: How did he react to your certainty?

Davis: (giggling) He gave me this look like I ran over his dog. It was so stupid, Lena, I swear. But when you're with a man, you have to put up with some dumb shit if you wanna keep the peace. It's not easy though. I'm tellin' ya'. Ben would make you want to pull your hair out! You dodged a bullet, Lena, you really did.

Lena: Well, any relationship has problems, even when it's good. You have to compromise; you have to learn how to fight and negotiate and then make-up. It's all hard work, even when it's very satisfying.

Davis: Ben gets that, Lena. He knows he can't control me and he's a good husband in that way. That's why I still tolerate his boring ass.

Lena: Davis… what do you want from Ben? What could he do that would make you happy?

Davis: I don't know. I feel like I only know what I don't want him to do.

Lena: And what would that be?

Davis: Well… it would be nice if he didn't hurt my feelings. I could put up with him more if he didn't hurt my feelings.

Lena: How does he hurt your feelings?

Davis: Like, I did this scene with Licky Linda, who I know Ben has a total boner for, even though he won't talk about it 'cause he's embarrassed. I was sooo excited about this 'cause I fucking love her. It was great for the web traffic and it made Inside Davis huge. But the thing I was most excited by was Ben. I wanted that scene to finally be a way for us to enjoy my porn. That's the main reason I asked her to do it with me.

Lena: So Licky was like your gift to Ben?

Davis: She even offered to have sex with him, but he fucking said no! He wouldn't even watch our scene when it was done! Can you believe that?

Lena: Maybe Ben just wants you to himself. If I were him, I would.

Davis: (disgusted) OH NO, I'd never be with someone like that! If there's one thing I fucking hate, it's monogamy. There's no reason to be monogamous with anybody, ever. That's pretty black and white, for me.

Lena: Does that mean you think I shouldn't be monogamous?

Davis: (passionately) Of course you shouldn't! You can't just exclusively own someone's sexuality. That shit is Victorian, Lena. I can't believe people still practice monogamy today. I mean it's 2016, for Chrissakes! Everybody needs to just fucking get over controlling people; that's bad for humanity.

Lena: Well, are you open to the possibility that Ben might secretly be monogamous? Like most people?

Davis: Well, he says I can trust that he's not. He begs me to trust him all the time, so I give him the benefit of the doubt.

Lena: He begs you?

Davis: Yeah, he won't risk ending our relationship. He likes having a family with me. I can understand that.

Lena: (sighing in frustration) Well… it could be that Ben isn't turned on watching you have sex with other people. That might be what's going on.

Davis: Maybe, but that still hurts me. It's not like I'm unattractive, you know? I read email after email from men telling me how lucky Ben is. I could easily be in relationships with any of them.

Lena: Well, is that what you want?

Davis: Ben could lose me, Lena. He's in danger of losing me. I tell him that every day.

Lena: I'm sure you do.

Davis: (angrily) But he can't see it! It's like he won't see it, no matter how hurt I am. It's like I can't fucking win with this man! Nothing and I mean NOTHING I do is ever good enough for Ben. Even Licky wasn't good enough for him! He rejected her and made her cry! She's never been rejected by a guy before – never in her life! And she's gorgeous!

Lena: Did that embarrass you?

Davis: It made me feel fucking ashamed.

Lena: Ashamed?

Davis: Yep. I was ashamed to be Ben's wife that day. That's how angry I was. You can't insult a beautiful woman like that, especially when you know she's had anorexia.

Lena: How does Max feel about Inside Davis?

Davis: Oh, he's worse than Ben.

Lena: How is he worse?

Davis: Well, he's not technically worse. He's not mean to me about my career. It's just the things he does… the things he does hurt me way more than anything Ben could ever do.

Lena: How does Max hurt you?

Davis: (sighing) Throughout his whole life, we were so so close, Lena. He never disobeyed me. He was always so curious and smart and well-behaved and just perfect. I didn't feel like I was hanging out with a kid, when I raised him. He was like a little old man, a sweet and gentle friend of mine that just totally understood everything about me there was to understand. We had that until last year.

Lena: What happened last year?

Davis: He just got very quiet, like he's disappointed in me.

Lena: Are you angry with him, like you are with Ben?

Davis: I try not to be. I try to cut Max some slack because I know why he feels the way he does.

Lena: And why is that?

Davis: He's fourteen.

Lena: (sighing in frustration) Yeah, fourteen is a hard age. I remember what you were like when we were fourteen.

Davis: Kids are so fucking self-absorbed when they're fourteen.

Lena: Do you ever talk to Max about your porn?

Davis: It's hard because every time I try and have a conversation about it, he says he'd rather not. He can be really rude sometimes.

Lena: How do you handle that?

Davis: I tell him if he wants to be rude, he can fucking be rude mowing the lawn. I don't let him get away with being a dick, just because he's fourteen. I won't let him guilt trip me just because his friends like Inside Davis.

Lena: That must be hard for Max.

Davis: What do you mean?

Lena: Well, I mean, his friends can see Mom having sex. That's not something kids normally have to deal with.

Davis: There's nothing to deal with. Sex is natural.

Lena: Well, sex is natural, but turning sex into a consumer product is a fairly new thing. It's not natural when the producers are your parents and the consumers are your friends.

Davis: (passionately) Yeah and why is that? It's 'cause the way things were throughout most of history sucked for women. I don't want to live in that world, anymore. I don't want to live in a world where women have to hide their sexuality. I don't want Max to grow up in that world.

Lena: I know you don't. I just meant that most kids don't worry about their friends seeing Mom have sex. That's the part of being Max that's hard.

Davis: But Max doesn't have to worry about anything.

Lena: I know he doesn't literally have to worry about anything. I was just thinking it might be embarrassing. Can you imagine how you'd feel if you were in his shoes?

Davis: Well, if I'd been raised by a family that didn't consist of backward, slut shaming misogynists, I'd know my friends were just being obnoxious little shits. If they put my mom down for her choices, I'd tell them to fuck off. I wouldn't be friends with people like that.

Lena: Yeah, but Davis come on: You're thirty-four. Not fourteen. When you're fourteen, you're not perfectly reasonable. Your hormones are crazy. Don't you remember what that was like?

Davis: What do Max's hormones have to do with my porn?

Lena: Well, he's fourteen. When you're fourteen, you want your parents to protect you.

Davis: I do protect him, Lena.

Lena: I meant when you're that age, you want your parents to keep their sexuality away from you.

Davis: (worried) You think I'm molesting Max?

Lena: (abruptly) No! I know you'd never hurt him! That's not what I'm getting at!

Davis: Then what are you trying to say?

Lena: I'm just saying… most people have a target audience for their sexuality. They flirt and seduce people who become their lovers. They don't seduce people they aren't interested in. They don't show those people images of them having explicit sex with strangers.

Davis: Yeah, but that's only because of social attitudes, today. At this point in time, we're still pretty backward in the West. I wanna move things forward.

Lena: But Davis, when most kids go through adolescence and start to develop their own sexuality, they want their parents to keep out of their social circle.

Davis: But I'm not in Max's social circle.

Lena: I know that, but your sexuality is part of his social circle.

Davis: (defensively) But that's true of any kid who has a hot mom! Why is it my fault his friends wanna fuck me?

Lena: It's not your fault, exactly. But you do encourage it.

Davis: (puzzled) How?

Lena: You consent to his friends seeing vids of you having sex. That's what separates you from all the neighbourhood MILFs.

Davis: But I don't consent to that! My vids are for adults.

Lena: Maybe you should be honest with yourself.

Davis: (confused) What?

Lena: You said you're an exhibitionist. You said you liked being able to get off any random person who happens to watch your porn.

Davis: (abruptly) ANY GROWNUP! NOT FUCKING TEENAGERS!

If I had my way, kids would have to use fucking finger printing to go on the internet, Lena. The only reason Max's friends can see me is because their parents are lazy. It's not because I'm trying to get them off! I don't do that.

Lena: (frustrated) Oh, come on Davis! If you make porn in 2016, kids are gonna see it. No one can keep teens from seeing porn anymore. It doesn't matter if you've uploaded it "for grownups."

Davis: But why is that my responsibility?

Lena: Well, it wouldn't be if you were single. But your son is a teenager and all his friends look at porn. But Max is the one kid with a mom they can all jack off to.

Davis: (defensive) But they could jack off thinking about any mom in Downey! It's not just me!

Lena: I know that, but Davis, you're *making* their jack off material *for* them. Are the other MILFs on the block doing that?

Davis: Well, in a way they are. Any hot woman who wears a short skirt is making their jack off material.

Lena: (rolls eyes) There's a difference between wearing a short skirt and uploading vids of you having sex.

Davis: But I don't make porn for fucking kids, Lena. My vids are specifically written and directed to please my fans – my *adult* fans.

Lena: (angrily) Oh, fucking get real! If you put porn on the internet, you're crazy if you think only adults will see it.

Davis: So should no one be making violent movies? Kids'll find a way to watch them too.

Lena: (adamantly) I'm not saying no one should make violent movies! I'm saying sex is different to violence in that when we grow up, we want to be at a distance from our parent's sexuality.

Davis: Max is distant from it, Lena. I never do anything in front of him.

Lena: (impatiently) It's still very close to him. Don't be stupid, Davis. Come on.

Davis: (defensive) But it's not close to him! I don't do anything anywhere near him!

Lena: (loudly) That's not what I'm saying!

Davis: I'm confused now.

Lena: (in stern voice) Then pay attention! I'm saying YOU are the mother of a fourteen-year-old son. You're making the porn you know his friends watch. Can't you read between the lines?

Davis: What's between the lines?

Lena: You're helping them cum.

Davis: ...Well, I don't see it that way.

Lena: (in condescending tone) So you think you control who gets off when you put porn on the internet? You think you can make sure the only people who cum are the folks you personally approve of?

Davis: My porn is made for a specific audience that doesn't include teenage dickheads. If they watch it and jiz in the bathroom, that's not my fault! My shit isn't made for them. If I had my way, there'd be better laws to keep minors away from anybody's porn. But those laws aren't there yet and things are the way they are now. I wish the internet was more regulated but unfortunately, it's not.

Lena: Davis, can't you predict what'll happen if you make porn and put it in a place that's swarming with horny teens? Can't you use your brain before you do this shit?

Davis: But kids are everywhere, Lena. They can see all kinds of crap that ain't meant for them. That doesn't mean I'm obligated to make family friendly entertainment. This isn't Iran, this is Southern California.

Lena: (irritated) I didn't say you should make family friendly entertainment! I'm just repeating back to you what you said. You said that you now have a successful career as an internet porn star. You also have a fourteen-year-old son that career makes uncomfortable because his friends watch you. And on top of that, your son has no say in any of this.

Davis: Max doesn't get to control who I fuck and when. That's my business and he knows that. He doesn't get to control any woman's sexuality. I'm teaching him to respect women.

Lena: Well, this is interesting. If Max isn't comfortable with your porn, according to you, that means he doesn't respect women.

Davis: (confused) What...?

Lena: You said any male who wants to control a woman's sexuality is disrespecting women.

Davis: So?

Lena: That means if Max wishes you weren't a porn star, he's a male trying to control his mother's sexuality. If you *really* think Max has no right to have any feelings about who you fuck and when, that means he's a dick for having any feelings about your career in porn. That's what you're actually saying.

Davis: (forcefully) But I'm not saying that! If there's one thing Max is not, it's a dick. He's an amazing kid, Lena.

Lena: (incredulous) Then why are you describing his feelings this way?

Davis: Because they're selfish and immature. I know he's fourteen, so I'd never be resentful at him for being immature. But it's my job to challenge those things in him. I'm his mother. I can't tolerate sexism in my own kid, even if he is wonderful in every other way. He needs to treat people fairly and especially treat women as his equals. That's the kind of grownup I'm teaching him to be.

Lena: (sarcastically) Again, this is very interesting, Davis. According to you, you're a good mother. You're a good mother even though you don't tolerate your son's feelings.

Davis: Are you saying I'm a bad mother?

Lena: (abruptly) Not at all! That's the last thing I would ever say!

Davis: Then why does it feel that way?

Lena: Because you're misreading me. I'm not saying what you think I'm saying.

Davis: (confused) Then just be straight with me, Lena! What are you trying to say?

Lena: I don't think Max is trying to control women by being uncomfortable with your porn.

Davis: If Max is secure in himself and his sexuality, he won't be uncomfortable with my porn. He won't need to control any woman's sexuality.

Lena: And how is he gonna get that security?

Davis: (defensively) I'm trying to give it to him with every damn thing I do. I'm teaching him.

Lena: What are you teaching him?

Davis: I'm showing him there's nothing wrong with sex: nothing wrong with straight sex, gay sex, non-monogamous sex and loads of other things people are still hung up about.

Lena: Well, maybe you should think about that in a different way.

Davis: Why?

Lena: It might be more useful to you.

Davis: (confused) What would be more useful?

Lena: Instead of thinking the problem is with Max, it might be more useful to think of him as a normal kid: a kid who wishes his friends couldn't see his mom fucking strangers.

Davis: (thinking hard) But …normal isn't always good.

Lena: (rolls eyes) What would you know about normal?

Davis: Normal means looking down on women for their choices. I don't want him to be normal that way, Lena. I want him to be better than normal.

Lena: (sarcastically) Gee, what a realistic expectation for a fourteen-year-old, Davis. Why haven't more parents thought of this?

Davis: Any decent parent has high expectations.

Lena: (with mocking laughter) You know, this is a really interesting take on parenting you've got here, Davis. It's fascinating, really.

Davis: What's fascinating about it?

Lena: (with disdain) You actually think a good parent makes her kid spend nights in the garage 'cause she's busy licking out porn stars on the family pool table.

Davis: (loudly) That's no different to what any mom does!

Lena: (irritated) Davis, lower your voice, please. You know there's other people in this café.

Davis: (quieting down) I'm sorry, Lena. I was just trying to say that… sex is sex. The location doesn't matter. Moms have sex in the bedroom and the kids can't come in that room when she's fucking whoever she chooses to be with. If kids find that awkward, that still doesn't make it abuse. It's just growing up with parents who have sex. It doesn't matter whether it's the bedroom or the pool table or anywhere else in the house. Sex is sex, not abuse.

Lena: I didn't say it was abuse, Davis. I just said it was awkward for Max.

Davis: Well, I wish Max didn't find it awkward, but he does. He's fourteen. Hopefully in a year or so, he'll change and we can be close again.

Lena: (sceptically) Do you really think he can be close to you again?

Davis: Of course I do. I'm his mom.

Lena: Then why are you making his life revolve around you having sex?

Davis: It doesn't revolve around me having sex. It revolves around his mom and dad's careers. His life revolves around his dad's work as much as it revolves around mine. That's part of growing up in a family.

Lena: Then why is Max only embarrassed by your career?

Davis: Because he's immature and selfish, but I can forgive him for that because I love him, Lena. He's a great kid; he's everything to me.

Lena: (mocking an empathetic response) Davis, what would be a mature way Max could *feel* about InsideDavis.com?

Davis: (not getting the sarcasm) I'd like him to be proud that his mother lives in a society where she can express her sexuality in a way that makes her feel confident and happy.

Lena: (sarcastically) How progressive of you.

Davis: I want him to be proud of me for being able to do something I love and still make money, especially when people today find that so hard in this economy.

Lena: (sarcastically) Max is so lucky to have you, Davis. Really.

Davis: (becoming irritated but not knowing exactly why) He should want to defend me when people give him shit about what I do! He should be grateful to have a strong and independent woman for a mother. He's got a mom who controls her life on her terms, Lena. So that's what I want him to feel. He's an amazing kid, so I want him to know that I'm amazing too. I want him to be proud of me.

Lena: Well, he might feel that way, in a perfect world where kids don't actually have totally natural feelings.

Davis: An ideal world is only ideal when you're too scared to make it happen.

Lena: (flabbergasted) God, is that what you really believe?

Davis: (passionately) Of course I do! You should never just accept things the way they are. You should always question everything and change whatever you can. Max agrees with me about that. We used to talk about this all the time. We could talk about this shit when he was eight, Lena. That's how smart he is. It freaks me out.

Lena: You shouldn't get freaked out by that. You're very lucky to have a son like Max. Most kids are boring.

Davis: I know, right? That's why I try so hard to be a good parent for him. He deserves a mom as good as the kid God blessed me with.

Lena: You really really love Max, don't you? I mean, every mother loves her son. But with you, it seems a little different.

Davis: It is different. We're not normal.

Lena: (laughing) Well, that's because you've destroyed all the normalcy in your family, Davis. I'm sorry but–

Davis: (interrupting) That's not what I meant. What I'm trying to say is… I've never felt like my son was a job. Ben feels like a job, but not Max. I never had a day when I felt exhausted by him, not even when he was a baby. When Max was in diapers, I always got scared of hurting him, but he never scared me. He's always been my rock.

Lena: (rolling eyes) Your rock?

Davis: He motivates me to do everything I do, Lena.

Lena: Even the porn?

Davis: Yeah. I think in a way, I'm trying to inspire him.

Lena: (in a patronising voice) Really? How does that work?

Davis: I'm teaching him he can be anything, that there should be no limits to how he wants to express himself.

Lena: (sarcastically) Of course! No kid should EVER have limits on how they choose to express themselves. Kids need to be wild and free. I forgot about that, Davis.

Davis: That's not what I'm saying, Lena. I'm saying there shouldn't be any rules when it comes to how consenting adults choose to express their sexuality. No one has a right to judge Max for his sexuality; that's what I want him to know. That's partly why I'm doing this.

Lena: (irritated) Oh, don't be a fucking idiot, Davis. You're the one who's judging him!

Davis: I would never judge him, Lena.

Lena: Yes, you fucking are. You're judging him for not being proud of you.

Davis: That's not judging him, that's teaching him.

Lena: Davis, get real. You think there's something horribly wrong with Max if he's not happy his mom is a goddamn porn star. That's how much you understand your kid's brain.

Davis: I didn't say it was horribly wrong. It's just him being fourteen.

Lena: (irritated) So he's immature because he's not proud that everyone can see you having sex in his house? Is that your idea of immaturity, Davis?

Davis: It doesn't matter who sees me and who doesn't. What matters is my choice and my happiness, Lena.

Lena: (sarcastically) Of course! It couldn't possibly matter that everyone he knows can see you fuck strangers. I mean, who gives a shit if all his teachers jack off to you at night; that doesn't matter at all!

Davis: If I'm a good parent, he'll know that what they think doesn't matter. He'll know it in his heart. He won't need to slut shame me.

Lena: (giggling) So if he's not proud of your porn, he's slut shaming you? You crack me up, Davis…

Davis: (with some ambivalence) …I can't hate him for that. He's a wonderful kid… the best kid I've ever known, honestly. But he's still a kid that hasn't learned to respect women yet. That's always a complicated process because it's never as simple as it looks. I try to teach him about women, but the culture pulls him away from the values I try to instil. As a parent, I'm working hard to fight against the culture.

Lena: (sarcastically) Yes, there are so many ways our culture tells Max to disrespect women. I mean, tampon prices are up this week…

Davis: Lena, the culture tells Max he has a right to control women's bodies, that women are there for his pleasure, that women are disposable when they get old and wrinkly. It teaches him that if women choose to have sex in ways he doesn't approve of, they're sluts and skanks and whores. The culture tells him that anything other than monogamy is selfish and that if a woman has an exhibitionist streak, she's damaged goods. That's how our culture tells him to disrespect women.

Lena: (sarcastically) Well, then I guess Max is utterly and absolutely disrespectful to all womankind, isn't he? I mean, not wanting your friends to watch your mom eat pussy. The gall of that kid!! How dare he!!

Davis: Lena, he's not a woman hater but he does have some misogynist attitudes. Everyone in our culture does and everyone needs to call them out and change them; not just Max.

Lena: This sounds like victim blaming to me.

Davis: Why?

Lena: Because you want Max to feel ashamed of his feelings. If you make him uncomfortable, that's his fault, not yours.

Davis: But Lena, sometimes it is his fault. Sometimes we should all be ashamed of our feelings.

Lena: (sarcastically) Of course! Silly me. How could I forget: shaming is the wave of the future! Everybody does it on twitter, so it must be good for parenting sexually confused teens. You should write for the Huffington Post!

Davis: Lena, the first time I saw two women kiss when I was eight, I thought it was disgusting. My dad's porn was so disgusting to me that I nearly threw up. But I was the one who was being disgusting. My feelings were disgusting, not Jodie Green and Cara Michaels.

Lena: (like a disappointed parent) Don't be a doofus, you were eight! You shouldn't have even been looking at Jodie Green and Cara Michaels.

Davis: I know I shouldn't have. That was my fault.

Lena: No, it wasn't. The feelings you have as a kid can't be informed by grownup politics, Davis. And even when you're a grownup, human feelings aren't always fair. You should know that by now. You're thirty-four.

Davis: I do know it. And that's why I want Max to get rid of a lot of his feelings.

Lena: (shocked at Davis's callousness) Are you serious?? You want your kid to practice emotional suppression??

Davis: (emphatically) Of course I do! Some feelings are just bad, Lena. A feeling isn't okay just because it's a feeling. Things like sexism, homophobia, biphobia, transphobia... those feelings are important to call out and get rid of! That's how we make a better world.

Lena: (sarcastically) That's so true, Davis. Why didn't I notice that before? Your job as a parent is to teach Max how to shut off his feelings! That's sooo healthy, Davis! I mean, why on earth doesn't everybody parent like this?

Davis: It's my job to help Max shut off *some* of his feelings. It's my job to stop him internalising the world's messages about women. I want him to understand he has no say in how any woman expresses her sexuality. He has no right to judge or disapprove or question any sexual choice any woman makes.

Lena: (in a sarcastic baby voice) And especially not his mommy. If Mommy needs to have an orgy, Max better be good and go to the garage. Yes, he should.

Davis: (irritated) He should go to the fucking garage! He should be proud that his mother's brave enough to do what makes her happy! I wish I had a mother like that. Who knows where I'd be now if I had that kind of mom.

Lena: (giggling) So when your face is buried in some woman's snatch, you want your kid to be proud he's in the garage?

Davis: (passionately) Yes, I fucking do!

Lena: (sarcastically) Yes, Max should be so proud of all that sexual imagery he's not even allowed to see.

Davis: (frustrated) That doesn't have anything to do with me! It would be against the law for him to see me having sex!

Lena: And have you ever asked him how he feels about that?

Davis: It doesn't matter how he feels. He needs to grow up and be a good person.

Lena: (like she can't believe how stupid Davis is) So Max being a good person means he has to be proud of sex he's not allowed to see? And then he has to turn off his feelings if he can't make himself proud?

Davis: Yep. Being a good person means not disapproving of how I or any woman chooses to express herself or earn a living. As long as I'm not abusing him, he has no right to judge anything I do. He should support me.

Lena: (holding in anger again) And what about your job to support him??

Davis: Lena, this *is* how I support him. I'm teaching him he can't control me or any other woman who happens to embarrass him. Being embarrassed isn't the end of the world.

Lena: (sarcastically) Yes, he's definitely controlling you, Davis. It couldn't possibly be that he's uncomfortable with some of your choices. What a bastard your son is!

Davis: (passionately) I don't care if he's uncomfortable, Lena. I don't want him to grow up feeling like because he's a guy, he's entitled to judge and cajole women into doing whatever the fuck he wants. I don't want him emotionally blackmailing his girlfriends. I can't stop Ben from doing that with me, but I can stop Max.

Lena: (rolling eyes) So Max is blackmailing you if he acts disappointed in you.

Davis: If that's not blackmail, what is?

Lena: (passionately) Davis, he's disappointed in you because you make something it would hurt him to see! Meanwhile, everyone he knows can see it and fantasise about fucking you. Your porn makes them want to fuck you, Davis. That's how it works. It's arousing them like a lover would and they're still just kids!

Davis: None of that's my responsibility, Lena. As I keep saying, no one's forcing them to watch me.

Lena: But we all know they will watch you. Can't you understand how that might make Max feel?

Davis: (frustrated with Patriarchy) Yeah, but those feelings are totally unhealthy! They're based on holding me responsible for shit that isn't my fault. Max's feelings are just mistakes Lena, unhealthy mistakes society encourages only boys to make.

Lena: (sarcastically) Oh yes, they're sooo unhealthy, Davis. They couldn't *possibly* be the feelings any fourteen-year-old would have about Mom if she fucking did porn. It couldn't *possibly* be that! Not in a million years!

Davis: (emphatically) If we accepted everyone's feelings, women wouldn't have the right to vote, gay marriage would still be illegal and trans people couldn't get the hormones they need!

Lena: (sarcastically) Yes and as every historian knows, none of those things changed because we started to value the feelings of oppressed groups.

Davis: No, Lena. They happened because those people have rights that need to be respected. Apart from that, feelings don't matter.

Lena: (mocking Davis) So everyone else's feelings: the men, the straight people, the cisgenders… all those feelings just don't matter! I mean, how could I not see that! Thank you for pointing that out to me, Davis!

Davis: Their feelings don't matter, Lena. I know it's not popular to say that right now, but people will get it as time goes on. Just like today, people understand that the feelings of slave owners didn't matter.

Lena: (giggling and shaking her head) So Max's feelings about your porn are like the feelings of slave owners? Jesus, Davis…

Davis: They actually are, Lena. I know that sounds harsh because I love Max so much, but that's just how it is. This is the culture we're dealing with right now. We have to fight this.

Lena: (mocking Davis) Tell me how we need to fight it, Davis? I must know! There's a national election in six weeks!

Davis: If Max or me or anybody else has feelings that deprive somebody of their rights, we have to accept that those feelings just don't matter. They're the wrong feelings to have.

Lena: (sarcastically) That's so true! It's so sad progressives don't know this already. It's so sad even *Democracy Now* would say Max's feelings DO matter. We need to put a stop to this now, Davis. Maybe you should email Noam Chomsky.

Davis: Lena, western society is still sexist and ashamed of female sexuality – even lefties. But it's the job of the left to move things forward now, especially those of us who are raising male children. It doesn't bother me that people on the left can't hear this yet. They'll hear it eventually.

Lena: You amaze me, Davis. I just can't believe the dumb shit that comes out of your mouth. It'd be hilarious if it wasn't so fucking horrible.

Davis: Why?

Lena: What would you say if Max falls in love with a woman and she cheats on him? Would you say he's not allowed to have strong feelings about that?

Davis: I don't think anyone should be monogamous, Lena. I told you that already.

Lena: But is Max even allowed to feel hurt if a woman cheats on him? Is he allowed to feel like she betrayed his trust?

Davis: I know it sounds like I'm being a hard ass, but no… he's not. No woman is obligated to have sex with him and only him. He has no right to expect that of any woman.

Lena: (sarcastically) Oh, of course not! Especially not a woman who says she loves him and tells him they're in a monogamous relationship. If he expects her loyalty, he's just a controlling prick! That must be what's going on!

Davis: If she changes her mind about who she wants to sleep with, he has to respect that.

Lena: (sarcastically) Yes and respecting her choice means he's not allowed to be hurt; not one bit. That would be sexist, wouldn't it?

Davis: Well, Max will be hurt if he feels like he has a right to control his girlfriends. I'm raising him to know that he doesn't have that right. I don't care if people don't understand that right now. I don't expect people to at this point in time.

Lena: (sarcastically) Yes, right now, it's not possible for ANY man to respect a woman's choice and still be hurt by it. That's like flying cars, isn't it Davis? We're just not there yet as a species, are we?

Davis: No, let me explain Lena: if Max is hurting because a girl has sex with someone else, that means he wishes she only had sex with him. And if he acts like those feelings are worthy enough to cry over, that means he's accepting them on some level. I want him to be better than that.

Lena: (with disgust) And you think he's capable of being as good as you want him to be! You think a fucking fourteen-year-old is capable of that!

Davis: I believe in my son, Lena. He's an amazing kid. I've never known anyone like him. I'm not just saying that because I'm his mom.

Lena: (sarcastically) And everybody knows amazing kids never have aaaaany limitations. They can do aaaaaanything. They can fly, if you push 'em hard enough, right? Isn't that what good parents do?

Davis: No, Lena. If we accepted everyone's limitations, we wouldn't have democracy, civil rights, human rights, or the most basic liberties. Progress happens because we push people to do what doesn't feel easy or comfortable. When we push people, everyone's happier in the long run.

Lena: So let me understand this interesting parenting philosophy of yours: if Max is upset because his girlfriend cheats on him or his mom is in porn, his feelings are sexist and wrong. He needs to get rid of them. His feelings are wrong, even if his feelings are like what most people in his situation would actually feel – even most women.

Davis: Normal isn't good just because it's normal. Jealous girlfriends are normal.

Lena: So, suppose you decide to fuck one of his friends in a few years. Is he allowed to be upset about that?

Davis: No. I mean, he might be, but I'll be incredibly disappointed; let's put it that way.

Lena: Are you allowed to be upset at him over who he chooses to have sex with?

Davis: That's different. I'm his mom.

Lena: Are you allowed to be upset if he jacks off to your porn?

Davis: (rolling eyes) Like Max would ever do that!

Lena: But suppose he did. Would that upset you?

Davis: Hell, yeah! I didn't make that porn for him to perv to. I'm his mom.

Lena: But what if you turn him on? It's not like he can control that.

Davis: He can control giving into those impulses. He doesn't get to act like trailer trash just 'cause his mom is sexually liberated.

Lena: I see how this works. You've given yourself permission to disapprove of both his sexual choices and his sexual feelings.

Davis: That's called parenting a teen, Lena.

Lena: But he's not allowed to disapprove of any of your sexual choices or feelings.

Davis: He's a teenager, I'm a woman. It's my job to parent him. The rules are different for us.

Lena: (sarcastically) Yes, it's part of the parenting rule book that teen feelings aren't worth shit. Especially feelings like embarrassment and humiliation.

Davis: Like I keep saying, my job is to help Max get rid of those feelings. His job is to obey me and try to understand what I'm teaching him. As a parent, I'm first and foremost a teacher. I'm also a role model.

Lena bursts out laughing.

Davis: What's so funny?

Lena: You've got chocolate on your face, sweetie. Come here.

Lena pretends to wipe a streak of chocolate off of Davis's eyebrow.

Lena: Look, Davis. I have a lot of shopping to do today. So maybe we should think about saying our goodbyes. Unless you want another cappuccino. If you do, it's on me, okay?

Davis: Why do you wanna buy me a cappuccino?

Lena: For being a good sport.

Davis: A good sport?

Lena: Well, for putting up with me today. I'm sure there are more fun ways of spending an afternoon.

Davis: No, Lena. I love talking to you. In fact, I needed to talk to you today.

Lena: I'm glad someone got something out of it.

Davis: Can we keep talking?

Lena: (surprised) You want to keep talking?

Davis: Yeah, if it's okay with you. This is like therapy for me.

Lena: I know it is.

Davis: (looking down) Sometimes I need someone to challenge me. No one ever challenges me anymore.

Lena: (not knowing what to say) So… should I get two more cappuccinos?

Davis: I'll have a water. I'm calorie counting right now, remember. I hate it, but I have to look better than most women.

Lena: (rolling eyes) So I've heard.

Davis: (matter of factly) You know I gotta pop those boners, Lena. It's my job.

Lena: (rolling eyes) And to think I had the pleasure of forgetting that for five seconds.

Davis: Anyway, go and order your cappuccino.

Lena: Okay, one cappuccino and one bottled water. I'm gonna have a croissant, I think. And maybe two chocolate cookies.

Davis: Are you sure you wanna do that?

Lena: Why?

Davis: Well, your face looks really puffy today. And your chin's way bigger than the last time I saw you.

Lena: (sarcastically) Thanks for telling me, Davis. I hadn't noticed.

Davis: Yeah, when you gain weight, it's really bad for your complexion. Go look in that mirror and you'll see what I'm talkin' about.

Lena: (sarcastically) It's okay. I trust you.

Davis: Don't you worry about gaining weight?

Lena: Only when I'm not celebrating.

Davis: What are you celebrating?

Lena: (smiling mischievously) I'm getting to talk to you, Davis. I didn't expect that today.

Davis: (genuinely smiling) I didn't expect it either. But I'm so glad you're here with me today. I just feel like… I really love you, Lena. I love you and I've missed you so much.

14. SEX: Pride

Lena goes to buy the bottled water, her second cappuccino, her croissant and two chocolate cookies. Three middle-aged, bookish men start chatting to Davis. They all have British accents. As Lena waits in line, she is also eavesdropping on their conversation. These guys seem to know a lot about politics, history and literature. Lena is impressed. She thinks of how much she'd enjoy spending her afternoon with them, instead of Davis. Lena loves listening to the three of them speak. They are all, in their own way, quite articulate, charming and polite.

One of them, Piers Waterfield, has a cool looking vaporiser in his hand, next to an old-fashioned chain watch which dangles out of his pocket.

The second bookish man, Angus Smart, asks Davis if she likes Alice Munroe, since Lena's books are now on the table where Davis is waiting for her. Angus is wearing a 1940s raincoat and has a wax moustache.

When Davis responds that she loves Alice Munroe, the third bookish man, Nigel Benn, says things which suggest he's read most of Munroe's works. Nigel is the wittiest of the three and he's wearing a cool pin stripe jacket that looks like it's from the early 60s. Nigel feels confident wearing this jacket, despite the fact that unlike his other bookish friends, he's not skinny.

Lena loves the fact that these are the sort of people you can randomly bump into in a place like Pasadena.

Davis just looks annoyed by these men. After a few minutes, she asks them why they decided to talk to her. Nigel says (with some irony) that he noticed what Davis was reading and thought she might be a good conversationalist.

Davis responds, "What a relief! 'Cause you know, in case you were wondering fellas, I don't fuck old men. Especially not fat dudes with man tits."

Davis smiles at Nigel sarcastically.

Lena rolls her eyes in absolute disgust.

The bookish men leave the café with offended looks on their faces. Nigel has tears in his eyes.

Lena then brings her tray with the water, the cappuccino, the croissant and the two cookies back to the table where Davis is waiting for her.

Davis is completely unaware of how Lena is feeling. Both women resume their conversation.

Davis: (annoyed) I hate assholes like that!

Lena: They weren't assholes, Davis. They were just British.

Davis: But they were interrupting our conversation! They can't just fucking do that without getting permission. This is America!

Lena: Well, from what I could see, it looked like they wanted to talk to you about Alice Munroe. They sounded like kindred spirits, to be honest.

Davis: (rolling eyes) They were trying to fuck me, Lena. Hello? That's all men ever want from me.

Lena: Possibly. But maybe they just wanted to have an interesting conversation.

Davis: If you have good game with chicks, you don't make it look like you're trying to fuck them. That's just creepy. Guys like that would never have a chance with me anyway.

Lena: (sighing) I didn't get a creepy vibe from them and I heard everything they said to you. All it sounded like was they wanted to talk about books and politics and maybe the European Union. It seemed like they thought you might be, I don't know… an interesting person. That's all I saw and heard. It was three nice, smart men who were looking to start a conversation with an attractive woman because she had some cool books beside her.

Davis: Well, even if that's true, they shouldn't have tried to start a conversation with me.

Lena: But why? Since when did men talking to women they find attractive become this horribly rude thing?

Davis: If a man wants to talk to a woman, he's gotta make sure she likes him first. That's how it is.

Lena: And how's he supposed to know whether or not you like him?

Davis: He's gotta be hot and wait for me to stare at him. If you noticed, I didn't do that with those losers. I wasn't staring at them. At all.

Lena: (sighing) …I did notice that, Davis.

Davis: I don't have to give gaga eyes to creepy fucking fat dudes. I have standards.

Lena: (emphatically) But aren't we allowed to talk to the guys that we like? We're not supposed to wait for them to make gaga eyes at us before we can speak to them, are we?

Davis: Of course not. Men and women are different.

Lena: You mean there's a different etiquette for men and women.

Davis: It doesn't matter whether or not it's etiquette. You don't talk to women before they talk to you. With women, you speak when spoken to. Those guys were fucking predators!

Lena: (sighing in frustration) They sounded pretty nice to me, Davis. They were much nicer to you than you were to them.

Davis: (smiling affectionately) Well, they weren't as nice as you. Maybe that's what I'm trying to say.

Lena: (looking down, with a look of confusion) I don't think I'm being very nice today.

Davis: Why?

Lena: I'm feeling things I don't normally feel.

Davis: Like what…?

Lena: (softly) I'm normally better than this. I don't normally feel hate.

Davis: (smiling) What are you talking about? You don't hate anybody.

Lena: You're making me feel… I don't know...

Davis: (confused) ...What is it? Tell me what you're feeling, Lena.

Lena: (confused) I'm feeling impulsive.

Davis: Impulsive?

Lena: Yeah, like I'm not in control. It's weird.

Davis: Is that why you got two cookies and a croissant?

Lena: (smiling) Maybe.

Davis: (smiling seductively) Well, let me tell you something Lena. I love making you feel impulsive. In fact, I wish I could make you more impulsive.

Lena: It's not just that. It's like I'm changing.

Davis: Change is good, Lena. I love change.

Lena: (smiling affectionately to Davis) I know you do.

Davis: You are such a control freak, though. You've been that way ever since we were kids. Every time we played a game, you had to make sure we were always sticking to the rules. I'm surprised I played with you as much as I did.

Lena: You were always breaking my rules.

Davis: (flirtatiously) Oh, I still am, Lena. I intend to break all your rules.

Lena: I think you already have.

Davis: Good 'cause I'm just so happy we ran into each other today. I never expected this to happen, today of all days. It's like a little miracle.

Lena: I'm happy you're happy.

Davis: I needed you to be here today. Subconsciously, I think I brought you to me.

Lena: What does that mean?

Davis: The universe always takes care of me.

Lena: (sarcastically) Yeah, it took you out of poetry and straight into porn.

Davis: I know this is weird, but my thoughts can get so crazy sometimes and there's no one in my life to help me understand them. There's nobody who can do that like you can. Ben can't do it. And I can't burden Max with it with anymore, now that he's a grumpy fucking teenager.

Lena: It's probably best not to burden him with it.

Davis: But you… you just get me. And when I lose that for years, it feels like in some way, I'm losing myself. Even when things are going really well.

Lena: Well, thank you sweetie. I appreciate that.

Davis: I've missed you so much, Lena. You know, there's so many fucking times I think about sending you a DM on Facebook.

Lena: Well, then why don't you?

Davis: I guess I'm just too nervous you might be busy. I don't want to bother you. I'm always afraid I'd be wasting your time.

Lena: You wouldn't be wasting my time, Davis. I've known you since you were five.

Davis: I just feel sometimes like… I'm not interesting enough to talk to you. You read way more than me. You know so much more than me about a million fucking things. You're like a professor now. In fact, that's not even true. You are a professor.

Lena: What does that have to do with anything?

Davis: You're just so… articulate and smart and successful. You do everything so well. You've got this like, encyclopaedic knowledge of so many books I wanna read and will never have the time to finish. You have a great new apartment, a great career and all these cool people you get to chat with all the time.

Lena: But why does that mean I can't talk to you?

Davis: It just feels like… you have everything in your life. It's like, compared to you, I'm really fucking boring. Even though I'm a huge celebrity, it's only online. I still live in Downey.

Lena: Well, I would never describe you as boring, Davis. You may be many things, but boring isn't one of them.

Davis: I hope not because I need you, Lena. I need you at the moment.

Lena: Why do you feel you need me?

Davis: My life just doesn't *feel* right. It doesn't feel right when you're not in it. I can't say it any clearer than that.

Lena: I don't really know what to say to that, Davis.

Davis moves her chair so that she's now sitting right next to Lena. She grabs Lena's hand underneath the table. While holding her hand, Davis looks at Lena with a lost, desperate look in her eyes.

Davis: There's no one I can talk to about Max. Ben doesn't get Max like you do. You've only met him once, but you totally understand him as a person. On Facebook, when you write on his threads, I read everything you say to him and it's like you just know who you're dealing with. You get Max and Ben. I can always tell when someone else can do that. I look at both of their threads every night. I'm always watching their Facebook shit even though I don't post anything.

Lena: (slightly worried) You know, I hadn't thought of that.

Davis: I see what you write on both of their timelines and it just floors me how good you are at talking to two such different people.

Lena: Well, Ben's a meat and potatoes guy. Max is complicated. That's who they are. That's how I navigate the two of them.

Davis: You know, I wish it was the other way around.

Lena: What do you mean?

Davis: I would find my life so easy if I had a simple son and a complicated, cerebral husband. That's what I always wanted. That's what I always thought would happen, when we were in high school.

Lena: But that's not what actually happened.

Davis: (looking very sad) I know it's not.

Lena: It may be a cliché, but you never know what you want until you take it.

Davis: That's probably true.

Lena: Anyways, it's pretty silly to try and predict what kind of romantic partner you'll wind up with. The person you fall for almost *never* turns out to be what you dream about, when you're fantasising. Your biggest crushes never want you back.

Davis: Yeah… I guess they don't, do they?

Lena: In the end, you just fall for the person who also falls for you, the person you'd never dream in a million years would be 'the one'. It's always a huge surprise. If you could predict the love of your life, there'd be no point in meeting that person.

Davis: That's sooo true. Nobody ever winds up with their type. They always wind up with someone you think they'd hate.

Lena: Is that why you hate Ben?

Davis: No, I don't hate him. I'd love him… if he were my son. He's like a nice, dutiful son I could be proud of. But I don't want a fucking son in my bed, I want a lover. I want to be with someone like…

Lena: Like who?

Davis: Like you, Lena.

Lena: (surprised) Me?

Davis: Yeah, I guess should come out and just say it. I wish I was in a relationship with someone like you. You are so my type, it's not even funny.

Lena: But I thought you said I wasn't pretty enough to be in porn.

Davis: I'm not attracted to you because you're pretty. I cum thinking about who you are. During the few times I still masturbate, I almost always think of you.

Lena: (shocked) You get off thinking about me?

Davis: I have for twenty years On and off.

Lena: (shocked and surprised) Jesus… I had no idea. Really, I mean–

Davis: (interrupting) Your mind amazes me, Lena. It's so deep and complex and mysterious. I could live inside your mind and let me tell you, that is SO fucking sexy.

Lena: (flattered) Really?

Davis: I could love you like nobody could ever love you.

Lena: (smiling) Well, you have a son who is a lot like me. You can love him, but that'll have to do.

Davis: What do you mean?

Lena: Unfortunately, my dear, I'm straight as an arrow.

Davis: (smiling) You're not straight.

Lena: No Davis, I am straight. Very, very straight.

Davis: (smiling) You're not straight, Lena. Not by a long shot. But you'll have to trust me about that.

Lena: (annoyed) How would you know whether or not I'm straight?

Davis: (smiling flirtatiously) Let me break it down for you, honey. A straight woman is just a chick who hasn't had the good fortune of having my tongue twirl around in her.

Lena: (sarcastically) Isn't there a name for this? Straight-erasure? Or is it heterophobia?

Davis: I've met so many chicks who think they aren't curious.

Lena: (rolling eyes) Of course you have.

Davis: Look at my tongue Lena.

Davis sticks out her long tongue for Lena to admire.

Lena: Yes, you have a long and pointy tongue. Big deal. It's kinda like… that old guy from Kiss. Gene Simmons, or whatever his name is.

Davis: (smiling) I told you I wasn't normal.

Lena: You certainly aren't normal! You're fucking crazy.

Davis: (smiling) I've always been crazy for you.

Lena: I think you're just crazy.

Davis: (looking into Lena's eyes) Then tell me you've never thought about having sex with me, Lena. I dare you.

Lena: (smiling flirtatiously) I've never thought about having sex with you.

Davis starts to stroke Lena's arm. Lena doesn't pull away.

Davis: (giggling) Well, fortunately for you, I'll never believe that. I'll never believe that 'cause I know you bitch. I know you way more than you think I do.

Lena: And what do you think you know about me?

Davis: I know what you're thinking. I can see it in your eyes.

Lena: (rolling eyes) What do you think you see me thinking?

Davis: (bringing her face close to Lena) I've seen you thinking about my mouth.

Lena: (with a raised eyebrow) Thinking about your mouth?

Davis: (smiling) Thinking… about… my mouth… doing this…

Davis slowly moves forward likes she's about to kiss Lena. When Lena moves forward, Davis pulls away and laughs at her. Lena is slightly embarrassed.

Davis: (giggling) I told you!

Lena: That doesn't prove anything.

Davis: It proves you've been thinking about my mouth, wondering about my legs, dreaming about my fingertips. It's in your body language. I can see it in you, right now. It's written all over you.

Lena: (sarcastically) And you complain about people sexually harassing *you*.

Davis: (flirtatiously) This isn't harassment, Lena. I know what you'd like me to do to you.

Lena: (incredulous) What do you mean you 'know'?

Davis: I can tell from the way you carry yourself, when you look at me.

Lena: Dream on, Davis.

Davis: (softly and with an intense look in her eyes). And you have no idea how much I'd like to touch your pussy right now.

Lena: Davis, this isn't really the place to–

Davis: (interrupting) I'd make you feel fucking amazing things, Lena. I'll make you forget who you are.

Lena: I prefer to remember.

Davis: (softly) Have you ever had a girl's tongue in you?

Lena: (giggling) I think you should lower your voice, Davis.

Davis: (giggling) You're talking louder than I am!

Lena: (giggling) …Maybe I am.

Davis: (smiling flirtatiously) Should I be quieter? Is that what you'd like from me, Lena?

Lena: (flirtatiously) Maybe. Maybe not.

Davis: Okay, here's some very quiet, very reverse psychology.

Lena: (sarcastically) You know about reverse psychology? I'm impressed!

Davis: (whispering with fake seriousness) Do not come to the bathroom with me, Lena.

Lena: (smiling mischievously) Why not?

Davis: (Davis leans over and whispers in Lena's ear) If you come to the ladies room with me, you'll make Davis very very angry. Then I'll have to punish you. I'll have to take you to a stall, pull down your panties, wiggle my big pointy tongue all over you and make you cum hard on my fucking face. Don't do it, Lena. Whatever you do, please don't come to the bathroom with me. Pleeeeease.

Lena: (smiling mischievously) Okay, I won't come to the bathroom with you.

Davis: (pouting like a child) It didn't work!

Lena: Does that mean you think I should come with you to the bathroom then?

Davis: Yes. I think you should.

Lena: But why-oh-why, Davis?

Davis: (matter of factly) Because I'm amazing at sex.

Lena: You've mentioned that already.

Davis: (smiling) I'm amazing, you're amazing… and I love you, Lena. But not just because I think we should have sex in a public place.

Lena: Why do you keep saying you love me?

Davis: (smiling tenderly) My body just needs to touch you. I can't help it.

It's like feeling broody or something. It feels spiritual.

Lena removes Davis's hand from her arm.

Lena: Are you feeling broody now?

Davis: No, I've only felt broody once when I was a teenager; that's why I had Max.

Lena: That's bizarre, Davis.

Davis: Yeah, it's amazing I was able to find a guy who allowed me to have a child at that age. I think it's terrible how girls are encouraged to wait until they're thirty before they have kids.

Lena: Well, I'm not so sure I agree with you about that. But I will say it again: your son is certainly amazing. He's one of the coolest kids I've ever met.

Davis: (with pride) He is amazing.

Lena: You know, I loved that essay he posted about Gabriel Garcia Marquez the other day. I read it twice. I couldn't believe a fourteen-year-old wrote that. It could get published and no one would know. It's that fucking good.

Davis: (smiling) It's such a weird experience having a kid like Max for a son. It makes me feel horribly inadequate, even though it's also pretty magical.

Lena: You shouldn't feel inadequate; you've influenced him a lot. That's why he's so cool. His mother knows a good book.

Davis: He's influenced me!

Lena: (smiling) I bet.

Davis: It's depressing though.

Lena: Why?

Davis: It sucks having a kid who's so much cooler than my husband. Max is more of a man than Ben could ever be.

Lena: Well, call me crazy, but I think your husband's a great guy.

Davis: Yeah, but being in a happy relationship isn't about being a good person. It's about finding someone you click with.

Lena: But you did click with Ben, very strongly. I saw it.

Davis: I don't think I did, Lena. I think I was just attracted to him and excited to be a mom. I think because of that, I projected this imaginary person onto him that turned out NOT to be the guy I wound up raising my kid with. Ben's not that person. He's a boring person.

Lena: I know you're bored of him now, but that can change. You could both go to counselling. What you're describing is very common.

Davis: I don't care if it's common, Lena. Being normal that way is tragic. It's like a Cora Sandel novel.

Lena: Well, like it or not, you didn't choose to fall in love with somebody like Max. You fell in love with Ben and had a kid who's a lot like the kind of guy you wanted to fall in love with. You have to deal with that, Davis.

Davis: I know I do. It's my life, whether I like it or not.

Lena: It's the life you created for yourself. If you wanted something different, something different would have happened.

Davis: At least I got Max out of all of this shit.

Lena: Exactly. There's something you can be happy about.

Davis: Oh God, I am so proud of him. Max is like… someone we used to crush on. He looks so old for his age. And he's so beautiful.

Lena: That's not exactly true.

Davis: You don't think he's handsome?

Lena: No, I meant when we were teenagers, people like Max were the age we are now. We never met anybody like that who was also a teenager.

Davis: That's part of why it's so hard to be a good parent to him. It's really fucking hard to know that a kid like Max actually thinks his mom is doing an okay job, you know?

Lena: Well, it seems like you want more than just to do a good job. You want Max's approval.

Davis: I'll get it eventually. We'll get close again. I'll make it happen.

Lena: His friendship is really important to you, isn't it?

Davis: Max is the only person in my life I always enjoy talking to, whenever I can get a conversation out of him. No one is more interesting; no one makes me laugh more; no one even looks after me the way he does, Lena. When I'm sick, he's the one who brings me chicken soup and gets aspirin. He takes my temperature. He does this way before Ben even notices I'm sick.

Lena: Well, he likes protecting you. You're his mom.

Davis: Max is the man in my house who used to tell me I was beautiful every day. It wasn't Ben. It was my fucking kid.

Lena: Well, that's not something boys typically do. Max is unique.

Davis: He could understand my writing. He could even understand why I'm not attracted to Ben. It's like Max always knew why I was pissed off about anything. He instinctively understood just what to say to make me feel good. He even knew the right words to use. And he could do all of that before he hit puberty, Lena. He's a fucking prodigy. It's scary how mature he is.

Lena: But why is it so important that he's proud of you? He's your son. Parents are supposed to be proud of their kids, not the other way around.

Davis: It's hard to explain it. All I can say is... he's the most incredible person I've ever met and he's my kid. That doesn't happen to most people. Most people tolerate their kids, but not me. I've never liked anyone as much as I like Max. I don't even feel like a mom. It feels more emotional than that. It feels deeper than anything I've ever felt about anyone.

Lena: Some people might say that's not so healthy though, Davis.

Davis: Do you know how most parents say they would die for their children?

Lena: Yeah.

Davis: I don't feel that way. I feel like I live for Max.

Lena: So, is your life, in a sense, his life?

Davis: Lena, I can admit who I am. I'm a difficult person. I know that. I'm creative but I'm also an attention whore. I'm spiteful and vindictive a lot of the time. I don't enjoy people unless they're useful to me in some way. Most of the time, people don't like me either and I don't fucking blame them. I'm the first to admit I'm not a good wife. The more I think about it, I actually can't stand my husband and aside from you, I don't really have any friends.

Lena: I didn't realise things were this bad.

Davis: So, what am I good at? I'm good at fucking and making films that turn people on. I can run fast, I have a high tolerance for pain and I'm a good businesswoman.

Lena: Is that all you think you're good for?

Davis: Well, there's a few other things. I'm good at getting people excited about shit. I'm good at co-ordinating events and being a hostess. I can do coding and sometimes design a decent website. Sometimes I'm funny, I'm really pretty and my body always looks great. But that's about it. I'm not even a good cook.

Lena: But Davis, you can always get better at anything you put your mind to. There are always ways you can improve yourself. I'm always improving myself. I'm never satisfied with where I'm at in life, ever. That's how I achieve things.

Davis: But I don't need to change, Lena. You know why?

Lena: Why?

Davis: Because I'm a good mother. That's the one thing I can give to another person that isn't sexual. I can fail everybody else, but not Max. He's the one person I can make proud of me.

Lena: Well… maybe the problem is you're not making it easy for Max to be proud of you.

Davis: I'm doing the best I can, Lena. Like I said, he'll come around eventually.

Lena: But how can he? Max isn't allowed to interact in any way with your career. How on earth can he be proud of you for it?

Davis: I can be proud of him for being a good husband in twenty years. I don't have to marry him to be proud of him for that. And he doesn't have to watch my porn to be proud of me for doing it.

Lena: Yeah, but you'll get to meet the bride. You get to go to the wedding. You'll get to have a relationship with the two of them. You might get grandkids.

Davis: So what?

Lena: And I was also thinking: If anyone talks to Max at school about you, it's probably to goad him and piss him off about his mom being a porn star. He probably gets bullied. None of that's very pleasant when you're fourteen years old.

Davis: Well, if I had my way, things would be different. People would be more tolerant and accepting, more sex positive. I hate the fact that society isn't there yet, but like I always say, that's not my responsibility.

Lena: Davis, let's try something.

Davis: What?

Lena: Let's try an imagination exercise.

Davis: Okay.

Lena: Imagine for a minute, that you were in the situation Max is in. Imagine you're a precocious and intelligent fourteen-year-old who looks about twenty. Imagine your beautiful mother loves you very much.

Davis: (thinking hard) Okay… I'm imagining this… I'm imagining having a dick. I'm imagining what it's like to pee…

Lena: Good. Now imagine you are pubescent and have a dick that gets hard when you look at porn. Imagine it gets hard, whenever you see porn, or whenever you think about sex. It gets hard whether you want it to or not… all the time.

Davis: (eyes closed, with her fingers on her temples, thinking hard) Okay, I'm imagining having a big dick that's hard. I've got a big dick that's hard and it feels good.

Lena: Now, imagine your mother's a beautiful porn star. She has sex with all the women who give you a hard on. All your friends can watch her and masturbate when she does this. So can all your teachers; so can all your future girlfriends. And most of them wish they could fuck her, especially the guys.

Davis: Okay.

Lena: Now, you're her son. That means you're the one person who can't fuck her. Not only that; you're also not allowed to watch her having sex. You're not even allowed to think about her having sex. If you ever even accidentally think about her in a sexual way, your job is to try your hardest to banish that thought from your mind.

Davis: I'm not allowed to watch Mom. Got it.

Lena: But imagine it's really important to your beautiful mother that you're proud of her. She wants you to be proud of her for being a porn star.

Davis: Okay. I can see this all really clearly, Lena. She's hot. She's almost as sexy as me. She's got great legs and a beautiful pussy. They're almost as good as mine and they don't smell. Well, they do smell, but they smell like baby powder.

Lena: Okay… is it easy to be proud of her?

Davis: Yes.

Lena: It's easy to be proud of her, even though your job is to make sure you never think of her in a sexual way?

Davis: I think so. Yeah.

Lena: It's easy to be proud of her, even though she's making something that's designed to make your dick hard?

Davis: I don't have to watch it. That way, I don't have to worry about her turning me on.

Lena: (smiling mischievously) But how do you know she won't turn you on? How do you know your beautiful porn star mother will never make you hard?

Davis: Because she's my mom. Sons don't get hard thinking about their mothers.

Lena: (innocently) Well, if that's true, you should be able to watch her porn without it affecting you. If sons don't get hard because of their mothers, even watching a porn film with mom in it won't change that.

Davis: That's true.

Lena: So in reality, the reason you can't watch her porn is if you did watch it, you'd get hard.

Davis: Maybe.

Lena: And that would be wrong, wouldn't it?

Davis: I guess.

Lena: (speaking slowly) So… wouldn't it be easier to be proud of your beautiful mother, if she did something you weren't supposed to completely stay away from?

Davis: I don't know…

Lena: Think about it: How can you be proud of someone for doing something that's designed to give you pleasure? But if you get pleasure from it, you're a bad person.

Davis: I don't know, Lena. I really, really don't know.

Lena: Well, that's the position your son is in. That's the position you put him in.

Davis: So you think I should let him see my porn?

Lena: (abruptly) I'm not saying that!

Davis: I can't hurt him, Lena. I don't want to be one of those moms who abuses their kids. That's really important to me.

Lena: You think I don't know that?

Davis: (sad and confused) I can't fuck him up, he's my son.

Lena: I'm not saying you're fucking him up!

Davis: I know. I know. It's just that I think I already fucked him up when he was younger, Lena. I don't ever want to do that again–

Lena: (interrupting) Oh, come on. What is abuse anyway? Have you ever even thought about abuse, as a concept?

Davis: Yes, I have. Abuse is when you do something to a kid that harms them, psychologically.

Lena: But isn't everyone different? Aren't we all harmed by different things?

Davis: I don't know. Are we all that different?

Lena: Well, lots of people would say that parenting a fourteen-year-old and doing porn is a form of abuse.

Davis: And that would be fucking bullshit.

Lena: Well, not if you take the definition of abuse at its word. There's no reason why having a porn star for a mother couldn't psychologically harm a teenage kid.

Davis: But it doesn't have to harm them. If the mother protects them from it and has a good relationship with that kid, it won't harm them.

Lena: And how do you know it won't harm them?

Davis: What do you mean, "How do I know?"

Lena: Well, even if you being in porn doesn't harm Max, suppose you were the mother of a very different kind of teenage boy, a boy that was much more sensitive than your son. How do you know it wouldn't harm that kid?

Davis: Because I'd always create an environment where he would know his mother's sexuality is natural. He'd know the freedom to express it how she wants is something he should celebrate. He'd know that deep down. No one could tell him otherwise.

Lena: Does this mean you think you can socialize a kid into being proud of his mother for being a porn star?

Davis: Yeah, I guess.

Lena: So that means you can socialise kids to cope with things they might otherwise find traumatic?

Davis: Maybe… I–

Lena: (interrupting) In a way, you've already done it a little.

Davis: What do you mean?

Lena: Well, think about it. Most normal kids would find Inside Davis traumatic. It would make them feel confused and disgusted by their own sexuality. But Max isn't like that. He's only embarrassed because his friends wanna fuck you. He knows intellectually that there's nothing wrong with porn. He at least knows you're not hurting him by doing porn, right?

Davis: I think so. I mean… I hope so.

Lena: So, you've conditioned Max not to be harmed by what you do. You've helped him cope with things more sensitive kids would struggle with. That's another thing you can be proud of. Your son is a cool, smart, handsome and charming little prodigy, but more importantly, he's not threatened at all by what his mother does. He's only embarrassed by it, right?

Davis: Well, he seems disappointed by it.

Lena: (condescendingly) He's not disappointed by your porn, Davis. You're so bad at reading people. You're ridiculous sometimes.

Davis: But you said he was disappointed by it! You said that before you got your croissant!

Lena: Well, now that I'm getting more of the facts, things are starting to look a little different.

Davis: Lena, if Max isn't disappointed by my porn, why are we no longer close? Why do I feel like I'm his annoying mom and not his friend anymore?

Lena: Well, part of that could be the fact that he's fourteen and teens naturally separate from their parents. Everything you're describing is totally age appropriate.

Davis: (sighing) I know, I know. I know that rationally; it's just fucking hard, emotionally.

Lena: Well, it's only one possibility. The other is Max feels shut out from your life.

Davis: (abruptly) But I don't shut him out! I talk to him every day. Anytime he wants, if I'm not working, we can watch 'The Wire' together, or 'Breaking Bad', or 'Twin Peaks'. The only thing I don't do with him is play video games. That's the one thing him and Ben have in common.

Lena: Davis, don't kid yourself. You shut Max out of the main thing you want him to be proud of you for doing.

Davis: (passionately) But that's because I'm his mom!

Lena: Then why are you doing it? Why are you recording yourself fucking strangers and putting it on the internet for everyone to watch?

Davis: (frustrated) You know why I'm doing it. I told you why. Why do you keep asking me this?

Lena: Because I'm curious. I'm curious why you're doing something that has to be so separate from Max? Why expect him to be proud of something he's forbidden from ever seeing?

Davis: Because I don't want to hurt him, Lena.

Lena: But you don't have to hurt him, Davis.

Davis: (passionately) I'm not hurting him!

Lena: (emphatically) I know you aren't! I'm just saying there are millions of career options you could have taken where it would be easy for him to be proud of you. When you used to write poetry, that was easy for him to be proud of, wasn't it?

Davis: It was so easy, it was crazy. He understood those sonnets better than I ever did and I wrote 'em.

Lena: And he was able to do that easily because he didn't have to be hidden from them.

Davis: Well, looking at one of my poems wouldn't hurt him.

Lena: Then why choose to make something that if Max saw it, it would hurt him?

Davis: Well, it won't hurt him when he's a grownup. He won't want to see my porn, but it won't hurt him when he's in his twenties. It's just because he's a kid. That's why it wouldn't be good for him to see my porn.

Lena: Davis, why do you think, at this moment in time, watching your porn would hurt him?

Davis: Because he's fourteen.

Lena: So you think fourteen-year-olds are traumatised by porn?

Davis: No, but I worry he'd be traumatised if he saw me in one.

Lena: But why? Are you afraid he'd be turned on by you?

Davis: You know, Lena, I can't answer that. All I can say is I don't want to even think about it.

Lena: Why?

Davis: (deeply disturbed) Because Max isn't supposed to find me arousing. He's not supposed to want to see me in the clips he jacks off to. That's not right.

Lena: But you said you wanted him to respect women. You said he couldn't be uncomfortable with your porn and still respect women.

Davis: I know that, Lena.

Lena: It sounds like you're saying that on the one hand, Max has to be proud of you for being a porn star. But on the other hand, he should be uncomfortable with your porn, too uncomfortable to ever watch it.

Davis: No, I don't want him uncomfortable. My porn is just me. I don't want him uncomfortable with that.

Lena: Then what is it you want Max to feel?

Davis: I guess I do want him to respect my porn and be proud of me for doing it, but also understand that it's not for him.

Lena: Okay, let me play devil's advocate here. Why is it not for him?

Davis: Because I'm his mom.

Lena: Why? What would happen if he watched your porn and got aroused?

Davis: Well, he'd be crossing a line and disrespecting his mother.

Lena: Would he also be disrespecting you if he wished you weren't making it?

Davis: Yeah, I guess he would.

Lena: If that's the case, remind me why you think you're making a product your own son should be proud of you for putting into this world.

Davis: Well, it's a good product that helps people and it's well made… so, I guess I think he should be proud of me for creating something, you know, that helps people.

Lena: How does it help people?

Davis: In a lot of ways.

Lena: What's the biggest way?

Davis: I guess it makes guys feel better than their girlfriends make them feel.

Lena: What about single men?

Davis: (thinking hard) Maybe it stops single guys from sexually harassing women. After they watch me, they aren't all pent up and sexually frustrated. So that makes women feel safer when they walk down the street.

Lena: So, would you say your porn is designed to make men want to look at it?

Davis: Probably. I mean my vids are supposed to turn on whoever sees them, even guys who just see the thumbnails. I design those to make sure even before a guy watches anything, he's hard as fuck.

Lena: How hard do you want a guy to be when he watches you?

Davis: (smiling) So hard he can't think straight. I want him fucking hyperventilating.

Lena: Okay. So we've established your porn is explicitly designed to make men want to see it… men who are sexual and attracted to women.

Davis: Of course it is.

Lena: Do you think Max is gay or bi?

Davis: He's definitely straight.

Lena: So he's a straight male. He's in the demographic your porn is trying to get hard.

Davis: Yeah, but it's different when it's your mom. Everybody knows–

Lena: (interrupting) So if Max watches porn you've designed to make him hard, that still means he's disrespecting you.

Davis: (confused) I wouldn't say that. I didn't design it so that Max would–

Lena: (interrupting in a condescending tone) You amaze me, Davis. You really do.

Davis: Why?

Lena: You're a fucking porn star, girl. You're drowning in hypocrisy.

Davis: I don't understand.

Lena: You're trying to turn on everyone in the world, except the one person you love more than anything. If his body responds to your sexuality, you want him to feel ashamed and suppress it, just like you say the world wants you to suppress your own sexuality.

Davis: But isn't Max being turned on by me bad for him?

Lena: Okay, let's explore that. Why is it bad for him?

Davis: Because it's incestuous. It's abuse. It fucks people up and ruins their lives.

Lena: Well, for most of human history, gay relationships would have done all of that too. Whenever any kind of human relationship is disapproved of, there are almost always pretty horrendous emotional consequences for the people in those relationships.

Davis: I know that.

Lena: Then can you think of a reason why, morally, it's wrong for Max to be turned on by you? An objective reason? Not a social convention, but an objective moral reason?

Davis: I don't know… Maybe because parents are supposed to create an environment where a kid can develop their sexuality in a way that's … totally separate from the sexuality of the parent?

Lena: (smiling like a teacher pleased by a pupil finally understanding something) You're onto something, my dear.

Davis: I'm trying to get this...

Lena: You can get it, Davis. Just follow the reasoning and you'll get it.

Davis: Okay…

Lena: So tell me Davis, what happens to a kid's sexuality if it's not completely separate from the sexuality of its parents?

Davis: Well, people say the kid's sexuality gets fucked up.

Lena: (smiling with an "I told you so" expression) You see?

Davis: (confused) Oh my God…

Lena: (laughing) If it's wrong for Max to be turned on by you, then you're one fucked-up mother Davis.

Davis: Am I a fucked-up mother?

Lena: (abruptly) I didn't say that. Pay attention to what I'm telling you.

Davis: I'm trying. This is just a lot to take in, Lena.

Lena: (irritated) Then concentrate! This is your son we're talking about. This is important.

Davis: (flustered) I'm trying to concentrate!

Lena: Then calm down and think this through. Just reason it out. Go on girl. You can do this.

Davis: Okay so… the whole incest taboo is based on the idea that kids need to be completely separated from the sexuality of their parents. Otherwise, they get fucked up in the head.

Lena: Yep.

Davis: And I'm a porn star.

Lena: Yes, you are.

Davis: And by being a porn star… I'm not really separating Max from my sexuality.

Lena: That's right, Davis. Now tell me why.

Davis: It's because… even though I'm not having sex with him, my sexuality is all around him. My porn's getting off nearly everyone he knows. Or at least, it could.

Lena: And why shouldn't Max watch your porn?

Davis: Because if he watched it, it could get him off too. Actually, my porn is so good, he wouldn't have a choice about that.

Lena: Right. Now tell me about all the other hot moms in the world. The ones who aren't porn stars.

Davis: The other hot moms… are completely separating their kids from their sexuality.

Lena: And how are they doing that?

Davis: By not trying to get off the whole world. By not showing everyone pictures of them having sex. By not filming porn so hot it could turn on their families.

Lena: (smiling) Yep.

Davis: So that's how I'm different to all the other hot moms?

Lena: You got it.

Davis: (having an epiphany) Wow Lena… this is fucking crazy.

Lena: It is crazy when you actually use your brain and think about what it is you're doing.

Davis: I totally get it now. I understand everything.

Lena: Good.

Davis: The incest taboo is fucking retarded.

Lena bursts out laughing again.

Davis: What's so funny?

Lena: …Oh, there's an old woman behind you with a funny hat. Look!

Davis looks behind her and there is indeed, an old woman with a funny hat wondering around the coffee shop. She orders a latte and sits down.

Davis doesn't understand why her hat is *that* funny.

15. SEX: Privilege

At this point in the conversation, Davis is beginning to feel like she's having many much-needed epiphanies about her life. This is one of the reasons she loves finally reconnecting with Lena.

Lena, on the other hand, is no longer taking the conversation seriously. She thinks there isn't any point. Instead, she's just having fun and being mischievous. Lena is surprised at how much she enjoys this. There's something about Davis's sheer cluelessness that makes Lena feel powerful, like she's finally getting her own private revenge against the disgusting slut who stole the hunk who should have been Lena's high school boyfriend. Making fun of Davis without Davis noticing is intoxicating. It's not only addictive and exciting for Lena; it even makes her feel kind of sexy.

Davis McFarlin, of course, is the farthest thing from what Lena Rodriguez would describe as a sexy woman. But Lena's ability to make Davis look foolish and pathetic is having an effect on Lena she never imagined it would, in all the years of knowing Davis.

Lena's panties are wet.

Lena: (smiling mischievously) So tell me about the retarded nature of the incest taboo. I'm sure I'm gonna love this.

Davis: (excited about her new epiphany) It's fucking retarded because… it's not really about incest!

Lena: What do you mean?

Davis: It doesn't just say don't fuck your kids, Lena. It says don't do anything that could ever turn them on!

Lena: Ah… so like… don't give hubby a sexy lap dance in front of little Johnny?

Davis: (enthusiastically) Yes! That's it! It's fucking retarded, isn't it?

Lena: (sarcastically) It sounds absolutely retarded, Davis. Like it was created by retards.

Davis: (shaking head) Most definitely. I mean, my God… just thinking about it…

Lena: (smiling to herself) What are you thinking, Davis?

Davis: (passionately) I just can't get over how… fucking sex negative it is!

Lena: (sarcastically) Yes, the incest taboo is very sex negative. Imagine that!

Davis: This is so, so crazy Lena. I never in my life thought about it this way before, but it's… just incredibly puritanical. I mean, it's disempowering to women.

Lena: (sarcastically) Oh, unbelievably disempowering.

Davis: In fact, you could go further than that. It's victim blamey. That would be a good description of it, right?

Lena: (sarcastically) Absolutely! I mean, why on earth should Mom be blamed for making the kids horny!

Davis: I know, it's fucking crazy, right? Think about what it implies!

Lena: (smiling mischievously) I have thought about it, Davis.

Davis: I'm so glad, because more people need to examine this stuff. If the incest taboo is right, that means any mom who wears a sexy dress is abusing her kid, or any mom showing cleavage, or being flirty on Instagram, or using words like 'pussy.'

Lena: (mocking Davis) That's hard to disagree with, when you put it so eloquently.

Davis: (proud of herself) And yet, we all take this reactionary shit for granted. Even I took it for granted, before I actually thought about it for two seconds!

Lena: (sarcastically) Even the bravest female role models can succumb to misogyny.

Davis: I know, Lena! My God, that's how powerful this culture is. Even I can't get away from internalising sex negative attitudes. They're everywhere.

Sexism is fucking insidious! It creeps up on you!

Lena: Maybe, but if that's how you feel, I don't see how you can be sex positive.

Davis: (confused) Why not?

Lena: If I'm not mistaken, sex positivity says that sexuality is good, provided that it's consensual. Is that not what it says?

Davis: Yeah, but what's wrong with consent?

Lena: Well, think about the shorts you're wearing right now.

Davis: What do my shorts have to do with consent?

Lena: Think about the three British guys you insulted. The ones that were hitting on you earlier.

Davis: What about 'em? What do they have to do with consent?

Lena: Davis, how do you think seeing your legs made those men feel? How do you think they felt when they looked at you?

Davis: I probably gave them a hard on. That's what happens to most men when they look at me.

Lena: And did you get their consent before you gave them a hard on?

Davis: (incredulous) Why the fuck should I get their consent for that?

Lena: Well, someone… not me, but someone… might say it's because their boners aren't really under their control.

Davis: Yeah, but who cares?

Lena: Well Davis, it's not like those guys could say to themselves, "This woman over here, she looks like an interesting and intelligent person I could have an amazing conversation with. She could be my soul mate, so I might as well get a hard on for her." Male bodies don't work that way.

Davis: So what?

Lena: Well, by wearing an outfit like the one you're wearing now, you're creating feelings in men they haven't chosen, feelings that don't express how they would ideally choose to feel. They get a hard on because an attractive woman like you does something sexy to give men hard ons. That's it.

Davis: But isn't that one of the best things about being a woman?

Lena: Well, it would be nice, if it weren't so sad.

Davis: Why do you think it's sad?

Lena: I guess it's just sad that… who you are doesn't matter. Your personality doesn't matter; what men actually like in a woman's mind doesn't matter; what they'd even prefer to get hard over doesn't matter. Their dicks just don't care about any of that.

Davis: But they don't need to. Sex is fucking animal passion. It's not about being a good person. You don't fuck hot guys because they have good character. If they're nice, it's just a bonus.

Lena: But a hot guy's dick might like you, even if that guy actually hates you. Have you thought about that?

Davis: (confused) Yeah, but isn't that just… human nature?

Lena: Well, rape is part of human nature. Should we be alright with rape because it's part of human nature?

Davis: No, I get what you're saying. Just 'cause something's normal… that doesn't make it good.

Lena: Right. That's what all the new the consent campaigns are about.

Davis: I've really been noticing that, Lena. People write to me about this. They say we all need to have a conversation about consent 'cause men need to take more responsibility for all the guys who rape women.

Lena: (giggling) That's hilarious.

Davis: So many fucking porn stars tell me that men just aren't doing a good enough job of stopping rape.

Lena: Well, that doesn't surprise me. You can't go to college today without taking at least some consent classes. I've had to sit in on a few.

Davis: People are obsessed with consent, with men subordinating women, with rape culture… and no one notices the obvious.

Lena: They never do.

Davis: If everyone gets obsessed with consent, society will become like, totally repressive to women. Women won't be able to give men hard ons…

Lena: …without first getting their permission.

Davis: (incredulous) Fuck.

Lena: It's a strange world we live in, isn't it?

Davis: (having another epiphany) Jesus… this means… sex positive people are actually sex negative. That's fucking nuts, Lena. Sex positive people are the real prudes!

Lena: (smiling mischievously) Well, you said it. Not I.

Davis: See, this is why I need to have conversations with you. You help me understand things I'd never be able to make sense of on my own. It's like I've got this foggy curtain in front of me that you pull to one side. After spending time with you, it's like I can see the world again. The dots get connected.

Lena: (sarcastically) Well, think of me as your dot connector, your brown dot connector.

Davis: (with a sweet enthusiasm) Oh, I do! You mean… so fucking much to me, Lena. I can't even tell you how grateful I am to just be sitting here with you right now.

Lena: So am I correct in assuming you're not actually sex positive?

Davis: You know, I don't think I am anymore. It doesn't make any sense.

Lena: Interesting.

Davis: If you're paranoid about fucking people without their consent, you're gonna be paranoid about other things, like popping boners. That just leads to madness.

Lena: So is consent unimportant to you?

Davis: No, it's important. I just think it's more of a body language thing. It's not about somebody telling you that you're allowed to make them cum.

Lena: So is your position that sexual consent shouldn't have to be explicitly verbal consent?

Davis: (confused) …I'm not sure.

Lena: What aren't you sure about?

Davis: (thinking for a few seconds) …I guess I'm only sure of one thing: it's the consent fascists who are repressive. That's who I feel strongly about right now.

Lena: (smiling) You should read Spiked Magazine. Have you ever heard of Luke Gittos?

Davis: (with purposeful zeal) I don't need to. I know who our enemy is. I've figured it out.

Lena: (trying hard not to laugh) So now we have an enemy?

Davis: Yes, we do. It's the consent fascists.

Lena: (sarcastically) Well, I guess that's better than fascists.

Davis: Consent fascists are the people we need to rebel against right now. These are the people who think you gotta ask dudes if it's okay to give them a boner.

Lena: You've encountered people like this?

Davis: They're called Christians, Lena. They think women are responsible for men getting hard. That's why they like modesty.

Lena: Okay, so let me get a handle on this: You think women aren't responsible for the sexual feelings of men?

Davis: That's right.

Lena: Are women ever responsible for the sexual feelings they… deliberately cause in men?

Davis: No, they aren't.

Lena: Does this mean a woman shouldn't have to ask a man whether or not she can give him a hard on?

Davis: Of course she shouldn't. It's not up to him whether or not he gets hard. It's up to her.

Lena: (with a raised eyebrow) What about a woman who makes a man cum? Should she ask his permission to give him an orgasm?

Davis: If he cums, that's his problem; not hers. And most of the time, it's never a problem, is it?

Lena: But what if a guy's married and you're both carpooling to work together. Let's say you start talking about how much you'd love to blow him. Let's say he wants to say faithful to his wife, but your words are turning him on.

Davis: (giggling) I've been in that situation so many times...

Lena: Okay, suppose the guy who is driving you to work asks you to stop. Let's assume he's asking you to stop because he wants to remain faithful to his wife and he doesn't like the fact that you're gonna make him cum in his pants. Let's say he only wants to cum in his pants when *she* talks dirty to him.

Davis: (matter of factly) Then that's her problem.

Lena: But what if he asks you to stop? What if he tells you you're making him uncomfortable?

Davis: Then I wouldn't carpool with him anymore.

Lena: But would you stop?

Davis: Probably not.

Lena: (smiling to herself) That's interesting.

Davis: This guy sounds like he deserves to be uncomfortable.

Lena: Why?

Davis: He's a misogynist.

Lena: What makes you say that?

Davis: He thinks his comfort is more important than my freedom. He sounds controlling.

Lena: So, you think any guy is controlling if he demands a woman *not* give him an orgasm?

Davis: Totally! All the sexual freedom women have today is there because we stopped men from telling us how we're allowed to make men feel.

Lena: Does this mean you think sexual freedom for women means men shouldn't have a say in how they get aroused, or have orgasms?

Davis: Of course. If that wasn't true, we'd still be in corsets.

Lena: But what about pregnancy? Should a woman have to get consent from a man if she decides to get pregnant using his sperm?

Davis: (giggling) If she did, half of us probably wouldn't be here.

Lena: What about teenage boys? Should grown women have to get their consent for anything?

Davis: Not for orgasms.

Lena: Why not orgasms?

Davis: 'Cause if women had to get consent for that, porn would be illegal; stripping would be illegal; filming strippers would be illegal; lingerie adverts would be illegal.

Lena: You think so?

Davis: Sex scenes in rated R movies would be illegal; girl/girl kisses would be illegal. We'd have to live in the fucking fifties.

Lena: Davis, I think lingerie adverts were actually legal in the fifties.

Davis: (rolling eyes) That's not the point, Lena. If women had to get the consent of teenage boys to make them cum, you wouldn't even see women on the beach. Bikinis would be outlawed. So would most bathing suits.

Lena: And why do you think that is?

Davis: (smiling) It's 'cause any beautiful woman, just by wearing shorts, is gonna make some kid make a mess in his jeans.

Lena: But why is it so important to you that women have the freedom to make that mess?

Davis: (giggling) Because if we can't control how our bodies turn men on, they can't control what we do with our bodies. It's just common sense!

Lena: Well, this is fascinating. It sounds like you're saying teenage boys should have no say over… how and when grown women make them hard. They shouldn't even get a say in how women make them cum.

Davis: What's wrong with that?

Lena: Well, it sounds like you're saying that the consent of teenage boys doesn't matter. It sounds like you're saying that if a grown woman is making a teenage boy have an orgasm, he doesn't have the right to ask her to stop.

Davis: Lena, if teenage boys had any say over female sexuality, they'd either rape us, or we'd have to wear fucking burkas. That's what the Islamic world is like.

Lena: Then what's the difference between raping a teenage boy and giving him an orgasm without his consent?

Davis: If a woman is touching a kid and he pushes her away and she keeps going, that's rape. But if she's doing something in front of him that turns him on or makes him cum, that's not her responsibility.

Lena: But why isn't it her responsibility?

Davis: Because if it was, she couldn't wear what she wanted to in public; she couldn't flirt with other grownups or say sexy things; she couldn't kiss her lovers on the street. She'd have to hide her sexuality.

Lena: So, because a woman and a teenage boy share the same public space, the boy has to put up with anything she does that makes him uncomfortable?

Davis: Boys aren't entitled to control what women do with their bodies, Lena.

Lena: Does this principle apply to a beautiful woman who happens to be the relative of a teenage boy?

Davis: Absofuckinglutely. Teenage boys can't police the choices of beautiful women – even their relatives.

Lena: Well, if that's true, no fourteen-year-old boy should ever ask his mom not to do a lap dance in front of him. That's your position, right?

Davis: I guess so…yeah. It's disrespectful to tell a woman how to express her sexuality, even if she is a relative.

Lena: And this would be because… regardless of whether the fourteen-year-old is uncomfortable or aroused, his feelings are never Mom's responsibility?

Davis: (thinking hard) That seems right. Beautiful women aren't responsible for turning on teenage boys, even if they are blood relatives.

Lena: Well, if this is how you feel, what are you gonna do about Max?

Davis: What do you mean?

Lena: Do you still think it's your job to hide your sexuality from him?

Davis: Well, it's illegal not to.

Lena: Well, homosexuality is still illegal in many countries.

Davis: I know that, Lena.

Lena: Remember: laws don't necessarily dictate the kinds of love that are good for people. Laws are social constructions.

Davis: I know that, too.

Lena: And remember: there are lots of gay people in the world. They fall in love and they don't do anything about it because they're afraid of the authorities. But then there are other gay people, gays that are braver and more radical. Those are the ones that actually change hearts and minds.

Davis: I get that, but I'm not sure this is relevant to me and Max.

Lena: I didn't say it was. I just think it's tragic when people don't take chances for love. Don't you think it's tragic?

Davis: (uncomfortable) Lena, I'm not doing anything sexual with my kid.

Lena: (abruptly) I didn't say you should do anything sexual with Max!

Davis: (confused) Then what are you saying?

Lena: I'm saying that… you should understand the relationship you've created with him.

Davis: I'm trying my best, Lena.

Lena: Look at it objectively. This relationship you have with your son… is a lot like an incestuous relationship. It's way more like that than what most kids have with their mothers.

Davis: Why?

Lena: Well, it's not technically incestuous, but it still has many of the features of an incestuous relationship.

Davis: (annoyed) What features? What are you talking about?

Lena: I think you know what features.

Davis: So… you think my relationship with my son is like an incestuous relationship. I'll try not to take offense at that.

Lena: Yes and before you take offence at what someone thinks, ask yourself why they think it. Ask yourself if you actually agree!

Davis: Is this 'cause I make porn that would get Max hard if he saw it?

Lena: Mmm… among other things.

Davis: Yeah, but come on, Lena. It doesn't matter if I stop making porn at this point. I'm all over the fucking internet now. There's probably fifty hours of footage floating around different websites.

Lena: Well, leaving the world of porn is one of your options. But it's not a particularly effective option, if the goal is stop Max from being so distant from you.

Davis: I know that, Lena. It would be pretty silly to stop doing porn, at this point.

Lena: I agree, Davis. I think it might be better to do something like what Max did for you, before he got all distant, before he became a teenager.

Davis: (slightly unnerved and not knowing why) So, should I just… talk to him and keep him company? Take care of him and tell him he's wonderful and amazing?

Lena: Well, sort of. I was actually thinking you could try and anticipate some of the things he wants and give them to him, before he asks you to give them to him. Isn't that what Max used to do for you?

Davis: All the fucking time, Lena. It was incredible.

Lena: Yeah, so surprise him with something that lets him know just how much you love him. Maybe that's what he's lacking right now. That could be why he's not connecting with you.

Davis: But I wouldn't know how to do that, Lena.

Lena: Well, that's not good if you want Max to be proud of you.

Davis: You know, you're right. Sometimes I wonder if he'd actually be proud of me if I quit porn and started writing again. That could be the cold hard truth.

Lena: Well, Davis, you shouldn't have to quit porn to make your own son proud of you. There are thousands of porn stars in the world, with plenty of children that are proud of Mom.

Davis: (nodding her head) I know. Jodie Green had kids and they turned out okay.

Lena: So, ask yourself this: How could you stay in porn and get Max to be proud of his sexy mother?

Davis: (thinking hard) Maybe act more like …being an exhibitionist is… totally normal for a mom?

Lena: Go back into his perspective again. If you were Max and your sexy mom was a porn star, what would make it easiest for you to be proud of her?

Davis: Like I keep saying, I really don't know how to answer that. It's hard for me to get in the head space of a teenage boy – or any man, for that matter.

Lena: Davis, your mom wrote children's stories. You were proud of her for that, weren't you? You were proud of her when you were a kid. Don't you remember?

Davis: I haven't thought about that for years, Lena.

Lena: When she first published that book of stories about the games you used to play, how did that make you feel?

Davis: (remembering with sadness) I thought… I guess maybe… Yeah, I was proud of her.

Lena: She never hid those stories from you, Davis. I remember you reading them aloud to me when you were nine. We used to read them together on my bed after school.

Davis: (smiling and remembering this for the first time in years) I used to love reading with you, Lena.

Lena: And it was easy for you to be proud of those stories. It wasn't because your mom was a good writer. It was something else.

Davis: (giggling) No, she was a terrible writer. Some of the worst children's literature I've ever seen. But it still made me proud, even though it was awful. Crazy, huh?

Lena: You were proud because this was something your mother shared with you, something she did she could show you, a way she could inspire you.

Davis: (suddenly feeling ambivalent about hating her mother) Maybe. I don't know.

Lena: Well, it would have been a lot harder to be proud of your mom, if she told you she was making something that would completely fuck you up. Imagine that, Davis. Imagine she made something you could never see, no matter how old you were. You'd have hated that.

Davis: (sighing) I know.

Lena: For all her faults, Davis, your mother never wrote anything you were forbidden from seeing. She never had to protect you from anything about her that would be disturbing to a kid, or an adult. She never had any dark secrets. She was easy to love. I remember how easy it was for you to love her.

Davis: I wish I could love her again, sometimes.

Lena: Don't you miss having her in your life?

Davis: Yeah, but I shouldn't.

Lena: Why not?

Davis: She's a bad person.

Lena: Is she really a bad person or are you just angry with her for still being with your dad?

Davis: (looking down) I'm angry because … she loves me. She only loves me.

Lena: What do you mean?

Davis: (quietly) She doesn't like me. She never liked me, Lena.

Lena: Maybe she just clashes with your personality, or maybe it's the exhibitionism. Maybe she can't get her head around the idea of a parent doing porn when their kid is a teenager.

Davis: (sighing) She thinks I'm a bad parent.

Lena: Well, you think you're a good parent. That's what's important here.

Davis: (shaking her head) I don't know what I am, Lena. All I know is the one thing I wish I had more of.

Lena: Which is?

Davis: …Love.

Lena: You don't feel loved?

Davis: (looking very sad) I'm not easy to love, am I? I know that's what you're trying to tell me, Lena. I'm not stupid.

Lena: (patiently) Davis, I'm trying to tell you how lovable you are.

Davis: (distraught) But I'm making a life that's bad for Max. I'm hurting him. Isn't that what this is all about?

Lena: No, it's about the fact that you're making something pretty awesome. And it's something you want him to be proud of you for making.

Davis: (with desperation in her eyes) I just want him to enjoy being around me again. I need that.

Lena: I know you do.

Davis: I need us to be close again. It's not enough that he's my son. I need companionship in my home. I can't function without it. I really can't. I'll lose Ben if I don't have Max back on my side. If I lose Ben, Max won't be living with a mother and a father.

Lena: Well, that's understandable. And it's not an unrealistic goal. I don't see why you and Max can't be friends again.

Davis: Maybe I should write again. I think about that sometimes.

Lena: (shaking her head) It's best not to live in the past, Davis.

Davis: But Max loved my poems, Lena. And maybe it doesn't matter if he's the only person who loves them.

Lena: (irritated) But Davis, come on. Think about ways of spending your time that are actually productive. It's not productive to write for an audience of one.

Davis: But in my case, that would be productive.

Lena: Davis, was your writing really that good? Do you really think you had any talent?

Davis: I don't know, but my writing was a way I really connected with my son. We had such a strong bond over that stuff. Maybe too strong a bond.

Lena: Well, you can write again if you want. But I honestly don't think you need to write shitty poems in order for Max to be proud of you.

Davis: Then how do I do it? How do I make him proud of me again?

Lena: Well, I can't tell you what you should or shouldn't do. All I can say is, if I were you, I'd get closer to Max, talk to him, be someone who he finds fascinating. And in doing that, I wouldn't change anything about myself or my sexuality. I'd have integrity.

Davis: But how do I do that when he's so distant from me?

Lena: Maybe you should stop pushing him away.

Davis: But how am I pushing him away? I don't even understand that.

Lena: What don't you understand?

Davis: (frustrated with herself) It feels like he's the one who's pushing me away. He won't stop pushing me away, Lena.

Lena: Davis, I'll say this as many times as I need to until you wake up and actually listen. You're pushing Max away from all the things you want him to be proud of.

Davis: ...Like porn?

Lena: Yes. You're definitely pushing him away from porn. You're not as innocent as you think you are.

Davis: (confused) But that's what I'm supposed to do. I'm his mother.

Lena: (giggling) Since when do you give a shit about what you're 'supposed' to do?

Davis: Well, I don't normally, but this is different.

Lena: How is it different?

Davis: (thinking hard) . . . You know, I don't know anymore. I'm so fucking confused now.

Lena: Davis, there's nothing to be confused about. You're a porn star; you're good at it. People say you shouldn't be a porn star and you defy them; you do it anyway. That's all Max has to be proud of!

Davis: I guess if there's one thing I want to teach Max, it's that he doesn't need to cave into peer pressure.

Lena: Absolutely. You're setting a great example.

Davis: . . . I really hope I am.

Lena: You want him to know he doesn't have to be like everybody else.

Davis: Definitely. He's too cool to be like everybody else.

Lena: He's amazingly cool.

Davis: I've never met anyone so cool. And so smart.

Lena: Max is brilliant and funny and mature in so many ways and it's all because of you.

Davis: Well, some of it's because of him.

Lena: You know, when I first talked to Max when he was ten, it was literally like meeting an adult. It was one of the strangest experiences I've ever had.

Davis: That's because he's not really a kid, Lena. His body's fourteen, but mentally… I think he's actually older than me.

Lena: You think Max is an adult? Like a genuine adult trapped in a kid's body?

Davis: (like she's amazed at what she's telling Lena) Yeah... if I'm honest, I think that's actually what I'm dealing with. I'm raising someone who doesn't need it. I don't know how you're supposed to parent a grownup. He's an old soul and I'm a young one.

Lena: I can't even imagine what that's like.

Davis: Most of the time, it's not even like being a mother. It's like hanging out with my best friend. That's how it was until last year. So now it's like my best friend doesn't like me anymore.

Lena: And what does that feel like?

Davis: (tearing up) It feels like I'm just his mom.

Lena: What's wrong with that?

Davis: (sighing) It was fine in the beginning… but not once he turned into Max.

Lena: What happened then?

Davis: I couldn't handle being a normal mother. It was too painful. We were way closer than that.

Lena: But why did you let your relationship with Max evolve like that?

Davis: I don't know, Lena. It was instinctive for both of us.

Lena: But you're the parent, Davis. That's your job.

Davis: I really didn't choose this. I wouldn't have chosen this. It just happened… and it stayed like that until last year. When I brought Inside Davis into our family home, everything changed.

Lena: Of course it did. Max felt like you were trying to make him a part of your sex life.

Davis: (shaking her head) You know, I'm such a stupid bitch sometimes. I make myself so angry. I sabotage the best things I've got going for me. I always do that.

Lena: Well, self-loathing isn't healthy, Davis. It's always better to forgive yourself.

Davis: But it's so hard for me to forgive myself sometimes. When I can see what I'm actually doing with my life, it can be so fucking painful.

Lena: But why are you in pain? What do you think you've been doing?

Davis: I've been giving Max double messages.

Lena: Well yeah, double messages tend to push people away.

Davis: I know they do. They're horrible.

Lena: You lose intimacy when you push kids away. And what you want more than anything from Max is intimacy, right?

Davis: (looking very sad) I hope that's not selfish of me. I know I'm supposed to be happy being 'Mom' but… I just can't do it, Lena…

Lena: But why? Why is it so hard to do what every mother can do?

Davis: (with tears in her eyes) He's not just my son.

Lena: He's your best friend? Maybe your only friend?

Davis: (sighing) …Yeah. It's stupid and sad but… he's the love of my life. I love him like… I don't know how to describe it except to say that it's not motherly. That's all I can say.

Lena: Do you know what this sounds like?

Davis: What?

Lena: It sounds like you want to be in a relationship with Max. It sounds like you're in love.

Davis: (speaking hesitantly) I guess… I am in love… But I can't let Max know that about me, Lena. It would hurt him so much.

Lena: Well, if somebody loved me the way you love him, I'd need to know it.

Davis: (worried) Even if they were your mother?

Lena: Of course! I'd want to know it in a clear and unambiguous way.

Davis: (shaking her head) I don't know. Max knows he's my angel. He knows that I love him more than anyone else in whole world, but he doesn't know that I'm in love and I think it should stay that way.

Lena: Are you sure he doesn't know?

Davis: I am sure. I hold that in for him.

Lena: Maybe you don't.

Davis: What do you mean?

Lena: Maybe you have a sexual outlet for those feelings. Maybe that's what Inside Davis is really about. It's your way of reaching out to Max.

Davis: I so hope that's not true, Lena.

Lena: Why?

Davis: 'Cause Inside Davis… just feels absolutely right. Being filmed having sex is like saying all the things I can't say in words. All the things that would hurt people.

Lena: But is that really fair?

Davis: (sighing) I don't fucking know… Life isn't fair.

Lena: I mean, you get to have this huge sexual outlet for all your feelings you can't express in words. But what do Ben and Max have?

Davis: (annoyed) I don't give a fuck about Ben's dick, Lena. He can fuck whoever the hell he wants. It's Ben who limits Ben.

Lena: And what about Max?

Davis: I can't help him fuck girls. He has to work that out on his own. I can make sure he wears a condom, but apart from that, I don't talk to him about what turns him on.

Lena: Never?

Davis: Once he said he likes women who look like older versions of me. That was the only time he ever told me anything about his sexuality. I find porn on his computer all the time. That's how I know he's straight.

Lena: What kind of porn is it?

Davis: It's MILF porn. Older women. But nobody I've done scenes with.

Lena: Do the actresses look kind of like you?

Davis: Less pretty, but yeah. Same build, same hair.

Lena: Well, again, it sounds like the porn that would get him off the hardest is the porn you don't want him to watch – the porn you're making.

Davis: (looking sad and scared) You could be right about that. I don't know what… or how I should–

Lena: (interrupting abruptly) Davis, this really isn't as complicated as you're making it out to be.

Davis: What's so simple about it?

Lena: Remember the imagination exercise we did?

Davis: Yeah.

Lena: If you were a fourteen-year-old kid with hormones going crazy from sexual frustration, it would be confusing to be told that the very porn that got you off the hardest was also the porn that would damage and hurt you. That's a total head fuck.

Davis: (shaking her head) That is a terrible head fuck.

Lena: And that's the head fuck that comes with having you as a mother.

Davis: I don't want to do this to Max anymore. It needs to stop. I can see that now.

Lena: Well, why isn't Max chasing other girls his age?

Davis: I think he's shy and embarrassed around girls his age. He's not socially confident.

Lena: And what are your thoughts on that?

Davis: I wish I could help him.

Lena: Why don't you then?

Davis: Confidence isn't really something you can teach. It just happens. It happened to me when I was about sixteen.

Lena: (giggling) Davis, I was there. You don't have to remind me you turned into the town whore. Your mom wasn't wrong about you.

Davis: (smiling) Yeah… it hurts to admit that.

Lena: Well, are you expecting Max to turn into the campus stud in a few years?

Davis: I don't know. I want Max to do what's right for Max. I want him to take whatever opportunities he gets from the opposite sex, but I don't want him to be pressured into anything he doesn't feel comfortable with.

Lena: Well, I wouldn't worry about that, honestly. He's fourteen. Right now, Max shouldn't really have any sexual "opportunities." Fourteen is too early to have sex. It's a better time to practice making out and holding hands with pretty girls.

Davis: Yeah, but this is Max we're talking about. I know for a fact he'd have uber game if he wasn't so fucking shy. If he started becoming more of an extravert, girls would be all over him, Lena.

Lena: I don't doubt that, Davis.

Davis: I know this is awful but if Max wasn't my son… if we weren't related and I met Max when I was a teenager–

Lena: (interrupting and giggling) You wouldn't have stolen Ben from me. You'd have started a family with Max! You'd fuck his brains out.

Davis: Isn't that just wrong?

Lena: No. It's kind of sweet.

Davis: (smiling) You think so?

Lena: Max is your perfect guy, Davis. He's what you always described, when you used to tell me about the guy you wanted to marry.

Davis: That's because Max is the guy I wanted to marry. It's like I'm being punished for what I did to Ben.

Lena: Why do you say that?

Davis: (sighing) I could have been with my dream man, Lena. I could be with that guy now, if I just had more self-control. I was so young and dumb when I took advantage of Ben… If I was nicer to you, if I was a better friend, I wouldn't be living in Downey. I'd live here in Pasadena and I wouldn't have met you on my own, in this bookstore. I'd be standing next to my husband, my dream husband.

Lena: (smiling sadly) And that's why I wish you didn't take advantage of Ben.

Davis: (looking sad) …I'm so, so sorry, Lena. I still feel terrible about all of this. I never wanted to ruin your life. That was the last thing I ever wanted.

Lena: You didn't ruin my life Davis, but I always knew Ben wasn't right for you. You made me doubt that for many years, but now I know what should have happened.

Davis: What should have happened?

Lena: You should have let me marry Ben. If you let me have Ben, you could have been with someone like Max, which is what you really wanted, isn't it?

Davis: (sighing with great sadness) My whole life… everything… it would all be totally different.

Lena: It would, Davis. You wouldn't have to either shove down your feelings or hide your body from the man you love.

Davis: I know! You could be with Ben and I'd be happy. I'd be living in Pasadena writing books or making movies. Who knows?

Lena: Well, there's no point in wallowing in regret. We are where we are now. I have to find a man. And whether are not you stay with Ben, you have to be your son's mom.

Davis: (tearing up again) I love Max so much, Lena. It scares the shit out of me… how much I love him. Sometimes I think he'd do better… being raised by someone else… I'm too fucked up…

Lena holds Davis's hand, looking deeply into her eyes.

Lena: Davis, you're no more fucked up than me. The difference is, you're also a wonderful mother to the most amazing kid I've ever known. He's proof of that wonderfulness.

Davis: (tears streaming down her face) But I'm not, Lena... That's why I'm a porn star.

Lena: What do you mean?

Davis: (crying) I think I did it to gross him out…. We were getting too close…

Lena: You don't think you were trying to reach out to him?

Davis: (quietly sobbing) I had to make him disgusted with me… I had to push him away from me, or else we would have done something… something horrible…

Lena hugs Davis and whispers in her ear.

Lena: That's why it's important not to push him away now, Davis. He needs you.

Davis: (crying on Lena's shoulder) And I need him… I need him more than I need sex….

Lena wipes Davis's tears with her napkin.

Lena: (in soothing voice) Then Max… needs to know… that there's absolutely nothing wrong with everyone in the world wanting to make love to his mother. You're not a normal mom, Davis. You're better than normal.

Davis: (sniffing) I know I am. I'm fucked up but I'm still better than most women.

Lena: Then don't be like most women! Don't use your career as an excuse to abandon your son.

Davis: (sighing) Porn isn't something that should push us apart, is it?

Lena: (smiling) It should bring you together.

Davis: It needs to.

Lena: I mean, what is Inside Davis? It's you. It's Max's mother, his best friend, the woman who loves him more than anyone.

Davis: It is; it's me. That's all it is.

Lena: It's recreation; it's fun and it's natural, like his own sexuality.

Davis: Of course it is. But sometimes it's hard feeling what you know is true.

Lena: Well, does Max know it's true?

Davis: I don't know but one thing's for sure: I can't just assume he knows it anymore.

Lena: I think you may be right.

Davis: I'm the one who needs to make sure he actually knows my porn is good for our family. Max needs to know this, backwards and forwards. I can't rely on Ben for that. I have to communicate.

Lena: Sex shouldn't be associated with shame, any kind of shame.

Davis: Absolutely. No woman's sexuality is ever a threat to Max – not even mine.

Lena: And Max should never be scared of his feelings, especially his sexual feelings, whatever they might be.

Davis: Yep. He needs to know any sexual feelings he has are absolutely okay.

Lena: Well, then are you okay with him having sexual feelings for you? Are you okay with him watching your porn?

Davis: I'm very much okay with it now. I'd prefer he watch me, to be honest.

Lena: (smiling) I'm starting to wish I had a mom like you!

Lena is surprised to find the idea of Davis having incestuous sex with Max deeply arousing. However, she is fairly confident that Davis wouldn't do anything that extreme in real life. Lena thinks Davis is an idiot, but she doesn't think Davis is *that* big of an idiot.

Davis, on the other hand, is feeling grateful to Lena for helping her see all the ways she can become a better parent.

Davis: I know I'm not perfect. I need to do more around the house, now. I get it. Max shouldn't be doing all this shit for me, when it's my job to make sure he's okay. I think I'll get a cookbook on Amazon this weekend. We'll do a shop and see what happens in the kitchen. I'll try and cook something.

Lena: That's a good idea. I would also suggest talking to Max about his feelings, especially about Inside Davis.

Davis: Yeah.

Lena: Talk to him about porn and what turns him on. I mean, he's a grownup mentally, so this would actually be an age-appropriate conversation.

Davis: Yeah, we do need to be more open about these things.

Lena: Max has to know that even though he's unconfident, his mother knows him well enough to give him what he needs, especially the stuff he doesn't have the confidence to ask for.

Davis: I'm gonna work so fucking hard at that, Lena. I know I'm not naturally good at reading people, but he deserves good communication from me. He deserves the best mom I can be for him.

Lena: Well, you have to read him, then. That's not optional.

Davis: (sighing) I know… I know… I'll learn it… I have to…

Lena: I mean, how on earth can you make him feel happy if you can't read him?

Davis: (determined) I need to make him feel good. I don't want him disgusted with me anymore. That's not good for our relationship.

Lena: Max needs his mom to make him feel good, doesn't he?

Davis: (shaking her head) It's so confusing… knowing what to do…

Lena: (speaking softly) You don't have to feel confused if you can make him feel good.

Davis: What do you mean?

Lena: Well, when Max was a baby, he was always in your arms. You were always holding him, kissing him. The bond between you guys was… tactile.

Davis: It was.

Lena: And now you've lost that bond and guess what? You can't even be close anymore.

Davis: I should never have lost that bond with him.

Lena: Maybe that's why he doesn't watch your porn…

Davis: I've been totally irresponsible with Max, Lena. But I can fix that now.

Lena: So, what steps are you going to take to repair your relationship with him? What are you gonna do, for instance, when you go home tonight?

Davis: I'm gonna talk to him about what turns him on. I'm gonna tell him jacking off to me is absolutely okay and that I want us to be close again. He'll know I'm not a boring, horrible mom. I'll prove it to him.

Lena: But you don't have to prove anything, Davis. It's already been documented in every bit of footage you've ever had sex in.

Davis: What do you mean?

Lena looks into Davis's eyes and strokes her hair with her right hand, just like a good mother.

Lena: (putting on a tender smile) If Max ever watches anything you've done, he'll see that he has the most beautiful, confident, and sensuous mother a boy could ever dream of. She's practically a goddess!

Davis: You really think so?

Lena: Well, think about it, Davis. If Max ever watches you eat pussy or take in a huge cock, what's he really looking at? It's not just sex, is it?

Davis: He's looking at the woman who loves him more than anyone, the woman who's teaching him he can be anything he wants to be.

Lena: (smiling) Exactly! He's looking at the woman who gave birth to him because she needed to give birth to somebody. She couldn't stop herself then, just like she can't stop herself now.

Davis: (feeling proud) I don't ever stop myself from doing anything I want. It's not in my nature.

Lena: And that's incredibly important, honey. That's why, if Max ever watches your porn, he'll be jacking off to the most courageous and daring person in his life; the one person who's not afraid to just put herself out there and show the world who she really is, from head to toe. That's why he'll cum so hard watching you, Davis. He'll cum harder than your biggest fans.

Davis: (wistfully) I hope so. I really, really hope so. That would be so wonderful…

Lena: You're beautiful and fearless and free, but you're still Max's mother. That's what everyone wants in a parent, deep down.

Davis: (deeply touched by Lena's words) You really think so? You think I'm that good of a mom?

Lena: Of course you are! Most women are boring prudes. They suppress their sexuality, once they start a family. And then they get boring and bossy.

Davis: I've noticed that, actually. Ben hates his mom. She can't think for herself and she's catholic.

Lena: (smiling tenderly) Well, ever since I've known you girl, you couldn't do anything except be yourself. In fact, I've never met a mom that's been so fucking brave. You've done things that would tear apart most families. Think about it!

Davis: (smiling) See, this is how I'm trying to inspire other women. I wanna reach out to teenage girls who don't have positive role models.

Lena: I think you're an amazing role model for teenage girls.

Davis: I hope so 'cause I don't want to live in a world where teenage girls feel ashamed of their sexuality. I don't! If a kid like me ever tells her mom and dad she wants to be a porn star, I want her to get love and validation. I don't want her to be shamed for it, like I was.

Lena: (smiling) Maybe someday… the whole family could sit down and watch the porn with her. Maybe they could validate her that way. It could be like a… Sunday dinner ritual.

Davis: (laughing) I don't know about that…

Lena: Why not? I mean, objectively speaking, scientifically speaking, you're maybe the sexiest women in America. If I was your mom, I'd feel blessed to know that I gave that to society. Forget about Max or Ben. It baffles me that your entire family isn't just drowning in pride. You're probably the most important person in your family.

Davis: (smiling) You really think so?

Lena: Well, you're probably giving more people orgasms than any person in your family ever will. That's an amazing achievement! I mean, you're not just getting off your co-stars. You're giving pleasure to anyone else who watches you – even the kids with lazy parents, or the hacker kids.

Davis: (uncomfortable) You know, that's weird. I never thought about the hacker kids. That's kinda fucked up. Some of them are like, nine.

Lena: (giggling) Davis, you were an amazing hacker kid! You could program before I learned how to plug in a fucking modem.

Davis: I was good, wasn't I? I remember showing you porn on my dad's computer back in sixth grade.

Lena: You managed to download forty seconds of grainy Jodie Green on your dad's PC, back in 1993, the day after Clinton got sworn in. I'll never forget that.

Davis: I remember, but it's still weird. The idea of children watching me. That's just–

Lena: (interrupting) But you looked at porn all the time when you were a child, Davis. You used to steal your dad's magazines and hide them under your bed.

Davis: (smiling to herself) It's wrong but I was a sneaky fucker.

Lena: (giggling) You still are, bitch.

Davis: I know, but children watching me today... That's not good. It's too early.

Lena: Well, maybe. But on the other hand, what harm did watching porn ever do to you? Did watching porn as a child ever stop you from doing anything you wanted to do in your life?

Davis: No, I guess it didn't, really. It sort of brought me to where I am today. I've always been fascinated by it.

Lena: Well, it's obvious why. Porn is a way people completely separate sex from intimacy and love. That's fascinating to me too.

Davis: Well, yeah. That's what sexual liberation's all about. Sex with no love and no boundaries.

Lena: Davis, I know at this point that you're like a huge internet celebrity and an important feminist icon. But do you see yourself as more than that? Do you see yourself as liberating people?

Davis: Well, people tell me I might be one of the most important celebrities on the internet, today. That's what's so amazing about Inside Davis.

Lena: And how does that feel? How does it feel to be so admired?

Davis: (enthusiastically) It's like, the biggest adrenaline rush in the world!

Lena: Tell me more about that.

Davis: It's exciting like… nothing you could ever imagine, Lena. It feels like being on drugs a lot of the time. Not acid. It's more like…snorting coke in the 80s, in a Duran Duran video.

Lena: (smiling) Sounds like it.

Davis: So yeah, on the one hand, it's totally awesome. But on the other hand… it would be nice if people showed some gratitude for what I do, you know? I give people all this joy and happiness, but you'd never know that, if you saw the way some of them treat me sometimes.

Lena: You don't feel appreciated by the public?

Davis: (annoyed) Not really.

Lena: What do they do that makes you feel unappreciated?

Davis: I just wish people were, I don't know, kinder and more sensitive towards me. More respectful.

Lena: How do they disrespect you?

Davis: (sighing) I just wish guys stopped assuming that because I'm trying to make them cum… that I would ever fuck them. And it would be nice if women actually looked up to me, instead of putting me down all the time. I could liberate so many women, if they listened to me.

Lena: Hmm… maybe the problem here is more philosophical.

Davis: (confused) What do you mean?

Lena: People confuse sexual liberation with democracy.

Davis: Are you talking about guys feeling entitled to women's bodies?

Lena: No, I'm talking about the fact that sexual desire isn't really democratic. Liberating desire doesn't mean that great sex comes to anyone who wants it. With sexual liberation, even nice people who deserve sex won't necessarily get laid. Erotic desire privileges attractive people over everyone else.

Davis: (emphatically) Totally! Sex isn't about equality. It's about how people are different.

Lena: Yeah and people assume sexual liberation means freedom for everyone to have more sex, especially the sex everyone fantasises about. But that, of course, is bullshit. The reality is only beautiful women ever get that freedom…beautiful women and the small number of hot people they choose to be with. Or in your case, the slightly larger number of hot people. (giggling)

Davis: (laughing) Jesus, you nailed it, Lena. You just put into words what I've been thinking for so many years.

Lena: Well, this is just the world we live in, sweetie. Sexual liberation was never about me, or the British guys you insulted earlier. It's about hot chicks. It's about people like you.

Davis: (nodding) Right and everyone benefits from that, if they don't let their egos get in the way.

Lena: (sarcastically) Of course we do! I mean, those of us who are out of your league, we all benefit so much from watching you. Don't we?

Davis puts her hand on Lena's shoulder.

Davis: (smiling reassuringly) Lena, you know you're in my league. Don't worry about that, okay? You know I think your mind is sexy.

Lena: But that's because you know me, Davis. If you didn't know me, I wouldn't be in your league, would I?

Davis takes her hand off Lena's shoulder.

Davis: (matter of factly) Probably not.

Lena: And that means if you didn't know me, you'd be pretty pissed off if I ever started hitting on you in a club or something. You'd feel insulted, right?

Davis: (shaking her head) Oh, more than that. I'd be enraged at you.

Lena: Really?

Davis: I'm sorry Lena, but I feel very strongly that people should stick to their own kind.

Lena: What, you mean racially?

Davis: No, in terms of beauty. If you have a sexy mind and a beautiful person finds it hot, that's maybe the one exception. But other than that, if you don't look nice, you should be realistic and hit on people that actually want you. That's what porn's all about, I guess. It keeps ugly men satisfied, so they don't try and punch above their weight and harass women they should stay away from.

Lena: You think porn lowers their confidence, when they approach a woman like you in real life?

Davis: (nodding her head) Hopefully it does. And the more I think about it… porn might actually do this for ugly women too, which is also pretty cool.

Lena: You think porn stops ugly women from hitting on hot guys?

Davis: No, it stops fugly ass chicks from hitting on women like me. It protects beautiful women.

Lena: Okay.

Davis: (definitely) And we need that! You'll never know what it's like being gorgeous, Lena. It's horrible. Everyone looks at you like you're a fucking piece of meat.

Lena: But Davis, when you say 'everyone' who do you mean? Do you mean people who aren't as beautiful as you? Is that what you're trying to say?

Davis: (shrugging her shoulders) Maybe.

Lena: Then… why is your whole career about trying so hard to make those people cum? Why are you trying so hard to get off people you'd never fuck in a million years?

Davis: I've thought about this a lot. I think maybe, deep down, I'd like to have a healthier relationship with people who look more normal than me. You know, people who look like you.

Lena: What does that mean, 'people who look like me'? People who are overweight? People with brown skin? Women that aren't gorgeous?

Davis: I mean people who look frumpy and unconfident, people who dress badly 'cause they can't pick out clothes that flatter their flabby bodies. You know, people who need self-control, people who can't stop eating shit that puffs out their face.

Lena: Is that how you see me?

Davis: Well, I'm not really attracted to Mexicans either, but that's not about body shape. That's more about skin pigmentation.

Lena: (with a raised eyebrow) My skin colour bothers you?

Davis: There's nothing wrong with your skin, Lena. It's just that most Latinos look dirty to me. I'm very sensitive about that kinda thing.

Lena: (confused) But if that's true, how could you be attracted to Manolo and Benji? Or Ben?

Davis: Ben used to have a beautiful face and a great body, so I could ignore his skin. I could ignore it until he started gaining weight and losing his hair. I don't have that problem with Manolo and Benji though. They have beautiful skin like me.

Lena: You mean they can pass for white dudes?

Davis: Yep.

Lena: Hmm… But aren't a lot of Latino men with brown skin… fans of your work?

Davis: (smiling) They fucking love me, Lena. Latinos are probably my biggest demographic.

Lena: Then are you doing porn because you want to have a healthier relationship with them? Do you think you have a good relationship with darker Latinos?

Davis: I think I do. I bring joy to their lives and I'm happy to do that for them, as long as they don't bother me.

Lena: (smiling mischievously) I suppose in a way, this is important work you're doing for the Latino community. You're helping people who look like me cope with the fact that they could never get with a white chick like you.

Davis: (feeling proud) Absolutely. What I do is like charity, in a way.

Lena: Well, yeah. It's your way of helping the less fortunate.

Davis: (thinking hard) I mean… in a broader sense, doing porn is about altruism. It's my way of giving back to society… Most of society isn't hot enough to fuck me, but I can give back by letting them watch me have sex and making sure they cum harder than anything. If they don't expect more than that, if they're respectful and polite and they don't slut shame me, I give 'em pleasure no beautiful woman would ever give them in real life.

Lena: You mean, no beautiful woman like you.

Davis: Totally! I'd rather die than fuck someone I'm not attracted to, Lena. I don't want to live in a world where women feel pressure to do anything they don't want to do. When it comes to sex, women should be in control.

No man should have sex with a woman he's not good enough for.

Lena: Davis, when you say 'women', do you mean 'women' or do you really mean 'beautiful women'?

Davis: (thinking hard) Beautiful women, probably. We're the ones that are most oppressed today.

Lena: That's an interesting take on things. Do you mind if I ask you why you think you're more oppressed than I am?

Davis: It's because men don't feel entitled to your body, Lena. They feel entitled to bodies like mine. That's who they wanna fuck: beautiful women.

Lena: (sighing) ...That's very sad, but you're probably right. Men are shallow.

Davis: (annoyed) It's not shallow to respond positively to beauty! That's what makes us human, Lena.

Lena: Then are you happy Max is beautiful?

Davis: It's a huge relief, honestly. I'd find it so hard to love an ugly child. I could do it, but I'd have to really push myself, you know?

Lena: (smiling to herself) I know.

Davis: Loving Max has never been a problem for me, no matter how old or young he is. When I look at him sometimes, it's like I'm staring into a strange mirror, like I'm staring at a younger version of myself, a male Davis with a deep voice. He's like a mini-me, you know?

Lena: I can see that. He does have your eyes.

Davis: He does! He's fourteen but he already looks like a fucking underwear model, Lena. Ben's been encouraging him to work out and oh my God, sweet Jesus, you should see his pecs! Do you wanna see a picture of him with his shirt off?

Lena: No, not really.

Davis: (with pride) Are you sure? The real thing's hotter than anything you could think up, Lena. Trust me.

Lena: I trust you. I'm just more curious about something else.

Davis: What?

Lena: Are you proud of the fact that your son doesn't have brown skin?

Davis: Well… I'm not racist, but I am happy he looks like me. So… yeah. I guess I am proud of that.

Lena: Would you find it harder to love him if he didn't look like you? Would you find it harder to love him if he looked like me?

Davis: (shrugging her shoulders) I don't know. Maybe…

16. SEX: Moving On

While in rush hour traffic, Davis thinks hard about the many issues raised in her conversation with Lena, as she drives back to her spacious home in North Downey. It's raining again.

For Davis, her encounter with Lena was not just important, but an emotionally cleansing experience. This cleansing was something Davis needed for many years. Like any long conversation with Lena, there were invaluable gifts in the exchange. There were pearls of wisdom to contemplate and mull over. Lena's advice once again seemed like the perfect tool for helping Davis sort her life out, allowing Davis insights into the world that she could never comprehend on her own.

Yes, Lena did give Davis some harsh truths. But they were the kind of harsh truths that were pathways into possibilities, possibilities Davis was far more excited by than the awkward and tense family life she had created for herself. As kids, Lena gave Davis many harsh truths and though these harsh truths were painful to hear, they always made Davis feel like she knew all the best choices available to her. Davis nearly always felt this way as a teen, when she and Lena would walk and talk on the streets of Pasadena.

In the years after Lena drifted away from her, Davis felt uncertain and confused about most of her choices. But after her latest conversation with Lena, Davis suddenly felt the thrill of certainty, once again. This was the same certainty she felt when Lena goaded her into doing self-destructive and dangerous things, back when they were students at Warren High School.

Before she arrived at Vroman's, Davis knew she needed a profound change in her life, a change that would make her marriage bearable, whilst making Max feel close to her. Davis had wanted this change for years, but she never understood what such a change could realistically be. None of the available options ever seemed terribly desirable. But after chatting to her old friend, one option suddenly seemed ideal, like it would magically solve all of Davis's problems. Lena never told Davis to take this option, but it seemed like everything Lena said suggested this was the best one.

This option had an additional appeal for Davis: thinking about it aroused her intensely.

She had never been so wet.

Davis was so close to having an orgasm that her pleasure was preventing her from concentrating on her driving. After nearly running over some Mexican children, Davis decided to pull over and stop at a McDonalds in the drab and grimy city of Pico Rivera. Pico Rivera existed somewhere between Downey and Pasadena.

While in McDonalds, Davis ordered a bag of fries and after quickly gobbling them down, she practically ran into the women's bathroom. Davis masturbated for a good fifteen minutes in one of the stalls, thinking of what she was going to do when she got back home. She came harder than she had cum in years, during what was one of the most intense multiple orgasms of her life. Frigging herself off in the woman's toilet, Davis's moans were loud and guttural. On her way out of the bathroom, an elderly woman stopped her to ask if she was in any pain. Davis replied that it was just a stomach upset she always got after having fries.

Driving past Pico Rivera into Downey, Davis was breathing heavily and smiling. She couldn't wait to get home. She especially couldn't wait to see Max and change both of their lives for the better. She was playing music from her iPhone, singing along loudly to 'Butts Tits Money,' a funky pop song from the 'Life' album by Knower. Davis loved this song, often playing it over and over again, while she was driving. Today, the song felt like an anthem, an anthem encouraging Davis to be a truly liberated woman, a woman unafraid to be courageous and daring, a brave and inspirational role model for 21st century girls everywhere.

As she finally pulled into the driveway of her Downey home, Davis turned off the music and absorbed the sounds of suburban silence, trying to calm down the waves of adrenaline in her body. For a minute, she thought about how one day, she was going to leave Southern California and bring Ben and Max with her to New York. Davis felt the Big Apple would suit the three of them far more than Los Angeles ever did. But this thought was interrupted as she started thinking about sex and love, once more. In a way that was completely out of her control, Davis's panties begin to dampen for a second time.

During the brief walk from her car to the front door, Davis was feeling extraordinarily impulsive. In fact, she'd never felt this impulsive before. It was as if something was taking her over. Her heart was racing and her palms were sweaty.

Two days later, Ben was filing divorce papers, while Max was absolutely and utterly devastated. Two days earlier, there had been an "incident" between Davis and Max. During that incident, Davis said and did things Max always assumed his mother would never say or do, things Max assumed no mother would ever say or do to her child. Afterwards, Max was shocked and horrified. Davis was shocked that Max was shocked and horrified. Davis was shocked by how much she hurt him and how quickly she destroyed their beautiful relationship. When Ben found out what Davis had done, he started crying and screaming. Ben screamed that Davis was disgusting, that he hated her and that he was going to kill her.

As Davis screamed back how sorry she was, Ben punched her hard in the face, knocking her to the floor. Davis blacked out before she hit the ground.

Luckily, she didn't hit her head when she landed, but in her unconscious state, Ben didn't check to see if his wife was okay. Instead, he screamed obscenities, repeatedly kicked her face and spat on her. Max screamed for him to stop, trying his hardest to pull his raging dad away from his unconscious mother. Ben was so angry he wound up also punching Max in the face. When Ben saw Max fall to the floor, he started shrieking and punching himself in the head.

Max got up and hugged Ben, as this was the only way to get his father's violence to stop. Ben wept and sobbed in his son's arms for a good ten minutes. This was one of the few moments in Max's life where he actually felt close to his father. It would also be the last.

When Davis awoke alone on her cold hard floor, she had swollen eyes and a broken nose. Although her face was bruised and covered in blood, she felt deep down that she deserved Ben's violence. For the first time since she could remember, Davis felt like absolute and utter trash, like she didn't deserve to breathe. Knowing the emotional pain she caused Max hurt her more than anything she had felt in her thirty four years of life. In fact, it was far more devastating to her than it was to Max.

It hurt so hard she couldn't even cry; she could barely move. It was as if Davis had stabbed her own heart – the blood slowly dripping over her internal organs. If Davis were stronger emotionally, she would have happily killed herself. That would be far nicer than the agonising pain of knowing how much she hurt the love of her life. Davis had never known pain so bleak and visceral; the physical pain of Ben's beating was mild in comparison.

After Ben calmed down, he immediately wanted to call the police. He was even willing to be prosecuted for the beating he gave his wife, so long as she paid heavily for what she did to Max. But it was Max who convinced Ben not to go down this road. Max, more than anything, didn't want to see his mother go to prison. So he told his dad that having to live with what she had done as a free woman would be a far worse punishment.

This wasn't true, but Ben was gullible enough to believe it. Ben's gullibility was one of the reasons Max always felt like he could never really relate to his father.

After the display of violence Max witnessed his father unleash upon his mother, Max went from feeling distant towards Ben, to actively disliking him. Watching Ben kick his unconscious mother's face, Max lost all respect for his father. The kindness Ben exhibited most of the time suddenly seemed like it was fake. From this point onwards, Max and Ben spoke to each other, only when they had to.

Lena was the second person to talk to Ben about what Davis had done. Unlike Max, Lena thought Davis should go to prison, but Ben was firm in siding with his son over anyone else, as Max was the true victim in all of this. Yet despite Ben's disagreement with Lena, she was still sympathetic and understanding when Ben sobbed over the phone to her. Ben told Lena he was simply in shock over what Davis had done, as it seemed out of character for his "sweet and loving" wife. When Ben said Davis was no longer the woman he had loved for fifteen years, Lena corrected him and said Davis was actually expressing her true character. Lena insisted that Davis was always quite sick and twisted. When Ben protested, Lena responded that Ben was just in denial, like she had been, until she found out about Inside Davis.

Lena said that Davis's career in porn should have a been a giant red flag for Ben. She said Ben was irresponsible for not having seen this red flag and not divorcing Davis immediately. Lena said that as soon as Inside Davis began, Ben should have been fighting hard in a custody battle for Max. Lena's overall message was that Ben was basically a negligent parent who endangered the well-being of his child, but she said all of this in such a nice way that Ben couldn't really take offence.

Although Ben was a math whiz, Lena was far more intelligent than him.

That's why he didn't question any of the things she told him, especially the things that made him feel good, or simply a sense of relief, after everything his family had gone through. Lena's 'take charge' personality made Ben feel happy. Ben felt happiest when a woman took charge. He felt safest when he trusted a woman to give him orders. Ben trusted Lena to give him orders because she was brilliant, successful and Ben knew she had both his and Max's best interests at heart. Ben had also known Lena for fifteen years and throughout those years, Ben had always wondered what it would be like to fuck her.

Lena was no raving beauty, but she did have a cute bubbly brown ass. Ben had a thing for bubbly brown asses: he'd always wanted to stick his dick in one, ever since he was Max's age. You could say it was something of a lifelong dream, but it was a dream Ben never thought he could make real. He was married to a white woman, after all. Ben would only stick his dick into a bubbly brown ass if it was attached to a woman who loved him.

This is why Ben, without question, quickly changed many of his beliefs in order to get love from Lena. The two of them quickly re-started the courtship that had ended in high school when Ben impregnated Davis.

Lena was no longer the shy and unconfident teenager Ben knew as a kid. Ben was now getting painful erections whenever he talked to the successful grownup who was now an English professor at UCLA. These erections were a nice distraction from the family trauma Ben was enduring on a daily basis. Of course, Lena knew this as well. This was why she was giving Ben those erections.

Throughout the last decade and a half, Lena had become a master at flirting, especially with people who were less intelligent than her. Because of these skills, Lena always knew exactly what to say to make sure Ben had a big boner throughout the day, no matter how many times he jerked it off. This helped Ben get over his habit of daily weeping.

Unlike Davis, Lena knew the secret to understanding Ben. In order to turn him on effectively and consistently, you had to compliment him. And when Ben was frequently turned on, you could get him to do whatever you wanted. During many conversations where Lena made Ben feel like a responsible and handsome father, she hinted that if he played his cards right, he could fuck her ass one day.

Lena knew Davis didn't like anal sex. The prospect of anal thus became a massive incentive for Ben to believe whatever Lena had to say about sex and parenting. As it turns out, Lena never did let Ben fuck her ass. But with the possibility of anal sex dangling in front of him, Ben found it easier to believe things his mind naturally railed against. This meant Ben found it easier to accept Lena's more socially conservative views.

Lena believed that when you're a parent, you should do whatever you can to keep your sexuality away from your kids. Being both a sexual exhibitionist and a parent was morally wrong, because an exhibitionist is someone who doesn't have a target audience for their sexuality; an exhibitionist tries to get the world off. Lena thought that, as a parent, you shouldn't try to get the world off, because your kids are a part of that world.

So if you're trying to get off the world, that means, at least indirectly, you're also trying to get off your kids.

Lena felt this was why porn stars shouldn't be allowed to raise children.

Raising a family with a working porn star parent, according to Lena, was child abuse. After what happened with Max, Ben found it hard to disagree. But he didn't feel guilty, in part, because Lena had convinced him that he had been manipulated by Davis. Lena told Ben that although he failed many of his duties as a father, this was understandable, given his circumstances. His circumstances were that Ben had impregnated a trashy and disgusting whore that was evil – a psychotic bitch who first raped Ben and then her own son, before either of them had reached the age of consent.

Davis too felt like a trashy and disgusting whore who happened to be a psychotic rapist, not to mention an evil bitch. She suffered greatly because of these feelings, but didn't want to blame anybody but herself for them. As it happened, she didn't blame Ben for their divorce. Nor did she blame Ben and Max for wanting her to move out of their home. She didn't even blame Max for not wanting to have any further contact with her, once she did move out. She expected all these things and felt she deserved them. Davis felt like a horrible person, the most horrible person she had ever known. She felt unimaginably horrible, like a walking piece of shit.

But Davis also could sense that her horribleness was because of the choices she made, choices that she and she alone had to take responsibility for. For the first time in her life, Davis started thinking seriously about her own responsibility.

After Davis moved out of her family home in Downey, she rented a studio apartment in Whittier. She immediately stopped doing Inside Davis and began a long process of soul searching, trying to isolate what things in her life had influenced her to repeatedly make such terrible choices, again and again. She couldn't come up with many answers. She expected not to, as Davis wasn't particularly adept at self-introspection. However, she was slowly getting better at it, much to her own ignorance. The fact that she expected to be bad at self-introspection, was evidence of growing self-introspection.

With her brief career in porn, Davis had amassed enough money to live without working for at least two years. But during these years, she couldn't find much to do that excited her. She couldn't write because her brain wouldn't allow her to concentrate enough to do anything creative. On most days, Davis watched movies in the afternoon, mostly older Japanese films like 'Roshomon' and 'Ugetsu Monogatari'. In the evenings, Davis would order pizza, clean her house for a few minutes and then cry on her living room couch.

After the crying, Davis would scarf down boxes of donuts, cookies and croissants, washing it all down with large glasses of coke. Before Davis moved to Whittier, she never used to eat like this, but after everything that had happened, she didn't see any point in looking better than most women. Davis couldn't be bothered to pop any boners; she actually felt asexual. This was the first time Davis McFarlin had felt asexual since she was a child. Even the thought of having sex made her feel nauseous.

Within six months of living in her Whittier apartment, Davis had gained forty pounds. For the first time since high school, Davis was no longer a hot woman most men wanted to fuck whenever she walked into a room. She almost had a twinge of empathy for Ben and his weight issues. She almost understood how hard it is to eat healthily, when you feel like you're failing the people you love.

Shortly after Davis moved to Whittier, Lena moved into Ben and Max's family home in Downey. Within a few months of Lena moving in, Ben proposed to her. Ben didn't know that Lena made him do this. She made him propose by making Ben feel like he couldn't cope as a father without Lena's help. Unlike Davis, Ben found Max very hard to be around. Lena convinced Ben that if he were to raise Max as a single father, he would fail miserably, as his son was far too complex for him to comprehend. Lena also didn't tell Ben that once they were married, she planned on having much more of an influence on Max than Ben ever could.

Max was the kid Lena had always wanted. Now she was going to finally parent Max the way he should be parented – the way she felt Max deserved to be parented. Lena had a vision and she wanted Ben not as a partner, but as a facilitator of this vision. She also appreciated Ben's accounting skills; it was nice to have a man who was good at looking after money. More intellectual men tended to be indifferent to money.

The day of Ben and Lena's wedding, Lena had a useful epiphany, an epiphany she kept to herself. She finally understood something that had always baffled her. There was a reason Lena never felt comfortable in relationships with intellectuals (men like the cardigan wearing preppies from Pasadena and Austin). Those men all wanted a relationship with a woman who saw herself as their equal. Lena never wanted this kind of relationship, as it pushed her too far outside her comfort zone, a zone where she had an iron grip on her lovers.

Lena enjoyed having male and female friends she could spar with intellectually. She enjoyed gay men she could talk to about fashion, food and the best clubs around town. But Lena never equated these things with feeling sexual. She only felt sexual towards straight men she knew would mostly do whatever she said, without question. She occasionally had sexual feelings for women, but only women she didn't respect – women she thought were bimbos she could run circles around, intellectually. Lena had an uncanny talent for making beautiful women feel unexpected bursts of confusion and self-doubt.

She was a good actress.

When Lena flirted with straight men, she behaved like the most wild and kinky harlot, but inside, she only felt arousal at the prospect of their obedience. And the most obedient straight men, while very kind, were also typically boring and bland. Lena felt incredibly powerful when controlling boring and bland men – guys like her new husband, but not so much like her new stepson.

As both of them accepted Lena into their home, she found it easy to make strange demands without Ben giving her much resistance. Max was a different story. So, whenever Max displayed any discomfort with these demands, Lena would threaten him with various things, most frequently the loss of his many privileges. This kept Max compliant enough with whatever she wanted to do.

Lena also didn't tell Ben or Max she was regularly texting Davis. Ben and Max were strangely forbidden from looking at Lena's iPhone; it was part of the house rules. Max thought this was weird and it made him feel nervous, but Ben didn't question it. Ben would never do anything to jeopardise the constant stream of compliments and orgasms his new wife gave him.

From Ben's perspective, he was the luckiest man in the world. He had a woman who happily stroked both his cock and his ego. It was relaxing; it made him forget his troubles. Very few men seemed to have that these days. But because Ben felt so happy and content with Lena, he didn't much care what Lena did when she wasn't being the wife he had always wished Davis would be. Lena may not have been beautiful or white, but in every other way, she surpassed Davis. Because of Lena, Ben could have sex like a teenager again.

After the two of them fucked and Ben was snoring, Lena would have half hour text conversations with Davis. Lena would tell Davis there was nothing wrong with what she did to Max and that society was too backward to appreciate the level of closeness Davis tried to create in her family. Davis disagreed with Lena but was always hopeless at winning an argument. Lena also encouraged Davis to try and seduce Max again. She suggested Davis send Max clips of her masturbating, while she said his name into the camera in her sexiest porn star voice.

Lena would text this repeatedly, as Davis repeatedly texted "No!" Lena was confident Davis would never show these conversations to the police, as she would be implicating herself in the crime of committing incest with her son. This fact made Lena feel giddy, like she had a free pass to say things to Davis she'd never dare say to another human being.

One night, Davis told Lena she felt suicidal and hopeless. Davis expected Lena to give her a myriad of reasons why she should value her life. She expected Lena to tell her, with eloquence and passion, that killing herself was the worst choice Davis could ever make. But Lena surprised Davis. She not only said suicide was a great idea, but also explained why suicide was an intensely erotic act. She even asked Davis to livestream it to her, so Lena could orgasm right at the moment Davis passed over into the great beyond.

After this conversation, Davis decided she would never commit suicide, no matter how erotic anyone found it. She also decided Lena was not a good person to have in her life anymore. Davis deeply regretted that this disturbed woman was now raising her beloved son, a son who steadfastly refused to see or talk to his biological mother.

Lena was now spending a lot of time with Max. From Lena's perspective, she had thoroughly replaced both Davis and Ben as his one true parent. Lena also did everything she could to influence Max to hate his mother. But as much as Max felt he should hate Davis, he just couldn't do it consistently. He could do it on most days, but not every day.

Max knew intellectually that he should love Lena and hate Davis. He knew intellectually that Lena deserved more of his love than Davis ever did. But in the reality of Max's head, it felt much easier to love Davis and dislike his new stepmother, a stepmother he knew was (objectively) a much better parent for him. This was all incredibly confusing.

Max appreciated Lena for being a much more practical mom than Davis had ever been. Lena also made Max feel safer than Davis, like his life wasn't always so unpredictable. With Lena, Max felt like he didn't have to be his mother's best friend, but instead could see her as someone who wanted to make sure he was always okay. These were all great qualities in a mother.

Because they were great qualities, they were supposed to make Max feel good. Max told himself repeatedly that being parented like this should feel natural, as it was like the parenting most of his friends experienced. But for Max, it felt horrible. It felt far more horrible than the relationship he had with his biological mother – the woman Max's stepmother, father, and extended family encouraged him to hate with a burning and continuous passion.

In this regard, everyone seemed to put an incredible amount of pressure on Max. It felt like he only got approval or help from his family, when he went on long rants about how much he hated Davis. Max even found it useful to say mean things about his mother as a way of calming them down, when they had become enraged with him.

After Lena came into the family, Ben and Lena were enraged at Max a lot. Max often felt like this was his fault; perhaps he wasn't trying hard enough to make Lena feel welcome in his family.

By the time Max was a senior in high school, he was trying hard to bond with Lena, even though she wasn't a very fun person. He respected both her intelligence and her success as a writer and he tried to learn from her. He also tried his best to initiate deep and interesting conversations, in the hopes of impressing her with his creativity and inquisitive mind. But surprisingly, Lena now showed little interest in connecting with him in a way that was cerebral or complicated. Max was now her son and this meant Lena got her greatest joys from bossing him around. In fact, Max often felt like him and his dad were simply Lena's minions. She now seemed to tolerate only brief conversations with both of them, in-between the many physical tasks she asked them to do.

Fun conversations were things she did with her friends… not her family.

Max and Ben got Lena's approval if they were quiet and always willing to drop whatever they were doing to complete one of her laborious tasks. It was normally a manly task, a task that involved lugging around heavy furniture or cutting down trees. It was rare that Lena did anything Ben or Max asked her to do. She was rarely even present on their birthdays. Lena's womanly tasks primarily involving yelling at Max in the afternoons, while making Ben scream like clockwork every night at fifteen past eleven.

Max knew that as long as Lena was having sex with his dad, Ben had virtually no free will. Ben was like a slave to this woman… more of a slave than he had ever been to Davis. Max could never be anyone's slave, even though he still tried valiantly to break down the emotional barriers between him and his stepmother.

But even when Max was doing what Lena wanted, she often made quite scathing and sarcastic remarks at him. On more than one occasion, Lena did an impression of Max's clumsiness that really hurt his feelings. She also teased him affectionately, making fun of his inability to get along with kids his own age. Sometimes he laughed at the way she teased him because he thought it might be Lena's way of showing him love.

Other times, her constant ribbing made Max want to cry, especially when it was about Max's nervousness around girls. Lena never seemed to care about Max's feelings, unless Max had feelings she approved of. Lena didn't approve of Max being hurt by her caustic wit, so she didn't care if Max was hurt by anything she found funny.

Here, we should be mindful that Lena would say that this characterisation of her was unfair. To be fair and balanced, we'd have to acknowledge that

Lena wasn't always unpleasant to Max. She gave him some useful tips on how to manage anxiety; she taught him how to effectively save money and she was quite adept at fastidiously protecting both Max and Ben during the brief military conflict between the United States and Russia that happened in the spring of 2020.

As Max developed into a young adult, Lena also gave him what seemed like good advice about women, advice Max thought was much better than the advice Davis had given him. Lena told Max that he had a right to expect sexual monogamy in any woman, once he started dating her. She told Max anything else was incredibly selfish and cold, or at least a harbinger of terrible things to come. Lena also told Max that sex was something one had to be extraordinarily careful with because even highly pleasurable sex could be traumatic for both women and men. Max agreed, as he had first-hand experience of this with his mother.

One thing Max grew to respect about Lena was how even handed she was in the way she looked at men and women. Unlike Davis, Lena never gave women sexual privileges she didn't also give to men. Hence, she gave both men and women very few sexual privileges. Lena discouraged Max from having pre-marital sex because of the risk of unwanted pregnancies and STDs. She also encouraged Max to wait until he was at least in his late twenties before settling down with a wife and family.

For Lena, there was nothing worse than being a single parent. She'd read several studies about how single parents were, on balance, more likely to have children who make less money than parents in stable nuclear families. Although Lena insisted she supported gay rights, she often claimed it was better that gay couples share their children with a parent of the opposite sex. Lena felt kids needed a mother and father, a man and a woman, a man and a woman who were married, had money, were monogamous and would never ever make porn.

Whenever Max thought about sex, he thought about Lena's numerous speeches to him about safe sex. He never thought about hot girls; he never even watched porn. He instead thought of all the risks associated with sex, risks Lena gave him almost daily reminders of. The way Lena spoke about sex, she made it seem cumbersome, complicated and unusually dangerous. To Max, this meant sex wasn't terribly appealing as a recreational past time and certainly nothing he could relax enough to have fun doing. Sex was terrifying. You could accidentally wind up becoming a parent, or a rapist, or someone dead in a few years, if you contracted HIV.

Max's love of films was much easier for him to deal with than sex. This is what he chose to major in once he went to college. In college and then grad school, Max had close friendships with a few attractive Caucasian women who all bore a striking resemblance to his mother. He preferred his relationships with women to be platonic, so he could get the benefits of friendship, without the risks of sex. His female friends were the ones who felt short changed.

Nearly all of them were waiting patiently for Max to finally cave in and decide to be their studious and handsome boyfriend. These friendships were extremely awkward for Max, despite containing lots of affection. Max's friends kept him company and often cooked for him, yet they frequently behaved as though they were trying to hold in a lot of anger. Sometimes it felt like they were secretly enraged at him, either for not being their lover, or simply not being whatever it was they wanted him to be. Whenever Max tried to defend his choices, his friends would scream at him, accusing him of either not listening, or being arrogant and condescending.

Max, however, didn't take offence. By the time he had become a young adult, Max accepted that this was just what women were like. Max was forgiving in ways he would not have been, had he noticed these same behaviours coming from men. When men acted like his friends, Max wanted to punch those men. But Max could never hit anyone…not after what had happened with his mother.

As a young man, Max communicated with his father out of a sense of duty, even though he secretly despised the man who once played video games with him in the garage. Ben was everything Max did not want to be. Ben was a failure at life; he was fake. And on top of all that, he was boring.

Max had no interest in male friendships because he thought that, like his father, most men were aggressively boring. Even intellectual men were boring to Max because they only ever used their intellect to defend the status quo. All the men Max knew personally were slightly subservient in their character and more than a little foolish, compared to the women who normally stood alongside them.

To Max, straight men were far more foolish and boring than gay or bisexual men. Straight men were obsessed with being desired by attractive women. Max couldn't think of anything more foolish than that.

It seemed to Max that whenever a straight man got in a relationship with a woman, he never treated her as his equal. He wanted her to instead be his second mother. A straight man wanted his woman to take care of him and have his children and in exchange for that, he would impress that woman with a level of obedience that was impossible in an actual child. It was as if straight men were constantly competing with their sons to be the most well-behaved little man in Mommy's life. If straight men had daughters, they'd mostly leave the parenting of the daughters to Mommy. Girls only got praise and adoration from their fathers.

A straight man also never talked about, or celebrated his own heterosexuality, if he was decent and honourable. Decent and honourable straight men were afraid of offending women, or at least afraid of women thinking their sexuality was disgusting. That's what supposedly made straight men more desirable to women than teenage boys. Women themselves were encouraged to celebrate their sexuality at every turn, expressing anger at men for not sufficiently joining in the celebrations. That was especially true when a fat woman was celebrating her sexuality.

Although Max was a highly attractive young man, he never talked about, or celebrated his own sexuality. In this regard, Max was much more like the straight men he disliked than he would care to admit. But he tried to convince himself he was different, reminding himself how he felt no need to get married or have children. His friends made him feel like he was already married.

By the age of twenty-seven, Max was a fascinating and charismatic, if soft spoken bachelor with beautiful and intense brown eyes. He was buff and clean shaven, often striking poses in coffee shops that made him look like an advertisement for expensive watches. But Max was not vain or materialistic. If you got to know him, you would discover that beneath his soft-spoken exterior was a charming, self-deprecating sense of humour that felt oddly more British than American.

When Max wasn't thinking about films or writing essays, he loved listening to 19th century piano music, playing chess and analysing Russian literature in his head. Max especially loved Dostoyevsky, although he felt loving Dostoyevsky was itself somewhat of a cliche. Max's one major vice was procrastinating whenever he had a task to complete that he found overwhelming. During such a task, Max would often stare for hours at images of famous paintings on his laptop. He particularly liked staring at paintings of women's faces by artists like Marlene Dumas, Alex Katz and Renee Magritte.

Between the day his mother moved to Whittier and the age of twenty-seven, Max had no contact with Davis McFarlin. This was how he wanted things and Davis certainly respected his wishes. This was partly because Max would always be her favourite person, the person she loved more than anyone she had ever known. Davis could never tell whether her love for Max was good or evil, like love to cherish or love to suppress. But because of this love, Davis would always do whatever she could to be thought fondly of by Max, even if that meant following his orders never to contact him again.

Max's friends tried to dissuade him from taking such a hard-line stance towards his birth mother. This was partly because Max never told his friends about the fact that Davis had sex with him. His friends instead thought Max wanted nothing to do with his mother because of her career in porn. Hence, Max's friends routinely encouraged Max not only to be proud of Davis's infamous career choice, but to also resume contact with her. They thought Max should feel lucky to have a mother who was such a trail blazer for other women. Max would respond that the last thing he ever wanted was to resume contact with the one woman in his life who hurt him more than any other.

His friends would shout, "But she's the reason you're alive!"

Max would reply, "I don't owe her my friendship just because I fell out of her."

Whenever his friends implored him to think of how much pain Davis might be in, Max would reply that this pain was her own fault. Sometimes Max's friends would speak more softly, demanding that he practice the art of forgiveness, using such forgiveness to repair a broken relationship with the woman who introduced him to so many of the things that he loved as an adult. Max would respond calmly that he didn't want to forgive her or repair the relationship. He'd say he could forgive many things, but not sexual abuse, especially from the woman whose job was to love and protect him. Max's friends were outraged that Max equated being a porn star parent with sexual abuse.

Max's friends continually brought up the issue of his estranged mother far more than Max himself wanted to talk about it. When Max repeatedly stated he didn't want to talk about it, his friends would accuse him of hurting himself. Max's friends thought that if Davis grew old and died without Max ever being in her life again, he would feel an unbearable guilt:

a painful, soul crushing regret he could never fully forgive himself for. Max would reply that these potential regrets were unimportant. If he felt them, that just meant his job was to make himself not feel them. They were the wrong feelings to have.

Because Max would never back down in this particular dispute, his friends frequently insulted him. They called him cold and misogynistic, insinuating he was the sort of man no woman would ever want to love. Max's friends believed that every man should have a deep respect for his mother, as unconditional love was only possible in light of this respect. Max would tell his friends that he didn't believe in unconditional love, after which his friends would shout that he was a prudish and controlling asshole. When Max pleaded with them to drop the subject, they'd get even louder, screaming how much they hoped to *never* have a son like him.

By the summer of 2029, Max had become a talented grad-student in film studies, doing a PhD on David Cronenberg's late works. Max's PhD was undertaken at USC, but he mostly did his research and writing at home. He had video conferences with his pedantic and prickly advisors and went to campus quite minimally. He didn't like most of the people at USC because they seemed competitive and snobbish, like his stepmother. This is partly why it was not a huge inconvenience that Max lived a long drive away from campus.

Max had a small apartment in Pasadena, near Colorado Blvd. He didn't really like the people in Pasadena, any more than he liked the people at USC. But he liked the city's shops, restaurants and bookstores. Like Davis McFarlin, Pasadena was pretty and the city reminded Max of some of the happier days of his childhood. Like it or not, Pasadena had something going for it that most Los Angeles suburbs did not: the city was interesting and unique. Whether a child, or a twenty-seven-year-old man, Max couldn't help but obsess over things he found interesting and unique.

As a bookish grad-student, Max had a set of routines he rarely deviated from. He wasn't hedonistic or someone who liked to party; he didn't drink; he hadn't even masturbated for four years. But every once in a while, Max got restless and did something impulsive, something almost out of character. He had one of these impulsive moments on the night of July 28th, 2029.

Shortly after 9pm, Max decided to visit Inside Davis, suddenly curious about what his mother's old porn looked like. To his surprise, Max found that Inside Davis was no longer a porn website, but instead a fan community platform discussing his mother's essays.

Perusing through this platform, Max found a few bits of information about his mother, particularly about what she had been up to in the intervening thirteen years. From what he could glean, Davis was now single and living in New York. She looked much the same as he remembered, but with a (slightly) more wrinkly face. She wore her wrinkles well and was still an unusually attractive woman in her late forties.

From what Max could see, it didn't look like Davis had anything to do with this platform. It was run exclusively by her obsessive fans, fans who didn't get that her writing was never ironic or satirical or 'meta'.

Max recognised a lot of Davis's older pieces but was curious about the newer ones.

One thing he immediately noticed was the change in titles. The older poems and essays always had quite melancholic and elaborate titles. The titles of the newer pieces were all very short and funny. A few of them made Max laugh out loud, which in turn, made him more curious to read them.

Max clicked on one essay titled 'Why I'd Never Want to Be a Nice Person'.

In this essay, Davis described, in lurid detail, all the things she loved about sex. Much of the language was vulgar; much of the imagery was titillating. But more so than that, the writing seemed distinctly unfeminine. It was like an essay about sex written by a dirty old man who liked to sexually harass women – the kind of sexual predator most women would be advised to recognise and stay far away from.

Yet what stood out most to Max was the essay's point of view. Davis loved sex for all the reasons Max found it cumbersome. She loved that it was dangerous and risky; she loved that it had the power to frustrate and hurt people. Davis even loved that sex could be manipulative: a way to control people, tease them and head fuck them into tears, heartache, violence, anxiety or depression. She loved that sex wasn't fair, that it was racist, that it wasn't politically progressive and that at base, sex was more exciting the less equal it was and the more it involved dominance, aggression, body shaming and things Max associated with pain.

This was fascinating to Max, as it seemed Davis had now dropped the pretence of being a feminist. The final page of her essay read:

> 'Fuck gender equality! Men and women are different and that's why they're so good at getting each other off.
>
> I understand this as a bisexual. For me, sex with a woman is only really sexy when it's like sex with a man. I despise lingerie, candles and anything with the word 'sensuous' in it. I do not like it when even beautiful women are gentle with me. And as a bisexual, I am the first to admit that many beautiful women are boring. I should know. I've had sex with over three hundred of them. And regardless of how interesting even the most beautiful woman is, there's always that fucking smell. I can forgive that smell, because I have been forgiven for many many things... much worse things.
>
> Despite what you might think, darlings, I am very happy to have done all the things I have been forgiven for. I have no guilt about any orgasms of mine...even my biggest ones, the ones that destroyed the boy I still love.
>
> That grown man, bless his heart, will someday read this essay. He will never be free of me. And when he reads it, I will own him. He will do anything for me, no matter how dangerous or depraved. I will make him my dog. He will even hurt himself, if I so much as ask him to. He will kiss my feet, suck my toes and beg for pleasures only I can give him. I am a woman, after all and he is a man. Like any man, he thinks he can see up my skirt, but that's only because of how much I look down on him.
>
> He himself looks up at the world with eyes that came from me. He grew because of me and this is why I can reduce him to nothing and smash his soul to pieces if I so desire. I might have done this already, but would gladly do it again, if it meant cumming hard on his big, beautiful cock.
>
> This is how I am not like you. I am not compassionate and I have no sympathy for those of you who are addicted to images of me. I do not care about you, darlings. I do not care if you are ugly; I do not care whether or not you hate yourself; I don't even care if you have cancer. I rejoice in your pain and death.

That's why you cum.

And that's why you love me.'

As Max finished reading this text, he began to remember things about his mother, memories came from around the time he was ten years old. He remembered how she would often say things to shock people, things that Max could never tell if she really meant. Max also remembered how attracted to her he was and how ashamed this made him feel. But Max also felt comfortable being ashamed of his feelings. Because of his shame, he could still say he was a good son, a loving son and a son who could be a good friend to even his crazy, sexy mom.

Max never loved his mother unconditionally; he liked her instead. Yes, Max thought she was sexy, but more so than that, he thought she was funny and fun to be around. She was, by far, the most interesting person he had ever known and the two of them had so much in common. It wouldn't be an exaggeration to say that Max was saddened by the fact that Davis was his mother. He wanted her to instead be his wife. He was even slightly angry at Davis for having chosen Ben as her husband.

Once Max turned eleven, Davis started to flirt with and tease him in a way that felt decidedly grownup. Max would try his hardest to be stoic and appropriate, impressing his mother by not flirting back. By this point, Davis was wearing inappropriately revealing outfits around the house and her language towards Max was peppered with sexual innuendos. To Max, it felt as if his mother was constantly trying to turn him on whenever the two of them were alone. Max could never tell if this was her true intention, or if she was suddenly wearing revealing outfits and speaking in sexual innuendos for the sheer fun of it.

Either way, Max was suddenly feeling like his favourite person and best friend was also a very bad parent. Yet Max himself couldn't be the son he wanted to be: he couldn't bring himself to ask Davis to stop her relentless teasing. He was addicted to it, as much as she was.

Max was also aroused by how brave his mother was and how distraught she could make anyone who got in her way. Davis had no qualms with making both her husband and son extremely angry. Whenever Davis could sense she had made anyone angry, she would always do something to make that person even more angry. Davis made Ben so angry, he was frequently in tears. Davis made Max so angry, he found it hard to speak.

Max was never angrier than when Davis told him she was going to start filming porn in their home. Yet despite (and because of) this anger, Max had reached a level of sexual obsession with her that was now terrifying to him. Max was so frightened by his desire for Davis, that he was also becoming obsessed with trying to find other women as desirable as his mother. He even tried to wean himself off his mother's image, masturbating to porn featuring women who looked vaguely like Davis, as these were the only women that could make him hard. This technique never worked. Max would watch these women and imagine they were Davis as soon as he was close to orgasm.

By the time Max was fourteen, his desire for Davis was stronger than anything Max had ever felt in his entire life. He had now given up on his quest to orgasm thinking about anyone else. Nearly every night, Max was falling asleep after having had an intense masturbation session, thinking about his mother seductively walking into his bedroom and nonchalantly asking if she could fuck his brains out. Max never imagined that Davis would actually do this on Sunday, September 25th, 2016.

Max always assumed he would refuse her in this situation, impressing his mother with his stoic resolve, turning away the ultimate temptation. Yet when Davis actually propositioned Max, he shocked himself, wilfully choosing to have unprotected sex with the woman who gave birth to him. Even more shocking was how good the sex was, despite it happening on what would quickly become the most painful and horrifying night Max would ever live through.

As Davis and Max began kissing and undressing each other, Max was secretly hoping that the sex itself would be creepy and horrible. If it were creepy and horrible, he would eventually be able to transfer his sexual desires to more appropriate targets. Seconds before entering his mother, all Max could think about was how bad sex would be a huge relief.

Unfortunately, things did not turn out this way. The physical pleasures Max experienced inside Davis were infinitely more intense than anything he had ever experienced while touching himself. Even worse, the sex was deeply emotional, containing a palpable warmth that felt natural, like Max was once again experiencing the maternal nurturing that made him feel so loved and understood, as a child. It didn't feel at all like Max was engaged in the naughtiest sex act with the most desired porn star of 2016. It instead felt like he was making love to his dream woman, the pleasures he gave her communicating things Max could never express in words.

It was horrible.

After Max came in his mother's vagina for the third time, she whispered in his ear, "This is why I had you so early. I wanted to do this with you, even when you were a baby. Do you remember the games we used to play?"

Upon hearing this, Max suddenly remembered the games they used to play when he was a small child.

He slowly put his hands around his mother's face like he was going to kiss her and then surprised her by squeezing her neck as hard as he could. Davis choked and screamed underneath him, her body flailing wildly like a dying fish. Within a few seconds, Ben ran into Max's room, violently throwing Max onto the floor and saving his wife's life.

Ben assumed that Max was high on drugs and had attempted to rape his own mother. Davis initially went along with this story, even though Max insisted he was innocent. An hour later, Davis started crying, confessing to Ben that the sex was consensual and that she and Max were in love with each other.

Max screamed that it wasn't consensual and that Davis had been abusing him since he was a small child. Ben started screaming and beating Davis, while Max found himself trying to protect the very woman he had tried to kill, an hour earlier.

As Max remembered all of this, he decided to do something extraordinarily risky. He decided to find his mother's email address and send her a few paragraphs of text. He wept as he wrote these paragraphs.

Max first apologised profusely for rejecting her from his life. Then he beautifully described how much he enjoyed spending time with her as a kid. He thanked her for giving him the gift of life. He told her that he still loved her very much, that he completely forgave her for what she did to him and that he wanted to see her again. Max suggested next time Davis visited LA, they have coffee at Vroman's bookstore. He even made these paragraphs sound profound, like something you might see in a book by Alice Munroe or Cora Sandel.

Max ended the email by telling Davis that her newer writings had inspired him, because of how much he related to what she was saying. After all these years, Max was realising that he too was tired of being a nice person.

He explained to Davis that his temperament was naturally more like Lena's, but this wasn't something he felt proud of. He described Lena as a pretentious and controlling bitch and Ben as an ignorant and petty man servant. Max told Davis he wished he could be more like his sexy mother, if just for the thrill of pissing off his other parents – the bland, nice, and unsexy ones. He knew this would make Davis laugh.

Here, Max was being slightly flirtatious. He was now regretting all the times he stopped himself from flirting like this with his mother. Max wished he had impressed Davis with how well he could flirt and not simply astonished her with how charming he could be. Max was now having vivid memories of making his mother laugh, helping her understand her own poetry, untangling her confusing thoughts, delighting her with loving surprises and even consoling her when she was upset. His heart was beating fast as he thought of what it would be like to do it all again.

As Max gathered up the courage to send his tastefully flirty email, he was also, in a more abstract way, feeling exhilarated by possibilities. Max could visualise a future for himself where he couldn't predict what might happen; where he wouldn't have to shut off his feelings, be conventional, or be ashamed of his desire for the one woman who stirred his deepest desires. In this boldly utopian future, incest between consenting adults was a cause like gay rights and even someone like Max could have guilt-free and consensual sex with the only woman who could now give him an erection.

Hence, Max abruptly came to his senses, believing such a future was nothing more than a silly delusion. The reality was the political elements of this future were silly, but the possibility of sex with Davis was very real.

If Max had sent her his email, she would have immediately written back and within days, the two of them would be together, catching up for lost time, weeping in each other's arms, talking over coffee, making each other laugh, sharing books, watching films and eventually fucking.

Hence, Max quickly deleted the beautiful and seductive paragraphs he wrote to his birth mother. He then stepped into an uncomfortably icy shower. Because of the piercing discomfort of cold water splashing against his body, Max's erection began to soften. Once he got used to the cold water, Max got hard once again.

It was infuriating how much Max's body responded to 'Why I'd Never Want To Be a Nice Person'.

However, Max didn't know that when his mother wrote this essay, it was actually composed at the recommendation of her therapist, Doctor Gillian Adams. Doctor Adams had encouraged Davis to write this essay as a form of spiritual healing. It was an exercise that would allow Davis to both cleanse her chakras and forgive herself for past transgressions.

When Davis first posted this essay online, she never considered the possibility that Max would ever read it. She just assumed that Max still hated her and had no interest in either her life or her work. Davis also didn't consider the possibility that Max would cum because of how well she described the carnal and heart pounding ecstasies of not being a nice person. She never imagined that from Max's point of view, her essay was like a porn film, porn she specifically designed to torture him.

Only a day after reading this essay, Max was masturbating compulsively, thinking about fucking his mother on an almost hourly basis. He wondered if this was what it felt like to be a hopeless drug addict.

If Davis knew the extreme impact that her words were having on Max, she'd be very happy. First, she'd smile to herself, beaming with pride at how erotic she could make a confessional essay. Then she would feel hopeful.

Davis would have hope for the first time since 2016.

She'd have hope that very soon, her beloved son would come back to her and the two of them would finally become what she deep down wanted them to be: secret lovers travelling the world, going on exciting adventures, leading a fun and bohemian lifestyle that celebrated pleasure and non-conformity.

Davis would visualise Max rubbing her feet, smiling and making her laugh, as they both sat on her stylish couch drinking coffee in her beautifully decorated living room, positioned in front of the many film posters Davis had hanging on her walls. In this visualisation, she and Max would live happily in her boho New York apartment, on the days they weren't travelling to Paris or London.

Davis's perfect chill day would be one where Max repeatedly told her she was still beautiful, while he cooked and cleaned for her, smoked weed with her, analysed her newest poems, behaved like a live-in therapist and made sure she was sexually satisfied.

Although Davis would also relish satisfying Max's sexual needs, she wouldn't do much else for him, apart from keep him company. That is, she would not behave like his live-in therapist, nor would she give him foot rubs, analyse his writing, or cook and clean for him. She would definitely not reassure him he was still beautiful, if he ever gained weight or started losing his hair.

This was because whenever Davis was in a romantic relationship, she expected everything to revolve around her own practical and emotional needs. She expected this, regardless of whether she and her man were having a chill day at home, or an adventure filled evening in another country. Davis's expectations were themselves a product of how she saw men and women.

Davis saw men and women as fundamentally different creatures, with highly distinctive needs. In the context of romantic relationships, Davis thought men didn't have any practical or emotional needs. They only had practical and emotional responsibilities: responsibilities to women.

For Davis McFarlin, sex was a man's only real physical need. Hence, she thought aggressively making a man cum was a woman's only real responsibility, once in a relationship with a man. The man's responsibility was to do all the things that made him earn the intense pleasures only his woman could give him on a consistent basis. The man earned his pleasures by looking after his woman, tending to her emotional needs, entertaining her, keeping her sexually satisfied and understanding that the relationship was more about her than him.

In Davis's vision of a healthy relationship, the man got to cum, while the woman who made him cum got everything else. This included many orgasms of her own, many of which came from other people. Davis still hated monogamy and thought there was no greater privilege for a man than to be with a sexually liberated woman, a woman who made a continuous effort to stay slim and make her man cum, as hard as she could. A man was jealous and possessive, if he expected such a sexually liberated woman not to sleep with other people. He was also ungrateful. Sexually liberated women were rare. Davis thought most women were boring prudes. In 2029, she still thought she was better than most women. Because she was so much better, Davis felt entitled to have sex with anyone she wanted to, under any circumstances.

Davis's therapist didn't agree with these beliefs and thought many of them were unhealthy – even narcissistic. Yet Doctor Adams did little to challenge them, because if she did, she knew Davis would discontinue their sessions. It was important to Doctor Adams to keep Davis as a client, as she had been a fan of Davis's porn since 2015. Doctor Adams was secretly using their therapy sessions as an opportunity to try and seduce Davis. Although this seduction was unsuccessful, the therapy did give Davis some skills she did not have, prior to seeing Doctor Adams. Davis had learned to play the harp, do yoga and practice transcendental meditation.

During these sessions, Davis revealed many of her deepest, darkest secrets. However, she did not reveal that she had had sex with her son when he was fourteen, or that she had sexually abused him when he was a small child. Davis told Doctor Adams that Max and Ben wanted nothing to do with her because she was a porn star. Doctor Adams replied that they were misogynists and Davis was actually better off without men like that in her life.

Max knew his mother well enough to know that in the years since they last had contact, she would see many therapists and become obsessed with her own mental health. Max also knew that none of this would ever stop her from being fundamentally selfish when it came to love and romance. On the evening of July 28th, 2029, Max still knew exactly what she wanted from him. He also knew exactly how much power she would have over him if he ever made the mistake of giving in to his lust. If Max ever became his mother's lover, Davis would quickly turn him into Ben.

Max would rather kill himself than be like his father.

This is partly why, on August 7th, Max would begin taking female hormones. Max was not liking the sort of person his male desires were making him: the sort of person, it seemed more and more likely, would find his way back inside Davis McFarlin.

As Max instead became a female person, he was surprised at how fast his gender transition wound up being. Everyone in his life congratulated him for being brave, as soon as he announced it. No one misgendered Max or used the wrong pronouns, even though it took over six months to stop looking like a man in a dress. Ben told Max he'd always wanted a daughter instead of a son, while Lena said she had a suspicion Max was too sensitive to be a successful husband and father. Even Max's friends were now less angry, as his new gender made them lose their resentment towards him for not being their boyfriend.

At the same time, Max worried that his decision to become a woman was possibly a mistake. He feared it might be a way of avoiding a deeper psychological problem, a problem it would take years to unravel with a decent therapist. To put it bluntly, Max hated his penis because of how it made him feel about his mother. Yet he didn't feel any deep psychological or physiological need to put a vagina in its place. Although Max felt ashamed to admit it, having his penis surgically removed seemed scary and unpleasant. Max wondered if perhaps the solution to his problem was a compromise: he would take female hormones, gender-present as female and leave his male anatomy intact.

Against this compromise was the fact that announcing his gender transition seemed to greatly improve Max's life. Both his immediate family and his friends had never been so nice to him. They talked over and over again about how much they admired his courage and bravery. Yet when he described how minimal his physical transition would be, they all seemed deeply disappointed, like he was letting them down. If Max was going to become a woman, he didn't want to do it in a way where he disappointed the people who loved him most.

The pressure Max felt to become an anatomically correct woman didn't always feel particularly liberating, either. Sometimes it felt like his family and friends were forcing him to conform to something, because they could sense how vulnerable and confused he was.

Even though Max was dutifully taking his "lady pills", he was even having doubts about whether or not he would like being a woman. A part of Max worried that he needed to love his male identity. That self-love was perhaps an important part of dealing with all his pain, as well as discovering what made his life meaningful. In his more paranoid moments, Max wondered if transgenderism was a way western society was encouraging more feminine men to erase themselves, using the latest medical technologies.

During the times Max confided any of these worries to his friends, they would politely accuse him of having internalised transphobia. They would also patiently explain to him that his ideas about self-love were just silly delusions. Max's friends were all devoted altruists, believing that what gave life meaning was to love others more than oneself. If Max ever expressed his fears about removing his penis, his friends would scream that Max was both a selfish coward and a hateful bigot making life harder for trans people.

Though it was hard hearing all of this, Max eventually trusted his friends. He trusted them because he knew just how much they loved him. Throughout the years, they were always there for him, always willing to talk to him, listen to him, and cook for him, no matter how much they disagreed with him, or how distant he got from them emotionally. Because of their relentless devotion and care for him over the years, Max knew deep down that they wanted nothing more than to make sure he was happy and healthy.

When Max finally told his friends that Davis had sex with him, they all unanimously changed their minds about her, agreeing with Max that his birth mother was toxic and dangerous. Max was impressed at how much his friends could suddenly be so reasonable, when presented with new information. Because of this, Max suddenly felt that whatever his friends had to say about his life must be true. If they said his dick needed to come off, then it really did need to come off.

As soon as Max's face began to look smooth and feminine, he was quickly treated to the full range of transgender surgeries, including the newer more controversial Adam's apple, facial, hip and vocal cord surgeries. These surgeries were all completed in a little over a year. Max's new vagina came with painful and embarrassing complications, but his friends convinced him this was still better than having a penis.

Although Max initially decided to go by the name Maxine, she eventually decided on Delilah, as this name better suited the shape of her new body – a female body that didn't quite look the way she hoped it would. Delilah would have ideally preferred for her physical transition to be slower, but the doctors were insistent that it all be done as soon as possible. If they waited, there was more of a chance Delilah would change her mind before the surgeries had all been completed. And if that happened, there was more of a chance Max would have to learn to love himself as Max. That self-love was absolutely unacceptable to everyone. Even advocating that form of self-love could get you a prison sentence.

This was because, by the final years of the 2020s, Western society was treating transphobes the way it used to treat sex offenders. Transgenderism was no longer even linked to having gender dysphoria. Anyone could get a sex change for any reason, under any circumstances.

Hence, Delilah was relieved at how truthful she could be when explaining to medical professionals why she wanted her surgeries. She could talk about hating men and hating being a man, without having to make up any lies about having been a child transvestite or someone who always felt like they were in the wrong body.

When it was all done, Delilah was mostly pleased with the delicate work her surgeons had completed, (apart from the weird squeaky sound of her new high voice, as well as all the complications that caused her pain and discomfort). Delilah accepted that she was now seen by society as quite an unusual looking woman. However, she still found that preferable to being seen as a handsome young man. Much to her surprise, Delilah didn't just like being a woman; she loved it. By 2030, it was fairly obvious why.

People were much nicer to you when you were a woman – any kind of woman. You were also far more likely to be forgiven when you weren't a nice person. And it was easier and more socially acceptable to express anger at other people, even people you loved.

This is why, once Delilah got used to her new gender, she quickly found the courage to tell all her friends to go fuck themselves and stay the hell away from her. By the end of 2031, she was feeling like she deserved some very different kinds of friends, friends who were less like Delilah's role models, growing up.

By the summer of 2032, Delilah had also decided that she no longer wanted to have any further contact with Ben and Lena. Delilah had come to the conclusion that both of them were far too much like Davis – thoroughly toxic people who brought nothing but nastiness to Delilah's mind and heart. Delilah could no longer keep Ben and Lena in her life out of a sense of duty. They were both far too damaged.

That same summer, Delilah finished her PhD and made the brave decision to move to the East Midlands of England after she was offered a job teaching film studies at the University of Leicester. Delilah didn't know much about the city of Leicester, except that it was the home of the only two contemporary writers she actually really enjoyed reading: Janet Waverley and Joe Pastorious.

Leicester was also the first place Delilah had ever lived where white people thought brown skin was beautiful.

After living in Leicester for a year, Delilah decided to permanently darken her pale skin.

PART FOUR: RETURN TO ROMANCE

"Gail is my best friend. If you can't deal with your husband or wife as a friend, you probably won't enjoy living together. Friendship (and I don't want to get sentimental here) is a very important dimension. I think a marriage without friendship is pretty boring."

- Frank Zappa

"Nostalgic longing is always for an elsewhere. Remembrance is the affirmation of what brought us here."

- Iris Marion Young

"If the Martians take the writings of moral philosophers as a guide to what goes on on this planet, they will get a shock when they arrive."

- Philippa Foot

17. ROMANCE: Patriarchy

Dear Reader,

July 28th, 2029, is an important date in our narrative.

This is partly because it's the 14th anniversary of another important date: July 28th, 2015.

During the late evening hours of July 28th, 2015, there's a violent and windy storm heading towards Leicester, announcing its arrival with bright flickers of white lightning interspersed with kettledrum bangs of pounding thunder. It's an unpredictable storm, although some might describe it as more exciting than unpredictable. It starts at 11:05pm and by midnight, it's still going strong.

At 12:04am, thirty-eight-year-old Joe Pastorious is in his office on the second floor of his Clarendon Park home, lounging in his underpants. His beautiful twenty-nine-year-old girlfriend Loraine Klein is in their bedroom, preparing herself for intercourse with Joe.

Earlier that evening, Joe was watching his favourite porn star Davis McFarlin, preparing himself for intercourse with Loraine.

But Joe has since lost interest in preparing himself for intercourse.

Joe is now sitting at his brown leather desk chair, doodling on a notepad, writing down the stages of something called a 'three-pronged stealth-attack massage.' The house Wi-Fi isn't working, unable to stabilise with the searing flashes of electricity that hover above the roof. Joe's laptop screen is frozen, making him feel disconnected to the world outside both his spacious, well-furnished home and the thunderstorm happening above it. Given all the drama in the sky, Joe can't focus on much else apart from the pointless list in his hands.

Writing down pointless lists is Joe's one hobby not even a broken internet can stop him from indulging in, especially during the times he is seriously frustrated with life.

Times like now.

Joe is frustrated by the fact that his own feelings get hurt so easily. He hates the fact that even sex with Loraine Klein can still feel like a burdensome chore. He also hates his fat, flabby body, his unsightly belly and the fact that he doesn't even feel like he deserves to share a bed with the leggy bombshell he's about to bang.

Joe feels like he doesn't deserve to be in Loraine's bed, partly because earlier that day, she bluntly stated that his unsightly belly was both "nasty" and "disgusting" to her. Loraine also said Joe embarrassed her with his weight, making her feel ashamed to walk alongside him in public. Joe was taken aback by these statements, having lived under the illusion that Loraine loved his body unconditionally.

Joe is now confused as to why Loraine continues to have sex with him so often, given how she feels about his physical appearance. The fact that Loraine can have sex with a man whose body she finds so repulsive is itself, quite disturbing to Joe. It makes him wonder why Loraine is in a relationship with him at all.

Joe's mind is now starting to wonder compulsively about many other things: things like whether he's as good an English teacher as his students tell him he is. Joe also wonders if his friends actually enjoy spending time with him. He wonders if they lie to him out of pity when they talk to him for hours in what seem like genuinely involving conversations.

Joe even wonders whether his friends would be all that upset if he died. Joe starts thinking that neither his best friend Claire or his girlfriend Loraine would be terribly distraught, in the event Joe decided to kill himself. He wonders if his suicide would make more of an impact if he hung himself in Loraine's newly decorated pink bathroom.

But these thoughts are interrupted as Joe hears Loraine yelling from her room.

Loraine: (yelling) Joe… what are you doing?

Joe: (yelling) I'm just organising our shopping list. The Wi-Fi's back on again.

Loraine: (yelling) It's midnight.

Joe: (yelling) I know that, just give me a few minutes to finish this.

Loraine: (yelling) Joe, I need to be asleep soon.

Joe: (yelling) Maybe you should try and get to sleep without me tonight. You don't want to become dependent on sex in order to fall asleep. There might be some nights when I'm not here.

Another ten minutes go by.

Joe doesn't know what to do. He feels like bursting into tears but doesn't want Loraine to see him drowning in such unmanly vulnerabilities. Such vulnerabilities would make him even less desirable than he already is.

Loraine: (yelling) Good night, Joe! I guess you'd rather finish that shopping list than spend the night fucking your girlfriend's pussy!

"Oh God, she's trying to turn me on," Joe thinks to himself, noticing just how unsexy he finds those words.

But he then thinks, "Come on, Joe. It's not Loraine in there; it's Davis. You're fucking Davis tonight. She'll make you feel better. Go on."

Joe slowly walks from his office into the house bedroom. Upon opening the door, he can see a smiling Loraine posing on their king-sized bed, wearing nothing but a blue robe and high heels. Joe can see Loraine's long curvy legs, spread open in a V-shape, while she rubs her clit with her right hand.

Loraine: Get over here, naughty boy.

Joe sits down beside Loraine, feeling like he wants to die. But he still does a clumsy impersonation of a happy, sexually aroused man.

Joe thinks that if he can get an erection, this impersonation will evolve into something that actually feels nice. Unfortunately, Joe's erection is completely inaccessible to him. For some reason, Joe can't visualise Davis McFarlin. All he can see is Loraine and all he can think about is hanging himself in her pink bathroom, once she has fallen asleep.

Loraine: I'm going to give you a reward for getting serious about your food plan, Joe. You'll like this.

Loraine takes Joe's hand and brings it to her vagina.

Loraine: (smiling mischievously) You won't be needing any more junk food. These lips are your candy store from now on. Pull them apart with your fingers, Joe. Smell your reward. Inhale it for me. Stick your nose inside...

Joe pulls his hand away.

Loraine: What's your problem?

Joe: I'm not really in the mood for this.

Loraine: (annoyed) Well fucking get in the mood!

Joe: I'm too uncomfortable.

Loraine: Why?

Joe: I don't feel comfortable with you talking about me that way.

Loraine: What way? I was trying to turn you on.

Joe: You're talking about me like I'm a child.

Loraine: What does that even mean?

Joe: It's like I'm a kid who you're giving sex to, in exchange for good behaviour.

Loraine: (smiling) That sounds like a naughty fantasy.

Joe: It might be as a fantasy. But right now, it feels like it's not a fantasy. It feels like that's how you see me.

Loraine: (confused) I see you as my boyfriend I'm trying to do something nice for.

Joe: Something nice?

Loraine: Yes, you're getting sex from your beautiful girlfriend who loves you.

Joe: Well, I don't know how I feel about that.

Loraine: Would you rather I not be nice to you?

Joe: I don't know

Loraine: Should I force you to take care of yourself in the other room?

Joe: Like I said, I don't know. Sex isn't something I want because you want to be nice to me.

Loraine: But I'm your girlfriend.

Joe: I don't want you to have sex with me because you want to be nice to me.

Loraine: Joe, you're confusing me.

Joe: I want you to have sex with me because you want to.

Loraine: But I do want to!

Joe: You want to so you can sleep.

Loraine: No, I also think you deserve some sex.

Joe: (shaking his head) Nobody deserves sex.

Loraine: Well, I know it was hard for you today, hearing how I felt about your weight. I thought I'd make it up to you and motivate you to continue on your healthy eating plan.

Joe: Motivate me? You mean manipulate me?

Loraine: (annoyed) It's not manipulation! I'm being honest with you. I'm *telling you* I'm trying to motivate you.

Joe: I don't like how it feels.

Loraine: (irritated) I don't like how it feels when you get stroppy when I try to help you grow and stop self-harming with food.

Joe: I know that but–

Loraine: (interrupting) But rather than get angry, I try time and time again to be nice to you. I'm not taking anything away from you because of your weight. You're getting pussy most men would kill for. Be grateful for that! It doesn't happen to just anybody.

Joe: That doesn't make me feel any better.

Loraine: (frustrated) I don't know how to please you. You're doing my fucking head in!

Joe: (loudly) I don't want you to have sex with me because you want to be nice to me! I want you to have sex with me because you want to!

Loraine: (loudly) But I do want to!

Joe: You want sex… to control me. You don't want sex because of me, Loraine. You don't want sex because you desire me.

Loraine: Well, if I only had sex when I felt desire, I wouldn't have had sex with you for most of the past year.

Joe: Exactly.

Loraine: (angrily) And you're angry because I gave you sex anyway? Do you realise how many men wish they were you?

Joe: I don't care. I want to feel like my girlfriend actually desires me.

Loraine: Well, then you should have made more of an effort not to be nasty. If you don't want pity sex, don't make a habit out of eating like a filthy fucking pig. Act like you care about yourself. It's not that hard.

Joe: (loudly) That's so fucking mean! Why should it matter what I look like? You're supposed to love me in all my frailties. If you can't love my faults, what kind of a relationship is this?

Loraine: (shouting) You're the one who's being selfish! You expect me to fuck you when you when you keep all that fucking fat on you?

Joe: (loudly) Food for me is an addiction! If you were addicted to heroin and looked like a rail, I'd still love you.

Loraine: (loudly) I do love you! But at least once a week, you do a big speech about how you feel unattractive. I try to make you feel good about yourself; I try to encourage you. But when I tell you to get on a diet plan, you ignore me! Then you shove that shit down your face the next night while I have to sit there and watch you. I want to fucking puke looking at you most nights we have dinner together! Do you think I like eating when I'm eating next to you?

Joe: Loraine, it's really hard for me to–

Loraine: (interrupting) But I let you continue to eat like that and I still fuck you! How the hell am I the selfish one? I'm the one who lets all that fucking fat roll against me every night! I'm the one who lets you body slam your big nasty hang dog of a gut into me over and over and over again! Do I complain? No! I even suck on your fucking tits 'cause it makes you cum hard! You think all of that makes me feel sexy? You think I like looking into your fucking eye patch?

Joe: (shouting) That's totally selfish! You don't like sex with me! You're only FUCKING me so you can fall asleep at night!

Loraine: (shouting) Falling asleep is the reason I tolerate it!

Joe: (shouting) But why tolerate it?

Loraine: (shouting) Because I'm a good girlfriend to you!

Joe: Jesus, do you realise how ridiculous you sound right now?

Loraine: I know I sound ridiculous, but it's because I'm trying to reason with someone I can't please. I can't win with you.

Joe: I don't understand.

Loraine: You go on and on about how love is selfless and about tolerating the imperfections of others. When I show you my weaknesses, you act disappointed with me. When I do things for you, you get angry at me because I'm not doing them for me! You go on and on about how you want honesty without manipulation, but every time I'm honest with you, you look at me like you want to cry. Everything I do is wrong when I do *exactly* what you say you want!

Joe: I never asked you to be so fucking shallow about bodies.

Loraine: (frustrated) That's one of my weaknesses! I know! I'm shallow. But that's who you chose to love!

Joe: That doesn't stop me from loving you. It just fucking pisses me off.

Loraine: If it pisses you off, that means you can't forgive me for it.

Joe: (loudly) I can't forgive you for it because of how it negatively affects me! It fucking hurts, hearing you talk like that!

Loraine: (laughing) You can't forgive one of my weaknesses because of how it negatively affects you. And you call me selfish?

Joe: I tolerated your shallowness for a long time. I didn't know until tonight that you were shallow about my body.

Loraine: Again, you forgave me for one of my weaknesses until it negatively affected you.

Joe: Anyone would be hurt by the things you said to me! Can you imagine what it would be like if a man said to a woman the things you said to me today?

Loraine: But I'm not a man and you aren't anybody. I'm with you because I thought you could handle me.

Joe: (angrily) So now I can't handle you?

Loraine: I thought you'd be different to all the other blokes I've been with. I thought you would man up rather than sulk like a little girl every time I say something you don't want to hear.

Joe: (holding back rage) You thought I would be fine with you hurling insults at me?

Loraine: I thought you weren't weak. I thought you weren't someone I should feel sorry for.

Joe: I'm not asking you to feel sorry for me.

Loraine: You know I fucking can't stand people who don't help themselves. I thought you were better than that. I thought you could handle a beautiful woman.

Joe: Well, I'm sorry but I don't think's it's terribly weird not to want to hear your lover call your stomach nasty and disgusting.

Loraine: Normal people don't like how they look, so they lie to each other. You're not with a normal person, Joe. You're with me.

Joe: So because you're beautiful, that gives you the right to body shame me? You think being beautiful gives you the right to say cruel shit to anyone you think doesn't look as good as you?

Loraine: I can say whatever the fuck I want! This is my house. If you don't like it, go sleep outside on the pavement.

Joe: (loudly) It doesn't matter that this is your house! I live in it with you and pay you rent!

Loraine: You don't contribute anything to this house except that rent. This house runs because of me! I do almost everything while you sit on your fat arse and gorge yourself with food.

Joe: (sighing in exasperation) Our routines aren't just my fault... You agree to do the things you do too...

Loraine: Yes, blame me instead of yourself.

Joe: (in frustration) You have a say in how this house runs, Loraine! You can ask me to do more if you're not happy with what each of us is responsible for!

Loraine: (loudly) Yes and you can take some initiative, so I don't fucking have to ask you! I swear, I feel like I'm living with a five-year-old.

Joe: That doesn't give you the right to treat me like shit and insult my body!

Loraine: I'm not insulting you, I'm just telling you the truth.

Joe: (loudly) You can tell me the truth without hurting me!

Loraine: But why should I? You don't fucking change without incentives. No one does.

Joe: I don't care. I'm fed up with you trying to change me. I'm fed up with your incentives. I'm fed up with your honesty. You use your honesty as an excuse to hurt me when I'm already hurting. You never make me feel better when I'm in pain. When I'm suffering, it's like you try and make it worse.

Loraine: (sarcastically) Well then helping you with my honesty is another one of my weaknesses. And surprise surprise: it's a weakness you won't tolerate!

Joe: (loudly) You don't tolerate the fact that I'm a human being! Whenever I show you my vulnerability, you belittle me and say the meanest shit! And it's not just me. You don't have a kind fucking word to say about anybody! I don't know anyone as intolerant as you.

Loraine: (loudly) My God, you are such a selfish fucking prick! You actually think you're the tolerant one in this relationship! You think you're the tolerant one even though I'm the one looking into an eye patch getting fucked by a human jelly baby. Half the time you smell like shit!

Joe: (shouting) Stop fucking saying those things to me! I've had enough!

Loraine: (loudly) Yes and you can say whatever pops into your head! I can see how this works.

Joe: (loudly) Unlike you, I don't say whatever's in my fucking head! If I did, you'd be devastated!

Loraine: Then you've been dishonest with me too! I'm finding out more and more things about our relationship every minute!

Joe: (shouting) If I was honest, you'd fucking leave me!

Loraine: Try me then. Do your worst!

Joe: Fuck off.

Loraine: No, go ahead! See how I respond to that honesty! You fucking owe me that given how much I've risked in being honest with you!

Joe: I don't owe you anything.

Loraine: That's right. (mocking Joe) "Relationships aren't bank loans. You don't have to pay back all that you owe."

Joe: You can make fun of me all you want. I'm still the only person in this relationship trying not to hurt the other.

Loraine: (angrily) That's fucking bullshit! I do whatever you say you want and then you're disappointed at everything I do! I feel like you're getting off on fucking with my head! It's easier for you to do that than actually tell the truth!

Joe: (boiling with anger) You want to know the truth?

Loraine: I don't think you have it in you to tell me the truth! You're a fucking coward. You don't want truth in this relationship. You just want what you like to hear.

Joe: (boiling with anger) Oh, you'll get the truth from me, you heartless fucking cunt!

Loraine: (mocking Joe loudly) Bring it on Joe! See if you can make me leave you! I'm sooo scared!!

Joe: You'll never leave me because you're too scared to be with someone you can't control. He'd throw you to the dogs.

Loraine: (loudly) You're with me because you're too scared to lose out on a piece of arse! You know I'm the only attractive woman that will ever fuck you. This is the best deal you're gonna get, fat boy!

Joe: (sarcastically) What a great deal! I'm with a woman who finds my body disgusting; I'm with a woman who's shallow and insensitive; I'm with an intelligent woman who wastes most of her day thinking about trivial bullshit. I'm with a woman who's small minded and petty; I'm with a woman who cares more about fixing our door frames than how much her words hurt people.

Loraine: (laughing at Joe again) You're gonna have to try a lot harder than that if you want to get rid of me.

Joe: (with seething contempt) I'm with a woman who's malicious… who's cruel... who focusses on physical attributes of people… they can do nothing about–

Loraine: (interrupting) If you're talking about my aversion to obesity, that's bullshit. Fat people like you can do something about being fat.

Joe: (yelling angrily) They can't if you tell them they're nasty and disgusting!

Loraine: (shouting) They need to fucking hear it!

Joe: (shouting) They do not need to hear that, Loraine!

Loraine: (loudly) Of course they do! Fat people are selfish fucking arseholes! They make themselves ugly and then force the world to lie to them! Everybody knows they're hideous! Everyone knows they look like fucking monsters, but no one's allowed to fucking say it!

Joe: (loudly) You think they like being hideous? You think they're not hurting inside?

Loraine: (loudly) They're not hurting enough! They're not hurting enough to stop eating bins of shit while the rest of the world has children in it who are fucking starving! Fat people are a drain on the health service. They're a drain on all the natural resources of this planet. And they get away with it because they make people feel sorry for them! No one's brave enough tell them they're greedy fucking bastards!

Joe: (loudly) But they're not greedy! They can't control how they eat! Being fat isn't like being a normal person! Being fat isn't a choice!

Loraine: That's so fucking stupid. People lose weight all the time! It's lazy people who stay fat. It's the pathetic fat blokes like you who get hurt when you finally notice most women think you're disgusting!

Joe: You don't have to remind me most women think I'm disgusting.

Loraine: (loudly) Oh yes, I fucking do! You think blokes can pull birds even when they don't look after themselves! That's insane.

Joe: (loudly) I don't earn sex by being thin, Loraine! Sex isn't like that!

Loraine: (loudly) Yes, it fucking is! You don't fancy bloated fucking cows! You like women who look nice!

Joe: I know that but being thin is so fucking hard! I can't express to you how hard it is. You know I would be thin if it was easy, but it's harder than anything. You'll never understand what that's like for me. I'm not just a big bloke who drinks too many beers at Firebug. I'm in pain… I wish I could explain how I feel.

Loraine: Fine, stay ugly. Be selfish.

Joe: (loudly) You are so fucking uncompassionate! When I'm out in public and see women I fancy, it makes me want to kill myself! When you told me how my stomach made you feel tonight, it made me want to crawl into a hole and fucking die!! It reminded me of when I was a kid!!

Loraine: Yes, you'd rather crawl into a hole than change. You'd rather die than lay off the fucking cheeseburgers. You'd rather be that disgusting fat bloke than treat me with some consideration!

Joe: (loudly) I can't lose weight if I feel like a worthless piece of shit!

Loraine: It's too bad that's what YOU are. It's too bad YOU have chosen that.

Joe: (shouting) I can't change if I hate myself!! I can't change if I want to die!

Loraine: Yes, the world has to cater to you in order for you to change anything about yourself. That's your big excuse for never changing anything.

Joe: (shouting) It's not an excuse! I don't need your fucking cruelty to lose weight! I need to have something to live for! I need to know that when I lose weight, I won't feel like dying!

Loraine: And what makes you think you're so special? Why do your feelings matter so much?

Joe: My feelings are all I've got, Loraine.

Loraine: You let your feelings ruin your life. You let them run you into the fucking ground.

Joe: (shouting) You have no right to say that to me! Every day I ignore my feelings to make you happy!! I shove them down for you!! I pretend I'm not hurting!!

Loraine: (shouting) Bullshit! You use your feelings as an excuse to take advantage of me!! You cry and then you eat! And then you turn yourself into a fat ugly pig with tits!

Joe: Why do you have to be so horrible?

Loraine: (yelling) Because you expect me to touch you!! You expect a beautiful woman to touch you!!

Joe: (yelling) You're the one who wants to have sex all the time!

Loraine: (loudly) And I fucking do it!! I swallow your rancid fucking sperm!! I let you stick your bloated fingers in me when you can't get a hard on!! I even suck you off when you haven't had a shower!!

Joe: (yelling) But you don't have to! That's not what I want! I want us to have good sex!

Loraine: Well, we're not having sex again until you lose four stone. I won't be degrading myself anymore.

Joe: (taken aback) What?

Loraine: You haven't earned a space on this bed, Joe. Until you lose four stone, you're sleeping downstairs. I'll be fucking my vibrator, not your tiny mushroom cock. And don't even think you can see me naked until you've lost at least two stone. I'm not putting nasty things inside me anymore; if you get horny, you can fuck your fat friends. See how nice that makes you feel.

Joe: (flabbergasted) Do you even love me? The shit you say is so hurtful–

Loraine: (interrupting and shouting) I wouldn't be saying these things to you if I didn't love you!!!

Joe: Then why am I not allowed to be hurt by them? Why won't you allow me that? Why is that against the rules?

Loraine: (shouting) Because I'm helping you! Fucking listen, for once. Stop obsessing over your fucking feelings and listen! You're making me hurt you!

Joe: (screaming) I can't help being hurt!!! I can't feel okay when you reject me like that! I'm a human being!!!

Loraine: (screaming) You're a fucking child that needs a wash!

Joe: (desperately) Loraine, I'm not perfect! I can't always be strong! Sometimes I'm vulnerable! Sometimes I'm like a child! I'm like every human being! Everyone has feelings!

Loraine: I have no sympathy for you, none whatsoever.

Joe: Don't you have feelings?

Loraine: Yes and I feel fucking disgusted at you. There's nothing more disgusting than self-pity; there's nothing more unattractive in a man.

Joe: (exhausted) Oh, here we go again…

Loraine: (loudly) Here you go again! You should get a vaginoplasty to go with your tits!

Joe: (shouting) Fuck you! I can't lose weight just because my partner is withholding sex! I can't lose weight because you tell me I'm a horrible piece of shit! I don't work that way and neither do most people who lose weight!

Loraine: (loudly) I don't fucking care if most people are lazy! I'm not! I work hard for this body! I value myself enough to care about my own health! I love you enough to care about actually turning you on!

Joe: (exasperated again) Then can't you love me enough to be sensitive towards me? I don't understand why you refuse to do that. I don't understand why that's such an unreasonable thing to ask of you!

Loraine: Your actions have consequences. If you eat shit, you can spend your life cumming in your hand. I will not be fucking a pig anymore! I'm going to start fucking men and women I fancy! I deserve that. I'm tired of turning down all the good people who want to fuck me. I'm going to start saying yes for a change. I might even fuck Sasha, just to teach you a lesson.

Joe: And what lesson would that be?

Loraine: (smiling sadistically) You'll know when I film it and email it to your students. Those thickos would love to see me fuck Sasha. I'm just not sure how the department might feel.

Joe: (nervous) ...I don't believe you would do that. You care about me too much.

Loraine: You forget that I can access your email from my computer. I could send your students anything I want.

Joe: (incredulous) You'd ruin my career because I'm fat?

Loraine: I'll do whatever it takes to get you to stop embarrassing me. I'm not afraid of you, Joe. You can't intimidate me because you're a bloke. I could fucking kick your arse!

Joe: (sarcastically) I'm so lucky to be with someone so kind.

Loraine: And I am very fucking kind to you! I'm the reason you're not as big as Claire! If it wasn't for me, you wouldn't even be living in this fucking house! You're the one who acts like an ungrateful shithead!

Joe: That's because it feels like you hate me.

Loraine: (loudly) I don't hate you! I just hate how you eat! I hate your excuses! I hate how you treat this house; I hate how you treat yourself; I hate your hygiene. I hate how you look, how you dress. I hate your goddamn daydreaming and I hate your pathetic fucking tears!

Joe: You do hate me.

Loraine: No, Joe. I love you. That's why I nag you for letting people walk all over you. That's why I wish you would stop teaching and get a proper job. Don't you get it?

Joe: I do get it: you hate me.

Loraine: (loudly) I don't hate you, Joe. I just hate living with a failure!

Joe: I'm not a failure.

Loraine: It doesn't have to be this way, Joe. It's all because you don't listen to me. You never do what I tell you to do. That's why you're a disappointment. And that's why no one will remember you after you die.

Joe: You're not listening to me, Loraine. I'm not a failure.

Loraine: What have you done with your life? What have you actually achieved?

Joe: I've achieved many things.

Loraine: Don't make me laugh – you haven't done shit except let yourself down. You've surrounded yourself with a bunch of ex-cons, cripples and fat bitches who tell you how great you are. But you're nothing, Joe. You're nobody. You can't get any job as a writer. You can't fucking look after yourself, you can't even manage a house without your fucking girlfriend doing everything for you. You can't stand up for yourself, you can't protect me, you don't make decent money. You're socially awkward and clumsy as fuck and that's not even half of it. You look and smell like a hairy fucking egg and fill your life with sick weirdos who treat you like a guru. Then you wonder why I don't take you to London with me anymore. I'm fucking embarrassed of you!

Joe: (tearing up) You think I don't know that?

Loraine: (with disgust) When people see me standing next to you, it's like being covered in shit! It's horrible!

Joe: (sighing) …I'm still the guy who loves you. I'm still the guy that never gives up on you.

Loraine: (yelling) You're the guy who ruins my whole fucking life! I'm ashamed to say I even know you! Half the time, I wish you were dead!

Joe: (holding back tears) …Why do you say things like that to me?

Loraine: (yelling) Because YOU need to hear them! You need help!

Joe: Hearing them doesn't help anything, it just hurts.

Loraine: (loudly) You are such a fucking liar! You'll ruin both of our lives if I let you! Anything you do well, you do because of me! I'm even the one who reminds you to fucking write! You wouldn't get up in the morning if I didn't wake you up!

Joe: There's a lot I do for us; there's a lot I do for you. You don't notice any of it.

Loraine: Oh, please. You are more useless than that whiny little cunt you keep talking about in that fucking novel you can't finish. She's more attractive than you anyway.

Joe: I don't want to be with someone who hates me, or my body.

Loraine: (loudly) I don't hate your body! I just want you to fucking change it!

Joe: I need to feel hope in my future. I need to believe we can be happy together and raise a family that's not totally dysfunctional. Otherwise, I can't go on. I feel like I'm drowning.

Loraine: We can create that happy family if you stop fighting me every time I tell you to do something!

Joe: I'm not fighting you, I'm just not as useless as you think I am. There are things I can do without you, Loraine. I can get healthy without you belittling me!

Loraine: I hope that's true because you're not going to be the father of my children if you don't get healthy. You're not just losing weight, Joe. I will not be gestating your sperm until you fucking stop smoking.

Joe: (annoyed) You know I'm quitting in three weeks! We've talked about that at least twenty times.

Loraine: (loudly) Yes and I can't go in my garden without breathing in your fucking smoke!

Joe: (loudly) I said I'm quitting!!!

Loraine: (angrily) You are going to fucking quit because you will not hurt our children! Once I get pregnant, you're going to do things right. You're going to be healthy even if I have to force you. I'll make you fucking eat right. I'll make you exercise. I'll say what needs to be said until you fucking hear it! You won't silence me anymore! I won't let you off the hook the way that I do now. I will be ON YOUR ARSE until you are good enough to be the father of my children! We're gonna have the family I fucking want! You will not spoil our kids! You will not feed them shit!

Joe: So you plan on being cruel to our children too?

Loraine: If you don't give them boundaries, that would be far crueller than I could ever be. Allowing a child to be fat is just horrible. Forcing them to have a fat parent is even more horrible; that's abuse.

Joe: (sarcastically) Yes, it's so much more abusive than burning cigarettes into their dad's neck.

Loraine: (shocked) What the bloody hell…

Joe: You're the one who brought up abuse.

Loraine: (shouting) You told me you would never bring that up again! You fucking promised me you would NEVER EVER bring that up again!

Joe: You promised you wouldn't hit me and then you threw boiling water at me. You're lucky I got out of the way.

Loraine: (shouting) You fucking prick! You fucking arsehole! I can't believe you're breaking your promise!!! I trusted you to never talk about that again! I fucking trusted you!!!

Joe: If you wanna talk about abuse, let's talk about abuse. Let's talk about all the things you've done.

Loraine: (screaming) I was fucking drunk!! And you know I don't remember any of those things!!! You know you can't talk to me about this!!

Joe: You're not the one who had all your clothes ripped to shreds. You didn't get a broken glass thrown at you. You don't have any scars, Loraine; I do.

Loraine: (boiling with anger) I can't believe you… I can't fucking believe this...

Joe: Believe it.

Loraine: (loudly) You sick fucking bastard… You're trying to make me feel guilty about my drinking! You know how hard it was to fucking quit… I trusted you to be supportive!! I trusted you not to make me drink again!!

Joe: You act like hurting me wasn't your fault because you don't remember what you did, like that absolves you of any responsibility.

Loraine: (shouting) It was my fault and that's why I STOPPED drinking! I actually changed something for you! I did something you asked me to do and you promised me you wouldn't fucking talk about it!!!

Joe: I know that, Loraine. It's just–

Loraine: (interrupting loudly) I know what you're doing! You're trying to bring me down!!!

Joe: (loudly) I'm not trying to bring you down!

Loraine: (screaming) YOU'RE TRYING TO GET ME TO FALL OFF THE WAGON!!

Joe: (loudly) Of course I'm not doing that! You think I want that?

Loraine: You want to fuck up my career! You'd love to see me fail and be like you!

Joe: Loraine, the last thing I would ever want is for you to fall off the wagon again!

Loraine: (shouting) Then don't ever fucking bring up my drinking! Don't ever bring it up ever again!!!

Joe: I was just trying to make the point that–

Loraine: (interrupting loudly) You don't have any points to make! You're trying to manipulate me! You're trying to make me feel like I'M the one who's letting us down! It's like you're getting off on hurting me, you fucking sadist!

Joe: That's what you said the last time you got hammered and smashed my laptop through the kitchen window, right after you said all that horrible shit to my dad on Skype. Or was that the day you got angry and killed our dog?

Loraine: (screaming violently) STOP IT!! JUST STOP IT RIGHT NOW!! IF YOU DON'T STOP, I'LL SMASH YOUR FUCKING HEAD IN!!!

Joe: (shouting) Do your worst! Hit me you fucking cunt! Go on then! Do it sober!

Loraine grabs a glass of water on their bedside table and brutally hurls it hard at the wall in front of her, smashing it into pieces that scatter across the room. This act feels violent, but Joe is relieved Loraine didn't throw that glass at him. After the glass breaks, Joe can see Loraine putting her face in her hands, crying. She's so angry she's shaking.

Joe: Do you think you've really changed since you quit drinking? Are you that much more calm and serene?

Loraine: (crying) You're the one who needs to change! Not me! I've done all the changing I need to do for you…You haven't done shit for me...

Joe: (sarcastically) And here come the tears.

Loraine: (crying hysterically) You want things to stay the same!!! You always get your fucking way!! I won't let you this time!! I won't fucking let you…

Joe: (shouting) Oh God, listen to yourself… you're wailing!!! Calm down!

Loraine: (sobbing) I won't let you make me feel guilty... I'm stronger than that…You can't fucking hurt me... not after what I've been through…

Joe: Stop crying and listen to me! I'm not trying to make you feel guilty!

Loraine: (crying) Yes, you are… You're killing yourself… I will fucking leave you… before I ever tell you that's okay… You want to be fat …and embarrass me so you can–

Joe: (interrupting) How many times do I need to say I hate my weight? How many times do I need to mention the fucking food plan? I'm trying to change my eating! I'm taking responsibility! I know what the problem is from my end. I know where I'm going wrong and I'm trying to do something about it! You, on the other hand, are not doing anything about that cruel shit that comes out of your mouth! You're just crying.

Loraine: (crying) I don't know how else to help you...

Joe: Well, I'm sorry but you can't help me by being a mean and punishing bitch. You have a sensitivity problem and I'm tired of it. I don't want a relationship with this much cruelty in it, Loraine. This is too painful for me.

Loraine: (wiping away tears) So now you don't want my honesty. You know that's how I show you my love... and you still don't fucking want it! You don't want me to love you! You want me to lie to you!

Joe: (irritated) Maybe you're right, maybe I don't want your honesty. Maybe you should keep some of your thoughts to yourself.

Loraine: (sniffing) You want me to lie! You want me to act like a good little wifey who does what she's told! If you could, you'd force all the women in the world to wipe the shit off your arse! You're a fucking misogynist!

Joe: Jesus, Loraine...

Loraine: (loudly) You don't want a woman who's your equal! You want a fucking slave who cleans your house and sucks your dick and lies to you! That's all you want from women! That's all you want from me!

Joe: You need to stop now, Loraine.

Loraine: (loudly) You're just like every other lefty! You think you respect women; you think you're sensitive because a woman can make you fucking cry! You want to call yourself a fucking feminist!

Joe: (shouting) I just want you to stop hurting me! I've had enough now! This has gone far enough!

Loraine: (loudly) You think you don't hurt me? You think I'm not hurting right now? You think I feel good inside?

Joe: You don't have to stay in this relationship, Loraine. No one's forcing you to stay with me.

Loraine: You think I like saying these things to you? You think I don't hate myself?

Joe: You shouldn't be in a relationship with me if you hate yourself.

Loraine: (sarcastically) Yes and we both know how much you love yourself.

Joe: (loudly) I said you don't have to stay with me! I don't feel good in this relationship anymore; it feels wrong. It feels like we're over; I feel nothing but contempt from you. I feel hated. I don't feel loved at all.

Loraine: Joe, I do love you. I just need you to change.

Joe: That doesn't matter. The things you feel about me you shouldn't be feeling about your boyfriend. You shouldn't be with someone like me.

Loraine: (annoyed) You can't fucking tell me who I should and shouldn't be with!

Joe: I am telling you. You've lost me, Loraine. You killed us. You killed what we had.

Loraine: Don't overreact to things, Joe. You know I didn't mean what I said about not fucking you. I'm just angry. You can fuck my arse tomorrow. I'll get some lube. We can sort this out.

Joe: I am sorting it. You're getting a new boyfriend, or you're taking time to be alone and figure things out. But you're not doing this to me anymore. I'm stopping this.

Loraine: Oh, you don't need to stop anything, Joe. I'm just being bitchy and you're being too sensitive. That's all that's happening here. I'm not trying to hurt you. I'm trying to help you. I'm your girlfriend!

Joe: That doesn't matter. If I stay with you, I won't be able to trust myself. I don't know what I'll do next time you throw a wobbler like this. It's getting dangerous, like I can't control my thoughts. This has to stop, Loraine. This relationship is over.

Loraine: (nervous) How are you gonna survive without me?

Joe: I'll be fine, okay? Don't worry about that. I can move into my old flat again. I make enough money to live and be happy, I don't need the dosh you need to feel okay. I'm not materialistic.

Loraine: (panicking) But what about me?

Joe: I think you'll be much happier with someone who doesn't disgust you the way that I do. You should be with someone you respect more. It's okay to leave me so that you can find that person, or at least get some therapy. I won't resent you.

Loraine: (loudly) But I don't want to fucking leave you! I can't!

Joe: Why not?

Loraine: ...You wouldn't understand.

Joe: Try me.

Loraine: You wouldn't understand.

Joe: I don't understand why you want to stay.

Loraine: You wouldn't believe me if I told you.

Joe: You'll never know that unless you tell me.

Loraine: ...I've never met anyone as kind or as giving as you.

Joe: Oh, come on Loraine. You can do better than that!

Loraine: It's true. You're a keeper.

Joe: How can you say that after–

Loraine: (interrupting) You're still here; that means you're kind enough. I'm still arguing with you; that means you're stubborn enough. I can respect you; you stand up to me.

Joe: I don't understand.

Loraine: You love me; you love me no matter what. I can be honest and you love me, I can show you my anger, I can be horrible to you, I can cry. You still love me even though I hit you and burned you. No one's ever loved me like that.

Joe: But I'm afraid of what will happen if I stay in this relationship. I don't trust myself.

Loraine: I don't care! I've never had love like this before. Very few people have loved me.

Joe: I don't get it. You act like I'm a nuisance, you say I'm useless, you hate my job, you say I don't protect you and I'm not a real man. On top of that, you don't fancy me. You hate the fact that I don't want your honesty: I just told you I don't like how you express your love for me. If I stay with you, I might hurt myself. On top of that, you think I'm a failure. I embarrass you; you hate how I cry. You think I'm gonna be a horrible parent and that being around me is like being covered in shit.

Loraine: (sighing) All true.

Joe: Why do you want that in a boyfriend?

Loraine: Because I love you anyway.

Joe: What?

Loraine: You might not deserve it, but I love you.

Joe: I thought you said unconditional love felt painful for you.

Loraine: It is painful, but I can't help it, I love you. I love you even though you drive me fucking mad! I love you even though I wish I could change a million things about you. I love you even though I think you are the most annoying person I've ever met, Joe. I can't stop loving you. I love you even though I hate your friends and I hate your body and I hate your fucking poetry. I love you even though I think you're a pretentious wanker and most of the time I can't even stand the sound of your voice.

Joe: You love me despite all of that?

Loraine: I love a poor, pathetic moron with an eye patch who won't help himself. I love a failure; I love an ugly fat idiot who will never amount to anything. And I can't stop loving him, or his small cock.

Joe: (tearing up) That's one of the sweetest things you've ever said to me.

Loraine: I'm happy I found something honest to say to you that didn't hurt you for once. I hate hurting you.

Joe: Then why do you do it?

Loraine: Because it's the only way to help you. You're lazy and I can help you get things done.

Joe: I don't need you to hurt me so I can make a decision about losing weight, Loraine! You keep ignoring me when I say that! You keep ignoring me and I'm scaring myself!

Loraine: There's nothing to be scared of. You just need to stop being a hypocrite. You want honesty; you don't want manipulation; you want to forgive me for all my imperfections. Why do you get so upset when I ask you to do those things?

Joe: Giving unconditional love is hard.

Loraine: It's fucking hard for me as well, you know! But I don't have a choice when it comes to you. I can't help but love you.

Joe: I know that; I have love for you like that as well. This relationship is too hard without unconditional love; it gets cruel without that. I can't handle all this cruelty, Loraine. I'm afraid of what will happen if this keeps going; I'm afraid I'll hang myself.

Loraine: (giggling) You are such a silly head.

Joe: I'm serious.

Loraine: Everything will be fine, Joe. You just need to be honest with yourself.

Joe: About what?

Loraine: Just admit that you're a man with eyes and a cock. You're with me because I'm a woman that stimulates your eyes and cock. There are other reasons you're with me too, but that's the main reason.

Joe: No, Loraine, that's not love. I'm going to love you when you stop stimulating my eyes. When I slim down you can get fat and I'll still love you. You don't earn my love with how you look.

Loraine: (loudly) But I do! I work hard to look this way! Don't make me feel like that isn't worth anything! I want to look nice for you! That's important!

Joe: It's more important that I love who you are.

Loraine: (frustrated) But that is who I am! I'm someone who works hard to make you feel good! I do that because I love you!

Joe: You don't have to be beautiful to make me feel good.

Loraine: Joe, Claire's your best friend. Answer me this: if I looked like her, would I be sitting here with you right now?

Joe: …I don't know.

Loraine: (giggling) You do know, you plonker.

Joe: It's horrible though. I don't want to think about that.

Loraine: Bodies matter, Joe. We're animals.

Joe: I'm not attracted to Claire… because she's like my sister. She'd be like that to me even if she was thin.

Loraine: That's bullshit and you know it. Claire's a selfish fucking cow. That's why you're not fucking that fat piece of shit. No one wants to fuck her. It's like eating rotten meat!

Joe: Why do you keep talking about people like they're pieces of meat?

Loraine: People need to be pieces of meat when they have sex! They need to be meat that looks and tastes fucking good.

Joe: I don't know, Loraine. What about women and objectification?

Loraine: Joe, the way I look is the reason you started loving me. It's the reason you love all the other things about me; it caused your love for me.

Joe: I don't understand.

Loraine: Being beautiful to you makes me feel good about myself. I can't handle it if you make me feel ugly! That's what pisses me off.

Joe: I don't want to make you feel ugly! But that doesn't mean I'm going to stop loving you when you get older, Loraine. I'll love you no matter what you look like. Don't you know that?

Loraine: Of course I do! But you have to stop being afraid of the reason you're in this relationship: you're not in this relationship because you wanted to love a friend! You've got plenty of friends. You wanted to love someone you could be happy fucking. You don't need me to have long conversations with you. You need me to live with you, be there for you and fuck you. That's what you need from me now and that's what you'll need from me when you're an old man.

Joe: Loraine, that sounds like... prostitution. I can't feel comfortable thinking about our relationship that way. Where's the romance?

Loraine: (frustrated) This is what actually works for men and women! Long conversations don't stop people from getting bored in a relationship, Joe. Long conversations don't get people hot when they're talking to someone they don't fancy. There is a difference between being a friend and being a lover! Don't you know that?

Joe: Of course I do, Loraine. I know best friends don't normally do well in relationships. I've had first-hand experience of that.

Loraine: Then you need to really listen to me. I can give you incredible things a friend never could: I can fuck you every night, I can look after you, I can tell you how to take care of yourself, I can give you a family. I can make other men envious of you.

Joe: You already you do those things for me, Loraine. In fact, you really are amazing at–

Loraine: (interrupting) Then stop doing my head in, Joe. Just do what I tell you to do and stop giving me so much shit about it! Stop over analysing everything! Stop being the one who gets in the way.

Joe: I'm trying, I really am. The last thing I want is to be in the way.

Loraine: Then I need you to appreciate how beautiful I am! I don't want fucking compliments. I need you excited to see me every day; I need to see it in your eyes.

Joe: I know that.

Loraine: I need to look into your eyes and see that being with me is more exciting than any time you will ever spend on your own, or with your weird friends. We can't have that if there's no good sex.

Joe: You know I want you to be happy, Loraine.

Loraine: (frustrated) That's why I need you to lose weight without taking it personally!

Joe: I know that! How many times do I need to–

Loraine: (interrupting) I can't feel like I'm beautiful if you're fat!! It's nasty and it's making me feel like I'm the one who's ugly!! I'd rather die than feel like that again!! Don't you understand??

Joe: (exasperated) Why won't you believe me when I tell you I'm going to lose the weight?? What do I have to do to get you to believe me?? Just tell me what I need to do to make you fucking believe me!!

Loraine: I'm starting to believe you, Joe. But it will really sink in when I know you accept the truth.

Joe: What?

Loraine: I'll know you accept the truth when you can look me in the eye and say, "Loraine, I need to lose weight because I am fucking disgusting. My gut is disgusting. My boobs are disgusting. My face is disgusting. I should never have embarrassed you in public by making myself so ugly. I've been insensitive and cruel, but I won't be anymore. I'm going to change without any excuses. Thank you for telling me I need to change, Loraine. Thank you for loving and caring for me."

Joe: Why do you want me to say that?

Loraine: If you can say that without hurting inside, or getting defensive, or feeling sad, I know you'll lose the weight.

Joe: Well, I can't say that. I can't control my feelings that well. I'm sorry but I'm flawed.

Loraine: I know you are. You're a fucking mess.

Joe: I have limitations. If you're going to be my girlfriend, you're going to have to accept my limitations. I can't give you anything more than that.

Loraine: I had a feeling you wouldn't be able to say what I need you to say. People I love always disappoint me; you aren't the first.

Joe: Well, I'm sorry I'm such a big disappointment. There's plenty of other guys who would be less disappointing to you. You don't have to stay with me.

Loraine: (loudly) But I don't want to be with any of those guys! I love you! I'm going to stay with you whether or not you lose the fucking weight!

Joe: I love you too!

Loraine: (exasperated) So please… please don't guilt trip me if I need to complain about you! Just let me have a moan, Joe. I'm human too. There's no reason to be scared.

Joe: Did you just say you're going to stay with me regardless of how big I am?

Loraine: Of course I'm staying with you!

Joe: You love me that much?

Loraine: I can't stop loving you Joe. I wish I could but I can't.

Joe: For someone who hates unconditional love, you may actually be better at it than me.

Loraine: (tearing up again) I love you because you're mine. You're the only guy I have ever known who loves me no matter what I say or do. No one has ever done that for me. I always get rejected sooner or later. You always stay with me; you always forgive me.

Joe: That's unconditional love, Loraine. You see? It's not about how you look.

Loraine: (crying) You can say as many nasty things about me as you want…

You don't even have to fuck me… I'll still love you back. I'll love you even if you hurt yourself. I'll try and stop you obviously but… I'll still love you!

Joe: (tearing up) That's all I've ever wanted from you Loraine. I just want to know that, no matter what, you'll always love me.

Loraine: All I want is a relationship where we can be honest with each other. Is that such a horrible thing to ask for?

Joe: No, I guess I want that as well. You are right that I need to develop a thicker skin. I need to be able to hear what you say to me without taking it personally and I need to forgive you for your flaws.

Loraine: You do!

Joe: I have to work on not getting so hurt whenever you show me an imperfection. I need to be stronger, mentally.

Loraine: We both want the same things, Joe. You just need to work on yourself if we're both going to have them.

Joe: I know, I know. I have a lot of work to do on myself.

Loraine: I'll be here for you throughout all of that work. I don't care how long it takes you to start doing what I tell you. I'll always be here for you, Joe. No matter what.

Joe: I'm so lucky to have you, Loraine.

Loraine: (wiping away a tear) You fucking are! Now come here and give us a hug.

Joe and Loraine embrace for a minute, crying.

Joe: (crying) I'm sorry I get so emotional and confused sometimes.

Loraine: (crying) It's okay, I get confused as well.

Joe: (crying) I love you.

Loraine: (crying) That's all that matters, Joe.

Joe: (crying) I want us to work.

Loraine: (crying) We can make it work because we love each other. I love you sooo much, baby.

Joe: (crying) I love you too. I'm gonna work hard to give you what you need from me. I know I need to be a better boyfriend. You need a boyfriend you can be honest with; you shouldn't have to be with a bloke you don't fancy.

Loraine: (crying) All you have to do is listen to me and everything will be fine, honey. You're my guy. You can be as good as you want to be.

Joe and Loraine hug for another minute.

Loraine: It's actually pretty late. All this fighting's made me knackered. I think I can sleep tonight without an orgasm.

Joe: Good. I'm tired too.

Loraine: Fighting can be sexy, but this was exhausting.

Joe: I know. I think I need to go online and look at some relaxation videos to calm my head down. I'll be back in about an hour. I don't have to work tomorrow, remember.

Loraine: That's fine if that's what you need to do, but just be quiet on your way in when you're done.

Joe: I will be.

Loraine: Joe…

Joe: Yes?

Loraine: I didn't mean what I said earlier today about your tummy. I was just angry at you for not listening to me. I was trying to make a point so you'd set up your new diet without me having to ask you thirty times. Your belly isn't nasty, really. It's kind of cute.

Joe: Well, I'm glad you feel that way. But what you said was still mean.

Loraine: Well, tonight you were mean too. It wasn't just me.

Joe: I know.

Loraine: Can you say you're sorry? It would make me feel a bit better. In fact, I think it would make you feel better too.

Joe: (sighing) …I'm sorry for being mean to you, Loraine. The last thing I wanted was to hurt you tonight. I was trying to communicate how I feel and I took things too far. I can be a dick sometimes. I know that and I hate it more than you do. Please forgive me.

Loraine: (smiling) You're so sweet, Joe.

Joe: Am I?

Loraine: Yeah, you are. I wish I was more like you.

Joe: (laughing) Well, you're not. You're nothing like me at all.

Loraine: That's why we're good for each other. We balance each other out.

It's still raining, but the thunder and lightning has temporarily stopped. The Wi-Fi is back on.

Joe goes to his office and decides to check his email one last time before he watches his relaxation videos. He sees an email from an address he does not recognise. The subject heading is:

'It's me, Janet'

Joe immediately knows who this Janet is and is frightened by her presence on his computer screen.

Joe initially thinks Janet Waverley is stalking him because she intends to kill him for some unknown reason. She's a psychopath, after all. That's what psychopaths do.

Joe's next thought is that he should immediately delete this email and block Janet's email address. Psychopaths can lie convincingly. Joe worries that whatever Janet says will be a skilful attempt at manipulating him, putting him in some kind of physical danger.

However, another part of Joe simply can't resist opening the email to see what it is that Janet has to say. That emotional part of him wins out over the much more rational part of Joe which knows Janet could kill him.

Hence, Joe irresponsibly opens Janet's email, allowing her many words into his head. The email is very long.

Initially, Joe is quite sceptical of the things that Janet is telling him. He sees ulterior motives in nearly every sentence. He even finds much of what she says offensive. Yet he keeps reading anyway. Towards the end of the email, Joe starts to feel a confusion – a confusion he can't fully understand. As he reads Janet's final sentences, Joe surprises himself. He does something he has tried desperately not to do since he last saw Janet.

He allows himself to miss her.

When this happens, Joe immediately brings his hands to his face and sobs. His sobs are loud and painful. He sobs for over forty minutes, crying his eyes out. Loraine hears Joe and assumes he is just having residual emotions from their previous argument. After Joe is done crying, he quietly goes back to bed with Loraine.

Joe is so exhausted from the emotional turmoil of the evening that he manages to sleep through the sounds of more thunder and lightning. He also sleeps through the sounds of yelling and banging coming from Eve and Alice, the lesbian couple next door.

As Joe drifts to sleep, he is no longer thinking about Janet. He is instead thinking about Loraine, feeling an awkward but still warm gratitude towards the feisty beauty sleeping next to him. If Loraine had not stirred up such intense anger in Joe, he would have hung himself in her pink bathroom after they had sex.

In the early hours of the morning, Joe has a long elaborate dream about his neighbours. In the first part of the dream, he dreams he is Eve, arguing with Alice about why they should remain a childless couple.

In the next part of the dream, Joe dreams he is himself, comforting Eve, after Alice pokes both of her fingers into Eve's unprotected eyes. In the last part of the dream, Joe gains an omniscient bird's eye perspective and observes Eve and Alice raising a daughter named Cara.

18. ROMANCE: Conditional Love

Throughout the morning and afternoon of July 29th, Joe is alone at home while Loraine is at work. Joe eats breakfast at 10am, pondering on his long elaborate dream about Eve and Alice. He wonders if this dream was partly inspired by the contents of Janet's email – particularly the bits about children.

By about 1pm, Joe is obsessively reading Janet's email over and over again – he can't stop reading it.

He hates the torrent of emotion this email is creating in him, but he can't stop thinking about Janet. Joe had planned to walk into town and have lunch with his friend Claire at 2pm, but he has cancelled that meeting by text, knowing full well he wouldn't be good company, unable to concentrate on Claire's quick and hyper-intellectual conversation. Joe feels like having lunch with him would simply be a waste of Claire's time.

Moreover, Joe does not want to tell Claire about Janet's email. Joe knows how much Claire hates Loraine: she tells Joe at every opportunity that he should get a more intelligent girlfriend who is less "normal", a girlfriend that other men aren't constantly throwing themselves at. Claire hates Loraine for being so much more "normal" and so much more beautiful than Claire herself is. Joe thinks this is quite a shallow reason for hating another human being. After all, Claire has never even seen Loraine when Loraine is rude or angry. If Claire saw those sides of Loraine, Joe thinks she'd have more legitimate reasons to hate her.

Joe knows telling Claire about Janet's email will simply start a heated argument where he will have to yet again defend his current relationship. A heated argument with his best friend is the last thing Joe is in the mood for today. Joe simply wants to be alone, eat some nice food, perhaps meditate, or go bird watching. Joe wants to do anything to restore peace and clarity, anything to remove the confusion and internal chaos Joe can feel in his brain and in his tummy.

But regardless of whether he meditates, listens to a tape of his mother's jazz compositions, or stares at birds through oversized binoculars, Joe cannot help but remember how happy he was when he fell in love with Janet Waverley and how much he consistently enjoyed her company as a young man. On the other hand, Joe can't stop reminding himself that Janet is a dangerous psychopath who poked his eye out in an act of uncontrolled rage. On top of these conflicting thoughts, Joe is embarrassed by the sheer immaturity of his newfound fixation on Janet. He thinks if he were a more emotionally mature person, he'd appreciate his current circumstances, feeling happy Janet is a long-gone part of his past.

Joe knows that the adult thing to do is delete Janet's email, block her new email address and never speak of her again. The choice of a grownup would be to live in the present moment without rehashing the traumas of the past – a past which cannot be changed. Joe also knows that telling Loraine about Janet's email will simply cause more headaches for him in the long run. It may cause another row and even a possible act of violence. Joe feels lucky Loraine was not violent with him the previous night, given how angry she was. However, Joe is feeling impulsive today. A part of him, despite his better judgement, is weirdly excited by the idea of Loraine reading Janet's email.

At 8:16pm, Loraine arrives home and proceeds to tell Joe about her long day at dance class. She begins the conversation by ranting about how parents today are too soft on kids. She's especially annoyed that some parents have recently accused her of bullying her less talented students as a way of motivating them to work harder. What they consider bullying Loraine considers teaching. Joe pretends to listen attentively, even though he's mostly trying to stop himself from telling Loraine about Janet's email.

At 8:30pm, Loraine stops ranting and complains that she's hungry, asking Joe where tea is.

Joe: (suddenly remembering his cooking duties) Oh, I'm so sorry, I totally forgot about that, Loraine. I've had a lot on my mind.

Loraine: (impatiently) What have you fucking had on your mind? I asked you yesterday to make sure something was on the hob before I got back from work!

Joe: I know you did. I'll make something fast, alright? I think we've got some vegetables I can turn into a Spanish lentil stew.

Loraine: (annoyed) No, don't fucking do that. It won't be ready for ages. You take too long to cook anything nice, Joe. We'll just order some food online.

Two white boxes of Chinese food arrive quickly and Loraine and Joe eat together on their Formica kitchen table. Joe has ordered a healthy vegetable dish. He makes sure to eat it slowly so as to not disgust Loraine. He also concentrates on eating slowly as a way of motivating himself to say anything other than the truth about Janet and her email.

Loraine: So what did you do today?

Joe: Not much, mostly wrote stuff.

Loraine: What did you write?

Joe: Just bits 'n' bobs. Stuff about life and human desire, paradoxes, love, that sort of thing.

Loraine: What, poems?

Joe: No, just things I needed to write down so I can get a better understanding of what I want in my life.

Loraine: What do you need a better understanding about?

Joe: What exactly I want.

Loraine: I thought all of this was what you wanted: our relationship, our home, our baby next year.

Joe: I still think I want some of that, but I want some other things as well.

Loraine: What "other things"?

Joe: I got an email from an old friend last night. It made me re-evaluate some aspects of my life; let's just say that.

Loraine: What old friend?

Joe: Someone who I don't necessarily want to be in contact with again, but someone who made me think about things in an interesting way.

Loraine: (getting irritated) Who?

Joe: My ex.

Loraine: (loudly) Which ex?

Joe: One who I've been afraid of for many years.

Loraine: (loudly) Oh God, that fucking psycho!

Joe: Regardless of what she is, her email was helpful in getting me to see some things.

Loraine: (loudly) Where the fuck is it? I wanna read it!

Loraine frantically gets up and goes to Joe's office room, bringing up his email account inbox. Joe is nervous and excited.

Loraine: (loudly) Don't you let this fucking bitch twist your mind! I won't let her manipulate you.

Joe: She can't manipulate me anymore. I'm with you, remember?

Loraine: (angrily) Make me a cup of coffee while I read this damn thing.

Joe: Okay, but before you read it, I think you should–

Loraine: (interrupting and yelling) DON'T TELL ME HOW TO FUCKING READ THIS! I DON'T NEED YOU TO INTERPRET IT FOR ME!

Joe: I'm sorry, Loraine.

Loraine proceeds to read Janet's letter.

Joe,

Let me start off by saying you have every right not to read this email. You have every right to delete it and if you do, I won't have any hard feelings. You have every reason to hate me. You have every reason not to forgive me for what I did to you.

If you choose to keep reading, I will tell you from the start that this is not a letter trying to elicit sympathy for me. I'm not writing this to try and convince you that you were wrong or that I'm somehow a normal person who isn't any different to anyone else. I have no delusions about who I am. I am a clinically diagnosed psychopath. I am writing this letter for purely selfish reasons, reasons that will become apparent as you read on.

Since we last met, I've had some pretty decent career success. I've travelled the world and met lots of cool people. I've had the opportunity to do creative work I find interesting and helpful to my fans in different ways, yet I haven't been happy through any of this. For a while, I thought the intensity with which I applied myself to my work would compensate for the feeling of emptiness that accompanied your departure from my life. It did not. As the years go by, I feel less and less like I can continue.

This last year has been particularly difficult. For the first time ever, my sadness actually stopped me from working at the pace I have become accustomed to. I've been struggling with mental health difficulties, I find it hard getting out of bed, I can't stop crying throughout the day and I'm finding it hard not to harm myself. I'm not telling you this because I want you to rescue me from it; I know that won't happen. I'm writing you because my thoughts are tinged with an unbearable guilt. I worry that I really damaged you the last time we spoke.

I bet you're thinking, "It's pretty obvious you fucking damaged me! You poked my eye out, you fucking bitch!"

If you are thinking this, I can't say I blame you.

I was a horrible person that day. The act of violence I committed against you was pure evil. It was one of the worst things I have ever done in my life, an act so awful I struggle to comprehend how it came out of me. It was wrong, it was cruel and it was terrifying (for both of us). It would be a cop out for me to say, "It wasn't really me that did that to you. Something took over me. My true self would never be capable of such an act!"

That, of course, is rubbish.

I take full responsibility for my actions. They were all me. What you saw that day was my worst self: a dark side I hid from you the moment I fell in love with you. I worry now that you think that side of me is the predominant one.

I'm also worried that my horrendous behaviour during our last conversation caused you to interpret the things I said in the wrong light. The things I said which were true, I said with such malice that I can't blame you for writing them off as obvious falsehoods. Still, I'm in turmoil over the negative consequences for you that might happen if you did dismiss it all. You always had a habit of substituting ideological crusades for instances where you should instead be standing up for yourself.

I remember you telling me many times that your mum made you feel like her love for you was conditional, when you were a child. Then you became very passionate about the importance of unconditional love. You'd give sometimes beautiful speeches about it. We would wind up discussing unconditional love instead of talking about how you needed to stand up to your mother because of how she was treating you.

I remember she once left a phone message for us where she said the amount of money you made was evidence you didn't have any potential when you were a kid. Instead of calling her back that night and telling her off, you had an argument with me about why you should just ignore that comment. You said you wanted to love her unconditionally and her comments gave you the opportunity to practice the art of forgiveness.

This was one of the few arguments we ever had, yet by the end of it, I could tell you were starting to see that your mother was actually being harmed by your forgiveness. I remember you calling her the next day and telling her, with confidence, how you didn't approve of the way she spoke to you.

She started swearing at you, screaming that she wished she'd never had a son. That was typical of her. But this time you yelled back, "Start acting like my mother and not like such a horrid fucking cunt!"

I was so proud of you in that moment. You were actually giving her consequences for her bad behaviour. Throughout her life, no one ever did that. When you slammed down the phone, you looked at me and said, "That woman does not deserve my love. She deserves a fucking beating." I smiled and hugged you for what seemed like ages. Up until that point, I never felt like I was able to help another human being the way I helped you. What made it even more special was you were also my lover.

During our last conversation, I'm afraid I undid all of that. I behaved coldly, with vindictiveness, making a virtual mockery of the importance of justice in any relationship. I made it seem as though anyone who values justice in a relationship is an unforgiving, self-righteous pedant.

Given what I know of you, I'm guessing you would see my behaviour as a vindication of the idea that unconditional love is the only healthy and humane way of loving another person. I can even see you taking on your 'unconditional love crusade' with renewed fervour. And yes, I can see you being a casualty of that crusade. I can see unconditional love being a way that people take advantage of you.

This may be paranoia on my part. Nonetheless, it's paranoia I can't get out of my mind. Maybe I don't know you as well as I think I do. Maybe you are happy and self-confident in ways that have nothing to do with anything I said to you during our last meeting. However, I can't bear the thought of you internalising a bad idea because my own inexcusable behaviour made it seem attractive.

If what you believe about love has nothing to do with what I said to you that day, feel free to not read any further. However, if you feel what I said negatively impacted your life in any way, give me a chance to explain what I was trying to say in a better way. I want to say it to you again, but this time clearly in a calm state of mind. If you disagree, you disagree and that's absolutely fine. Nonetheless, I want you to see what I was trying to express in a way where my words aren't coming out of a person behaving like a psychopath. This is the only way I can deal with my guilt and try to turn it into something positive.

So here goes:

Every human being has faults. Any kind of relationship with an adult requires a lot of slack cutting from both parties. People can indeed be grumpy and unsociable on many days when the best response to such a mood is patience. However, there are limits to the amount of patience one displays before the patience becomes a way of normalising abuse. This is why constant forgiveness is bad for any relationship. If you have to constantly forgive, that means your partner is constantly doing something you have to forgive.

If that's the main dynamic in your relationship, the relationship isn't fair to you. It's not fair to you whether it's your spouse, your friend, your parent, or your child. If the forgiveness in any relationship consistently goes one way, that means someone is giving way more to the relationship than they are getting in return. When that happens, the relationship instantiates a kind of injustice. The injustice becomes abusive when there are no boundaries in place to stop the forgiven behaviour from becoming cruel behaviour that is also forgiven.

The biggest threat to the boundary which keeps a relationship just, is the idea that adult relationships are grounded in unconditional love. When you love someone unconditionally, you love them irrespective of who they are or what they do; you love them whether they treat you fairly or whether they abuse you. This is why I believe unconditional love is the lowest form of love. It's a love necessary for infants and small children because they need to be forgiven for consistently bad behaviour. This constant forgiveness is necessary for them in their journey towards goodness.

The same is not true of adults.

Unconditional love reduces adults back into the infantile state. It teaches adults that they don't need to bring things to a relationship that are proportionate to what their partners bring.

Worse still, unconditional love teaches adults that it's okay to treat everyone's pathology equally. This is another hallmark of abuse. When someone's messy bedroom is treated as the equivalent of someone else's punches, the relationship is actually harmful to the parties involved. Nonetheless, this abuse gets normalised because the person with the messy bedroom wants to love their partner without expecting anything in return. The outcome of this pathological desire is enabling.

Enablers use disturbing language that reflects their particular insanity. They will say things like "We need to treat each other better" when referring to an unclean kitchen which had prompted a blow to the head with a hammer. The enabled abuser will say things like, "Your hyper-sensitivity isn't good for us" when referring to the enabler's meek complaints about the blow. What's often unnoticed is that physical violence isn't the only context in which this dynamic is present. The enabler may also complain about being hurt by emotional sadism on the part of the enabled abuser. The enabled abuser will respond that the enabler is being emotionally sadistic, merely in complaining about it.

Whenever the enabler complains about the abuse, the abuser will reframe the issue as though the enabler is at fault. The abuser may even demand that the enabler should choose to interpret the abuser as someone who gives the enabler "tough love." When the enabler expresses reluctance to accept this interpretation, the abuser will accuse the enabler of placing conditions on their love. The enabler, wanting to love unconditionally, will do anything to remove the appearance of these conditions. Thus, the abuse cycle will continue, often getting worse and worse.

When there are no conditions placed on love, neither partner has any incentive to treat the other as an equal. In any relationship, these incentives are necessary. There also needs to be additional incentives to motivate both parties to treat their partners with kindness. These kindness incentives must be juxtaposed against still further incentives that motivate dignity and self-respect for and from both parties. Unconditional love removes all of these incentives in one fell swoop. For adults, it is toxic and dangerous. Something for nothing is nothing indeed.

I suspect the reason why unconditional love remains a popular delusion among the adult population is that adults have a romanticised view of infants and children. Adults talk about infants and children as though they are more valuable or precious than other adults. They use words like 'innocence' to describe behaviours in children that would more accurately be described as naïve and immature. Temper tantrums in toddlers may be something we find cute for evolutionary reasons, but temper tantrums in adults are the source of everything that's wrong with the world. Like children, adults need boundaries. Unlike children, adults are better at undermining those boundaries by exploiting the compassion of those whose job it is to reinforce them.

As an adult, when you can be loved for having met certain conditions, you know you deserve that love. You know that love has been given to you because you've helped someone, touched someone, entertained someone, amused someone, impressed someone, cared for someone, sacrificed for someone, inspired someone, or simply loved someone.

If you're a bad human being and you get love anyway, that love is tragic and pedestrian – a love for infants and dogs.

It is a love for what you are, not a love for who you are. Conditional love is love for the individuality of autonomous adults. Unconditional love for adults is a de-humanising form of pity. This is because when unconditional love is given to an adult, pity rather than affection is the reason it's given. No one wants to love a serial killer because they feel warm towards the killer, nor do they love the killer because they appreciate the killer's inner qualities. The killer's individuality expresses itself in a way which is destructive. Unconditional love is given to the killer as a way of saying, "I hate how horribly you behave. Let me reward you with what you don't deserve so that I can change your behaviour. Let me help you be nice to me. Let me lick your arse to stop you from shitting in my mouth."

Because of the ludicrous condescension of this gesture, it rewards the killer rather than stops the killing. Even more importantly, the unconditional love is given begrudgingly. It's given for the purpose of stopping behaviour which is hated. It's given as a tool to achieve something else. It's the furthest thing from a spontaneous affirmation of a person's individuality. It's a Pavlovian manipulation and an ugly one at that.

So for me, conditional love is an end in itself. It is given to reward rather than manipulate. The reward is not given to ensure future good behaviour. The reward is given out of awe and respect. Awe and respect are the main ingredients of a healthy companionship. Companionship, to put it bluntly, is roughly symmetrical mutually self-satisfying behaviour. Companionship would be totally symmetrical were it not for the flawed nature of human beings. Yet the behaviour must be roughly symmetrical in order for the companionship not to degenerate into an instance of one person treating another like a beggar waiting to be pissed on by a drunken rich man. This is why the term 'self-satisfying' is so important. You can't be in a relationship for the sake of your partner. You both have to be in the relationship for yourself.

In my view, love is not a favour or an obligation: it's a gift. And like any gift, what matters is that (a) the gift is given so that it can be reciprocated and (b) the reciprocal exchange is roughly equivalent. If someone buys you plastic turds and you buy them a mansion, this makes for an awkward Christmas.

I hate how people pretend that Christmas is about giving. It's obvious Christmas is never fun when the gifts aren't roughly equal. Giving only feels good if you know you are giving in proportion to what you are getting. This is the true meaning of Christmas – a lesson society would gain from acknowledging rather than denying in shame. If you want proof of this, imagine Christmas had a different set of rules. Imagine Christmas gift giving involved half of the participants being givers and the other half being only receivers. Would people still do Christmas if these were the rules? Of course not! Unfortunately, most people celebrate Christmas in a way which is far worse. A typical Christmas has become a ritual where adults wilfully harm children.

Think about what happens at a typical Christmas when the older members of the family give gifts to the children without expecting anything in return. They are spoiling an entire generation! They are teaching the extraordinarily harmful lesson that the children are entitled to receiving without giving. The older generation isn't simply selling themselves short here. They are enablers, creating a generation of privileged and self-absorbed arseholes, arseholes who deserve pain instead of material items.

The reason why good parents force their children to give presents is so that their children can experience Christmas with the asset of likability. Without likability, Christmas is psychologically painful for a child. This pain is good. It's the means by which the child learns to be more likeable next year. In a healthy Christmas, children experience shame and humiliation when they don't give the equivalent of whatever they receive. Father Christmas punishes greedy children, in much the same way that the law would punish bankers and thieves. It's not a coincidence that Father Christmas is red. Father Christmas is justice, or to put it another way, a rebuke to consumerism and unregulated capitalism.

This is why I think a healthy Christmas is a good model for judging when relationships are healthy and unhealthy. The justice of the healthy Christmas is in its expected proportionality. The achievement of justice is through the recognition that giving is inherently about receiving. Receiving works when everyone is aware of what is in their interests and can communicate that with partners who they have affection for. The affection arises because the partners are likeable to each other. This likability arises from each partner displaying qualities that are themselves presents for the other partner.

It doesn't work if one partner is intelligent and kind, while the other is a fucking moron. Moronic attitudes can't and shouldn't delight a good person. In any relationship, a good person needs a partner with qualities that are equal to their own. Otherwise, the relationship is like an imbalanced scale. When a relationship attains balance, everyone in it can be happy in a way where no one is deluding themselves. The best strategy for never deluding yourself is to recognise that for 99% of the things that matter in life, acting in your self-interest is what makes you a good person. Self-interest is what makes you happy, healthy, successful and likeable.

The other 1% is where altruism comes in. Altruism is what happens when people are too flawed to do what is in their self-interest. They can still do the right thing, but in a way which is crippled and half-hearted. The soldier who fights the Nazis is too flawed to find pleasure in blowing up Germans who clearly deserve to die. So the soldier has to rely on an altruistic desire to die for his country. He is motivated not by his own pleasure at enacting justice, but by the thought of democracy defeating a racist totalitarian regime.

Although the soldier takes the life of another human being, he is too weak to experience it in the fullest way. He can't see that his execution should be cruel, that the violence should be joyous, that his own heart should delight at the crimson blood spilling out of his enemy and that he should swoon at the screams and sobs of the wife, the mother and even the children of the Nazi scum he's just vanquished from the earth. But of course, he can't. Mimicking a coward, the altruistic soldier can think only of helping others when he pulls the trigger.

A similar thing happens when couples who are victims of terrorists are forced to choose between their own lives or those of their partners. Individual members of the couples sacrifice themselves not because they gain pleasure out of it, but purely for the sake of their partner's continued existence. Here, they are too weak to enjoy their own death, a death responsible for the continued life of their beloved. Because they are weak, they can only think of the beloved when they die. They aren't strong enough to think of the fortunate violence ensuring their beloved's continued existence.

There's nothing wrong with any of this, mind you.

However, it's only in these exceptional circumstances that humans actually draw upon genuine altruism. These occasions are so rare that altruism has nothing to do with whether or not anyone is a good or bad person.

I came to this conclusion because I am capable of being a good person even though I have a psychology most people believe prohibits that. I know my unusual brain is the reason we broke up. I admit I was unwise in hiding so much of it from you during our time together. I'm sorry I allowed you to be in a position where the revealing of my mind's inner workings frightened you so much. This is the thing in my life I regret most.

I never felt like I got a chance to fully explain the mind I did reveal to you. I told you about my diagnosis and that I was completely self-interested, though that wasn't really the whole story. I held back from explaining as much as I should because I felt like I was defending myself the evening you broke up with me. I was defending my love for you, rather than explaining how it happened or how it felt. I wish more than anything that I could have done things differently. All I can do is try and acquire something like peace of mind about the end of our relationship. This is partly why I needed to communicate with you again. I need to explain to you who I am. You need to know who you fell in love with for those three years.

I'm a person with many skills and talents others envy. I am extraordinarily creative, extremely productive and good at getting others to do things for me. I've created a career for myself that requires a level of hard work, people skills, ingenuity, logistical know-how, entrepreneurial talent, impeccable taste and social insight one normally finds in a team of people. As you may remember, I also have a photographic memory. I can remember nearly every detail of any day I have ever lived through. This is how I am not like a normal person.

Normal people are not like me in that they can easily be kind, decent and sensitive to one and other. These character virtues come so easily to them that they don't have to think about character virtues, most of the time. Normal people can expend most of their mental energy on their careers and life projects. I am the opposite of this. For me, re-inventing the wheel is child's play. Being nice to people is like climbing Mount Everest. This is why my greatest achievement in life has not been my career.

As a child, my parents told me that I would be a bad person unless I could do things for other people. As a result, I spent most of my childhood and adolescence feeling angry and dejected. I didn't bond with anyone; I hated most adults I knew. I didn't like or care about any of my peers at school and I was angry with most of my teachers. I coped by trying to temporarily behave in ways where I got people to give me what I wanted. I wasn't yet very good at it.

The problem was I didn't get much pleasure from doing things that other people demanded of me. I also had tremendous problems reigning in my impulses. I couldn't turn down a dare no matter how destructive or dangerous it was. I misbehaved, played pranks on others and was often spiteful and sadistic. By the time I was a teenager, I was living with my Auntie Becky and Uncle Raoul because my parents couldn't cope with me. Even Auntie Becky nearly put me into foster care, when I made the mistake of confessing that I had once drugged the two of them with sleeping pills and set fire to their house.

During this time, I also suffered my first bout of depression. I wanted so badly to be a decent person, but I couldn't help but be mean and horrible. I often thought about killing myself, but I couldn't tell if I wanted to kill myself because I was angry at the world, or angry at me.

At the age of fifteen, I had an epiphany. I figured out that I actually wanted to be loved by people. I thought it was unjust that my self-centredness made people hate me when they seemed just as self-centred as I was. I hated these hypocrites with a passion. I spent many afternoons daydreaming about exploding a pipe bomb in my school canteen and blowing everyone to bits. Yet I knew that if I did that, I'd be depriving myself the opportunity to lead a decent life. I didn't know what a decent life for me would be, but I knew I only had one chance to try and live it. It would be stupid to cock up that chance.

By the time I was seventeen, I had disciplined myself to mostly reign in my worse impulses and become academically successful. I was motivated by the idea that I deserved a chance no one else was giving me. I wanted to prove to the world that I could be someone who deserved love as much as anyone else. I taught myself how to behave well in classrooms to get the desired responses from teachers. I saved my cruelty for other girls at school who struck me as shallow, obsessed with their looks, or taking pleasure from bullying others they saw as less attractive.

I hated these girls with a piercing intensity. I didn't hate them because I was unattractive (far from it). I hated them because they made no effort to modify their most basic drives. It's true that, biologically, women are predisposed towards vanity. We innately dislike the sight of people who are ugly (especially men) and want to ostracise them. However, this impulse is irrational. There's no reason why anyone who is unattractive is a lesser quality human than anyone else. There's also no reason to think a fat or ugly person is less hurt by this ostracisation. Because they receive it frequently, they are probably more hurt by it than the rest of us. This is why the urge to give preferential treatment to beautiful people is something any humane person will fight against. It may be a biological urge, but it's a callous one.

Shallow girls, to a much greater extent than shallow men, take pride in their refusal to rise above this urge. They use their sexuality to take advantage of others: to manipulate men, to humiliate other women, to insult those who are unconfident, to kick those on the lowest rungs of the mating hierarchies, all the while eroding trust and responsibility in the name of women's rights. But make no mistake: shallow girls are products of consumerism. They are agents of the Patriarchy, counterfeit revolutionaries and what sensible feminists would describe as dirty whores, unfaithful lovers and future abusers of children.

This is why I spent so much of my youth bullying and humiliating shallow girls. It was easy to bully them because it was easy to turn people against them. They ruled by fear until someone else actually stood up to them, without fear. It didn't hurt that the person standing up to them was a cute lass lots of the boys fancied. I was cleverer than my enemies and I could be crueller than they could ever be. Two shallow girls committed suicide because of me. That's how effective I was, at bullying the worst bullies.

To my surprise, my reputation for standing up to bullies didn't make people think fondly of me. In fact, my reputation for cruelty far exceeded any reputations of the bullies I took down. Initially, I thought this was unfair. Then I realised something rather important: I was harming people.

Harming people makes others dislike you.

Even people harmed by the people you harm dislike you when you harm those people. So, if you want to lead a good life, you need to make it one of your top priorities to minimise harm. If you prevent harm, this raises your social capital. Because high social capital is an effective tool for achieving your dreams, I knew I needed some high social capital if I was going to do anything meaningful with my life. So, by the time I entered the world of higher education, I had a new personal motto: MINIMISE AND PREVENT HARM.

During my first year at uni, something happened that was completely unexpected: I started really liking people. I didn't like them just because they did things for me, I started liking them because of their personalities. I started to enjoy their humour, their patience, their intelligence and their moral and political attitudes. I became very excited about collecting friends. Yet as soon as I would collect a friend, I would normally lose them, abruptly. Although I didn't know it at the time, I possessed a terribly acid tongue. I had what you might call a sensitivity problem.

Initially, I thought it was simply a case of my friends not having a thick enough skin to cope with my honesty. What I began to realise was that my honesty was harming people. It was incredibly inconsiderate on my part. I assumed that because my skin was unusually thick, other people should be able to handle whatever it was I chose to say to them. I wasn't adjusting my words for what I could reasonably predict would hurt the feelings of others.

Kindness, I learned, is an important and benevolent form of manipulation. Kindness is when you adjust the information you give to others on the basis of what you can predict will hurt them. Sometimes it's necessary to hurt others. However, in general, it's best to sugar coat the harsh truths that need to be said and refrain from asserting the harsh truths that don't. This is the best overall strategy for resolving problems with other people, getting them to do what you want and helping them grow.

If you say things to people without any consideration for what might hurt them, your words become a kind of violence. Psychological violence can be just as damaging as physical violence.

My experiences with my friends taught me that even my well-intentioned words could be an unjust form of callous cruelty. Because I wanted friends so badly, I knew I needed to push myself to my limits in order to keep them. Learning the art of tactfulness took an incredible amount of focus, hard work and self-restraint on my part. Somehow, I managed to do it. The idea of someone caring for and enjoying me was a fantastic motivator. If someone with a brain like mine could be a good friend to someone, I thought this vindicated my chances of leading a good life and being a good person.

In my early twenties, I wanted to be kind more than anything – I was driven to the point of madness. I felt like kindness could somehow justify my parents having had me. I felt that if I could be kind, this was what could make up for all the havoc I caused in their lives as a kid. I needed to know that I deserved to be on this planet. So, I was determined to be a good friend to someone even if it killed me. Yet the one human emotion I did not think I was capable of experiencing was romantic love. I assumed romantic love was completely tied up with altruism and thus outside the realm of my neurology.

That is, until I met you.

When I first met you during that seminar on Elliot and Hemingway, I knew I loved talking to you. Nonetheless, it didn't feel like talking to my friends. Talking to you felt strangely compulsive, like playing a slot machine. We met a few times for coffee in the afternoon and I remember our third coffee turning into an eight-hour conversation. I never felt so much excitement in being able to say something to someone else and wait for what they had to say in return. The engagement I had with your mind felt visceral.

Everything you said became an idea I could play with the way I would play with a Rubik's cube as a small child. Every look in your beautiful eyes drew me into you like an ornate row of tiny symbols I could barely understand but wanted to see more of. Talking to you made me feel like we weren't talking; it felt like moving. Our conversations were like a ballet of ideas, the kind of dance where the roll and sway of surprises never fails to be otherworldly and beautiful at the same time.

We would talk and I found myself wanting to kiss you, hold you and make you feel things as intense as the feelings inside of me that spiked through my nerve endings when I so much as thought of you. It was terrifying – terrifying and exhilarating. Exhilarating because I felt I had access to something I thought I was always excluded from. Terrifying because I worried you would find me out.

I worried that when you saw my normal day-to-day self, you would see my lack of kindness and reject me. This fear and exhilaration spurred by having a lover I actually loved back aroused me tremendously. The adrenaline rushes made our sex life feel explosive in its intensity. Yet I still couldn't imagine our relationship lasting for more than about six weeks. I was fairly certain that within two months or so, you would reject me.

Despite all of this, I knew you genuinely loved me. That thought motivated me in a way nothing else had ever done before. You were the most amazing person I had ever met and you loved me. That meant you deserved love from me. The thought of you not having that love was unbearable.

I felt like my life actually had a purpose: to love you in a way that was deep and passionate and to make our connection work despite how different we were. But of course, that was the paradox of our relationship. We were so similar, so well suited and yet different enough to feel exotic to each other no matter how comfortable our days together became.

From your perspective, you were falling in love with a young woman who was mad about you. From my perspective, I was fighting myself to be good enough for you. I was fighting for you, fighting for me and going against my nature to love you just enough to keep you from noticing how hard I was fighting. No matter how difficult it was on some days, the satisfaction of even our most mundane moments made me push even harder.

After a year, it stopped being so hard. Loving you started to feel second nature. That was when I took the ultimate risk and moved in with you. Again, I thought you would reject me. But I needed to know for certain, one way or another.

Despite all my gloomy expectations, you seemed genuinely happy when we lived together on Charles Street. During our two years together in that flat, we did have the odd row. We did have the occasional day where one of us was bitchy or in a bad mood. Yet on the whole, our behaviours felt in complete synch with each other. I felt I could be myself and tell you my thoughts on nearly everything and I loved it. For the first time, I could be honest about most things and my honesty actually made someone happy. I had never experienced that before. Whether we were in each other's presence or far away, it felt like you were the other half of my heartbeat.

That isn't to say I didn't sugar coat various things I expressed to you. I was kind, remember. Not blunt and tactless the way I was during our last conversation. The only thing I was not completely honest with you about was how my mind worked. I do remember debating with you about how some of your views on altruism were unhealthy, yet I never told you that I couldn't do it. I never told you that my lack of altruism was the cause of an incredibly traumatic childhood and adolescence. I never told you that friendship and love were such relatively new experiences for me when I met you. I told you about events in my past. I gave you plenty of information that would allow you to eventually suss out that I am completely self-interested. Yet you always believed in my altruism, despite everything.

I remember you thinking I was selfless and giving because I was a socialist. I am only a socialist because I think making people dependent on the market is unjust. You thought I liked justice because I put other people above myself. The reality is, I like justice merely because of how it makes me feel. If justice didn't give me pleasure, then I wouldn't like justice. In a similar way, if I didn't get pleasure from you, I wouldn't like you either.

The tremendous quality of our relationship was wonderful, but something that began making me feel on edge as we moved into our third year together.

"It's too good be true," I would think to myself. I saw so many people with normal psychologies in relationships that lacked the connection, intensity and co-operation that ours had. On some level, I think I was worried I didn't deserve you. This worry eventually made me start to feel like I was losing control of my behaviour. As you know, I started gambling and I racked up some debts for us, debts it took some crafty manoeuvring to sort out. I decided to go to therapy because my impulse control problems had the potential to destroy our relationship. The therapy was useful, but it ended with me being diagnosed as a psychopath.

I suspected as much before I went into therapy, yet having the diagnosis become official made the one secret I kept from you much more perspicuous. It was the one dark cloud in an otherwise idyllic relationship. I spent three weeks deciding what to do. The turmoil I felt was stomach churning.

The morning I finally informed you of my new label, I explained it all in copious detail. Yet you said very little, looking frightened and confused.

Later that evening, you sat me down on our settee and presented me with my greatest fear: you rejected me.

I argued with you. I tried to make the best case I could as to why we should stay together. I even let you see me cry and scream.

You didn't budge.

The next day, when I understood that your decision was final, I changed my demeanour. I reacted nonchalantly, like I didn't mind. That was the first time I put up a completely false front in your presence. It wasn't a partial lie of omission; this was a full blown and genuine lie. Inside, I was devastated.

Your rejection of me made me feel like I had mistakenly convinced myself for three years that I was worthy of you. It felt like you loved me when I showed you my love but rejected me when I showed you my brain. The best thing in my life, the thing that had given my life vibrancy had quickly spiralled into a colourless present of despair.

I couldn't cope with the pain. I knew I could no longer control my feelings or behaviour.

After we split up, I moved in with Julie, the woman we met at the Oxfam conference earlier that summer. Julie pretty much looked after me throughout the next eighteen months. During this time, I wasn't in my right mind. It felt like all the work I had done on myself throughout the last decade had completely disappeared. I was a teenager again. I acted either with aggression or in a depressed state of melancholia.

That meant I was either in bed or being cruel and selfish. I wasn't acting in my own interests. I was like a pulse, alternately sleeping and bursting with rage – unreasonable rage. Julie was patient with me, but I am grateful that her love for me was not unconditional. She made it very clear that I had to make an effort to work through my problems with mental health professionals or else she would not continue to be my friend.

So I worked harder than I had ever worked in my entire life to reclaim my behaviour. Yet all that was changing was that I could be creative and productive as long as I didn't interact much with others. I became obsessed with writing and drawing every day. I wrote my first graphic novel in Julie's basement on an old computer. I was told by a publisher for RZM Press that they loved the manuscript and were interested in publishing it the following season. This made me feel a bit of happiness for the first time since we broke up. I may not have been worthy of love, but I could still contribute to the world in other ways.

Then I got your two emails. I had avoided you for over a year and a half because I didn't feel confident in my ability to keep up the lie that I wasn't completely destroyed by your rejection of me. More importantly, I still didn't have the strength to control my behaviour and I didn't want you to see me in such a dismal state. Yet when I read your second email, I felt incredibly sad and guilty. What you sent me was a big excuse for all the things your mother subjected you to throughout your life. You wrote at length about how even her physical violence towards you was understandable, given her upbringing.

You justified the way she would hit your sister over the head with iron cords when you were both in primary school. You justified how she would punish you by making you carve a pig mask out of an egg carton and wear it standing in your front garden. You justified all the ways she tried to blackmail you. You even justified the sexual abuse. You defended horrific things, like the time she stabbed your father and then called the police, claiming she was defending herself from him. I knew you were having some sort of a breakdown.

You ended the email by saying you wanted to carry on her legacy by having kids of your own, after she died. That was particularly painful to read because you told me you didn't want children the night we had our first kiss.

Do you remember that night we walked in our hammer and sickle jumpers through St. Martin's Square, even though it was quite cold? It's actually one of my more vivid memories. You had just bought me a stack of Frank Zappa CDs for my birthday. I was carrying them in my little white bag with your portable gold CD player in it. We were wandering about, looking for a shop to replace the batteries.

You said, "I know it's really early to mention this, but I need to get it out before things get more involved with us. I'd rather risk an awkward moment than hurt you in the long run. I don't want to have kids, Janet. I love the idea of being married but I don't want to raise a family. I've always felt that way. If a family is something you want, we should just stay friends."

You were tense and nervous when you said that. I could tell you were worried I was going to reject you. So I made you laugh.

I said in my best dead pan delivery, "Joe, I fucking hate

children."

When I saw you laugh, I took your hand in mine and said, "Well, that's not exactly true. I like really, really old children. Really, really old children who I'm free to tease without having to censor myself the way I would with a younger child."

You giggled and replied, "You like teasing ex-children!" with a big grin.

I responded, "I don't have to hold back when I tease ex-children, Joe. I can give them everything I know they want." I smiled and stuck my tongue out at you.

You looked at me flirtatiously and said, "What do you think I want?"

I said, "You want... to be able to love who you choose to love. You don't want it to be expected of you that you will devote your life to a stranger. You don't want it to be expected of you that you will magically find children interesting when they spit and cry, are incapable of having decent conversations and have horrible taste in everything. You don't want to have to pretend that you find dirty nappies and first words interesting when you could be living in a beautiful flat surrounded by amazing books. You don't want to devote your life to loving a demanding and ungrateful shit just because they share your genes. You want to be able to choose to love the best of humanity because you want to, not because you are responsible for them. You don't want to feel guilty for that. You don't want to feel guilty for wanting to love people because they make you happy. And when you find a woman who makes you happy, you don't want a crying, attention seeking bore who won't appreciate either of you to become the focus of your lives. You want to focus just on her."

As I said these things, I could see tears welling up in your eyes. I put my hand on your face and asked you why you were crying.

You said, "I just feel so guilty. I agree with everything you said but it feels so horrible actually saying any of it. I was going to tell you I didn't want kids because I'm going to have a career where I won't have time for them. I didn't want you to think I thought any of the things you just said, Janet. But you said it all before I could lie! How did you do that?"

I said, "It's pretty obvious why you don't want kids, Joe. You hate the suburbs; you hate mundane shit; everything you write just screams that. That's why I love your writing."

You were smiling but I could see you were still upset. I asked why you have such a hard time accepting the things you want.

You replied, with a dark look in your eyes, "I just feel so selfish and horrible, Janet. I feel intolerant, like I don't give children a chance. I feel narrow minded and judgemental. I don't know, it's hard to explain. I feel like I can't make peace with the fact that people are flawed. I feel like I expect too much of people."

I responded, "That's a stupid way of looking at things, Joe. All you are is a wonderful person who wants love that makes you happy. You're no different to everyone else who wants children. You're just a little odd in what makes you happy. I'm the same as you. That's why I'm so happy I met you."

When I said that, your eyes lit up and you told me "I love that I met you, Janet. I needed to meet someone like you."

I smiled back and replied, "It's weird. I feel like I was supposed to meet you too. I've never met a bloke our age who knew they didn't want kids. Everyone says "I don't know what I want" and then normally changes their mind when they hit thirty and give up on life. They blame it on their instincts when it's really just a choice they've been pressured into. Most people are delusional. They think that their genes will give them this intelligent and precocious, well behaved little person they can show off to the neighbours like a party trick. They won't admit to themselves that having a kid is like playing the lottery. If most people thought about what being a parent entails, most people wouldn't have children."

You then responded, "You know Janet, I've never even told my mother I don't want children. I don't think she'd ever talk to me again if I did. She'd think I was disrespecting her."

I abruptly replied, "You don't need stupid people like that in your life, Joe. If your mother won't talk to you because you won't breed, fuck her! She's an idiot. People like that shouldn't be allowed to have children."

You became slightly irritated with me. I could see it in your face. You started lecturing me about how I should be more tolerant of people that don't share my political views. So I tried to lighten the mood.

I interrupted you by saying, "I was just kidding, Joe! You know I didn't mean it when I said 'fuck her'. You know I'd much rather fuck you than fuck your mother. You haven't even kissed me yet!"

You laughed and said, "I'd very much like to kiss you right now."

I giggled at you and brought my face close to yours. I said, "Well Joe, whether you kiss me or not depends on the choice you make. It depends on the choice you make after I bring my lips... right up next to yours... and open them like this..."

I grabbed your crotch for the first time, squeezing your cock. I also mocked you with my eyes while I brought my open mouth directly in front of your chin. I knew what I did to you when I surprised you this way. I could feel your frustration and it was delicious. I pushed out my tongue and touched your bottom lip. You quickly pulled my hand off and stepped back, with a nervous smile on your face.

I knew I was making you hard in public and this made you embarrassed, even though you were trying to kiss me. You slowly moved in for a more conventionally romantic smooch and I moved my head towards you like I would make it easy. Then I surprised you and quickly pulled back, laughing at your earnest attempt to 'be the man' during our first embrace. When I saw how confused and helpless you looked, I brought my lips close to yours again.

I whispered into your mouth, "Are you gonna feel guilty... or are you gonna take what you want?"

Before I had a chance to pull my head back, you shoved your tongue in my mouth and kissed me hard. You finally let go and took me the way I knew you could. Everyone could see us, but you didn't care. I could literally feel your courage. I could taste you not giving a fuck. It was an attitude I could feel on my tongue and in my chest and in my hands. And I loved that it was me bringing that out of you. In that moment, in that first kiss, I knew that I loved you. I saw how love could come out of and through me. I knew I was the only woman that could ever make you really happy. Even your hard cock and I were soulmates. I can still see it whenever I touch myself. I can feel it waiting for me.

Hence, my photographic memory is both a blessing and a curse.

When I read your disturbing second email about how Jodie was dying and you wanted children, I felt like you were pissing on all my precious memories of you. You were going against everything you stood for when we were together. Your sentences felt violent, like you were emotionally disfiguring yourself. I knew you were forgiving your mother and deciding to become a father because of the trauma that our break-up had caused in you. Or at least I hoped this was true because I would then be able to help you in some way. I should have known I couldn't help you see that your mother was a terrible person.

I couldn't help you see that having children would make you miserable. I wasn't mentally stable enough. Yet despite my better judgement, I couldn't resist the chance to see you again.

The morning of the day we last met, I got an email from RZM saying they had rejected my book. I went to meet you in an already foul mood, an even bigger mistake. As I sat waiting for you outside that little cafe, I did breathing exercises to try and get a sense of calm. When I saw you moving towards me, I nearly didn't recognise you because of how much weight you had gained. At first, I felt relieved. I thought the weight would help me lose my attraction to you. Yet when you sat down and started speaking to me again, this relief quickly went away.

All my feelings for you came flooding into my throat. I kept swallowing water to keep myself from bursting into tears. I immediately wanted to sob because I knew in my heart that I would never be able to move on from you. Even after what you did to me, I wanted you as much as I had always wanted you. I wanted you fat or thin, young or old, nasty or nice. My feelings made me angry because they were a reflection of how I was no longer in control of my love. I wasn't loving you because you did or didn't deserve it anymore. I had lost my integrity.

I worried my love for you had become unconditional. This worry filled me with rage. It wasn't rage at you; it was rage at me. Yet I took it out on you and for that I am deeply sorry. I should have let you explain yourself and apologise to me that day. I'm sorry I deprived you of that. I'm also sorry I said incredibly hurtful things about your weight. I'm sorry I said cruel and vicious things about your character, things I hoped you could tell I didn't mean. And yes, I'm sorry I poked your eye out. I did that I think because you told me a truth I couldn't handle hearing. You said I was going to die with justice while most of the world lives with love.

At the time, I thought this would happen to me because no man would ever want to be with someone who had a brain like mine. I have since found out this is not the case. The reason I am going to die alone with justice while the rest of the world lives with love is because I have only ever felt romantic love for one person, a person who couldn't cope with being in a relationship with someone who had a brain like mine.

You could make a strong case that this love is unhealthy. I know I have good reasons to move on and find someone else. I have a successful career. You rejected me because a relationship with me didn't make you feel safe. Over a decade has gone by since we last saw each other. A year ago, I was making progress in my attempt at moving forward. It was becoming easier for the first time since I last saw you to be kind and sensitive to people. I was making friends. I still hadn't met anyone I had any romantic feelings for, yet I was learning to enjoy my work and new companions in a way that was making me feel that perhaps I could live happily without another romance.

One afternoon, I was feeling edgy for a reason I couldn't articulate. I impulsively googled your name and found you on Facebook. I saw that you were in a relationship with a woman called Loraine Klein. The first thing I noticed was how beautiful she is. The second thing I noticed are the vicious comments on her Facebook page about celebrities she thinks are ugly. I then went to her blog and read several of her posts where she talks about how much she hates Muslims and transgender women.

I saw all the articles she re-tweets about how good it is to smack children. I saw the picture she posted of herself wearing an 'I bathe in male tears' t-shirt. I saw all the selfies she took with Nigel Farage. I read the insulting ways she described you during the early phases of your courtship. I noticed how every time she posts a picture of you, she always calls you 'Fat boy'. But even that doesn't scratch the surface of how disdainful she is of you, especially the comments where she mocks your writing and teaching.

A week after I discovered your hot girlfriend, I noticed that Loraine uploaded a fresh new post with three pictures of you in it. The first picture was a close-up of your stomach. The next picture was a close-up of your chest. The third picture was a close-up of your shrivelled penis after you'd just had a bath. Underneath was a comment from Loraine which read:

"Fat boy is the luckiest boy in the world. Thanks to me, this ugly fat pig gets to fuck the most beautiful woman in Leicester. And you know what? He doesn't even pay me. He expects me to fuck him even though he looks like a pregnant woman. Most of the time, I can't even feel his tiny cock inside me. I can't stand how he smells. His hairy tits are fucking disgusting. When he cums, I want to be sick. I even hate his puffy fingers. But sex is still better than having a conversation with him.

I get fuck all from him in this relationship and I'm sick of it. When I look at him, I don't feel like I'm looking at a human being anymore. I see a hairy lump of shit I'd like to flush down a fucking toilet. When he cries, I honesty fight the urge not to kick him in the balls. I wish he would hurt more and cry harder. But there's no time I hate him more than when he tells me he loves me. That's when I wish he was dead.

I know he's not all bad. He's good at running errands for me and can cook a decent curry. I taught him how. But the fact that I share a bed with him makes me so angry. I don't know why I do it. It's like I'm lowering myself to his level. When I fuck him, it's like having sex with a cockroach. When he kisses me, I want to be sick in his mouth. When he holds me, I think about stabbing him. Sadly, I would never stab this piece of shit because I'm a good girlfriend. I always do the right thing and fuck him all the time like a robot. I've even agreed to have his babies.

People tell me this is what love is, but I just don't fucking understand it. Love is nothing but a complete and total mystery to me. My love has become the reason Fat boy is the luckiest boy in the world. I'm insane."

When I saw this, something horrible happened in me that I can't really explain. It was like my world turned upside down. I started worrying about you obsessively. I couldn't think about anything except what this woman might be doing to you. I even worry about the effect she's having on your mental health. Over the past year, those worries have become intrusive thoughts. I can't sleep because these worries batter my brain even during the moments I'm trying to drift off into unconsciousness. But even then, I dream about you and the worries are as real there as they are when I'm awake.

I worry that Loraine wants to make sure you don't lose weight so that she can use your weight to leverage power over you in your relationship. I worry she will trap you into a permanent attachment to her because of a family you don't want. I worry she preys on your low self-esteem and makes you normalise cruel behaviour. I worry that she also commits acts of violence towards you. I worry you tolerate her violence because you think you should feel lucky to be with someone so physically attractive. I worry you think your weight gives her the right to hurt and publicly humiliate you.

I worry that the bad light I painted conditional love in has made you an easy target for someone like Loraine. I worry that your desire to give her unconditional love will stop you from placing any expectations on her behaviour. I also worry that your desire to be loved unconditionally will make you complacent with yourself. I worry that it will stop you from working on your weaknesses. I worry that you may eventually become as bad as Loraine. I worry that your kids will be very, very dislikeable. I worry she will abuse them too.

I know you broke-up with me because you didn't feel safe in a relationship with a psychopath. With hindsight, I can't be angry at you for doing what any normal person would have done in your situation. If you really trusted me, my diagnosis wouldn't have mattered. It did matter because I didn't make you feel that trust. Despite my best effort, I just didn't make you feel how much you deserved my love. I can accept that now. But I worry you are also with Loraine because of that same failure of mine. I worry that your experience with me has convinced you that someone like Loraine is what you deserve. It isn't, Joe.

You deserve someone who treats you with kindness, respect and dignity. You deserve someone who is open minded and sensitive to other people. You deserve someone who isn't an uncompassionate bigot, someone who actually understands and loves what you bring into the world. The last thing you deserve is a cruel and mean-spirited bully for a wife. You deserve to be with a woman who actually loves you. You don't have to be like your dad: your masculinity doesn't depend on you tolerating female abuse.

In fact, you owe it to yourself not to tolerate it. You owe it to Loraine as well.

I know there's little chance you agree with any of the things I'm saying about her. I know I'm making myself look presumptuous and arrogant. But I'd rather look like that than not tell you these things. I know you may think I am full of shit. You may think I am a terrible person and not trust a word I say. I can understand how this email might cause anything from confusion to anger in you. I can even understand if you are indifferent to it. It's possible you might not have even read far enough to get to this very sentence. Yet here I am, writing another sentence underneath it.

I know our relationship is done. I can't have you anymore. Yet I can't bear the thought of not doing everything in my power to make sure you are okay. I'll risk you hating me even more if there is just a small chance I can help you when you need help. I don't want to see you taken advantage of, I don't want you to suffer anymore because of me; you're too important a part of my life. You motivated me to be my best self. I don't know if you understand how important that is to me.

Because of you, I got to experience what it's like to be happy, fulfilled and loved for three years. That is, by far, the greatest thing I have ever done. As a child, I never in my wildest dreams thought this would ever happen to me. You also taught me how painful it is to lose all of that. I am still in that pain now, but I don't regret knowing you. I can't regret that; you're too special. You're the first person who ever made me feel human. Feeling human is the hardest and greatest thing a psychopath can ever experience.

I know my brain makes it difficult for me to effectively communicate my feelings. Maybe I appear selfish and manipulative, even when I'm doing my best to project kindness. Maybe I'm not a very lovable person. But being with you made me feel like I could cope with that. I could cope because you allowed me to do something I always thought was impossible: You made me love you even though I'm me. You made me love you even though I can't do altruism. You made me love you even though I'm completely self-interested. You made me love you even though I might not be able to love anyone, my experiences of love being nothing more than a mirage. I don't understand any of this.

I don't understand how you made me love you with everything – with everything that I am and everything I could be. I don't know how you brought that out of me. I don't know why I gave you everything and you made me feel mad. I don't even know whether or not I actually am mad. I don't understand if my feelings are real or fake. I can't grasp the metaphysics of love or the conditions that make love genuine. I've never been able to do any of that. All I know is that whenever I think of you, I feel a deep and devastating emptiness, like an important part of me is missing. This is why I find myself crying so often. This is why most of the time, I try my hardest not to think of you. But today, I couldn't help it. I didn't have the strength to turn off my feelings. I couldn't help writing this ridiculously long email. And no matter how much I write, I still don't have the words to tell you how much I love you.

I can only say that, from the bottom of my heart, that I wish you could feel that. I wish I could somehow put you inside my feelings. If you could feel that love, you'd know just how much you deserve it. You wouldn't be happy in a relationship with someone who hates you. You'd respect yourself. You'd only be happy being treated like what you are.

You are not pathetic. You are not an ugly fat pig. You are not a hairy lump of shit. You are an amazing and beautiful human being, my favourite human being. Because of you, I'm still alive and fighting to be here.

You're the reason I can do that. You're the reason I can love.

Janet

19. ROMANCE: Empathy

At 10:16pm, Joe is closely watching Loraine as she reads Janet's long email. Loraine does not look happy. Joe doesn't know what Loraine will do once she finishes reading Janet's ridiculously long email, a laborious text which is part romantic confessional and part undergraduate philosophy paper. Joe is also uncertain of how he will react to Loraine's reactions.

Joe is aware that Loraine may become enraged at him for even having read Janet's email, rather than simply deleting it. Joe also knows that Loraine may get violent, despite her sobriety. The other possibility is that Loraine will become defensive, denying that her vicious blog is something she actually wrote. Janet, after all, didn't provide a screenshot or link as evidence of Loraine's authorship. But Loraine can't deny that the hateful descriptions of Joe certainly sound like something she would write. Nor can she deny that, shortly after the beginning of their relationship, Loraine began taking nude photographs of Joe.

As Loraine finishes Janet's email and has a sip of her coffee, there is a razor's edge of silence, a moment where it feels like literally anything could happen. 'Anything' includes the possibility that Loraine will break up with Joe, giving him the opportunity to re-unite with his favourite person, a person he hasn't spoken to in eleven years.

Joe Pastorious is still passionately in love with Janet Waverley. If you asked him, he would fervently deny this: he would agree with both society and the mental health industry that psychopathic women are damaged goods and best to keep far away from. But deep down, Joe doesn't care whether or not the love of his life is a clinically diagnosed psychopath. He doesn't even care about the fact that she nearly killed him.

Joe loves Janet. He loves her in all of her imperfections. He loves her in all the ways they are alike and all the ways they are not.

And even after everything that has happened, Janet is still Joe's dream woman.

Loraine: (thinking about Janet) What an evil fucking bitch.

Joe: She's not evil.

Loraine: (loudly) Of course she is!! Did you not read this??

Joe: I don't agree with most of what she says but she's not evil.

Loraine: Oh fuck off, you stupid fucking prick.

Joe: (loudly) No, fuck you, Loraine! I'm not the one who posted naked pictures of my partner in a blog that could get me sacked!

Loraine: (yelling) That blog was only up for FIFTEEN FUCKING MINUTES!

Joe: What?

Loraine: (defensively) I wrote that blog the day you snogged your fucking boss. I wanted to bloody kill you, but instead I wrote my feelings down. I did what you told me to do!

Joe: (yelling) I DIDN'T TELL YOU TO POST THEM ONLINE NEXT TO NAKED PICS OF ME!!

Loraine: (loudly) I was fucking angry! I had a cup of tea and then I took it down! Your psycho ex is stalking me, Joe. She's screenshotting everything I publish like she's getting ready to kill me!!

Joe: (angrily) She wouldn't have been able to see that blog if you showed the tiniest amount of restraint.

Loraine: Well, she did see it and so did some other people. Fucking get over it. It was nearly a year ago. It's not up anymore.

Joe: (shaking head) I just can't believe how fucking vicious you were! I can't get my head round how you thought it was okay to share your complete and total disgust at me, with everyone we know, with the whole fucking world! No one's ever hurt me like that, Loraine. It was bloody disgraceful. I can't even express how violated I feel. I feel like I've been raped!

Loraine: (yelling) YOU FUCKING CHEATED ON ME!! YOU EXPECT ME TO BE NICE TO YOU AFTER THAT!!??

Joe: (yelling) I DIDN'T SLEEP WITH CHLOE! WE JUST SNOGGED!!

Loraine: Kissing is cheating you fucking dickhead!

Joe: (sighing) …I was feeling vulnerable that week because you kept laying into me about my snoring. You made me wear that white mask and said I couldn't sleep next to you 'cause I looked like a Nazi doctor. I was feeling rejected; I was feeling rejected and hurt and spending time with someone that actually wanted to kiss me.

Loraine: (with disdain) You have excuses for everything.

Joe: I'm sorry but kissing someone in a moment of vulnerability isn't as bad as what you did.

Loraine: (loudly) Then you have no idea how much you hurt me! I only get that angry when I'm fucking hurting!

Joe: (exasperated) I'm sorry I hurt you. I say it practically every night, but I'll say it again.

Loraine: (angrily) I can't even express how much you hurt me when I saw you kissing that ugly old slag! That blog I wrote was nothing compared to what I was feeling! Nowhere near it!

Joe: How could it hurt you that much?

Loraine: I was crying for three hours before I burned your diary.

Joe: I never saw you cry.

Loraine: (loudly) I didn't want you to see me cry then! I couldn't cry in front of you until a few months ago.

Joe: You didn't want me to see you cry but you were happy to post naked pictures of me. You were happy to tell the world I make you sick and you wish I was dead.

Loraine: (loudly) Only for fifteen minutes! I wasn't thinking straight. I took it down!

Joe: Loraine, normal women don't do things like that. Even when they're angry, they don't post shit like that about their boyfriends.

Loraine: (angrily) NORMAL MEN DON'T CHEAT ON THEIR HOT GIRLFRIENDS WITH A COFFIN DODGER!

Joe: (loudly) She's not a coffin dodger! She's only sixty-eight!

Loraine: (loudly) Yes, and how do you think that makes me feel? I'm fucking beautiful and my boyfriend would rather kiss a pugged nose fucking prune with a hairy face. You think that's good for my self-esteem?

Joe: I know it wasn't good for your self-esteem, but it wasn't as bad as your blog. You'll never convince me those two things are equal, Loraine. Especially since I apologised to you over and over again for about six months.

Loraine: (with contempt) Your apologies don't count; they were lies! And they weren't the only fucking lies you've told me. You never treat me with any fucking decency. You lie over and over again to shut me up! You make me feel like I'm a goddamn burden!

Joe: (loudly) You know that's not how I feel!

Loraine: (yelling) Then why the fuck did you read Janet's email?? Why didn't you just delete it?? Why did you let that bitch back into your head??

Joe: Because I wanted to know what she wanted to say to me.

Loraine: (loudly) She wanted to tell you fucking lies! She wanted to convince you the sky isn't blue!

Joe: Not everything she said was rubbish.

Loraine: (yelling) My God, YOU ARE SUCH A STUPID FUCKING PRAT!

Joe: (yelling) I'M NOT STUPID! I JUST HAVE EMPATHY!

Loraine: (yelling and banging her fist) YOU HAVE EMPATHY FOR A FUCKING PSYCHOPATH, JOE! SHE'S SCARY AND DANGEROUS AND YOU'RE LETTING HER INTO OUR LIVES! YOU'RE LETTING IN SOMEONE EVIL!

Joe: I can't believe she's evil, Loraine. Not anymore.

Loraine: Joe, she just told you she made two people kill themselves. She almost burned her fucking family to death! Are you seriously okay with that?

Joe: You don't know her, Loraine.

Loraine: (loudly) She doesn't even know me and she says I'm abusing you! She said I'm trapping you into a family you don't want!

Joe: I think she's wrong about you too.

Loraine: She's lying about me, Joe. That's what psychopaths do. She's a user and a manipulator. She's good at getting people to do things for her. She said it herself!

Joe: But she's also suffering. She didn't want to send me that email but it was the only way she could move on. She's obviously depressed.

Loraine: (exasperated) Oh, Jesus!! How can you not see what she's doing?

Joe: I don't know what she's doing and I don't care. There's pain in that email.

Loraine: (angrily) You make me so disappointed in you, Joe. I wish you had the courage to man up and get the hell out of my life. All you do is fuck everything up!

Joe: (calmly) Janet isn't normal and I know she can be manipulative. But I care about her and she's hurting. You know what it's like to be depressed, Loraine. You know what it's like not to be able to get out of bed. You can feel empathy for Janet. I know you can!

Loraine: (loudly) Every day she's out of action is a day she's not hurting people!

Joe: (loudly) She doesn't just hurt people! I've seen her on telly giving speeches! I've read reviews of her books! I've seen her vlogs! She does a lot of good in the world, just like you do!

Loraine: None of that shit makes you a good person.

Joe: I don't care, Loraine. I'm not in a position to judge her. I'm sure if you pick away at my life, you could find loads of reasons why I'm not a good person either.

Loraine: Now you sound like a loony.

Joe: (angrily) That's not what you said last night. Last night, you said I was a failure!

Loraine: (loudly) That doesn't mean you're not a good person! The fact that you're a good person is more important than whether or not you're a fucking failure! I wouldn't be with someone who didn't have a good heart! I'm only still with you because you're good, Joe.

Joe: Loraine, I'm not a good person.

Loraine: (definitively) You're the nicest person I've ever met!

Joe: That's not saying much. Your friends are arseholes.

Loraine: (loudly) I'm a better judge of character than you are! I didn't fall in love with someone who tried to poke a fucking hole in my brain!

Joe: I don't think that's what happened. I think–

Loraine: (interrupting) Psychopaths like her control people, Joe. They stop you from thinking for yourself. They can't help it – you know that. You know Janet's jealous 'cause I'm prettier. You know she wants to isolate you from the people you love. She wants you to forgive her when you know you should fucking hate her and protect me from her! She could hurt us!

Joe: I care about Janet, Loraine. Just because she has problems and I can't be friends with her, that doesn't mean I'm indifferent to whether or not she's in pain.

Loraine: (loudly) But she's lying! She can't fucking feel pain! That's why you broke up with her! Don't you remember all the things you told me?

Joe: I don't think I understood her then.

Loraine: (yelling) IF YOU THINK SHE'S A GOOD PERSON, YOU NEED TO BE SECTIONED!!

Joe: I don't care what you think, Loraine.

Loraine: (shocked) What?

Joe: I'd rather be fooled than doubt someone when it looks like they're in pain. I don't ever want to do that again. If that means I'm easy to manipulate, I'm easy to manipulate. If that means I'm mentally ill, I'm mentally ill.

Loraine: (sarcastically) That's just great. I feel so safe and protected by you.

Joe: (loudly) We're not in any danger! She's just–

Loraine: (interrupting loudly) She stabbed you in the fucking face!

Joe: (loudly) She apologised for that!

Loraine: All it takes is an apology for you to forgive that? You're under her control more than I thought.

Joe: (loudly) I AM NOT UNDER HER CONTROL!

Loraine: Yes, you fucking are. She wrote a long fucking email trying to convince you to get back with her. And now you're gonna do it.

Joe: (loudly) I wouldn't go back with her in a million years! That email wasn't something she wrote–

Loraine: (interrupting) Just make sure you don't make her mad! Don't come crawling back to me when she forks out the other eye and blinds you.

Joe: (yelling) SHE DOESN'T WANT ME TO GO BACK TO HER!! SHE'S WORRIED ABOUT ME!!

Loraine: (loudly) Of course she wants you to go back to her! That email is about how you misjudged her, how I'm a complete cunt and how much she still loves you. It ends with her trying to convince you that you were wrong about her, that she can love you like a normal person. It's pure fucking bullshit!

Joe: Did you ever consider the possibility that she needed to write those things down? Sometimes you need to get thoughts out of your head in order to cope with life when things are really bad. You of all people should know that!

Loraine: (yelling) Then she should have written them down and not sent them to you! You're in a fucking relationship she knows nothing about and has no reason to judge!

Joe: I know that. I know she was completely unfair to you in her email. And I don't agree at all with what she said about unconditional love. Loads of other things she said were horrible; that's not up for dispute. But there's pain in her words as well. It's not black and white.

Loraine: (with disdain) Why should you feel sorry for her? She fucking mutilated you. She stabbed you and left you there to bleed to death in front of everyone! She didn't even call an ambulance!

Joe: She's a complicated person.

Loraine: She's a self-centred bitch who wants to ruin our relationship. You can convince yourself that she's more than that, but you can't convince me.

Joe: I don't know what she is. All I know is I couldn't be with someone like her again. I want to be with you. Her letter helped me see that.

Loraine: (irritated) No, it fucking didn't.

Joe: Yes it did, Loraine. It reminded me that I'm really lucky to be in a relationship with someone who isn't so pompous and arrogant. That aspect of our relationship was so annoying. Psychopath or not, she can be very judgemental.

Loraine: (loudly) Then why didn't you delete her email? Why didn't you at least tell her to fuck off and never contact you again?

Joe: Because I care about her. I care about her and her email helped me see some things that could improve our relationship.

Loraine: (flabbergasted) Oh my fucking god!

Joe: It made me see that I want more kindness from you.

Loraine: (irritated) You're taking advice from her about kindness? Are you fucking insane???

Joe: I want to lose weight, but I want you to encourage me without hurting me. I don't want you to threaten to withhold sex. I don't want you to tell me I'm disgusting. I want you to reward me, not punish me.

Loraine: (angrily) What is going on here? Did you fucking message her on Facebook? Have you been talking to that bitch while I'm at work?

Joe: I don't want to remain in contact with her anymore.

Loraine: (yelling) THEN WHY THE FUCK ARE YOU TAKING ADVICE FROM HER??!!!

Joe: Because she's insightful about some things.

Loraine: I can't handle this. I don't know what the fuck is wrong with you, Joe. I feel like I've lost you.

Joe: Loraine, I need you to hear me now: I agree with what Janet said about kindness; that's why your words hurt me yesterday. I'm not the one who should have apologised to you, you should have apologised to me.

Loraine: (loudly) Oh, fuck off! Not this again!

Joe: Yes, this again.

Loraine: (yelling) I SAID WHAT I SAID TO YOU YESTERDAY BECAUSE YOU NEEDED TO HEAR IT! I'VE TRIED BEING NICE BEFORE AND IT DOESN'T FUCKING WORK! I WON'T HELP YOU HURT YOURSELF ANYMORE! I'M YOUR GIRLFRIEND! I'M SUPPOSED TO HELP YOU!

Joe: (loudly) And your good intentions don't excuse your fucking insensitivity! You're not loving or kind when you try to help me. You're like an abusive fucking parent and you need to take some responsibility for that! You need to say you're sorry sometimes!

Loraine: (angrily) SO YOU DO THINK I ABUSE YOU!!

Joe: (loudly) Yes, I fucking do! Are you happy now? I think my beautiful girlfriend who loves me also abuses me. I'm in an abusive relationship. I can see it, anyone who goes online can see it. Even Janet can fucking see it!

Loraine: (shouting in a panic) THAT'S BECAUSE SHE'S TRYING TO TURN YOU AGAINST ME!

Joe: You're the one who's turning me against you.

Loraine: (yelling) I've never done anything to you that's worse than what you did to me! I never cheated on you! I never wrote a forty-page poem about how much I hate you! You fucking read that poem in front of all your friends last week! You even used my name in the title!

Joe: Okay, we're as bad as each other. We're in an unhealthy relationship. We're abusing each other.

Loraine: (yelling) We're in a normal relationship! She just wants to fucking split us up! She's making you paranoid!

Joe: (angrily) Anyone who saw that blog you wrote would be worried about me! She's not unusual in worrying about me!

Loraine: (loudly and in desperation) She can't worry about anybody except herself!! Why do you keep ignoring me?!! Why won't you fucking listen to me?!!

Joe: (angry and with a sense of resolve) Because I know Janet! She can feel bad if people she cares about are suffering. I've seen it with my own eyes! I've seen her cry because people she loves are in pain. Being self-interested doesn't preclude that!

Loraine: (loudly) Being a psychopath does! Those tears were fake! She told you they were fake!

Joe: Not all of them were fake, Loraine. And that diagnosis was wrong. She's the furthest thing from a psychopath.

Loraine: (loudly) Bloody hell, she was fucking diagnosed by a team of clinicians!

Joe: I think her therapist just didn't get Janet. That woman's biases influenced all of the other people who were working with her when they evaluated Janet. Maybe they all had their own preconceptions that stopped them from understanding the good parts of Janet. Maybe they focussed on Janet's youth. Maybe they didn't take stock of all the ways she changed when she became a young adult.

Loraine: Clinicians are trained not to do that.

Joe: They did this time, they must have. Her email isn't something a psychopath could have written.

Loraine: How can you say that? Everything she wrote in that email was scary! She thinks people should be more cruel and violent! You think that's a nice person?

Joe: You can't say someone isn't a nice person because they say things you disagree with. I don't like a lot of what you say and I don't accuse you of being a horrible person.

Loraine: (loudly) You don't need to! A doctor never diagnosed me that way!

Joe: (passionately) I know there's something wrong with Janet. I know she's dangerous. But I also think the mental health system failed her. Whatever she is, she's not a psychopath. She's not a horrible person. She's not cruel.

Loraine: (shouting desperately) WHY CAN'T YOU SEE WHAT'S RIGHT IN FRONT OF YOUR FUCKING FACE!!

Joe: What am I not seeing?

Loraine: (loudly) She's telling you a story to make your heart melt! She's fucking seducing you! She's talking about how much she wants to grab your cock!

Joe: And you know what? That makes me feel fantastic, Loraine. Having a woman tell me she thinks I'm sexy makes me feel wonderful. You haven't done that for me in ages.

Loraine: (even more exasperated with Joe) SHE'S USING HER SEXUALITY TO BREAK UP A RELATIONSHIP! I would never do that to another couple! That's psycho bitch behaviour.

Joe: (adamantly) SHE IS MOST DEFINITELY NOT a psycho bitch! She's complicated and strange! But she's been suffering over what happened between us and she wanted to reach out to me! Janet's worried I hate her! I can understand that.

Loraine: (loudly) Why didn't she do that eleven fucking years ago??

Joe: She probably thought I was frightened of her. She probably didn't want to scare me.

Loraine: (yelling) SHE DIDN'T GIVE A FUCK ABOUT YOU!

Joe: No, she does care about me, or else she wouldn't have written that email.

Loraine: (frustrated and banging her fists) SHE'S GIVING YOU A FUCKING ROMCOM FANTASY!

Joe: What are you on about?

Loraine: (in an American accent) "The crazy cunt with a heart of gold; the psycho bitch who learns love and becomes a good person. Coming to a theater near you."

Joe: Loraine, I believe she can be something like a good person. And even if she can't be, she wants to be. She wants to be a good person very much. For me, that's what counts.

Loraine: (angrily) That's because she's manipulating you! You're letting her ruin your life, just like you kill yourself with food!

Joe: I saw her every day for three years. I lived with her for two of those years.

Loraine: That doesn't mean shit. That bitch can lie.

Joe: She's not a horrible person, Loraine. She's not someone I can be with, but she's not a horrible person. I know her.

Loraine: (loudly) How the fuck can you say that? How can you say that after everything she did to you? How can you say that after seeing everything she wrote about me?

Joe: When she attacked me, she wasn't well. She was struggling with the emotions of our break-up. She couldn't control her behaviour.

Loraine: (annoyed) And you're daft enough to actually believe that?

Joe: I saw her every day for three years, Loraine. She was never the way she was the last time I saw her. The day she attacked me, she was like a different person.

Loraine: (loudly) That's because she hid herself from you every day until you fucking broke up with her!

Joe: No, no person can do that. You can't put on an act every day for three years.

Loraine: (shouting) You can if you're a fucking psychopath!

Joe: (passionately) But I saw her on the days she was super mardy! I saw her on the days she should have let the mask slip and showed me this terrible human being. She never did. She was no different to everyone else I've ever known when they get mardy. Compared to most women I've ever seen in a foul mood, Janet was cordial and apologetic afterwards. She always apologised if she said something she knew upset me. She wasn't like you.

Loraine: (loudly) That's because she was lying! She had more control over her behaviour than a normal person. She's fucking fake and you fell for it! That's what you told me!

Joe: Loraine, on most days, Janet was friendly. She was funny, a great conversationalist and someone with a lot of high energy and a great imagination. She had great ideas, a great mind for politics, wonderful taste in music and films and books. She was always really creative and talented. I loved her drawings and the little essays she would write. I loved all of that before she got famous. I still love all the stuff we wrote together.

Loraine: That doesn't make her a good person.

Joe: I know that, but she was also really sweet and forgiving! Much more so than me. She was patient with me on many occasions she had no reason to be: she defended me when she didn't have to; she negotiated with me when I was wrong and most people would have lashed out at me in anger.

If she knew I was upset or hurt or anxious, she spent however long it took to make sure I was okay. She even took days off of work to look after me when I was having panic attacks.

Loraine: (shaking head) That's because she was trying to make you dependent on her. She wanted you to feel like you needed her to feel good about yourself. All her love for you was a big fucking lie and you've known that for eleven years. But now she's making you doubt yourself and it's putting my life at risk!

Joe: (definitively) I wasn't the only person she was nice to, Loraine! She was patient and loving towards people I found it hard to be around! She was even good with my mother! Before they fell out, she got along better with Mum than I ever did. That's why Mum wanted to see Janet when she was dying. Janet was the only person that could help Mum actually have fun. She was the only person I ever knew that could bring out the good side of my mother, before she got sick. She made Mum actually want to be nice to me! Janet made her feel like another woman actually wanted to be her friend. I know Janet has impulse control problems and can say really horrible things. I know she can be arrogant and judgemental, but on most days, she's an unusually kind person.

Loraine: She hates your mother, Joe. She was never her friend. She lied to her.

Joe: No, she loved her and hated her. I loved Mum and hated her too.

Loraine: (loudly) That doesn't make any sense!

Joe: (loudly) People are complicated!

Loraine: (loudly) No, they fucking aren't! People lie and make it look like things are complicated!

Joe: Loraine, you are very very complicated. You're one of the most complicated people I've ever met.

Loraine: What do you mean?

Joe: Whenever you talk about the kind of people you hate, the kind of people who completely drive you mad, who are you describing?

Loraine: What does that have to do with anything?

Joe: (emphatically) You're describing me! You hate people like me and you love me!

Loraine: No, you're different to those bellends. You're a sweetheart, you don't have a fucking lumberjack beard, you don't have twenty nose piercings and a big hole in your ear, you don't wear a dress so you can get a hard on pissing in the girl's loo, you don't read Lena Dunham, you don't follow Russell Brand on Twitter, you're not an anarchist, you don't drink absinthe, you don't go to hipster bars and pay ten pounds to eat a bowl of cereal. You're just a fat wanker who's lazy.

Joe: Then tell me why you're not with a gorgeous, intelligent and hardworking hunk who isn't a wanker.

Loraine: Because no man like that will have me. I work with what I can get.

Joe: No, it's not as simple as that. You're attracted to qualities in me that you don't like. The fact that they irritate you makes you want to be with someone like me. If what I'm saying wasn't true, this relationship never would have happened. If you truly hated the things in me that really piss you off, you'd be happy being single. You'd be happy having one-night stands whenever you got horny.

Loraine: What does that prove?

Joe: (smiling) It proves you want to be with a wanker, Loraine. It proves you're pretty fucking complicated.

Loraine: (shaking head) It just proves I'm an idiot.

Joe: You're not an idiot, Loraine. Deep down, you like people who challenge you.

Loraine: I don't like hardly anyone anymore.

Joe: (enthusiastically) Oh yes you do! You just think you don't!

Loraine: (rolls eyes) Whatever.

Joe: If Janet wasn't my ex and you met her on the street, I know what would happen.

Loraine: What would happen?

Joe: You'd get to see what it's like being around another strong woman and you'd love it. You'd be best mates. Janet's tough as nails, just like you are. One night, she was making a salad and she accidentally chopped off her left index finger. There was blood everywhere and she didn't even wince. She looked at me with this big smile on her face. She had the finger in her right hand and said, "Oops..." like she was a four-year-old who'd just wet herself on purpose to be naughty. I was freaked out and got her into the car and rushed her to A&E, but she kept laughing at me. On the way there, she was giggling and making jokes, doing impressions of me being scared. I was panicking but she eventually started to make me laugh too and then I could calm down. She kept doing these really funny impressions of Nigella Lawson. By the time we drove into the carpark, there was blood all over the car and we were both laughing our heads off. She can laugh about ridiculous things, Loraine. She can make anyone laugh their head off.

Loraine: (loudly) How can you think that fucking bitch has a sense of humour? Whenever I make a joke about you on Facebook, she says I'm being "disdainful" of your writing and teaching! Is that what you think of me?

Joe: No, but she thinks that because some of your jokes don't always translate well online.

Loraine: (emphatically) You know I think you're an amazing teacher! When I joke on Facebook about you repeating yourself to your students, I'm being affectionate. I take the piss out of you because I think you're ace! I call you 'Fat boy' because being fat doesn't make me stop wanting to be with you! I call you Fat boy because I love how sweet you are and that's more important than how you look! I've never met anyone as sweet as you. I never knew people could be as sweet as you!

Joe: She doesn't get your humour. Your humour is like a teenage boy. Janet doesn't get teenage boys.

Loraine: You don't get teenage boys either.

Joe: Yes, but when a woman talks to me like that, I think it's fucking hilarious! It's so camp. She doesn't understand that, but you can't really blame her for that. That's not something most people understand about me and you.

Loraine: She thinks I'm a bigot. She thinks I'm a bully. She thinks I'm trapping you into a family you don't want. She thinks I'm using my beauty to leverage power over you. She thinks I'm an all-around piece of shit! You think I shouldn't blame her that? Is that how much you love me?

Joe: (loudly) She's depressed Loraine! When you're depressed, you don't think clearly and you're unreasonable! You know what it's like to be depressed!

Loraine: She's not depressed. That bitch is fucking character assassinating me and so are you.

Joe: (loudly) She's not character assassinating you! She's worried about an ex of hers who she saw being degraded and humiliated by his girlfriend!

Loraine: (losing patience) You keep making excuses for her. You still won't hate her! You won't hate her even though she hates me!

Joe: (angrily) She's only worried because of what you write in your blogs! Even your mum thinks some of that stuff is horrible. It's not just Janet!

Loraine: (shouting) Don't bring my mother into this! You know she wishes she never had me!

Joe: (loudly) She doesn't wish that! Your mum just thinks you do things sometimes without thinking about other people! She loves you!

Loraine: (shouting) SHE DOES NOT LOVE ME! She doesn't care at all about what it's like to be me! She only cares about other people having to put up with me! Neither of my parents ever cared one fucking bit about me! They were self-absorbed, unkind fucking snobs who acted like raising a child was some kind of prison sentence! That's what I fucking had to grow up with!

Joe: I know that but–

Loraine: (interrupting loudly) Growing up like that hurts!

Joe: I know it hurts. I know they weren't the best parents for you but–

Loraine: (interrupting loudly) Your psycho ex sounds just like my mother!

Joe: (loudly) Loraine, they are two totally different people! They are nothing alike at all!

Loraine: (loudly) Neither of them give a shit about what it's like to be a beautiful woman with a fat boyfriend! They don't give a shit about how my beauty affects me!

Joe: Your beauty is an amazing privilege, Loraine. How can you see it any other way?

Loraine: Notice how Janet didn't write: "The only thing about Loraine that makes Joe seem genuinely excited is her beauty. He makes no effort to make himself hot and still expects Loraine to fuck him most nights. I worry about Loraine. I worry Joe doesn't really like her. I worry she's being treated like a cum bucket by a man who uses unconditional love as an excuse to lie to her. I worry she's being abused."

Joe: Is that how you see me?

Loraine: That's what she would see if she actually lived with us instead of screenshotting the blogs I take down.

Joe: I can't believe you actually think I don't like you.

Loraine: (loudly) You act like you don't fucking like me! You act like it every damned day and it makes me feel like shit!

Joe: (frustrated) I do like you, but I SEE you every day! That's why it sometimes looks like I don't like you, but that's normal. No one gets ecstatic when they see their partner. That's not what life is like. I wasn't even like that with Janet!

Loraine: (shouting) YOU ARE SUCH A BOLD-FACED FUCKING LIAR! HOW CAN YOU LIVE WITH YOURSELF?

Joe: (loudly) I don't know what you want from me! I don't know how I'm supposed to communicate that I'm jumping for joy every time you walk into a room!

Loraine: (loudly) The only thing that excites you when I walk into a room is how I look! That's the only fucking thing!

Joe: (loudly) That's not true. You know I love your character! I love everything about you!

Loraine: (shouting) GO FUCK YOURSELF! You love HER character!

Joe: What?

Loraine: You still want her. I can see it in your face.

Joe: (exasperated) ARE YOU DELUSIONAL?? LOOK AT WHAT SHE DID TO ME!!

Loraine: Yes and you can make excuses for her because you're still hard for her pussy! You're hard for a fucking ice queen with a heart of stone! That's how much you love yourself.

Joe: (yelling) I DON'T EVEN WANT TO BE IN CONTACT WITH HER! I'm with you because I wanted everything she isn't! I wanted to be with someone who's a giver!

Loraine: (loudly) I don't believe you. You still like her! I can see it in your fucking face. You like her more than you like me!

Joe: (definitively) I CAN'T LIKE HER!! I HATE people who only care about themselves! That goes against everything I'm about! People like that ruin this fucking country! Everything I do is about trying to give back to the communities I work with! Every poem I write is about how we should come together in society and practice empathy instead of greed! I have empathy for Janet, but I still can't fucking like her! She stands for everything I think is reprehensible. She's a misogynist!

Loraine: Now you're fucking lying to yourself. You bloody like her.

Joe: (emphatically) I really don't, Loraine. If I liked her, I wouldn't have given up on her when I found out about her diagnosis. If I liked her, I would have forgiven her for what she did to me. I'd still be her friend today if I like her.

Loraine: You're blind to yourself, Joe. You don't even know you like her and you do.

Joe: (loudly) I don't!

Loraine: You like her for the same reason you like how beautiful I am.

Joe: What does that mean?

Loraine: You like my beauty because you can't make yourself attractive. You like her because she's everything you're afraid to be.

Joe: (loudly) I know what it's like to be fucking self-centred! I was a kid once! You think that scares me?

Loraine: You like her because she's not afraid of being happy; you are.

Joe: Why do you say that?

Loraine: (tearing up) Because you act like it every fucking day! That's how you talk, that's how you behave, that's what it looks like when you look at me. Even when we're having a good time, you look at me like you're trying to hide the fact that you're disappointed. You smile at Jill and Claire; you don't smile at me. Not anymore.

Joe: Loraine, I get a lot of happiness from watching you be yourself. I know I should show it more but watching you be you does give me a lot of joy! I know I'm not good at showing it. I know I need to work harder to show it better.

Loraine: (crying) I don't understand how you can get joy from me.

Joe: Why?

Loraine: (crying) I don't understand how you can get joy from someone so angry with you. I don't understand how you can get joy from someone so different to you.

Joe: I get joy for loads of reasons. I love the hard work you put into teaching your students. I love how you fixed Claire's shower last week even though she didn't ask you to and you don't even like her. I love how you always put away everyone's rubbish bins on our street at 6am. I love how whenever any kid in our neighbourhood wants to go to a party, you always give them a ride, so they don't have to buy a cab. I love all the work you do raising money for cancer research. I love all the volunteering you did last year for charities that help children with brain diseases. I love how you're always there for me, no matter how fucked up my head can be. I know I need to communicate how much I appreciate you more. I know I need to make more of an effort to show you how much I love those things.

Loraine: (wiping away tears) I fucking hate that word so much.

Joe: (flustered) What word?

Loraine: 'Love'.

Joe: Why do you hate the word 'Love'?

Loraine: 'Cause you loving all those things about me isn't important.

Joe: Why do you say that?

Loraine: Because you don't *like* them; they don't excite you. They don't make you feel happy and neither do I.

Joe: (passionately) Of course those things make me happy! They make me feel safe and loved and like I can count on you!

Loraine: Joe, everything you say you love about me gives you far less joy than a ten-minute conversation with one of your friends. You have more fun texting your friends than spending an evening with me. Open your eyes.

Joe: (emphatically) But I don't trust someone with my life because I have fun conversations with them! I don't need to be constantly entertained by you! I love you because you're there for me and you help me grow! I love being there for you too! Don't you know that about me, Loraine?? Don't you know that's what I've always wanted??

Loraine: You don't know what you want.

Joe: (loudly) Loraine, you know I want someone I can settle down and have a family with!! We've talked about this over and over again!! I want someone I can have a legacy with that both of us can be proud of!!

Loraine: I'm finding that hard to believe after reading that email, Joe. You fell in love with that bitch 'cause you both fucking hate families.

Joe: (definitively) I didn't want a family when I was twenty-three! I didn't know myself then, Loraine! I didn't realise how wonderful children were!

Loraine: (loudly) You never told me you hated children when you were twenty-three!

Joe: I didn't think it was relevant. I was in a different place then.

Loraine: (angrily) You never told me you laughed when she said, "I fucking hate children!" You fucking laughed at that, like you agreed with her! You were both holding hands and giggling over how much you both hate innocent and helpless toddlers! That's fucking horrible!

Joe: (loudly) I was laughing because I knew she was having me on!! She doesn't hate children at all!!

Loraine: (loudly) You expect me to believe that? She could write a fucking book about how much she hates children!

Joe: Loraine, when we were together, we spent a lot of time with her niece Emily. I told you about Emily before. Janet was a great influence on Emily.

Loraine: That's because Emily was a precocious, well behaved little girl who was doing her Masters at LSE by the time she was seventeen. That's not a normal kid!

Joe: Why does that matter?

Loraine: Janet would hate spending time with normal kids. She'd hate spending time with any girl who'd like to play with dolls or dress up in pink; she'd hate spending time with any boy who'd like to play sports or smash toy cars or run into walls.

Joe: That doesn't make her hate kids. I wouldn't enjoy spending time with those kids either.

Loraine: (sighing) That doesn't make sense.

Joe: What?

Loraine: Why in the world do you want to have kids if that's how feel?

Joe: You can't control the kid you get when you become a parent. So you can't expect to get a kid you enjoy. That's not what matters. What matters is that you're totally there for the kid you do wind up with. You gotta love them unconditionally. You love them even if you can't stand spending time with them.

Loraine: Do you actually believe that?

Joe: Of course I do!

Loraine: (angrily) I'm confused now! I'm fucking confused!

Joe: Why?

Loraine: (shouting) WHY DID YOU EVEN WANT TO BE A DAD??

Joe: Well, I–

Loraine: (interrupting loudly) We've spent so much time talking about having kids and you've never even told me why you want 'em!

Joe: (loudly) You never asked me why I wanted them!

Loraine: (loudly) I didn't even know there was a time in your life you didn't want 'em! Not until I read that fucking email! I've known you for over two years, Joe!

Joe: Loraine, I didn't want children when I was younger because I thought I wouldn't make a good dad.

Loraine: (loudly) Why did you think that??

Joe: Because I didn't like being around children and they mostly irritated me. I didn't really like being around other children when I was a child. Like I told you, I didn't have any friends until I was a teenager.

Loraine: What made you change your mind?

Joe: When my mother died, I started thinking about our family's legacy. I started thinking about how I could make peace with Mum and my memory of her. I started thinking about unconditional love and how children are the ultimate test of that. I started thinking I needed to learn to be more patient. I started thinking about how I needed to learn to get along with people better who were very different to me.

Loraine: I think I understand now.

Joe: What?

Loraine: You want children because you want to love people you can't stand.

Joe: That's hardly how I would describe thinking about my family's legacy.

Loraine: (shouting) Children aren't your family's legacy! They're fucking people!

Joe: (loudly) I know that!

Loraine: (shouting) No, you don't!

Joe: (loudly) Why are you so angry about this? My reasons for wanting children are the reasons most people have!

Loraine: (shouting) I don't care what most people want!

Joe: (shouting) What gives you the right to judge what most people want?

Loraine: (shouting) The fact that you don't know makes my decision for me!

Joe: What decision?

Loraine: (loudly) I'm not fucking having kids with you!

Joe: What?

Loraine: You heard me. I'm not having kids with you. Or anyone.

Joe: I thought you wanted kids as much as I did.

Loraine: I was doing it because I thought it would make you happy. I didn't realise what kind of a dad you're going to be. I can't believe what an absolute gorm I've been.

Joe: (confused) You don't want to have kids with me because I want my bloodline to pass on?

Loraine: No, it's because I know you. You'll treat our kids the way you treat me. You'll love them even if you don't get the kind of kid you want. If that happens, they'll be able to tell that all they're getting from their dad is love. Fuck that! I know what that feels like.

Joe: I don't understand. You don't want kids with me because I'll love my children even if I don't have much in common with them?

Loraine: It's so much more than just that.

Joe: You don't trust that I can love them?

Loraine: Joe, you are bad at nurturing people. You don't give people boundaries. Someone like you shouldn't be a parent.

Joe: (irritated) There you go again, being fucking cruel.

Loraine: Joe, listen to me! You would not make a good parent. You don't want kids for the right reasons.

Joe: (shouting) BUT MY REASONS ARE THE REASONS OF MOST PARENTS!

Loraine: (yelling) I don't fucking care! Too many children suffer because of parents who have them for those reasons. I was one of those children! You won't make me do that to a child! No one should have to grow up like I fucking did! No one!

Joe: Why is it wrong to want to have a legacy? Why is it wrong to want to learn patience you don't have before you become a parent? Why is it wrong to want children because you want to grow?

Loraine: (loudly) Because you're playing with their lives! You're treating their lives like an experiment where you can prove to yourself that you can do something you hate! You're putting them in fucking danger!

Joe: (loudly) What danger??

Loraine: You send too many mixed messages. The people you say you love you treat like burdens. You get no joy from them on most days. You say they constantly hurt your feelings. Seconds after you whinge about your hurt feelings, you tell them you love all their imperfections. You say shit like, "I wouldn't change a single thing about you." Then you write fucking poems about how stupid and boring they are. I can handle that but not a kid! That would fuck with a kid's head. I don't want to do that to someone innocent.

Joe: But don't you trust that I can work on myself and change?

Loraine: I trust that you will try. I don't trust that you'll actually do it. You've disappointed me too many times.

Joe: (sarcastically) It's nice to know you have such faith in your boyfriend. You're being sooo considerate of my feelings right now.

Loraine: (shouting) FUCK YOUR FEELINGS! I HATE YOUR FUCKING FEELINGS! YOUR FEELINGS MAKE YOU HURT YOURSELF!

Joe: (shouting) Oh, I see how this is! ONLY YOUR FEELINGS MATTER!

Loraine: (loudly) I might not be able to stop you from hurting yourself, but I won't let you harm a kid!

Joe: (loudly) You think it's me that would harm a kid and not you?

Loraine: It's not a fucking competition 'cause it's not going to happen. Get over that or find someone else. I'm tired of this shit.

Joe: We don't want the same things, do we?

Loraine: (loudly) We fucking don't! Now what are you going to do about that?

Joe: What do you mean, what am I going to do about that?

Loraine: Do you want to stay in this relationship or leave?

Joe: Of course I want to stay with you, I–

Loraine: (interrupting) Joe, think about what you're saying! You're committing yourself to a relationship with someone who won't have a family with you. You're with someone who won't have a family with you because they think you're damaged. Is that what you really want?

Joe: Why do you want to be in this relationship?

Loraine: I don't if this relationship is going to hurt us.

Joe: (surprised) I thought you said you were going to love me no matter what. Last night you said nothing I could ever do would make you stop loving me!

Loraine: You're not the only person who got something out of that email.

Joe: What?

Loraine: Love is only good if people don't delude themselves. Janet's right about that.

Joe: You think I'm deluding myself?

Loraine: Our relationship isn't making you happy. It's making you miserable. I'm making you miserable.

Joe: (frustrated) That's not important! I still want to work on it. We've been happy before and we can be happy again!

Loraine: Love isn't good if it doesn't make you happy. It just hurts.

Joe: If you love someone, you work hard so that the relationship does make you happy.

Loraine: Sometimes you can't. I do care about you, Joe, but that doesn't mean I can be in a relationship with you.

Joe: (loudly) Breaking up with me isn't showing me that you care about me!

Loraine: (loudly) I'd only break up with you because I'm trying to help you. That is me caring about you!

Joe: No, that's patronising. Love is about doing the hard work to accept another person. It's supposed to be difficult! You can't honestly say that you love your child if you stop seeing them because it's exhausting. That's not love; that's taking the easy way out!

Loraine: Joe, you're not my son. You're my boyfriend.

Joe: (emphatically) It doesn't matter! Love requires dedication and compromise! You can't leave a person on their own because you can't bring yourself to be there for them in a healthy way. That's a bloody cop out! If you love someone, you do the work you need to do so that love can go on. You make the relationship healthy! You control that!

Loraine: I'm trying to make our relationship work, Joe. I really am. I just feel like I don't have whatever it takes to fix it. I'm missing whatever it is that makes us be happy together. I feel like I bore you, you just make me angry and then I hurt you. I don't feel like I'm good for you.

Joe: (definitively) The success of our relationship has nothing to do with you not being good enough for me!

Loraine: Then what's wrong with me?

Joe: (loudly) You need to make more of an effort to stop acting like a fucking bitch! You need to think before you speak! You can't fucking belittle me for my weaknesses; you need to accept them and help me overcome them! That's what you do for the person you love!

Loraine: I do want to help you with your weaknesses, Joe. But I don't feel like I'm in a relationship where my weaknesses are being helped. I feel like a fucking obligation.

Joe: You said you felt very loved yesterday.

Loraine: I do feel loved. I don't feel liked.

Joe: (sighing in exasperation) …Isn't love all that matters? Love is what gives us the strength to work through our problems. I can like you because I love you.

Loraine: That's not how I see it, Joe. I cherish your love but it's not enough. 'Like', not 'love' is what gives me the strength I need right now. Loving me might make you feel good about yourself, but it doesn't help me solve our problems. I need 'like' at the moment. Not 'love'.

Joe: I do like you, Loraine. But I am hurt by some of the things you say to me.

Loraine: Isn't most of what I say true?

Joe: I don't know. It's hard for me to decide that. A lot of the time, I think I agree with you. But even when you say things I mostly agree with, I feel like I'm being cut open. Your words are like razor blades. When I look into your eyes, I just see pure hatred staring back at me.

Loraine: (passionately) But that's who I am! That's who you chose to love.

Joe: I know.

Loraine: Then why are things between us so rotten? Why does it feel like we're constantly tearing each other apart?

Joe: That's not how I would describe our relationship.

Loraine: How the fuck else would you describe it?

Joe: It's a relationship where I'm tested and I like that. It makes me a better person.

Loraine: Then why do I feel like I don't give you what you want?

Joe: That's part of what I like about our relationship. You test me.

Loraine: I test your patience?

Joe: You test all sorts of things about me.

Loraine: (definitely) I don't want that.

Joe: Then what do you want?

Loraine: I can cope with testing you if I feel in other ways that we enjoy each other. I need to feel like my boyfriend isn't just tolerating me.

Joe: (frustrated) Loraine, I do so much for you! I don't eat meat in the house, I listen to music with headphones on, I've even given up music on weekends, I've agreed to meet my friends outside of the house, I've agreed to cook for you before you get home from work. We have sex whenever and however you want. I even let you say things to me that really push the boundaries of what I'm capable of hearing! I'm staying with you even though you don't want to have children with me.

Loraine: (thinking hard) Okay, I see the problem now.

Joe: What do you see?

Loraine: I'm angry because I don't feel like you're excited to be with me. That makes me resentful towards you because of things you do that fob me off.

Joe: Okay.

Loraine: I make you promise that you'll try to do less of those things. But that doesn't solve the problem. You're still not excited to be with me.

Joe: I wouldn't say that I'm not excited, I would say that I'm frustrated–

Loraine: (interrupting) You're not excited to be with me because I'm making demands on you, but there's no demands coming from you towards me. You're resentful because you feel like you're bending over backwards to appease me.

Joe: Maybe.

Loraine: So here's what we have to do. You need to tell me some things I need to do for you, things that will make it easier for you to like me.

Joe: (confused) Are you serious?

Loraine: Yes, deadly serious.

Joe: What kinds of things? What kind of things do you wanna for do for me?

Loraine: Well, I'll make a deal with you: I'm not going to censor myself and stop being honest with you. You'll always have to put up with that if you choose to be with me. But I can do some other things for you.

Joe: Like what?

Loraine: Whatever would make your resentment go down. Whatever would make you enjoy me more.

Joe: You know you don't have to do anything to make me approve of you. I already think you're wonderful.

Loraine: (angrily) This isn't about you fucking approving of me! This is about you liking me! I don't need you to be my friend, but I need you to like me! I need you to tell me things that will make you like me more!

Joe: Okay.

Loraine: This is the only way I can see our relationship working.

Joe: (passionately) I'll do whatever you need me to do, Loraine. Anything. Just tell me what you need and I'll do it.

Loraine: Like I said, I need you to tell me some things I can do to make you like me more.

Joe: (thinking hard) Okay… here's one thing: I don't mind seeing Jill and Claire at Starbucks, but I'd like you to see me read my poems occasionally at the Crumblin' Cookie. I know you don't understand them, but I'd like the moral support. I won't read any of the poems about you that are nasty.

Loraine: I'll come and see you perform. I can do that for you.

Joe: I'd also really appreciate it if you reserve judgement about whether you like a poem until you've spent a few days trying to understand it.

Loraine: So if I hate a poem, I say to myself, "Wait for three days. Then decide if you hate it." Is that what you want?

Joe: Yes, that's a great way of thinking about it. And during those three days, really try and think about what I was trying to say. If, after those three days, you still hate the poem, you can tell me you hate it.

Loraine: Done.

Joe: Here's another thing. I'd like to watch one film a week with you that I like or want to see. We can watch it on my laptop or go to the cinema.

Loraine: That's fine.

Joe: Like the poems, I want you to wait three days before you decide whether or not you like the film. I want you to really think during those three days about what the filmmaker was trying to do. I don't want to hear you complain about the film, if you complain at all, until three days have passed.

Loraine: That's fine. What else?

Joe: Here's something: you're really beautiful, but lately you've been wearing these baggy dresses that are really unflattering. They don't do you or your figure justice.

Loraine: You mean my new orange dresses?

Joe: Yes. You look best in your black shorts and your grey porn star T-shirt. I'd like you to go online and order five or six more of those shirts. Make sure to buy them in a smaller size so that they really cling to your body. Also, it would be really nice if you could buy one of those 'Playboy Bunny' t-shirts we saw at Primark the other day. And make sure that all the shirts cut off just below your breasts so people can see your stomach. People need to see that. It's important to me.

Loraine: Why?

Joe: Because it's a work of art. Your stomach is unbelievably sexy, Loraine. You have the most beautiful stomach on any woman I've ever seen.

Loraine: But all the Pakkis will never leave me alone if I dress like that.

Joe: Well, I don't get jealous, Loraine. I'm proud of you.

Loraine: But what if I want them to leave me alone?

Joe: You said you wanted me to like you, Loraine. Having to talk to men who hit on you isn't exactly agreeing to never have a family.

Loraine: (nodding her head) ...You're right. It isn't.

Joe: Besides, when we're outside, you can wear a coat if it's raining, or when it gets cold in a few months. What's important is that indoors, people see your stomach and your legs and your face.

Loraine: Okay, as long as I don't have to wear fucking heels in the snow.

Joe: You don't. In fact, you look really good in white trainers. It doesn't matter the time of year.

Loraine: I can wear trainers.

Joe: Sandals aren't flattering because your toes are too big. But with good trainers, your legs can be really beautiful, even if they look kind of empty.

Loraine: They look empty?

Joe: Well, they look nice, but they would look even better with a really good tattoo.

Loraine: A tattoo of what?

Joe: Me.

Loraine: You want me to tattoo your name on my leg?

Joe: No, I'd like an image of my face tattooed on your left thigh.

Loraine: Are you winding me up?

Joe: Not at all. I want to show you off when we're out together. And when I'm not around, I want people to know that you belong to me. I don't want it to be a small tattoo of my face either. I want it big enough to cover your entire thigh. And I'd like you to get a second tattoo above your navel which says, 'Just 4 Joe' in green letters. I want a black arrow next to it pointing to your crotch. That's partly why I want your tummy on display.

Loraine: But I'll feel like a cow that's been branded.

Joe: I hope you do feel that way, Loraine. I want you to feel like a branded cow that I love and want to make people jealous of because of how proud I am. I want you to feel like the best tasting cow in the world, the cow most men and women wish they could taste in their wildest dreams!

Loraine: (laughing) At least you're being honest with me about what I can do to make you happy.

Joe: I want to be more honest with you.

Loraine: I like that. When I know you can love me and still look at me like a piece of meat, that turns me on.

Joe: (rolling his eyes) More truth comes out: I can still turn you on, despite my weight.

Loraine: (smiling) A little bit, yeah… if you're honest with me about how you see my body. There's nothing that turns me off more than when you talk about how much you love me.

Joe: (sarcastically) That's good to know. No love talk.

Loraine: I get that you love me, but sex isn't about that; it's about feeling fucking wanted. When we have sex, I don't want to feel like I'm some princess being rescued by a loving prince in shining armour who's working hard to treat me like a delicate flower. I don't want it to feel like I'm making love. I want it to feel intense, like two tigers ripping each other apart. I don't want to talk during sex or play any bloody games. I want it to feel like we're ferocious fucking animals, fighting to the death! Every time I cum, I imagine we're both dying. That's how I can ignore your body some of the time.

Joe: (surprised) You've never told me this.

Loraine: Having to explain what I want completely turns me off! I want a guy to just know. The problem is no guy has ever figured it out on their own. I always have to spell it out.

Joe: (sighing) Neither of us like telling the other what we want. I guess we have to though, if either of us are going to start getting it.

Loraine: Totally on board with that, Joe. Now, what else do you want from me?

Joe: I want you to help motivate me lose weight in a way that works for me.

Loraine: What would work for you?

Joe: Well, here's what I'd like: between Sunday and Tuesday, we have sex that you want, or no sex at all. It's up to you. But on Wednesdays, Thursdays and Fridays, I want you to use your vibrator if you're horny. I want those to be my days off.

Loraine: I can do that, but I don't understand how your weight loss figures into that.

Joe: I will weigh myself every Friday. If I don't lose a pound, Fridays and Saturdays are days I don't have sex.

Loraine: Okay.

Joe: If I lose a pound, I have sex with you on Saturday. But it's sex exactly the way I want it.

Loraine: How do you want it?

Joe: I want to role play some fantasies with you. I might want to buy some Halloween costumes I think you'll look sexy in. There's a William Shatner mask that would be so hot if it had your body poking out of the neck. I want you to wear that mask and I want to play some Star Trek episodes on my laptop while I'm fucking you. I'll plug the laptop into our stereo speakers so we can hear the dialogue and music booming through the floor. That'll be so fucking horny!

Loraine: That doesn't really get me off, but I can do that for you. I've still got Sunday until Tuesday for me to get the sex I want.

Joe: That's true. But on my days, I'm not holding back Loraine. I'm taking everything I fucking want from you.

Loraine: Fair enough. Is there any other kind of sex you want on Saturday? Or is it gonna be you, me and Captain fucking Kirk?

Joe: Hmm… sometimes I'll want us to act out a scenario where we pretend we're different people before we have sex. Other times I might want you to read an erotic story to me while I wank.

Loraine: That's not a problem. You know I'm good at reading bedtime stories to my little cousins. I'm a good actress.

Joe: Your talents will come in handy, I assure you. When you read me a story, I want you to put some bloody effort into making it good. Pretend it's a dance you're getting just right. I want to see skill and artistry, Loraine.

Loraine: You'll see it. Trust me.

Joe: When I tell you I'm ready to cum, I want you to stop reading and fuck me to orgasm. I want you to be really responsive to my body in those moments. I want to feel you pushing hard and fast with those strong hips.

Loraine: (smiling mischievously) You don't know what hard and fast is.

Joe: Well, after I find out, you're going to read me a second story and repeat the process. I'll want at least two orgasms from two different stories that I pick during the week.

Loraine: (giggling) I feel like I'm about to host my own late night radio show!

Joe: It'll be more like a radio drama.

Loraine: This actually sounds really fun. I used to love doing voice over work.

Joe: It will be really really fun… FOR ME.

Loraine: Well, I can't guarantee anything, but I can only say from the bottom of my heart that I hope you love it. You having fun with me… is more important to me than anything right now.

Joe: Well, you owe it to me. If I owe you my health, you owe me some joy, on my terms. That's what a girlfriend's for.

Loraine: I know that now, Joe. I really do.

Joe: Well, that's not how you act, Loraine. You stopped acting like that after I moved in with you.

Loraine: (sighing) It's because I can't do it anymore, no matter how hard I try. That's why I hate your fucking friends. They make you happy. I can't ever do that. I can't ever make you feel creative, or inspired, or naughty or...

Joe: (interrupting) They don't make me feel naughty.

Loraine: Yes, they do. Just not in a sexual way.

Joe: Why do you say that?

Loraine: Because I'm like your mum and they're like the kids you get in trouble with. I hate that. It's so different to how I thought things would be. I wanted to be like… your sexy fantasy mother. But instead, I'm like a real mum. It's embarrassing.

Joe: You're not like Mum, Loraine. I didn't want to fuck her. She was the one who wanted to fuck me.

Loraine: (smiling sadly) I wish she was still alive and you could hide me from her. I wish you were fourteen and hot and I could be the age I am now. I wish I could have an affair with you and break the law and risk everything, maybe go to prison. I wish I could scar you for life and still be your dirty little secret.

Joe: …I don't need any secrets. Not anymore.

Loraine: I just wish I wasn't me sometimes. I'd rather be a bikini poster on your bedroom wall or some wet dream – something more exciting than old hags or fat bitches or… pointless conversations.

Joe: (irritated) They're not fucking pointless! I get ideas from those conversations! My friendships make me happy in ways you can't! You don't do depth or imagination, Loraine. That's not what you bring to the table.

Loraine: (looking up in disappointment) I just wish I did. I wish Claire was your girlfriend.

Joe: Why?

Loraine: I wish Claire was your girlfriend and you were secretly falling for me.

Joe: Well, that's definitely not what I would want.

Loraine: And I'd love it if you were obsessing over me and hurting her, the way she hurts me. It'd make me so happy if you'd betray her and make her feel like she couldn't believe in anything. I wish you'd fucking destroy her, Joe.

Joe: Loraine, that's not–

Loraine: (interrupting) I wish she'd slit her fat fucking wrists. I'd want to be there when she got scared. I'd want to be the one she needed to call 999. I'd laugh. I'd watch her fucking die and spit on her.

Joe: When you talk about Claire like that, it makes it hard for me to like you.

Loraine: (smiling seductively) Well, that's too bad, 'cause if I had my way, it'd make you hard... harder than when you watch Davis.

Joe: Well, you're the reason I'm not hard. It's you and your awful fucking behaviour.

Loraine: (wistfully) I just wish I was like this dangerous drug… or piece of forbidden candy. And I wish you would just fucking take me, before I even knew what was happening. I wish you wanted me so bad, it hurt.

Joe: (irritated) Then you actually have to try to be a decent lover! You can't be half-hearted about getting me off anymore. You have to be sexy and seductive! It's not just me that should do all the work!

Loraine: I know that, Joe.

Joe: (angrily) I'm so sick of you assuming that because you're a woman, I'm the one who needs to do all the work. You need to give *me* your best for a change. And stop complaining about me all the time!

Loraine: I'll give you more than my best, Joe.

Joe: How do I know I can trust you about that?

Loraine: Because it's important to me. I feel like I need to prove myself to you.

Joe: Well, you do. Things need to change around here.

Loraine: I need to be better at something than Claire, even if it's just making you cum.

Joe: (authoritatively) Then here's what you need to do: when you role-play with me, always stay in character. Even when I'm cumming.

Loraine: (nodding) I'll stay in character.

Joe: Don't ever stop being that character, Loraine. Even if it's a character with a helium voice. We'll get you some balloons so you can swallow air that makes your voice go high.

Loraine: I'll swallow anything you give me, Joe.

Joe: Good. Because if you're doing a character with a helium voice, I want to hear that fucking voice when I'm cumming.

Loraine: Don't worry. You will.

Joe: I want to hear it right at the moment the semen starts popping in your fanny.

Loraine: (smiling) You are such a weirdo.

Joe: That's who you chose to love.

Loraine: I know.

Joe: Anyway, that's what I want every Saturday night if I lose one pound.

Loraine: What if you lose more than one pound?

Joe: (smiling mischievously) If that happens, you're gonna get a golden ticket into Willy Wonka's chocolate factory.

Loraine: (smiling) Why am I frightened?

Joe: On Saturday night, if I lose more than one pound, I want you to give me a three-pronged stealth-attack massage.

Loraine: (rolling her eyes) What's a three-pronged stealth-attack massage?

Joe: It's Japanese. It would suit us perfectly because you're taller than me.

Loraine: Just tell me what it is.

Joe: It's a nude massage where you massage with both hands and your tongue but the person you're massaging can't see you.

Loraine: I hope this isn't what I think it is.

Joe: It's based on the idea that erotic power stems from creating sensations that the body can't anticipate using visual cues. For the first prong, we both get naked. I bend down in front of you in a doggy position, facing away from you. You get behind me. You spit three times on both of your hands and do a wrist prayer about forgiveness. Then you use your right hand to alternately toss off my cock and rub your palms against my balls.

With your left hand, you alternatively pinch my nipples and rub your palms all over my chest in a rapid motion. Then you do a little prayer about atonement that starts the second prong.

Loraine: This sounds really complicated.

Joe: It's something you can have fun with once you really get into it. The fun will help you ignore what you'll be doing with your mouth.

Loraine: Don't tell me that you want me to–

Joe: (interrupting) Yes, that's the chocolate factory, Loraine. The third prong of the massage involves you licking my arse while you use your hands to do the other things.

Loraine: (shouting) NO FUCKING WAY!

Joe: Loraine, it's not as bad as you think. The anus, when it's clean, is much more hygienic than the human mouth.

Loraine: (loudly) You can fucking forget that! I am NOT RIMMING YOU…

Joe: Can't you just concentrate on other things the way you do when we have sex?

Loraine: (adamantly) No way! Rimming is fucking disgusting!

Joe: Is it really that much of me to ask of you?

Loraine: It fucking is! I wouldn't even do that to Brad Pitt! I do not clean out arseholes with my tongue.

Joe: (angrily) Then let's fucking list the things I'm doing for you:

1. I'm trying to lose weight!
2. I don't smoke in the house!
3. I'm agreeing to not have my friends over the house on most nights!
4. I'm agreeing to cook for you before you get home from work!
5. I'm agreeing to spend my weekends with you!
6. I'm agreeing not to make you have to listen to music I love that you hate!
7. I'm agreeing to give you the sex you want on Sundays, Mondays and Tuesdays!
8. I'm willing to accept the abusive language you use in the ways you express yourself to me AND
9. I'm agreeing to stay with you even though you won't give me a family!

Loraine: I can understand what you're saying but–

Joe: (shouting angrily) Now let's fucking list what you're doing for me!

Loraine: Calm down!

Joe: (yelling and adopting a physically threatening pose) DON'T YOU TELL ME TO FUCKING CALM DOWN! I SAID LET'S LIST ALL THE FUCKING THINGS YOU'VE AGREED TO DO FOR ME!

Loraine: I get your point!

Joe: (aggressively with hatred in his voice)

1. You've agreed to come to a fucking poetry reading!
2. You've agreed to watch some fucking art films!
3. You've agreed to wear clothes that make other men want to talk to you!
4. You've agreed to get some tattoos that will help you look nice!
5. You've agreed to help me lose weight by giving me some sex I want EVEN THOUGH you're getting WAY MORE OF THE SEX you want!

That's five against fucking nine, Loraine!

Loraine: I know it's five against nine. I just don't see why you need me to do something that disgusts me.

Joe: (shouting in a rage) YOU SAID LOVE BETWEEN US WAS NOT ENOUGH! YOU SAID I NEEDED TO LIKE YOU!

Loraine: But why do you need me to rim you in order to like me?

Joe: (shouting loudly and menacingly) YOU FUCKING OWE ME THIS!! YOU OWE ME THIS FOR EVERYTHING YOU'VE PUT ME THROUGH!! YOU OWE ME THIS FOR EVERY DAY YOU HURT ME!! YOU OWE ME THIS BECAUSE I FUCKING LOVE YOU!!

Loraine: Joe, I've never seen you like this before. You're scaring me!

Joe picks up a glass and smashes it on the ground next to Loraine's feet. Loraine screams.

Joe: (screaming menacingly and coming closer to Loraine's face) YOU WANT ME TO FUCKING RIP YOU APART?? IS THAT WHAT YOU WANT? IS THIS WHAT TURNS YOU ON!

Loraine: (scared) Joe please stop!

Joe: (screaming in a rage) YOU'RE GONNA GET WHAT YOU WANT, YOU SELFISH FUCKING BITCH!!

Joe grabs Loraine by her shoulders. Loraine struggles to get away in a panic. Loraine can see pure hatred in Joe's eyes, staring back at her.

Loraine: (screaming) GET OFF ME!! GET THE FUCK OFF ME!!

Joe: (screaming) NO!!

Joe slams Loraine hard against the corner of Joe's office door. Loraine hits her head and is nearly knocked unconscious.

She quickly stumbles away from Joe towards the back of the office, feeling dizzy and trying to remain upright.

Once against the wall, Lorain is in pain, terrified, breathing heavily and experiencing a huge adrenaline rush.

Loraine: (frightened) What are you doing? Why are you doing this to me?

Joe suddenly stops his aggression and smiles at Loraine.

Joe: (in normal tone of voice) You should be careful what you ask for Loraine. You might get it.

Loraine: (shouting) I DIDN'T ASK FOR YOU TO DO THAT!!

Joe: (loudly) Oh yes you did! You said acting like an animal trying to kill you gets you hot!

Loraine: (loudly) I meant I wanted sex to feel that way! I didn't want you to fucking act like that here!

Joe: Get over here.

Loraine: Why should I trust you?

Joe: I want to show you something.

Loraine: (scared) Joe, I'm freaked out. I think I'm bleeding.

Joe: (calmly) There's no reason to be scared. You know I love you. Now come here, I want to show you something.

Loraine: (nervous) You're not going to hurt me, are you?

Joe: (calmly) No, Loraine, I love you. You're my partner. The last thing I would ever want to do is hurt you.

Loraine: (softly) Please don't hurt me. Please...

Joe: I won't hurt you. You know you can trust me. I've never hurt you before now.

Loraine cautiously steps towards Joe. Joe sticks his hand down her knickers and feels her lubrication with his fingers. He then sticks his fingers in Loraine's face.

Joe: There's wetness there Loraine.

Loraine: (sighing) I know.

Joe: You don't like it when I'm nice to you.

Loraine: My body responds to you when you're aggressive.

Joe: I knew it!

Loraine: (loudly) That doesn't mean I wanted you to be aggressive here! I can't get off if I'm fucking terrified! It doesn't matter how wet I am! That's not what I want!

Joe: Then what do you want?

Loraine: (angrily) I want you to be aggressive in bed when I tell you to be aggressive! I just want you to do what I fucking tell you to do, Joe. I don't want to feel scared in my own house!

Joe: I see.

Loraine: (loudly) Just because I like aggression, that doesn't mean I want to feel like I'm on my way to a battered women's shelter! Pretending is one thing, but this wasn't pretending! This was fucking real! You fucking hurt me!

Joe: (suddenly confused) I take your point. I don't know why I just did that.

Loraine: I know why you did it.

Joe: Why?

Loraine: I made you really fucking angry.

Joe: Maybe.

Loraine: (loudly) But you can't behave like that just because I make you angry! I'll punch you in the fucking throat if you ever come near me like that again!

Joe: (feeling like something is taking over him) I don't know what just happened to me. I've never done that before… to anyone. I've never been that angry with anyone before…

Loraine: I made you that angry?

Joe: (sighing) Yes. You did.

Loraine: (smiling) I know you won't believe me when I say this… but that actually makes me feel good.

Joe: What?

Loraine: It's a relief.

Joe: Why?

Loraine: Because it means it's not just me that gets really angry.

Joe: I'm probably angrier than you, Loraine. I just hide it better.

Loraine: But do you even realise how hard I have to push you to get you to show me any of your anger?

Joe: (shaking his head) I try to hide my anger from you when I can. I want to be a gentleman.

Loraine: Well, maybe I don't want you to be gentle with me. I don't crumble when you get angry with me, Joe. I didn't crumble last night. You don't have to either shove down your anger or act like a fucking wife beater. There's a middle ground.

Joe: I know but finding that middle ground is hard for men. It's hard for me to say what I want without hurting women.

Loraine: Joe, I can handle the truth about what you want! Just remember to be kind afterwards.

Joe: (smiling) Kindness? YOU… want kindness? LORAINE KLEIN wants kindness?

Loraine: Everyone needs a bit of kindness, even me. I know I never ask for kindness because you make me so fucking angry all the time. But if you can be honest with me and not hold shit in, I might not get so angry. When I'm not angry, I actually enjoy being nice to you.

Joe: You are nice to me sometimes, Loraine. More than you think.

Loraine: Sometimes I want to be nice to you. It doesn't matter whether you always deserve it. Sometimes, I just enjoy watching you be happy.

Joe: (feeling a strange sense of deja vu) I never expected that to come out of your mouth.

Loraine: You know, I'm not as different to you as you think I am.

Joe: What do you mean?

Loraine: Sometimes, I love giving you things you don't deserve. Sometimes I enjoy getting angry with you just so that I can enjoy forgiving you.

Joe: You can hurt me all you want as long as I know you'll forgive me in the end. As long as you love me, I can take anything you throw at me, Loraine. I've decided I'll never complain about you hurting my feelings ever again. I was being petty earlier when I said you needed to apologise to me.

Loraine: Thank you Joe. That makes me feel good.

Joe: I'm happy I can make you feel good. I was beginning to doubt I could do that anymore.

Loraine: (smiling playfully) Today, you not only made me feel good, you just fucking made me wet! We weren't even fucking and you made me wet! It was scary but you did it!

Joe: (distraught) I honestly don't know what happened to me… I've never ever done anything like that before. I'm so so sorry. Please trust me when I tell you I'll never ever do that again. I would never ever want to frighten or hurt you. I need you. You mean more to me than anyone.

Loraine: I know all of that, but it's not what's important. What's important is you know you can get me wet before you slim down. I can complain about your body and you don't have to feel hurt about it.

Joe: (shaking his head) But Loraine, I scared you and smashed your head against the edge of a door. There's blood on your neck.

Loraine: (annoyed) I know that! But if you could release that aggression when I tell you to, it wouldn't be scary. It would be fucking hot! Don't you get it?

Joe: Aren't you upset at me?

Loraine: (thinking hard) ...I was for a minute, but now I'm mostly just relieved. You know you can turn me on and I can still be honest with you. I couldn't ask for anything more than that, really.

Joe: So...are you saying you like it when I'm angry and violent?

Loraine: I guess I do. I need you to stand up to me sometimes, Joe. I hate knowing I can walk all over you. I want to be with a man, not a scared little girl. I've already been a scared little girl.

Joe: (speaking hesitantly) But isn't this like… abusive? Aren't you asking me to abuse you?

Loraine: It's only abusive if I decide I don't want it.

Joe: (confused) Okay… so what does this mean? Does this mean you want me to act like a maniac next time when we have sex?

Loraine: I'd honestly love that, Joe. I'd love it if you could do that for me. But don't throw my head against a door. That could cause brain damage. I'll figure out something else for you to do, though. Something sexy. Maybe you can punch my stomach or drop kick me. I'll have to think about it.

Joe: We'll need safe words. I'll need to know if I'm going too far.

Loraine: (rolls eyes) We'll get you some fucking safe words.

Joe: This is weird, Loraine.

Loraine: What is?

Joe: I feel like I'm learning about all these different sides to you that I never knew about. It's like being on an adventure.

Loraine: Don't you think I feel that way as well?

Joe: It's just that when you're with someone for as long as we've been together, you think you know them. You think you can always guess what the person wants or is going to do.

Loraine: You never really know anyone. You're always getting to know them, every day.

Joe: Sometimes I feel like I know me less than I know you.

Loraine: I feel the same way. Funny that.

Joe: I know myself enough to know that I love you though. That never goes away.

Loraine: (smiling) It never goes away, no matter how much you sometimes want to kill me.

Joe: We don't really know why we love each other, do we?

Loraine: (sighing) Your guess is as good as mine.

Joe: So… where do we go from here?

Loraine: First, you're going to clean up all that fucking glass on the floor.

Joe: Yeah, that would be a good idea.

Loraine: Secondly, I'm going upstairs to watch some telly. You can do what you want: come up later if you want to, write poems on your computer if you want to, listen to music, wank to Davis. Just be quiet on your way in if I'm asleep.

Joe: Thank you Loraine.

Loraine: Thirdly, you're going to try your hardest to lose less than two pounds next week.

Joe: Why less than two pounds?

Loraine: Because I don't want to spend next Saturday evening with my tongue darting in and out of your arsehole.

Joe: (excitedly) You mean you're going to–

Loraine: (interrupting firmly) You are going to sit in soapy water for at least forty minutes before I even come near you!

Joe: (smiling) You are an amazing fucking girlfriend!

Loraine: (rolling her eyes) I am an amazing girlfriend. I'm going in the chocolate factory, you fucking weirdo.

Joe: I'll do whatever I can to make this as painless for you as possible.

Loraine: Just make sure you're clean. Other than that, don't worry about me.

Joe: As much as I'm looking forward to this, I don't know if I can go through with it now.

Loraine: (annoyed) Why are you fucking with my head again?

Joe: I just realised something.

Loraine: What?

Joe: I can't enjoy it if I know you're disgusted.

Loraine: But I'm a good actress.

Joe: I know you're a good actress, but–

Loraine: (interrupting) Joe, you have to put up with my honesty every day! Let me act for you for one night.

Joe: You want to act for me?

Loraine: I never get to perform for you. I'm always performing for other people and being honest with you. I love performing. I want to be able to share that side of myself with you.

Joe: You like performing because you like impressing people.

Loraine: Totally. You know I wanted to be a magician when I was a kid.

Joe: (wistfully) I'd love it if you could find some way to work magic into our sex life. That'd make me so fucking hard.

Loraine: (smiling) Honey, you look like a fat pig. So when you get me wet, that is a fucking magic trick.

Joe: (laughing) Sex is magic, isn't it? It's like magic for grownups.

Loraine: You can't impress someone or delight them or turn them on if you never do any magic to them. Too much honesty ruins shit. People need to have fun; people need to act and perform for each other, once in a while. That's why dancing is so beautiful. It's not real.

Joe: It's acting.

Loraine: Yes it is, just like the best porn.

Joe: (mischievously) And speaking of acting, tell me how you're going to play your arse eating character?

Loraine: She'll be a total slut… but not just any slut.

Joe: (smiling) Oh?

Loraine: (suddenly doing a cockney accent) "She'll be the one slut who knows how to do it right. The one slut who won't rest until the job is fucking done proper."

Joe: (giggling) I think I've already type cast you.

Loraine: (smiling) I don't mind being type cast as long as my performance teases you into all those naughty little feelings your body isn't expecting. If I'm acting, that means my big tongue is acting all over you. And if I'm rimming you, my tongue will be acting like it's over the moon to wiggle up your nasty big bum just to make you fucking cum hard all over the floor. I'm a dancer, Joe. I act by moving my body on stage for a living. All of my body is very limber, especially my tongue. Remember that.

Joe: (excited) I'll remember.

Loraine: I'll pretend I'm putting on a ballet for bedridden fat kids that can't clap for me. If I can give them a hard on, that's how I'll know they want an encore.

Joe: And what's the encore?

Loraine: (with seductive eyes) Fun and frolics for the whole family.

Joe: (surprised) Wow.

Loraine: What?

Joe: You're really making me hard right now. And you're doing it with words. I've never seen you use words like this. It feels almost like Janet.

Loraine: (smiling) Janet's got nothing on me.

Joe: (giggling) I don't know, Loraine. She may be fucked up and dangerous but she's very good with words. She's also very good with her tongue.

Loraine: I still think I have the edge on her.

Joe: Why is that?

Loraine: (smiling confidently) I'm better than her at making you feel things. Yesterday, you said I made you want to crawl into a hole and die. Today, I made you feel like you'd been raped, then I made you violent. I made you throw me against the edge of a door and hurt me. Janet could never do any of that. She could never make you feel the things I make you feel.

Joe: No, she couldn't, Loraine. You do something to me when we have sex that she never did.

Loraine: What's that?

Joe: You make me feel like I'm stealing something. Sex with Janet just felt like fucking someone who instinctively knew how to get me off, really really hard. It was like wanking with another person's body instead of my hand, except the orgasms were way more intense. A few times I passed out.

Loraine: I told you she was trying to kill you!

Joe: Well, that's not the point. You give me something totally different to her. When I fuck you, it feels like I'm robbing a bank. I love the fact that it's me fucking you and not some handsome bloke with a big cock and rock-hard abs. I feel like I'm stealing you from all those beautiful men and rubbing their fucking faces in it. That's far more exciting than anything Janet ever did for me.

Loraine: (suddenly feeling aroused again) I like the idea of you breaking into me and stealing something.

Joe: (smiling with pride) It's like a battle I'm always on the verge of winning. I can't ever leave you no matter how much you hurt me. I can't let myself lose; I have to win. You make me want to fucking conquer and defeat you. No woman has ever done that; no woman apart from my mother.

Loraine: (seductively) You know you can't live without the things I make you feel.

Joe: It's true. I can't.

Loraine: That's one of the reasons I still have sex with you, even though your body disgusts me. I love the days we fuck and you're angry with me. I know you try to hide it and be gentle, but you're a horrible actor. I can always tell when there's rage in you. When I can really feel it, that's when your body doesn't bother me. That's when I cum.

Joe: So when I'm angry, you can ignore the fact that I look like an ugly fat pig?

Loraine: When I feel you fucking hate me, the fact that you're an ugly fat pig only makes it hotter.

Joe: Really?

Loraine: (giggling) Last night, when you were saying all those horrible things about me, I had to work so hard to stay angry. I had to cry to keep myself focussed on being angry instead of–

Joe: (interrupting) You were gagging for it last night??

Loraine: I came three times after you left. When I heard you crying, I came a fourth time.

Joe: (surprised) You're having me on!

Loraine: Nope.

Joe: So my inner turmoil and pain gets you off. Not just my anger.

Loraine: That's who you chose to love.

Joe: But if that's what gets you off, why is it so important to you that I lose weight?

Loraine: (suddenly feeling sad) I don't feel good getting turned on this way, Joe. I know what it's like to cum because you like me and I want that again. I don't want what we have now. I need to know you'll put in some effort to look nice for me. I can't feel liked if I don't see that effort coming from you. I can't feel beautiful if you don't like me. I feel ugly and you know I can't handle that.

Joe: But why do you need me to like you in order to feel like you're not ugly?

Loraine: (speaking hesitantly) When I was a kid… my mother used to tell me I was a beautiful little girl that was fooling everyone. She said none of my friends actually liked me; she would say they just wanted to be my friend so they could be popular; she said some kids were only friends of mine because they were scared of me. When I got kicked out of school for the first time, I started to believe her. When my pedo uncle finally told me my parents wanted me to move in with him, I just didn't want to be alive anymore. That's why I gained all that weight when I was fourteen. I wasn't brave enough to kill myself, so becoming ugly was the next best thing. … But being ugly felt worse than being dead. Being ugly is what gave me the courage to die. That's why I was hospitalised.

Joe: Why haven't you told me this before?

Loraine: (sighing) I didn't want you to know my mum is right about me.

Joe: (loudly) Your mum isn't right about you!

Loraine: I'm not beautiful, Joe. I'm ugly.

Joe: How can you say that? You're the most beautiful woman I've ever seen!

Loraine: Only on the outside. Only while I'm young and exercise.

Joe: That's rubbish, Loraine.

Loraine: No, I'm an ugly person. I can't do anything about that. I can just distract myself by doing other things.

Joe: You're the furthest thing from an ugly person!

Loraine: I can distract myself by being healthy and looking beautiful; I can distract myself by helping people and working hard. But I'm horrible and you know it. You live with it.

Joe: But you're not horrible at all, Loraine. You're just a normal woman! You're like what most women are like, behind closed doors.

Loraine: I fell for you because you were the first man I ever met who actually liked me. I know we don't have anything in common and I'm not someone you would be friends with.

Joe: (tenderly) You have no idea how much I'd love to be your friend, Loraine. There's nothing I want more but I don't know how. I don't know how to get you to let me in.

Loraine: I don't know either. I'm not a good friend to anyone, really. I'd never make a good mother. I can only dance and help people and make people feel good when they look at me. That's it; that's all I can do. I'll never be able to lead a decent life. Most people who get to know me wind up hating me.

Joe: That's so NOT true, Loraine! You have no idea how loved you are by so many different people.

Loraine: They don't really know me. My friends don't really know me.

Joe: That's because you don't let them know you. You keep them at a distance.

Loraine: They'd hate me if they knew me.

Joe: No, they wouldn't. They're similar to you.

Loraine: (shaking her head) They're not as angry. They don't have fantasies about stabbing people.

Joe: How do you know they don't?

Loraine: I don't even know. There's so much anger in me that I don't understand. It comes out if I'm really close to someone. That's why I'm only close to you. I have absolutely no clue why I have all this hate in me. Most of the time I'm not angry, I feel like I'm dead inside. Hardly anything or anyone makes me feel good anymore. It feels like I can't love other people, Joe. I can't even love you, if I'm honest.

Joe: (shocked) What?

Loraine: I said it, didn't I? I guess I should say it again: I don't love you, Joe. I'm sorry but I can't love you.

Joe: But I don't understand. You tell me you love me nearly every day.

Loraine: I say I love you but I don't, really. I want to but I don't know how. Saying it is the closest I can get to actually doing it. I tell myself that if I say I love you enough times it will eventually happen, but it never does. It's like a deaf person trying to understand music.

Joe: So why are you in a relationship, then? Why are you in a relationship with a guy you don't love?

Loraine: (looking down in shame) Because you made me feel like I could be beautiful inside. No man ever liked me after we started seeing each other for a few months. You did. You liked me even after you saw how ugly I really am.

Joe takes Loraine's head in his hands and stares lovingly into her sad eyes.

Joe: Loraine, I liked you because you needed me to like you. It doesn't matter what you're like on the inside. I don't do conditional love. When I love you, it's not something you have to earn. It's a gift.

Loraine pulls away from Joe's hands and turns her back to him.

Loraine: Well, it's a gift I'm not getting anymore. You've had to put up with the real me for too long. You only love me now because you feel sorry for me. You can't make yourself like me anymore.

Joe: Loraine, right now, I like you a lot. I like you more than I've ever liked you.

Loraine turns around and faces Joe with a lost desperate look in her eyes.

Loraine: Why? Why do you like me? How can you like me?

Joe: So many reasons. It's hard to put it all into words…

Loraine: That's why I don't believe you, Joe.

Joe: (speaking hesitantly) Loraine, I like you because… you make me feel all those things I'm not supposed to feel. You actually do make me feel naughty, Loraine. You make me feel like I'm getting away with something. You're not like my friends; you're actually the most honest and passionate person I've ever known. You're honest and passionate even when it hurts people. Being with you feels electric. Being hurt by you feels electric. And when you hurt me, you don't stop, no matter how much pain I'm in. You always keep going.

Loraine: (sighing) I know I do. I can't stop, Joe.

Joe: It's fucking amazing.

Loraine: (incredulous) You think it's amazing?

Joe: (smiling) Of course I do. You're like James Bond. You could easily torture the bad guys in order to save London from being blown up by a hidden bomb. Other agents would stop when the suspects started crying, but not you. You'd go all the way and burn their bodies to ashes. If any of them gave you any jip, you'd castrate their friends. You'd suffocate their mums. You'd even torture their children and enjoy it.

Loraine: I know it's terrible, but I would enjoy that. I've always wondered what it would feel like to kill someone.

Joe: I know you have, Loraine. And I know it shouldn't make me feel this way, but I'm just in awe of you.

Loraine: Why?

Joe: I'm gobsmacked when I think about who you are. I can't believe how strong and beautiful you are. You impress me so fucking much, Loraine. You achieve everything you want in your life; you help so many people; you never get tired or bored with anything you're doing. You work so hard at absolutely everything. You're like a drill instructor with your students but they listen to you because you're so bloody good! And you're not just a harsh taskmaster, you're also really kind and supportive when they need your help. I can't count how many times you've had a kid over the house crying in your arms because of something that's going on with their parents. You have so much more patience with kids than I do. I can't believe you think you'd be a bad mother when I see how you are with kids. You're so protective and loyal. You always go the extra mile to make sure everyone you care about is okay. You tear people to shreds when you think they're even taking the piss out of me!

Loraine: (giggling) Only I'm allowed to take the piss out of you.

Joe: I know. That's why being with you is like… having a guardian angel. That's why whenever I think about how cruel you can be, I can never be angry for very long. You hurt me so badly and I know a lot of it is abuse, but at the end of the day, everything about you just makes me go gooey inside. That's why I sit there and take it when you say horrible things to me. That's why I never get fed up and leave. I feel protected. I never got that from my parents.

Loraine: (softly) ...You haven't left me. It's amazing to me that you haven't.

Joe: I'll always do anything to be back in your arms, Loraine. You should know that about me by now… I'm in love with you. You're my lover and my lioness protector, my enemy and my ally, my teacher and my bad habit, my boss, my bedroom fantasy and my atom bomb blast of out of this universe hotness that makes all womankind look like shit on your heels. You're my fucking dream woman, Loraine. You're my dream woman and I'm so happy you're in my life. You're like a superhero to me.

Loraine: (tearing up) Oh, Joe.

Joe: (tearing up) I'm so fucking proud of you. I know sometimes it's all for the wrong reasons and I know I'm seriously fucked up in the head, but I've never met anyone who makes me feel like you do. I want you for all the reasons that make people on the street love you and I want you for all the reasons that would make them hate you if they ever lived with you. But I don't care what they think, either way. To me, you're wonderful and helpful and sassy and so powerful it makes me want to cry. You're like a hard and bright diamond: you're so strong and so unique and you never break, no matter what. That's like being perfect, Loraine. To me, you're just fucking perfect.

Loraine: (tears streaming down face) I've never been perfect to anyone.

Joe: (crying) You're perfect just the way you are.

Loraine: (crying) I never knew any of this. I never knew you felt this way.

Joe: (crying) I didn't know it until today. I didn't know it until you said we should break up. When you said we should break up, everything I was feeling flipped on its head. Going back to Janet suddenly seemed like a horrible punishment. Losing you seemed like it would be the biggest mistake of my life.

Loraine: (crying) You've just made me feel beautiful for the first time in over a year.

Joe: I'm glad. I want someone I like as much as you to feel beautiful.

Loraine: (wiping away tears) Joe…

Joe: Yes…?

Loraine: I believe you now. I believe you when you say you like me.

Joe: (smiling and wiping away tears) If I didn't like you, I wouldn't have started loving you. If I didn't love you, I would have broken up with you by now. You've given me a million reasons to break up with you.

Loraine: I know. Compared to you, I'm not a very good person. But it's okay because you still love me. No one's ever loved me like that.

Joe: I know they haven't. You give me strength most men will never know.

Loraine: That's why you can handle me, isn't it?

Joe: It is. Being with you makes me strong enough to turn off my feelings when I need to. Very few men can do that.

Loraine: At least I'm honest about myself, though. I would never lie to a guy and say that being in a relationship with me is easy. One time I made a guy so angry, he punched a hole in his car window and split his hand open. Another time, a guy told me I was the reason he got really bad fucking plastic surgery. I've made so many blokes cry in front of me, Joe. Girls as well. I've never tried to hurt anyone though. I've never wanted to hurt anyone. These things just happen to me, no matter what I do.

Joe: They don't just happen to you, Loraine. When you've got a cob on, you can be a cruel fucking bitch (laughing).

Loraine: (giggling) You're probably right.

Joe: But you're a cruel bitch that's helped me see something very important about myself.

Loraine: What's that?

Joe: I am not a civilised man.

Loraine: (smiling affectionately) I wouldn't be with you if you were.

Joe: I know that now. I know why you're with me.

Loraine: I'm glad. You knowing that might make our relationship easier.

Joe: I want it to be easier. I want us to be happy with each other.

Loraine: I want that too, Joe. I'm sorry I haven't been appreciating you so much lately.

Joe: I understand. I'm sorry for being so lazy with my eating.

Loraine: And let me just get this out of the way: I'm really really really really fucking sorry about that blog post. I know it was only up for fifteen minutes, but it was still fucking nasty. I'm sorry I wrote it. I'm sorry I let other people see it. I should have held back. It was mean to you. You kissed Chloe because I was mean to you and I feel like such a horrible fucking cunt. I don't want to ever do anything like that again. I want to be the best girlfriend for you that I can be.

Joe: (speaking softly) I'm not upset about it anymore. I know why you wrote it. I know how much I hurt you when I cheated on you. I won't ever hurt you like that again.

Loraine: (sniffing) There's nothing that hurts me more than you getting something from someone else you could have gotten from me. There's not much I can give you, Joe.

Joe: I understand that and it's not a problem. What you do give me is more than enough. Just be you and I'll be fine.

Loraine: You know, if you ever decided you wanted to be with someone else, I'd want you to just be truthful with me about it. If I could see it wasn't a load of cobblers and you were really in love with another woman, I'd let you go. I'd be in bed for weeks but I'd still let you go. I wouldn't ever want to stop you from being with someone who loves you. I'd want to kill the fucking bitch, but I'd hold back for you. I'd hold back so you could have her. Sometimes I feel like that's the greatest gift I could give you.

Joe: But that's not the gift I want from you. The only gift I want from you is you.

Loraine: (smiling) I'm so lucky to have such a good bloke.

Joe: I'm not a good bloke. I'm just a bloke who loves you.

Loraine: I appreciate that. I'd like to love you someday. I'd like to learn how to do that.

Joe: Are you sure you don't love me, already?

Loraine: I'm sure and it makes me feel fucking horrible.

Joe: It really shouldn't. You can only do what you can do.

Loraine: But you love me, Joe. Me not loving you isn't fair.

Joe: It's fine, Loraine. I have to accept and cherish what I have from you. Life is largely about learning to be happy, appreciating the things you are lucky enough to experience. You can't always get everything you want, but you can still be happy anyway. That's how you become wise.

Loraine: (shaking her head) I don't fucking care. It feels like you're hurting yourself. I hate it when you do that.

Joe: Why do you think I'm hurting myself?

Loraine: Because I can't give you the one thing you want from a woman.

Joe: No one can give anyone everything they want. That's a fantasy.

Loraine: Maybe. But I feel like I should be your friend. I feel like I should be able to talk to you for hours. I feel like, by not loving you, I'm letting you down.

Joe: Loraine, last night you said all that mattered was that you fuck me and were loyal to me. You said that was what worked for men and women.

Loraine: But you're not like a man; you're like a woman.

Joe: What does that mean?

Loraine: You want to be with someone who loves you.

Joe: But loving someone else is more important than being loved.

Loraine: Joe, you want to be with a woman who loves you. That's what you've always wanted, since you were a kid. And then when you grew up, you finally got it. Janet loved you for three years and she still loves you now. No one else ever loved you, before or since. Your mum didn't love you. I don't love you. Pamela never loved you.

Joe: But that's not important. I'm with you. I'm with my dream woman, Loraine. Very few men can say that.

Loraine: But that isn't what's important. You deserve better than your dream woman.

Joe: True love isn't about what you deserve. It's about loving the person you chose to spend your life with; it's about learning to develop the empathy and patience it takes to do that. It's about accepting who you love without needing them to change; it's about accepting who you love even if someone comes along that's more attractive to you and gives you more of what you want from a partner. It's about loving your partner, no matter what, loving them without conditions, loving them with all your heart even if it turns out you love them way more than they love you!

Loraine: (rolling her eyes) I've heard all this before. Love isn't fucking fair, is it?

Joe: Nope. It's not fair and it's not just. It's not even ethical, if you think about it.

Loraine: (sighing) Love is some sad shit.

Joe: But you don't have to feel sad about it. Love makes the world go round, Loraine.

Loraine: ...I feel sad for you.

Joe: Why?

Loraine: You're choosing to love someone who doesn't love you back.

Joe: (smiling tenderly) That's not sad. That's the purest kind of love.

Loraine: You're choosing me over another woman who loves you.

Joe: I know that.

Loraine: But you're rejecting her. You're never going to talk to her again.

Joe: That's right.

Loraine: I don't know what to think right now. I feel weird.

Joe: Why?

Loraine: (confused) ...Things turned out the way I wanted them to. You made the choice I hoped you would make. I fucking hate Janet. She's a psycho bitch.

Joe: Then you should be happy.

Loraine: I know I should... but I'm not.

Joe: Well, how do you feel?

Loraine: …Very sad.

Joe: Why?

Loraine: I don't know what's happening to me.

Joe: What's happening?

Loraine: I feel very very sad.

Joe: But why?

Loraine: It's stupid.

Joe: Your feelings are your feelings. Don't ever be ashamed of them, Loraine. Just tell me why you're sad.

Loraine: …I can't say it. You'll think I've lost the plot.

Joe: No, I won't. You can tell me anything.

Loraine: (quietly) I'm sad for her.

Joe: What?

Loraine: (tearing up) I feel so sad for her.

Joe: Why are you sad for Janet?

Loraine: (crying hysterically) ...Because she's fucking perfect for you! I can feel it in her words… It's not normal… It's like how my mum loved my dad…

Joe: (sighing) I know that, Loraine. I have to admit that I do still like her. You were right about that.

Loraine turns her back to Joe again, her head in her hands.

Loraine: (sobbing) I hate her… I fucking hate her but I can't stand the idea of hurting her… I hate hurting her and I don't know why… I wish she'd hurt me instead… I feel like I'm losing my mind…

Joe: You're not losing your mind. You just have empathy for her. I knew you had empathy for her.

Loraine: (crying) She loves you… She loves you so hard… and you're throwing her away to be with a woman who can't love you… That's so sad it's fucking cruel!!

Joe: But that's life! People get rejected for all sorts of reasons. It builds character.

Loraine: (crying loudly) …I don't want to build her character! I don't want to be this person anymore! I don't want to take you away from her…

Joe: You don't mean that, Loraine. Come and have a glass of water.

Loraine: (crying painfully) I want to tell her how sorry I am… for everything… I want to tell her I'm so, so sorry…

Joe: But you haven't done anything to her!

Loraine: (sobbing loudly) I feel like I've taken my dad away from my mum… It's like being a kid again… I feel so horrible… I feel worthless… I feel like I'm not good enough to breathe…

Joe: You're not worthless and that's not what's going on! I'm doing what's best for Janet. I'm helping her.

Loraine: (crying) No, you're not… She needs you and you're fucking crushing her! … You're crushing the one woman who loves you…!

Joe: (abruptly) But I'm helping her! I'm doing her a favour! I'm giving her the chance to be with someone who won't crush her. I'm giving her the opportunity to get over me, once and for all, Loraine. When that happens, she'll be able to be in a healthy relationship with a nice, decent bloke who's normal. She'll be happy!

Loraine: (crying and screaming) BUT SHE'S NOT NORMAL!! YOU'RE NOT NORMAL!!! SHE'S YOUR WOMAN!! SHE'S YOUR SOULMATE!! IT'S HER!!

Joe: It's not her, Loraine. I'm horrible for her and that's why you're crying. She's suffering but that's only because she hasn't moved on from me yet. I'm making the right choice. I'm giving Janet a chance to find love. Remember, even the best choices can be difficult. But don't be sad for me and Janet when I'm not sad. I'm actually very happy right now. Come here.

Joe is looking into Loraine's eyes, wiping the tears from her face. Her expression is one of utter hopelessness. It's like the expression one sees on the face of a person about to take their own life. Joe recognises this expression.

Joe: (tenderly) Don't forget how happy I am that you're in my life. Think about who you are, Loraine. You're the person I've chosen to love; not Janet, it's you. You're the one in this house with me. We built a home. You're the woman in my life, in good times and in bad. You can do anything you want to me and still be that woman. You're the woman I love, the woman who wakes me up every day. It doesn't matter that we don't have anything in common; it doesn't matter that I can't talk to you. I fight and cry and let you hurt me because you're my woman! It's not Janet. It's you. I've chosen you!

Loraine pulls Joe's hands off her again and steps away from him.

Loraine: (sniffing) I'm sick of hurting you.

Joe: But it's okay! I don't mind, honestly.

Loraine: I mind. It's not right.

Joe: (exhausted with Loraine) Loraine, you have a man in your life who loves you. Think about that. He'll do anything for you! He worships the ground you walk on! He even lets you hurt him, over and over again. That's what every woman wants!

Loraine: I don't care.

Joe: But why can't you be happy? I don't get it. Why can't you just appreciate what we have?

Loraine: (looking down) I don't deserve to be happy. I feel like I shouldn't have been born.

Joe: (passionately) None of us deserve to be alive and we're still here! It's like God is loving us all. It's the ultimate example of unconditional love.

Loraine: (quietly) I don't deserve love… from anyone.

Joe: But you do! You're an amazing person!

Loraine: (shaking her head) I was a mistake.

Joe: (reassuringly) You're not at all a mistake, Loraine. Not at all. You're wonderful and I feel nothing but gratitude for the fact that you're here with me. We all exist, despite all the things that could have happened in the universe to prevent us from ever evolving and being born. Isn't that beautiful? Isn't it beautiful that by random chance, we're both alive at this time and we found each other?

Loraine: (slowly) No, Joe… It's fucking tragic…

Joe: Don't you think you're being a bit selfish?

Loraine: (softly) No.

Joe: Loraine, think about what I just said.

Loraine: I am.

Joe: Then why can't you give of yourself? Why can't you appreciate the love that I give you?

Loraine: (quietly) …'Cause you want me to hurt you, Joe. You'd rather be abused than have love. That's what your mum did to you.

Joe: Well, I can't tell you how you should or shouldn't feel. I can't make you happy if you choose to be unhappy. All I can tell you is that there's nothing that makes me happier than knowing that whenever I'm hurting, you'll be there with me. You make my life so beautiful, no matter what's happening in it, no matter what I'm facing. That's how I live with all my struggles, that's how I cope with being sad, that's even how I cope with you acting like such a mean and punishing bitch.

Loraine: That makes sense.

Joe: (definitely) Of course it does! It's love!

Loraine: It's not love; it's abuse. I'm abusing a man because I'm a beautiful woman and people think my fat boyfriend should consider himself lucky to be with me.

Joe: (emphatically) But it's not abuse if the other person wants it! That's what you said.

Loraine: No one sees it when an attractive woman abuses a man. No one wants to.

Joe: But that's okay! Everyone interprets abuse differently. Abuse is subjective!

Loraine: (shaking her head) It's not subjective. It's fucking horrible.

Joe: It's still love and it's better than being alone. I'd rather die than not have you in my life.

Loraine: (sighing) I don't want to hurt you anymore… I'm hurting myself…

Joe: (irritated) Hurting me is obviously better than being alone, Loraine. Don't be stupid.

Loraine: It's worse…

Joe steps closer to Loraine. Loraine is walking backwards, moving away from Joe. Loraine suddenly does not like the look on Joe's face.

Joe: (frustrated with Loraine) I think you're forgetting what it was like to be alone. Remember all the weeks you couldn't get out of bed? Remember all the meds you were on? Remember all that pain?

Loraine: ...I remember.

Joe: (getting angrier) Do you seriously want to go back to that? Do you want to be in pain again, with no one to look after you?

Loraine: No.

Joe: (angrily) And you think you can just FIND someone else?? You think any self-respecting man would put up with you??

Loraine: …It's not likely.

Joe: (loudly) Then FUCKING BE HAPPY! BE HAPPY WITH THE LOVE I GIVE YOU! CHERISH AND PROTECT IT!

Loraine: (tearing up again) But I don't want it anymore… You should be with Janet...

Joe: (yelling) DON'T EVEN GO THERE!!

Loraine: (crying) What's wrong with you…? Why can't you be with your dream woman…? She needs you to love her!

Joe: (screaming) YOU NEED TO LOVE ME!! I'M NOT LIVING WITHOUT YOU!! I'M NOT!! I'LL HANG MYSELF!! I'LL DO IT TONIGHT!!

Loraine suddenly pushes Joe, slamming both her hands into his tits.

Loraine: (screaming) DON'T YOU FUCKING DARE!!!

Joe: (screaming) WHY SHOULDN'T I??!!

Loraine: (screaming) 'CAUSE I WOULD NEVER FORGIVE MYSELF, YOU FUCKING TWAT!!

Joe: (screaming) WHY NOT??!!!

Loraine: (screaming) I FUCKING LOVE YOU!!!

Joe stops screaming and smiles.

Joe: (playfully) What did you say?

Loraine: (deeply embarrassed) ...I said I love you.

Joe: (teasing Loraine) Would you mind saying it again?

Loraine: (suddenly smiling) Fuck you.

Joe: (smirking) You wish.

Loraine: You wish!

Joe: I kind of do. That was horny.

Loraine: It was.

Joe: Why did you try so hard to convince me that you didn't love me?

Loraine: (sighing) …I wanted to know you knew I was lying.

Joe: Well, you're a good actress.

Loraine: I know I am.

Joe: You're also quite sexy, for someone who isn't a psychopath.

Loraine: I'm a shallow girl. I'm sorry Joe, but that'll have to do. (laughing gently)

Joe: Nah, you're more of a prick-tease than a shallow girl. You believe in monogamy and you do far too much slut shaming.

Loraine: (nodding her head) I do hate dirty fucking whores.

Joe: (teasing Loraine) Can I trust you not to abuse any children?

Loraine: I won't be abusing anyone, ever again.

Joe: (playfully) Not even if I ask you to?

Loraine: Nope. We're gonna be nice to each other. And we're gonna get some counselling.

Joe: That's probably a good idea.

Loraine: (definitively) And if I notice either of us abusing each other again, verbally or physically, we're over. We're done. That's it.

Joe: (nodding his head) That's depressing but it sounds like a good idea too.

Loraine: I think we should sit down and write a list of things we both think are abusive. We need some clear guidelines to work with.

Joe: Okay.

Loraine: This is why I'm not getting any tattoos; I'm not a fucking cow. And you're gonna have to tell me if I'm hurting your feelings. We can't always assume your feelings are wrong. We both have to take your feelings far more seriously. Otherwise, you'll kill me one day.

Joe: (nodding his head) You're right.

Loraine: And you have to tell me when I'm going too far in the things I say. This brutal honesty shit isn't working for us and it's not good that I can't stop hurting you once I start. I have to practice being more sensitive to you and dealing with my own feelings in a healthier way. I have to work at being a kinder person and you're gonna have to help me with that, Joe. We need to do a lot of work – both of us.

Joe: (sighing) …That's a lot less sexy, but okay.

Loraine: (definitively) If you wanna be abused, there's a woman waiting for you in London. She won't make you do any work on yourself.

Joe: (quietly) I know.

Loraine: If you still love her, go get her. I won't stop you.

Joe: Why are you so certain she would abuse me?

Loraine: 'Cause she doesn't trust that you love her for who she is. Otherwise, she wouldn't talk about wanting to grab your cock. If you know a guy loves you, you don't need to do that shit. And if Janet was really worried I was abusing you, that's all her email would be about and she would have sent it to you a year ago. But that wasn't the email she sent you yesterday, was it? That email was about why you should forgive her and how much she wants to grab your cock.

Joe: (laughing) Yeah, it was kind of transparent.

Loraine: (giggling) It was sixth form psycho bitch.

Joe: But you don't think she's just… a really loving person that's also really sexual? You know, someone who shows affection by being sexual?

Loraine: (rolling her eyes) People would only describe a woman that way.

Joe: What do you mean?

Loraine: If you thought a bloke was abusing Janet, would you send her an email where you talk about fingering her?

Joe: No.

Loraine: Why not?

Joe: I don't know... It would be creepy.

Loraine: (adamantly) Exactly! And that's why she doesn't get to do that to you without me thinking she's a fucking creep. Just because a chick makes you hard, that doesn't mean she's not crossing a line and acting like a fucking dickhead. Telling a bloke in a relationship you want to grab his cock is dickhead behaviour. She's a fucking slag.

Joe: But what if she loves you and thinks you're being abused by your current girlfriend?

Loraine: Then she should be better than your current girlfriend. You're not a starving animal she can control by dangling pussy in your face; you're a human being. She says you're her favourite human being and she talks to you like you're a salivating dog. Do you honestly think she respects you?

Joe: (smiling) You know, it never ceases to me amaze that you think you'd be a bad mum.

Loraine: Well, no, I'm childfree like Janet is. I'm just not hateful about it. I don't hate children the way she does. I don't see the point in that.

Joe: (laughing gently) I know you don't, Loraine. And I can't say that I'm not sad that you're childfree. But I guess... it's good for the environment. And if I'm honest, I'm not sure I'm dad material either. It's hard enough having you as a girlfriend.

Loraine: And it's even harder having a boyfriend who needs a mum.

Joe: I don't want another mum. Just a sexy fantasy mother.

Loraine: Well, what kind of a sexy fantasy mother do you want?

Joe: (smiling mischievously) One who does all the naughty things a mum isn't supposed to.

Loraine: (with seductive eyes) We can always role play.

Joe: Oh?

Loraine spontaneously begins to do a sexy porn star monologue, where she sensually rubs her hands up and down her body.

Loraine: (in a fake American accent) "We can pretend you're my thirteen-year-old son and I've decided right at the moment you're getting your first boners that I'm gonna be the sexiest porn star in the world! And I'm gonna start filming porn in our family living room and livestream it to the whole world so you get a sex positive feminist upbringing where you'll be so proud of the fact even your momma's rich gynaecologist wants to stick his tiny dick inside her AIDS infested cooch!"

Joe: (laughing) You sound like Davis!

Loraine: (imitating Davis McFarlin masturbating) "Oh sweetie… I'll be fucking… all your favourite porn stars… (panting)… while you play video games… with your crying cuck of a dad… in the garage… OH GOD... YES"

Joe is laughing quite hard. The is the hardest Loraine has made Joe laugh in months.

Loraine: (imitating Davis having an orgasm) "…Oh, yes, baby… I'll make your dad… feel like a broken… worthless… failure… OHHH JESUS!! I'll make you go through life… only having boners… when you think about… ME!!… (screaming) OOHH GOD… I'M SUCH A GOOD MOM!!!!………"

Joe: Do you think she's like that, in real life?

Loraine: Nah, I'm just mucking about.

Joe: You know, you are making me laugh, but this isn't a mum/son fantasy I could get off to.

Loraine: (with a raised eyebrow) Why not?

Joe: It's too much like Mum. If Mum was alive and still acting like that today, I wouldn't want to fuck her. I'd want to beat the living shit out of her.

Loraine: (smiling with pride) That's my boy.

Joe: (mischievously) I thought you didn't approve of violence, anymore?

Loraine: Well, I don't, but you're still my boy and you still make me proud.

Joe: (sighing) I am your boy, in a way. But I wanna be your man, Loraine. I'm tired of being a boy. I'm nearly forty.

Loraine: I thought you hated gender roles and masculinity?

Joe: I never hated masculinity. I hated *my* masculinity. I just thought I hated all masculinity, until I met you.

Loraine: What happened then?

Joe: (smiling warmly) I realised that the most beautiful woman I've ever seen is also the most masculine person I've ever met.

Loraine: Is that a problem?

Joe: Only for people who hate men.

Loraine: (playfully) Do you know what?

Joe: What?

Loraine: I think we should stop talking and you should have a bath.

Joe: Why?

Loraine: (smiling seductively) 'Cause I want you to sit in soapy water for forty minutes.

Joe: (shocked) Are you serious? You want to rim me?? Now??

Loraine: I think I need to do some more acting for you.

Joe: But why now? Isn't it kind of late?

Loraine: It is, but I need you to feel something, tonight. I don't want to just say it to you. It's important to me that you feel it.

Joe: What do you need me to feel?

Loraine clasps Joe's right hand with both her hands and brings it to her chest, looking deep into his eye.

Loraine: (slowly) I need you to feel how hard I can make you cum. But I also need you to feel how much I love you, respect you, cherish you and how much I want you to be in love with me again 'cause you're *my* favourite person. You're my only real friend, if I'm honest, Joe. You're my only friend who knows me and all my blokiness. You know me and still love me. That's the most precious thing anyone's ever given me.

Loraine can see Joe beginning to cry again. Loraine releases Joe's hand and starts stroking the back of his head.

Loraine: I could never hate you, you know. I don't ever want you to think that I hate you. You're the reason I can have love from a man, babes. The fact that I can be in a relationship is insane. Who else is gonna love me? I'm a fucking cunt! (laughing)

Tears are now streaming down Joe's cheek.

Loraine: You are such a girl.

Joe nods his head.

Loraine: (smiling) It's okay, really. You don't have to be sexy all the time.

Joe is deeply embarrassed by his tears. He believes he is very unsexy in this moment, drowning in unmanly vulnerabilities.

Loraine agrees that Joe is unsexy in this moment but still wants to rim him anyway.

Both Loraine's acting and the limberness of her tongue give Joe the biggest orgasm he's had in years. It's so intense, Joe nearly passes out. Loraine hopes Joe finally understands just how much she loves him.

After Joe's orgasm, he and Loraine go to bed, falling asleep in each other's arms. As Loraine drifts off to sleep, she thinks about how happy she is that she is finally better at something than Claire. Joe falls asleep more quickly than Loraine. He has a long elaborate dream about Davis McFarlin.

In the first part of the dream, Joe is Lena Rodriguez, a chubby Mexican writer Joe imagines is Davis's best friend from high school. In the second part of the dream, Joe is Davis's son Max.

In real life, Davis McFarlin is the porn star name of Beth Stewart. Although Beth Stewart now lives in Los Angeles, she was born and raised in Austin, Texas. Beth's political leanings are libertarian. Although she is 'sex positive', she doesn't self-identify as a feminist, believing this political movement unjustly equates female empowerment with persistent man bashing. In 2016, Beth Stewart reluctantly voted for Donald Trump as president of the United States, believing Trump was the lesser of two evils.

In 2017, Beth abandoned her career in porn to become a stand-up comedian. Although Beth is quite funny, her shows are regularly protested, because of her right leaning political views. Beth doesn't believe in systemic racism, is a strong supporter of Israel and is very vocal in her opposition to minors being given puberty blockers.

Many of Beth's original fans now hate her and regularly post vicious comments about her on social media. Although a few of them give her regular death threats, most of them insult her appearance. Since leaving porn, Beth has gained forty pounds. She now has a double chin.

Beth is married to a Korean woman named Kyung-Soon Park. Kyung-Soon Park's porn star name is 'Licky Linda'. Kyung-Soon has a fourteen-year-old daughter from another marriage named Alice. Alice spends half of the week living with Kyung-Soon and Beth and the other half living with her father Ted. Alice and Beth have a difficult relationship. Alice has a relationship with Kyung-Soon that's filled with even more animosity and tension.

Much to Beth's dismay, Alice is deeply ashamed of her mother.

She is deeply ashamed of her mother for being a registered Republican.

20. ROMANCE: Unconditional Love

Joe Pastorious first entered into a relationship with Janet Waverley in the autumn of 1999. Both Joe and Janet fell in love in a place called Leicester, which is a small city in the middle of England. Many things have been said of Leicester, but one thing that is not said enough is it is a fantastic place to fall in love. It was the perfect place for Joe and Janet to fall in love. This is true, despite the fact that Joe and Janet's love is anything but perfect.

When in the present, one can't predict the future. Hence, the present is the best place to understand imperfect people. When people are dead and we know absolutely everything they have ever done, this creates an illusion of certainty the present thankfully wipes away. You can't trust a corpse, because there is nothing about a corpse's decisions that may hurt or disappoint you. However, you sometimes can't trust the past, either.

Janet Waverley didn't initially fall in love with Joe Pastorious because the two of them had a deep, cerebral connection with each other. The email she sent him on July 28th, 2015, made it seem as though that's what happened.

But that's not how Joe remembers it.

When Joe thinks about falling in love with Janet in 1999, he remembers being a young man packed with hard muscles and testosterone. Even though he suffered bouts of anxiety, his anxieties had no relation to the fearlessness with which he navigated the external world. Joe felt anxious when he worried what his mother might be doing to his other relatives. But he worried much less about breaking laws, or accidentally hurting himself.

When Joe wasn't thinking about his mother Jodie, he regularly worked out, went mountain climbing and would often say shocking things to provoke a reaction from people. The way Joe swore and made insensitive remarks about people's appearances made more middle-class types feel uncomfortable in his presence. The people Joe made most uncomfortable were middle class women he thought were unusually beautiful.

Although Joe was initially quite nervous about actually touching any woman in a sexual way, he was the furthest thing in his conversation from a polite gentleman. He said things which regularly celebrated his virile heterosexuality, he talked about his penis having its own needs and described women's bodies in ways that were crass, vulgar and objectifying.

He loved porn and inappropriately described his favourite porn scenes to any attractive woman who would have a conversation with him. He even played football and occasionally started drunken fights in pubs.

These were the reasons Janet Waverley fell in love with Joe Pastorious. Once in the relationship, Janet also loved the deep intellectual connection she had with her sexy boyfriend. But Joe's intellect wasn't the aspect of Joe that turned her on. Janet was aroused by Joe's shocking rudeness and quite brutish masculinity. Joe's masculinity aroused Janet, while she in turn, gradually removed any inhibitions he had about acting on his more masculine impulses.

Joe remembers Janet encouraging him to lick food off of her breasts in public, getting the two of them kicked out of many local restaurants. Joe even got an anti-social behaviour order for frightening some children, at Janet's request. This ASBO made her quite proud of Joe; she was proud of the lengths he was willing to go to turn her on. The more aggressive and dangerous Joe became, the more Janet lovingly encouraged him to be aggressive and dangerous.

By 2001, Joe was no longer making any effort to check whether Janet gave him her consent, whenever he decided to have sex with her. Every night, whether she wanted it or was tired, Joe regularly fucked the shit out of Janet. He would bite her neck, pull her hair, slap her face, call her a disgusting slag and make her orgasm hard, over and over again. Yet the orgasms he gave her were nothing compared to the ones she gave him afterwards – orgasms that were so intense he found it hard not to hyperventilate.

Joe remembers having sex with Janet regardless of whether she was sober, or so drunk she could barely stand up. She was never angry afterwards; she normally smiled and asked him to do it to her in a more extreme way. If Joe decided to stick his small hard penis inside Janet's arse and quickly ejaculate, she'd ask him to do it again more slowly, while squeezing her neck with his strong and small hands. Once it became apparent Joe was choking Janet, she'd ask him to choke her even harder, after which Joe would become frightened and start panicking. Seeing Joe get so distressed would make Janet giggle. Then she'd say something that would make him laugh and Joe would feel safe again.

He'd feel both safe and incredibly loved.

The fact is, Joe had never felt so safe and loved in another woman's arms.

Before he received Janet's love, Joe had never experienced love which felt so overwhelmingly like love. Janet's love felt otherworldly, like the purest and most intense love a human being could have for another. Some of Joe's friends didn't like Janet and insisted the otherworldly love she made him feel was actually the means by which she controlled and manipulated him. Whenever any friend of Joe expressed any discomfort with Janet, Joe would insist that they didn't really know her and couldn't see her good side. Janet never knew that some of Joe's friends intensely disliked her. In fact, Janet liked all of Joe's friends as much as Joe did.

This was one reason Joe Pastorious genuinely believed he found the perfect girlfriend in Janet Waverley. But just because he believed Janet was the perfect girlfriend, this didn't mean Joe believed she was a perfect human being. Janet did make Joe angry on some occasions; she had a gambling problem, after all. And during the times she made the mistake of telling Joe about the high debts she had racked up, Joe didn't hesitate to punch her. Whenever Joe punched Janet, she'd become sexually aroused. The harder he repeatedly punched her, the more sexually aroused she became.

After being violent with Janet, Joe would always apologise with tears in his eyes, begging her to break up with him and find a boyfriend who wasn't so damaged. Janet would smile gently and explain to him that he was overreacting, that he couldn't really hurt her and that she was proud of him for being so strong and passionate. When Joe told Janet how much he was scaring himself, she would hold him tightly and kiss him tenderly, like a mother reassuring a small child there were no monsters in the dark.

By November of 2002, Joe Pastorious hated himself, while Janet Waverley was oblivious to the fact that her boyfriend hated himself. Janet could only see that her boyfriend was sexy and that she was giving him extreme pleasures; she inferred from this that they were in a healthy relationship. Janet saw herself as an imperfect, but still amazing girlfriend for Joe. Joe saw himself as a violent rapist who was a danger to those he loved.

It wasn't until Janet decided to send Joe her ridiculously long email on July 28th, 2015, that she had fully come to terms with the fact that her young self was not an imperfect, but still amazing girlfriend. Janet now understood for the first time that she and Joe were in an abusive relationship. Worse still, that relationship contained abuse she enabled and encouraged for completely self-interested reasons.

Janet was telling the truth in her email, when she said that she found it hard not to harm herself. But she omitted that this was because of her crippling guilt over not only disfiguring Joe, but encouraging his worst traits, turning him into a person he couldn't help but hate. Janet believed that Joe's relationship with Loraine was a product of Joe believing he was a terrible human being, a human being who deserved to be abused and denigrated by a woman who hated him, for the rest of his life.

Janet was devastated in 2014 when she saw Loraine's hateful blog post about Joe, partly because it was the opposite of what Janet was hoping to see. To convince herself she was a benevolent influence on Joe's life, Janet wanted to see that Joe had finally found another woman like herself. She wanted to see Joe with a far less damaged version of Janet, a Janet who was not a clinically diagnosed psychopath. The last thing Janet wanted to see was Joe in a relationship with a woman whose behaviour bore more of a resemblance to Joe's mother Jodie Green. The only thing Janet was still proud of about her young self, was that she was never like Jodie Green.

Despite her numerous flaws, young Joe was attracted to young Janet because she was beautiful, charming, interesting, intelligent, creative, courageous, funny and a great flirt. Janet was crazy about Joe for similar reasons. They had great conversations together.

Joe thought Janet was an amazing lover and had more fun with her than he had with any other person in his entire life. Janet shared all of Joe's important religious and political views. She had similar tastes and shared his hobbies. Joe could spend long periods of time with Janet without either of them getting on each other's nerves.

Janet helped Joe improve some of his weaknesses. Joe and Janet liked most of the same people for the same reasons. Janet always considered Joe's advice and very much respected his opinion. She often gave Joe good advice and shared a perspective with him that helped him see things he was sometimes blind to on his own. Both parties took their commitment to one another very seriously. Both of them would only leave the relationship if they thought it wasn't working. Joe and Janet only said things to each other that were true. They did this while frequently combining their honesty with tact, so as to not hurt the other's feelings.

When they wanted to lie to each other, they did so by not saying what was true: lying by omission. In Janet's 2015 email, she lied by omission, quite a lot. She didn't tell Joe how much she wanted to be in a second relationship with him, a relationship where she could use her newfound maturity to actually be a good romantic partner, rather than encourage and enable Joe's violence. Janet didn't mention this in her email to Joe, partly because she worried that if she did, it would destroy the possibility of that second relationship.

On November 5th, 2017, Joe Pastorious finally wrote Janet Waverley his own ridiculously long email. This email comprehensively responded to everything she wrote to him, two years earlier.

Joe began his 2017 email by apologising to Janet for not writing her sooner. He then quickly explained that he had no hard feelings about the fact that Janet had stabbed his eye with a cake fork in 2004. He had already spent thirteen years being angry about this and was now ready to let the anger go. Joe also explained how he and Loraine had greatly benefitted from reading Janet's 2015 email. He wrote many paragraphs detailing how the two of them went to counselling because of Janet and that both of them, for the first time in their lives, were working hard to be their best selves.

Loraine was working hard to be kind and sensitive to others, while Joe was learning to stand up for himself, take more responsibility for his life, self-publish his first novel and maintain his now healthy weight. Joe also stated emphatically that Janet was mistaken in her belief that Loraine hated him. Joe described in detail how much Loraine loved, respected and cherished him and then explained that this was why Loraine eventually broke up with Joe on April 10th, 2017. The decision to end their relationship was mostly mutual and far less painful than either Joe or Loraine expected it to be.

Shortly after breaking up, Joe and Loraine quickly became good friends – much better friends than they had ever been while they were a couple. Joe was quite shocked at how well they got on, once they stopped being romantic partners. This confirmed to Joe what he had always suspected: he and Loraine were best suited as house mates who cooked and cleaned together, gave each other advice and occasionally made each other laugh. Becoming Loraine's house mate (rather than her lover) also made Joe feel a deep sense of gratitude. He felt grateful to have a friend like Loraine, as she was his only friend who could be honest with him about harsh truths it was important for him to hear.

Joe told Janet one harsh truth he had come to accept was that Loraine needed to be in a relationship with someone who thought more like she did. Otherwise, Loraine couldn't relax and feel like she could just be herself, without also feeling like a nuisance to her partner. Joe could only relax and feel like he could be himself with his own friends, Jill Patel and Claire Widerlich. Joe described Jill and Claire to Janet as two highly intelligent, highly creative women he loved dearly but was not attracted to. Joe also described to Janet how in the last six months, he was finding it harder to relax around either of them, as Joe's weight loss and new status as a single person was producing changes in their behaviour he found periodically awkward.

Just a week after announcing he had broken up with Loraine, Jill seemed to resent Joe for not suddenly falling in love with her. It was as if Jill felt entitled to be Joe's girlfriend, while Joe himself had no say in the matter. Claire, on the other hand, started obsessively flirting with Joe in a way that felt creepy. Claire was constantly peppering her words with sexual innuendos to see if she could give Joe an erection. Every time they hung out, Claire couldn't stop herself from describing how amazing fat women were in bed and how every one of her lovers was gobsmacked at her ability to deep throat a cock until it spurt copious amounts of semen down her throat. Although Joe was happy for Claire's lovers, he had no desire to spurt copious amounts of semen down her throat.

Joe did think Claire had a pretty face and would be attractive if she lost even five stone. However, Claire's current weight made Joe think she resembled a stuffed white bin bag. Joe reassured Janet he would never tell Claire how he saw her, because doing so would be needlessly cruel. Yet Joe also said that he felt ambivalent about whether he was being a good friend, in avoiding the harsh truth that Claire needed to lose weight. Claire, after all, was constantly boasting about what a fantastic lover she was, even though she made no effort to make herself look attractive. Since Joe was now making that effort, Claire was suddenly looking very selfish to him. Her selfishness was unattractive to Joe, just like it had been repulsive to Loraine.

Joe had recently suggested to Loraine that she ask her friend Sasha Glasser if he was interested in seeing her romantically. Joe knew Loraine fancied Sasha and thought the two of them would make a good couple. Within days of telling Loraine this, she and Sasha were not only spending a lot of time together, they seemed to be falling in love. Joe told Janet he had never seen Loraine so happy and carefree, now that she was actually falling in love with a man she was both physically attracted to and who she could delight by just being herself. Sasha and Loraine had so much in common.

Joe explained to Janet that he was quite happy for Loraine, even though he thought Sasha Glasser was incredibly boring and bland. However, Sasha was very kind and hardworking and this was fundamentally more important to Joe than how interesting he found Sasha's conversation. Sasha had a successful career as a local fitness instructor, but he still told Joe how much he appreciated the fact that it was Joe who encouraged Loraine to make the first move.

Even though Sasha and Loraine had been friendly acquaintances, Sasha was too nervous to tell Loraine he had a crush on her. He was far too intimidated, both by Loraine's extreme beauty and brash personality. Although Sasha was handsome and surrounded by attractive women every day, none of them were half as beautiful as Loraine. Joe was not surprised when Sasha told him Loraine was the most beautiful woman he had ever seen. But Joe was surprised to hear that Sasha initially found it quite difficult to even make eye contact with her. Until they started seeing each other, even looking at Loraine made Sasha feel nervous and inadequate.

Much to Janet's surprise, Joe explained that it was Loraine who encouraged Joe to be brave and finally send Janet the very email she was now reading. Loraine said that if Joe waited until Janet was in a happy relationship before having the courage to send her an email, he would regret it for the rest of his life. Joe agreed with Loraine, even though resuming contact with Janet was quite difficult for him. Joe was honest about this, telling Janet in the most tactful manner possible, that he was frightened of letting her back into his life. Joe was frightened of how much Janet could physically (and psychologically) hurt him, if she ever had impulse control problems again.

Joe also told Janet that, despite his deep fears, she was a risk worth taking. This was what motivated him to finally send her all these pages of text, text explaining in great detail what was going on in Joe's life, how much he missed Janet and how proud of her he was for becoming the writer and public intellectual he always knew she would be. In the most beautiful words Joe could think of, he told Janet that, regardless of whether they would ever become a couple again, he would always love her. And it wasn't unhealthy love, either. Joe insisted that Janet deserved to be loved by him and many other people, because she was a truly amazing person.

Joe, however, didn't tell Janet she was his favourite person, because he wanted to tell it to her in person, once he knew for certain they were going to become a couple again.

Joe instead thanked Janet for telling him how much she wanted to grab his cock. He humorously described how much Loraine hated that bit of Janet's 2015 email, but then explained why he fundamentally disagreed with Loraine. Joe didn't like the idea that romantic language was the only way a woman could prove to a man she wasn't manipulating him. Since sex was what separated romance from mere friendship, Joe thought it was important for any woman to tell the man she loved just how much she wanted to make him cum. For Joe, love talk without sex talk, was fundamentally manipulative. It was talking to a romantic partner the way you should talk to a friend.

Joe also said he didn't want to just jump into a second relationship with Janet, without first seeing how well the two of them got on in 2017. It was important to Joe not to simply repeat their first relationship, because in many respects, he understood it was deeply unhealthy and abusive. Joe apologised profusely for beating and raping Janet and insisted that he wanted to prove to her that he had become a completely different person since they last saw each other. Joe said he could only be with Janet if she too had become a different person, a person who would encourage him to be a better, rather than worse, human being. It was Loraine who taught him that this is what he wanted most from a romantic partner.

In order to know Janet could be this romantic partner, Joe would need to spend a lot of time with Janet and get to know her again, now that the two of them were both forty-one. Joe described, with eloquence and wit, how he needed to know for certain whether he and Janet were best suited as lovers, friends, or people who loved each other enough to leave each other alone. But he still concluded his email by saying he hoped he was good enough and brave enough, to be with someone he loved as much as Janet Waverley. Joe then spent his final two sentences describing how much he missed fingering Janet under the table at middle class dinner parties, when no one was looking.

As soon as Janet finished reading this ridiculously long email, she laughed and smiled. Joe had always been good at making her laugh and smile. But fifteen seconds later, both her hands were covering her face, as Janet was blindsided by an uncontrollable burst of tears. It suddenly hit her what she had just read and what it actually meant. After all these years, Joe Pastorious not only still loved Janet; he was thinking of getting back together.

Since not receiving a response to her 2015 email, Janet had convinced herself that Joe hated her. Despite this, Joe's love was the one thing Janet secretly wanted more than anything else in her life. Thus, seeing Joe's renewed romantic interest in her felt somewhere between experiencing a divine miracle and being punched in the face. It was so overwhelming emotionally, that Janet wept and sobbed like a little girl.

As she wept, she thanked God over and over again, having never in her life felt such an overwhelming rush of gratitude, for absolutely everything. Janet thanked God profusely for giving her the gift of life, for having created Joe, for having created love itself and for giving even a clinically diagnosed psychopath the greatest thing that could ever happen to a human being: love.

Janet promised God that if she and Joe were to begin a second relationship, she would never stop fighting the worst parts of her character. She would give their second relationship absolutely everything she had, drawing from every bit of fairness, loyalty, courage, tenacity, sensitivity, tenderness, warmth and compassion she had within herself. Janet promised God she would love Joe as hard as she could, even giving him her life, provided he did the same for her.

Janet was so overwhelmed with these intense emotions, partly because Joe sent her his email on November 5th, 2017, exactly fifteen years after he first broke up with her. November 5th, 2002 was the second most painful and horrifying day Janet had ever lived through. The most painful and horrifying day was August 7th, 2004. That was the day she disfigured Joe, momentarily believing she had actually murdered the love of her life.

Although Joe was enraged at Janet for disfiguring him, he still couldn't tell the authorities what really happened that day. No amount of rage within Joe was powerful enough to compete with the power of Joe's love for Janet. It was true that after Janet stabbed Joe's eye with a cake fork, he believed that Janet had simply revealed to him that she was an evil person. Yet he also knew deep down that this belief was false. Whether she was a psychopath or not, Janet Waverley couldn't be evil; she had far too much love inside her.

Janet's love for Joe, after all, is what prevented Janet from killing Joe's mother. Janet could have easily killed Jodie Green and made it look as though Jodie had killed herself. Between 1996 and 2000, Jodie would send periodic emails to various people in her life she had abused or threatened, terrifying them with claims she would commit suicide if they refused to comply with various demands she made. Jodie sent many of these emails to Joe and Janet. By June of 2000, Joe himself was planning on murdering

Jodie, because he knew he could easily make it look like a suicide. Joe was keeping this a secret from Janet.

Yet it was Janet who ultimately convinced Joe to try and manipulate his mother into being a nicer person. Joe was amazed at how effectively Janet could manipulate Jodie, even creating moments when Joe actually enjoyed being in his mother's company.

Because Janet had inspired Joe not to kill his own mother, he instinctively knew he would someday forgive Janet for nearly killing him. And not only would he forgive her, but he'd also forgive her for good reasons. Joe knew Janet enough to know she would eventually earn Joe's forgiveness by atoning for her mistakes, becoming a thoroughly amazing human being and demonstrating to Joe just how much she still loved him. Joe, however, couldn't admit any of this to himself...not until November of 2017.

Yet even on August 7th, 2004, both Joe and Janet knew they would one day become a couple again. What neither of them expected was that Janet would one day convince Joe that feminism had evolved into a deeply misandric, authoritarian hate movement. Janet was the last person to predict that her politics would change so radically, between July of 2015 and November of 2017. She was also unaware that she wasn't ready for Joe in 2015, partly because the feminist movement she identified with was denigrating Joe's masculinity, as well as normalising the female abuse he had suffered for most of his life. 2015 Janet couldn't even see that feminism was largely at odds with the kind of relationship she ultimately wanted. Janet never wanted children, but she did want something else that was decidedly patriarchal.

As early as 1999, Janet Waverley knew she would one day get on her knees and propose to Joe Pastorious, asking him with tears in her eyes, to be her husband. Twenty years later, on September 2nd, 2019, Joe said yes to this proposal and the two of them were married on Valentine's Day, 2020. This was not a religious wedding, because although Joe and Janet believe in God, they both intensely dislike organised religion.

Joe and Janet's wedding reception was held (unsurprisingly) at Firebug, one of Joe's favourite hangouts. Alice Adler helped with the catering and did magic tricks to amuse the other guests. Joe and Janet invited Eve Fenn, Alice Adler and their daughter Karen Adler, but only Alice was present at the wedding.

Alice loves weddings and any party where she can flirt with people and be the centre of attention. This is why she attended Joe and Janet's wedding, despite having a fever, stuffy nose and persistent cough. When speaking to the wedding guests, Alice made no effort to cover her mouth when having coughing fits. She even repeatedly wiped her nose onto her own hand, instead of getting a tissue, as she handed food and drinks to people. Four days later, Alice would be in hospital, breathing on a ventilator.

Fortunately, this same fate did not befall any of the other people at the wedding. However, Alice did infect Joe, Janet and twenty-three other guests with COVID-19. The next week, most of these wedding guests had what felt like a mild flu. Joe and Janet had no symptoms.

Jill Patel and Claire Widerlich were not invited to Joe and Janet's wedding, as Joe had recently fallen out with both of them. Joe would quickly regret this decision, finding out a week later that Claire had suddenly died of a heart attack. After hearing of Claire's death, Joe was devastated. Janet, however, was still happy Claire was not invited to their wedding. Janet didn't want anyone at her wedding that she knew would be seething with jealousy and resentment.

Because Janet could see how distressed Joe was at Claire's passing, she kept these feelings to herself. Janet instead tried to be emotionally supportive during Joe's time of grief. Janet, after all, had promised Joe she would always do her best to be emotionally supportive, during their wedding vows.

Joe and Janet's wedding was very different to the one they would have had, if they had gotten married in their twenties. Young Joe and Janet hated Valentine's Day, seeing it as a consumerist ritual that reduced romance to a vulgar capitalist industry. By 2020, Joe and Janet had accepted that consumerist rituals produce economic growth and such growth generally reduces crime and poverty. Both Joe and Janet were no longer lefties, having thoroughly made peace with both capitalism and the importance of traditional rituals. However, they saw their wedding less as a ritual solidifying their commitment to one and other and more as a gesture of gratitude to their guests. The wedding guests were all people Joe and Janet greatly appreciated for being so supportive in both of their lives.

The only aspect of the wedding that was unpleasant for Joe and Janet was having to deal with Sasha and Loraine. During the reception, Sasha and Loraine got in a drunken fight that was so loud and so vicious, Joe had to ask both of them to leave. But this didn't stop either Joe or Janet from having a good time afterwards and treating their remaining guests with kindness, respect and dignity. Joe and Janet even danced to cheesy pop songs they didn't like, for the sake of helping their much-appreciated guests have a good time.

This was because, by the day of their wedding, Joe and Janet had come to terms with the fact that social norms are valuable and sometimes worthy of respect. Both of them finally understood that even eccentric humans like themselves sometimes have obligations to respect social norms, rather than constantly demand that the social norms cater to them, at the expense of everyone else.

During the coronavirus pandemic that overtook Britain shortly after February 14th, 2020, many people expected that British society would begin to see the world more like Joe and Janet.

It did not.

However, British society did watch a lot of porn.

21. ROMANCE: Moving On

Throughout the eighties and nineties, Jodie Green was the UK's most well paid and successful porn star. Between June of 2001 and October of 2002, Jodie Green and Janet Waverley were secret lovers. Until Jodie's death on August 12th, 2004, millions of men and women also wanted to be Jodie's lover. Even Beth Stewart had her first orgasm thinking about being Jodie's lover.

Joe Pastorious, however, never wanted to have sex with his mother. From the time he was fourteen until he was twenty-three, Joe consistently refused all of her sexual advances.

These refusals enraged Jodie. Joe, after all, was refusing what Jodie saw as a great gift, a gift millions of men and women fantasised about, a gift she thought very few sons were lucky enough to have offered to them by their mothers. Despite how much Joe enraged Jodie by refusing this gift, he still tried in vain to be a good son – even a son his mother could be proud of.

Joe tried hard to bond with his mum, relying on the fact that both of them were quite intelligent and had similar taste in music, movies and literature. Jodie was a big influence on Joe's taste, introducing him at a young age to John Coltrane and Eric Dolphy records, Ingmar Bergman and David Lynch movies and books by Alice Munroe and Cora Sandel. Unfortunately, by the time Joe was in his teens, Jodie had come to believe that music, movies, and literature were relatively trivial aspects of life – temporary diversions from what truly mattered.

For Jodie, what truly mattered was demanding things on behalf of women and minorities, making people bend to your will, making lots of money, raising beautiful children and making others envious of you.

Joe couldn't competently do any of these things. However, he was an unusually handsome teenager who was constantly wanking. Jodie was confident that if she was aggressive enough in her pursuit of Joe, he would eventually cave in and fuck her. Jodie was convinced that if Joe had sex with her, this would give him first-hand experience of what an amazing mother he had. In her mind, this would make up for all the cruelty Jodie exhibited towards Joe, as he transitioned from being a child into being a teenager.

Shortly before twenty-three-year-old Joe Pastorious met Janet Waverley in 1999, Jodie stopped trying to seduce Joe. Jodie began to suspect that Joe did not want to have children. Joe never told his mother that he was childfree, but Jodie could suddenly read it in his body language, whenever she talked about grandchildren. When this happened, Jodie switched from trying to aggressively turn on Joe, to instead expressing anger and criticism at every opportunity.

By October of 2002, Jodie had convinced herself that it was Janet who manipulated Joe into believing he didn't want to become a father. This was why Jodie stopped being Janet's lover and threatened to tell the police Joe was beating Janet unless he quickly broke up with her.

Jodie, however, convinced herself it was Janet who was responsible for all of Joe's quite brutal beatings. Jodie believed that Janet was so manipulative and controlling that as long as Janet was his girlfriend, Joe had virtually no free will. Jodie became extremely paranoid, convincing herself that Janet was responsible for everything Joe believed and did.

Joe's submissiveness to Janet was disgusting to Jodie. Yet she was far more disgusted with Joe than with Janet. Joe, after all, was giving Janet control over him Jodie thought was rightfully hers. Like many mothers, Jodie believed only she could control her son in a way that would ensure his future success.

Hence, it was incredibly important to Jodie that Joe break up with Janet and find a nice girl who would convince him to have children while he was still in his twenties. Having children in his twenties would allow Joe to both carry on his mother's legacy and make Jodie a grandmother while she was still a highly attractive woman. By being childfree, Joe was crushing Jodie's big dream of being the most youthful and sexy granny the adult film industry had ever seen.

By November 1st, 2002, Jodie was now much crueller to Joe than she had ever been. But no matter how badly she treated Joe, he still couldn't help but love her. After Joe broke up with Janet and started gaining weight, Jodie tormented him with consistently vicious emotional abuse, doing her best to make him as miserable as she could. The only thing that made her back off slightly was she could sense that Joe was becoming suicidal. If Joe committed suicide, Jodie wouldn't get her grandchildren.

Joe's twin sister Wendy was not like Joe.

Wendy hated her mother with a passion, refusing to have any contact with her. After nearly dying as a result of one of Jodie's brutal beatings, Wendy began living with her grandmother in the summer of 1990, at the age of fourteen. Thirteen years later, Wendy was a well-respected and much-loved police officer engaged to Chico Venturi, a rich and famous Italian violinist. Wendy married Chico on November 25th, 2003. However, she forbade Jodie from attending her lavish and expensive wedding. Wendy knew this wedding would make Jodie proud and thus wanted her to know about it, while simultaneously communicating the message that Jodie was forbidden from entering the church premises.

Wendy Venturi would give birth to twin girls on September 11th, 2006: Mia and Irene.

Both of Wendy's daughters would have a lifelong obsession with the life of their grandmother.

Mia was ashamed of the fact that her obsession with Jodie Green was privately erotic. Irene, on the other hand, was not aroused by Jodie, but instead inspired by her.

Irene Venturi would enter the adult industry at age twenty-three, in July of 2029. After Irene began making adult films, her mother disowned her. Once Wendy disowned Irene, she changed her porn star name from Kayla Clitnibbler to Jodie Green.

Irene wanted to punish and humiliate Wendy, in much the same way that Wendy wanted to punish and humiliate her own mother with her lavish wedding. But although Irene was quite angry at her mother, she didn't quite hate her.

Wendy, on the other hand, thought her mother Jodie was, by far, the most vile and disgusting human being she ever had the misfortune of knowing. When Wendy found out that Jodie had passed away, she didn't feel even the smallest twinge of sadness. She instead wept tears of joy, feeling like a huge weight had been lifted from her shoulders. Unlike Wendy, Joe didn't feel happy when their mother died, but he also didn't cry.

When Jodie gave birth to Joe and Wendy in 1976, at the age of twenty, she was a much nicer person than the person her children would remember her being. Teenage Jodie was rebellious and intelligent. She read voraciously, was composing jazz tunes on the piano by the time she was fourteen and spent hours practicing Karate in her small dirty bedroom.

Jodie Green grew up in a working-class suburb of London and regularly fought with her overbearing and verbally abusive parents, Frank and Gail. It was Gail, rather than Frank, who gave Jodie severe beatings as a child, beatings which often landed Jodie in hospital.

Jodie learned martial arts as a way of intimidating her mother, so that Gail was too frightened to lay a hand on her by the time Jodie was an unusually tall and skinny adolescent.

Despite Jodie's burgeoning knowledge of martial arts, Gail and Jodie still verbally antagonised each other. Both of them would often have huge rows where each would try their hardest to insult the other in the cruellest way they could think of. Frank did nothing to stop these rows, mistakenly assuming this behaviour was normal in mothers and daughters. Frank made an even bigger mistake: he assumed these rows were an expression of love between Gail and Jodie. Frank equated brutal honesty with love and intimacy.

Jodie first met Mateo Pastorious on February 2nd, 1974, when she was eighteen and he was twenty. Jodie fell in love with Mateo because he was quiet, soft-spoken and kind, unlike the members of her own family. Jodie had never known a man as kind as young Mateo, nor had she ever met a man so compliant with her whenever she decided she wanted to do things that made him uncomfortable. In 1974, Mateo was not in a frame of mind where he found it easy to stand up to people, especially not a beautiful young woman who was attracted to him.

On March 2nd, 1973, both of Mateo's parents had died in a car accident. Mateo was understandably traumatised by this event and initially found his new relationship with Jodie a great source of comfort. Mateo also enjoyed being with a young woman who had such a domineering personality. This was partly because Jodie's intelligence and ability to fight for what she believed in were deeply sexy qualities to young Mateo. These were qualities he had only ever encountered before in his own mother Ida. In a strange way, being loved by Jodie felt like having a mother who was still alive. Jodie often spoke to Mateo like he was her son.

Jodie convinced Mateo to marry her within five months of meeting each other, in a cheap impromptu wedding in Blackpool on July 27th, 1974. Much to the disappointment of her parents, Jodie kept her surname, because she thought the tradition of a woman taking on a man's surname was deeply sexist. Mateo was also hurt that his wife wouldn't take on his surname, but fundamentally, he thought this was better than not having Jodie as his wife. Her prickly personality was a worthy price to pay for her beauty, her confidence and all the pleasure she gave him.

Jodie Green was a fantastic lover.

During the first two years of their marriage, Jodie pressured Mateo into getting arm tattoos he didn't really like, one of which was a large drawing of her face. Jodie was also angry at Mateo for wanting to wait until he finished uni before starting a family. She poked holes in their condoms, tricking Mateo into impregnating her before either of them could financially support children. As a result of this, Joe and Wendy Pastorious were both born on October 9th, 1976.

In 1977, Mateo dropped out of university and got a low paying job working long hours as a cook, rarely spending time with Jodie or the kids. Mateo found the stress of his job overwhelming; he soon began taking speed to cope with his long days in a fast-paced bistro kitchen where the head chef was constantly screaming at him for being too slow. Mateo even worked on weekends, having no days off.

Jodie spent most of her days looking after the kids at home and obsessively playing the piano. Jodie wanted to have children while she was young, so that she could form a jazz trio and tour America, while she was still in her thirties. Her musical ambitions were admittedly less artistic than competitive: Jodie wanted to show the world a woman could be a better pianist than most men.

Between 1976 and 1982, Jodie Green was a controlling, short tempered, but still very loving young mother to Joe and Wendy. She made sure that both of them could read and write by the time they were five years old. She constantly played an eclectic range of music for her children, rented a movie projector so she could teach them how to watch movies with subtitles and often devised imaginary games the two of them could play while she was busy at the piano. For her own amusement, Jodie taught both Joe and Wendy how to put on make-up and pretend they were fashion models, strutting down a catwalk.

Like most young mothers in the late 1970s, Jodie would sometimes scream at and hit her children when she was angry. But most of the time, she found joy in teaching and playing with these two new humans. She loved being silly and making them laugh. She also gave them lots of hugs and kisses and often fell asleep cuddling both of them tightly in her arms. All of this would begin to change in 1983, shortly after Jodie began appearing in porn films.

Her brash decision to become an adult film actress was initially a way of financing Mateo's new coke habit. When Mateo was at work and Jodie was busy filming her scenes, Jodie's parents would often look after Joe and Wendy. Yet they were both unaware of what Jodie did to make extra money for her family.

Mateo was initially enthusiastic about his wife's new job, not simply because it facilitated a steady stream of drugs; he also found it highly arousing. Within the world of adult films, Jodie became successful very quickly, as she was both more attractive and a more charismatic performer than most of her contemporaries.

Jodie was also unique in the adult industry in that she used her actual name. Jodie Green wanted people to know who she really was, that she was proud to be a porn star and that she thought society was stupidly judgemental towards sexually exhibitionistic and promiscuous women. She said so in many interviews.

Jodie was never promiscuous as a teenager, but as an adult, she was finding her life in the adult industry quite exciting and, in its own way, addictive. It was far more addictive than even playing the piano. Being a promiscuous porn star initially felt sexy and powerful, but then stranger emotions began to emerge; it was as if Jodie was having a spiritual transformation. She started to believe that she was not only more desirable than most women, but also that she was braver and more historically important. The more movies Jodie made, the more convinced she became that she had no obligations to adhere to any basic social norms.

Because of Jodie's new income, Mateo was now no longer having to work weekends and could spend much more time with his family.

At the bistro where Mateo was becoming an increasingly incompetent cook, he still frequently bragged about his wife's new career as a porn star. The other staff would often tease Mateo, calling Jodie a slut and a whore. But Mateo delighted in this teasing, because he knew deep down that they were jealous of him. Between 1983 and 1985, Mateo felt like he was living the life that every man secretly fantasised about.

Mateo thought that the only reason society disapproved of sluts and whores was that most men were angry at them; men were angry because sluts and whores tended to fuck only the most successful and attractive men. Mateo thought men fantasised about sluts and whores because in real life, most men weren't good enough for them. But Mateo felt unique in being one of the few ordinary blokes who was good enough for an actual porn star. Jodie agreed with Mateo, now believing she was better than most men, as well as most women.

During this period, Mateo and Jodie were suddenly having sex two to three times a day – sometimes in public places and sometimes in front of Joe and Wendy. Even at work, Mateo often had a thick erection, just thinking about Jodie's scenes. He was constantly excusing himself to go to the men's room, quickly masturbating to get his thick erection to subside enough for him to focus on the meticulously coordinated food preparations he was responsible for. In February of 1986, Mateo was finally sacked from his now part-time job.

After this sacking, Mateo stopped feeling superior to other men, even though he was still married to a woman who was quickly becoming one of the biggest sex symbols in the UK. Because of his new inability to work, Mateo began to feel a powerful self-loathing, a self-loathing Jodie took advantage of, because it made him more compliant when she made various demands on him. One of those demands was that Mateo have sex with other men, while she watched. Another was that Mateo get a nose job.

He complied with both of these demands, even though Mateo was heterosexual and had no desire to cut up his face.

Although Jodie regularly gave Mateo quite powerful orgasms, she also berated him for being a bad husband and father, frequently telling him he was lucky to be with a woman so beautiful, successful, and sexually liberated. By 1988, Mateo was agreeing with Jodie. He felt he was incapable of doing anything meaningful with his life, as he was now a hopeless drug addict who depended entirely on his wife's money. Sex and drugs became the only things that were powerful enough to distract Mateo from the overwhelming sense that the world would be a better place if he were dead.

Being so focused on sex and drugs made Mateo oblivious to something else that was happening in his home: the more Jodie was winning awards and breaking records in the adult industry, the more she was exhibiting cruel and violent behaviour towards her children. It was as if Jodie's sexual exhibitionism and her cruelty to Joe and Wendy somehow reinforced each other.

Mateo dutifully tolerated his wife's cruelty, before finally deciding to divorce her in 1994. But between 1988 and 1990, Mateo felt like he deserved to be abused and denigrated and even encouraged Jodie to repeatedly abuse, denigrate, frighten, humiliate and beat Joe and Wendy. This would allow Mateo to be 'the fun parent' whose company his children preferred. This strategy worked until Joe and Wendy were teenagers and could see the obvious truth that Mateo had no intention of protecting them from their mother.

By the spring of 1991, Wendy was living with Jodie's mother Gail, while Jodie herself was beginning to sexually harass Joe.

Fourteen-year-old Wendy was now adamant that she had no desire to see either of her parents, ever again. Gail knew about the beatings Jodie gave Wendy, but refused to alert the police, as she didn't want to see her daughter go to prison. Wendy was allowed to live with her grandmother on the condition that she kept her mother's violence a secret. Mateo agreed with Gail.

Mateo was also well aware that Jodie was now trying to seduce and fuck Joe. But like Gail, Mateo was frightened of the prospect of his family being permanently torn apart and his wife being sent to prison. Even after Mateo divorced Jodie, he still didn't alert the authorities about his ex-wife's violence or her numerous attempts at committing incest with their son.

Mateo stubbornly believed that the most important thing in Joe's life was that he have access to his mother. Mateo, after all, no longer had access to his own mother. Mateo was still heartbroken over Ida Pastorious's untimely death, wishing more than anything that he had appreciated his mother more, when she was alive. He felt this way, even though, like Jodie, Ida was often cruel and violent.

After Mateo divorced Jodie, Joe promised his mother that he would no longer have any contact with his father. Jodie was now adamant that Mateo was psychopathic and would poison Joe's mind and turn him against his mother, if Joe continued to have any contact with him. Jodie repeatedly stated that she would no longer love Joe, unless he chose to live with her in

Kensington and make a lifelong commitment to completely shunning both his father and his sister. Joe agreed to all of this, because it was still better than not having his mother's love.

Joe communicated with his father and sister in secret, until the beginning of 2004.

In August of 1997, Jodie married a porn director called Matt Hancock. Matt also divorced Jodie in November of 1998, after it became obvious to Matt that Jodie was something like a psychopath. Nonetheless, Matt would remain a lifelong friend to both Joe and Wendy. He was at both of their weddings.

When Matt left the world of porn in 2000, he became a journalist who detailed the corruption and abuse within the adult industry. After the widespread use of the internet, porn was suddenly becoming fashionable and mainstream, much to Matt's dismay. By 2001, he considered his career in pornography the single biggest mistake of his life. Matt did not, however, consider his marriage to Jodie a mistake. That marriage, after all, allowed him the chance to become a father figure to Joe and Wendy.

Matt didn't merely feel an obligation to treat Joe and Wendy as his own children. He genuinely liked both of them and instinctively felt they were both people he would be friends with, even if he had never met Jodie. Matt advised, financially supported and protected Joe and Wendy far more than Mateo ever did. When Joe and Janet moved into their first flat on Charles Street, in the summer of 2000, Matt agreed to pay half of their rent. He wanted both of them to live somewhere nice, even though Charles Street was slightly out of their price range. Matt was well aware that Jodie refused to help Joe financially. He didn't know that Jodie would have happily paid for all of the rent, if Joe and Janet agreed to have a baby.

Matt was also unaware that during his marriage to Jodie, she was constantly pressuring Joe to fuck her, whenever the two of them were alone. Joe kept this a secret, because he too wanted to protect Jodie from the consequences of her behaviours towards him. Like his father and grandmother, Joe worried that if he told anyone about Jodie's attempts at seducing him, she would go to prison.

Six years later, when Jodie announced she had terminal cancer, she had destroyed all of her friendships and almost every living relative she had refused to have contact with her. The one relative who loyally still stood by her was Joe.

This is why, towards the end of her life, Jodie began pretending she was quite fond of him. Jodie started saying things to Joe to make him believe she had always been proud to have a son like him, a son so intelligent and kind and giving. Jodie said that Joe's good heart was more important to her than whether or not he had a proper job, lost weight, or made her a granny while she still had her looks. Joe believed all of his mother's lies, more so because he wanted to than because they were believable.

Jodie tried her best to treat Joe with kindness, respect and dignity. This was the first time in Joe's life since he was a child that Jodie had ever tried to consistently treat her son with kindness, respect and dignity. Unfortunately, she was only doing it because she was terrified of dying alone. Jodie was terrified of dying in a hospital bed, without someone who loved her, holding her hand.

On August 12th, 2004, once news broke that Jodie Green had died of bladder cancer at the age of forty-eight, the only people in her life to say nice things about her were the many porn stars she had sex with. These were people she had deliberately kept at a distance.

On the night of August 11th, Joe Pastorious sat beside his mother's hospital bed, holding Jodie's hand with a tense look on his face. He could see that something inside his mother was changing.

Although Jodie was now only minutes away from the end of her life, Joe could sense that his mother was not ready to die. Her tired face was filled with terror, terror at something that throughout her life, she had refused to admit to herself.

Staring into her son's new eye patch, Jodie was terrified of what the rest of Joe's life would be. She was terrified of how many years of pain and suffering he would inflict upon himself because of the way she had treated him, throughout their time together.

At 9:11pm, Joe blurted out the only words he could think of:

Joe: Mum, this is awkward. You're not at peace, are you? You're thinking about how much you hurt me. I can see it in your face.

Jodie nodded her head, slowly.

Joe: (reassuringly) Alright, I understand but… you really need to let it all go now. It's in the past and it really is time to let it go. You have to remember, Mum… I know you.

Jodie: (sighing) I wish you didn't, Joe. You should hate me. I don't even deserve to–

Joe: (interrupting) That's not what I'm saying.

Jodie: (confused) …I don't understand.

Joe: (warmly) Then please try and understand… that I know the person you wanted to be… I didn't see her very often, but I always knew she was there. You gave me her, remember. And she'll always be with me, even after you go. She'll be in every book I write and every woman I love. She gave me everything I need, okay?

Jodie could see Joe begin to smile.

Joe: She gave me my love of books… She introduced me to jazz and Bergman films… She taught me how complicated people can be… And don't forget that I still love her, despite everything… That's why I'm sitting here now, holding her hand… I love this woman you wanted to be, Mum… I know her and I love her very very much… and I'm so happy she's finally here with me.. I'm so happy I can tell her how much I love her.

Jodie: (whispering softly) But I wasn't her… I was horrible to you… and you… never stood up to me… You never… told me off… Just once, you–

Joe: (interrupting) She's lovely, Mum. You've just forgotten. You don't remember how lovely you can be and that's okay. But I remember. And I'll never forget who you really are. I can't. That's a part of me now, Mum… She's a part of me. She'll always be in my heart.

Upon hearing these words, Jodie suddenly felt an overwhelming and intense love for her son, a love she hadn't felt since the day he was born. All the tension, agitation and fear suddenly left her body, as a life she never led flashed before her eyes. Jodie could suddenly see everything she wished she had done with Joe and everything she should have been as a mother.

Jodie looked down at Joe with tears in her eyes.

Jodie: (slowly) I still… wish… you made love to me… I still wish… you'd cum inside me… I so wish… we had a baby together…

Joe: (nodding) I know, Mum. And you can fuck off. I'm your son. If you love your son, you don't say that to him. And if that's your idea of love, I don't fucking want it. If this is what love is, I don't ever want to be loved again… I'd rather be hated.

Joe suddenly let go of Jodie's hand and proceeded to walk briskly down the hospital corridor, taking the nearest lift to the ground floor carpark.

Jodie died at 9:46pm, alone.

Dying alone wasn't as frightening as she thought it would be.

Later that night, Joe played a cassette of old jazz compositions that his mother wrote and performed on her living room piano. This was a cassette Jodie made for Joe on his ninth birthday, at his request. Joe hadn't listened to this tape for seventeen years and was shocked at how good this music was.

Jodie's playing was technically dazzling, deeply artistic and influenced by everything from reggae baselines to the orchestral works of Paul Hindemith and Henri Dutilleux. The chords never went in directions Joe's ear was expecting, the rhythms were odd yet funky and the scale choices in the improvised sections were complex, imaginative and played with speedy precision. Some of the music was dissonant, some of it was quirky and eccentric, some of it was lush and beautiful, and all of it sounded quite creative and new. It sounded creative and new, even though it was recorded on October 7th, 1985.

Although the tape was hissy and poorly mixed, Joe could hear that his mother had given him forty minutes of music that was on par with Coltrane, Dolphy and any critically acclaimed jazz pianist he (or she) had ever been impressed by. He could also hear his mother's sense of humour in the music. The last piece was an odd, up-tempo rendition of 'Happy Birthday' with quite jarring chromatic chords underneath the familiar melody.

After it was finished, Jodie spoke into the tape recorder, giggling at her last wrong note: "Sorry dear, messed that one up."

Two seconds later, Jodie took a breath and spoke again: "Anyways love, happy birthday. There it is. This is the music you asked me to record for you. I hope you liked it. I won't be upset if you don't. It's not for children, really. However... if you do like it... and if, by chance, you do love it later in life... I want you to know that you'll never love it... as much as I love you, baby. Happy birthday Joseph. Happy birthday, my clever little son. You're nine, now. Bloody hell!"

Jodie giggled once more and turned off the tape recorder.

As Joe listened to the end of this tape, he thought of how pleased he was with how he spent his final moments with his mother.

On the one hand, he finally stood up to her, after years of being submissive. His submissiveness to Jodie had been to the detriment of himself and many other people.

On the other hand, Jodie Green was an amazing, if underappreciated jazz pianist and composer. On the night of her death, Joe told this brilliant pianist and composer that he loved her, that she had influenced and inspired him and that she would always be in his heart.

In her hospital bed, Jodie Green died peacefully, with a smile on her face. She was deeply impressed with how her son finally stood up to her, after she tested him one last time.

Jodie was also hoping that in the afterlife, she could help Joe write a book that was both technically dazzling and deeply artistic.

In 2017, Joe did write that book. He dedicated it to his mother – with the deepest love and gratitude.

And then he woke up.

PART 5: LOVE

"Love is the difficult realisation that something other than oneself is real."

- Iris Murdoch

"The truth will set you free, but not until it is finished with you."

- David Foster Wallace

"Beyond the fiction of reality, there is the reality of the fiction."

- Slavoj Zizek

22. LOVE

Joe awakes on the morning of March 6th, 2021, after having had a long elaborate dream where he was married to a woman called Janet Waverley. In Joe's dream, Janet was a psychopath, but somehow simultaneously a nice person and a loving partner for Joe.

Unfortunately, Joe only half-remembers this incredibly detailed dream, a long series of dreams within dreams.

Joe's girlfriend Loraine was in it, Joe's ex-wife Pamela was also present, as was Joe's favourite porn star, Davis McFarlin. But there were other imaginary people: a bohemian bartender named Alice, an art history lecturer called Eve and a Mexican writer from Los Angeles named Lena Rodriguez. Parts of Joe's dream were erotic, parts of the dream were scary and parts of the dream made Joe feel sad to wake up. Joe's mum Claire was in the dream, except she was his annoying friend, rather than his mother. And Joe's dream mother was somehow a porn star called 'Jodie Green' who looked exactly like Loraine.

After Joe adjusted his eyes, looking up at the ceiling fan, he took a moment to remember everything he could about the dream's events, so he could write them down on his iPhone. Joe always wrote down his dreams, as he was planning on someday writing a novel based on the imagery that came from his quite vivid and strange unconscious. Joe felt that his dreams were much more creative than anything he could come up with in his waking life. However, after he wrote down two paragraph's worth of what he could remember, Joe decided that this particular dream was silly and stupid.

Janet Waverley, within the logic of the dream, was supposed to be far less attractive than Loraine. Janet even gave impressive speeches and wrote long emails about how looks didn't matter. She was a passionate advocate of the idea that you should always love people for their inner rather than outer beauty. Yet when Joe recollected Janet's physical appearance, she was stunningly beautiful. She looked like Audrey Horne from Twin Peaks. Janet was at least as beautiful as Loraine, if not more so. And by the end of the dream, she seemed more like a romantic fantasy than a real person.

After yawning into his hand, Joe looks over at Loraine, who is wearing nothing but a blue robe and high heels. Loraine fell asleep with her back to Joe the previous night, after the two of them had a vicious row over Joe's weight. During that row, Loraine claimed that Joe didn't deserve to share a bed with her. She also bluntly stated that Joe's belly was both "nasty" and "disgusting" to most women. Loraine even said that Joe's body was a huge embarrassment, making her feel ashamed to walk alongside him in public. She then insulted the size of his penis.

Joe was taken aback by these insults, as they suddenly made him feel as though he could no longer trust Loraine. Joe had lived under the illusion that Loraine was attracted to him and had at least as much fun as he did, whenever they had sex. After Loraine suddenly blurted out her true feelings about his body, Joe immediately decided he needed to do two things:

1. Start exercising
2. Break up with Loraine.

Joe was by no means a fat man. Yet he still thought he would look much better if he lost about two stone. Nonetheless, Joe was adamant that he would not be in a relationship with anyone who fat shamed him, as a way of motivating him to become more physically healthy. Loraine had already said many nasty things to Joe before yesterday's row but trying to make him feel ashamed of his body was the last straw. Joe had enough, realising that no amount of love was worth putting up with someone who felt entitled to be cruel, whenever she was in a bad mood.

Joe met Loraine Klein on January 27th, 2016.

They met in a Tesco Express, where Loraine was yelling at some teenagers for purposefully tripping Joe and laughing as his groceries flew out of his hands. Loraine helped Joe to his feet, put his groceries into a basket and even paid for the bottle of red wine that broke and splashed its contents across the white floor.

Joe thanked Loraine profusely for her help and then offered to buy her a drink at a nearby pub called Firebug. Much to his surprise, Loraine said 'yes' and the two of them spent the rest of the night drinking and talking about how much they hate bad parents. Before Loraine walked back to her flat, she gave Joe a long hug that ended with a sensuous kiss on the side of his mouth.

By the next morning, Joe had developed an intense infatuation with Loraine. A mere two days later, Loraine confessed to Joe that she was falling in love with him. A day after that, Joe and Loraine began a relationship together.

Joe was elated.

In the first twelve weeks of this new relationship, Joe was happier than he had been in many years. However, by the summer of 2016, Joe's happiness began to fade. He became acutely aware that although Loraine was an amazing person, she was also very demanding. When Loraine was in a bad mood, she was frequently verbally abusive. And on a few occasions, after drinking too much alcohol, Loraine got violent. She would throw sharp objects at Joe, rip up his clothes and kick their dog Max. Joe tolerated this behaviour because Loraine was, in most other ways, the person he wanted to spend the rest of his life with.

By the time Loraine moved in with Joe on April 10th, 2017, her career was skyrocketing. By the end of 2020, Loraine was not only a best-selling author of politically motivated graphic novels, she was also becoming quite a charismatic public intellectual.

Loraine was regularly wheeled out by the BBC to make television appearances on current events programmes. She also did eloquent and heavily viewed vlogs in addition to making quite mesmerising speeches at rallies and university campus halls. Loraine championed causes like universal basic income, the plight of the Palestinian people against Israeli aggression, feminism and green energy. She also did TED Talks on subjects like the benefits of globalisation, new revenge porn laws and body positivity.

Joe's mother Claire was convinced that Joe had hit the jack pot with Loraine. Claire couldn't believe what an amazing daughter-in-law she might have, if Joe would ever commit himself to settling down with a woman and raising a family. Loraine herself was ambivalent about marriage and children. She could see herself enjoying life as a wife and mother, but she was also perfectly happy to remain Joe's live-in girlfriend, without the responsibilities of kids, or the planning of an elaborate wedding. Loraine didn't think marriage or children were relevant to the question of whether or not she was committed to Joe. Loraine told Claire this many times, but Claire assumed Loraine was simply lying, so as to not insult her son. Claire couldn't understand how a woman as attractive and successful as Loraine could be happy without a family.

In some ways, Claire enjoyed Loraine's company more than the company of her own son.

Claire's biggest worry was that Loraine might one day get wise and leave Joe for a man who would truly commit to her. Claire thought that Loraine was out of her son's league. She felt strongly that her son was truly lucky to be with Loraine, as he was not a published writer, artist, or charismatic public intellectual. Unlike Loraine, Joe was also not rich, or particularly good looking. Joe wasn't ugly, either – just average.

Yet although he was rarely appreciated for it, there was one respect in which Joe Pastorious was far above average.

He was an excellent English teacher for adults with special needs. He not only taught effectively but also inspired many of his students to become better people. Joe was proud of his work, which he found much easier to navigate than his confusing romantic relationships.

Before Loraine, Joe had only been in one other relationship – an utterly tedious fifteen-year slog with an academic named Pamela Cassard.

Joe had met Pamela in July of 1999, dated her for three years and eventually married her on November 8th, 2002. Pamela was an art historian who spent most of her time arguing with Joe. Within a few weeks of their relationship, it dawned on Joe that Pamela actually enjoyed this. She loved constant debate for its own sake, even saying things she didn't believe because she found debating so much fun. Pamela would have much rather argued with Joe than give him a hug. Joe found this incredibly frustrating. It made forcing himself to stay in the relationship much more difficult. But Joe stayed with Pamela, for as long as he did, for the sex.

Pamela was quite attractive. Joe thought regular sex with an attractive woman was not an easy thing to acquire, particularly since Joe was average, in so many respects.

On November 8th, 2014, on the evening of their twelfth anniversary, Pamela confessed to Joe that she had three affairs throughout their marriage. The reason she gave for having had these affairs was that she was never physically attracted to Joe and needed to have sex with men who could satisfy her. Joe thought Pamela was callous in the way she explained her infidelities, but he also felt strangely relieved. The two of them were, by then, so disconnected from each other that they were no longer even interested in sex. Although Joe couldn't admit it himself, it was actually exciting to break up with Pamela. By 2014, Joe thought of her as nothing more than an annoying ball and chain around his neck.

Loraine was much more difficult to leave, even though she was not Joe's wife. Joe had never loved a woman the way he had been so obsessively in love with Loraine. From the day he met her, Joe felt intuitively that she was his one true soulmate, the one woman he was actually desperate to spend the rest of his life with. Like his mother Claire, Joe felt lucky to be loved by Loraine. It was as though he was in a relationship with someone who was superior to him, in (almost) every way.

Loraine was beautiful, charming, interesting, intelligent, creative, courageous, funny and a great flirt. She could be warm and nurturing in ways that Pamela was not. She was even artistic and creative in ways Joe was not. But Loraine was also cruel and Joe knew he could no longer tolerate a relationship with someone who was persistently cruel. It no longer mattered how much Joe loved spending time with Loraine when she wasn't angry. It didn't matter how fantastic so many of her other qualities were. She had crossed a line.

While in bed, Joe tugged at Loraine's shoulder, gently giving her time to wake up. He went downstairs and made her a coffee with some toast and marmite and quickly brought the food back to Loraine on a small green plate. As she began to talk and move slowly, it didn't seem as though she was still angry with Joe. Like any morning where Loraine would wake up next to him in their bed, she slowly ate the food Joe had prepared for her, smiling as though they hadn't been at each other's throats, the night before. If anything, her demeanour was one of quiet appreciation for Joe.

Joe, on the other hand, was anxious, waiting for Loraine to fully wake up, so he could finally explain why her behaviour was absolutely unacceptable. He was nervous, but he also felt a strong resolve within himself.

Joe was going to be as kind as he could, yet as firm as he needed to be, when explaining to Loraine why their relationship was conclusively over. Joe expected Loraine to be manipulative, doing everything she could to convince Joe she could change and that their relationship could still work, if they both gave it their best. But Joe wasn't about to show any weakness. He was determined to be strong in all the ways he couldn't be, in his silly, stupid dream.

Joe wanted to be a man and act forcefully, without sentimentality.

That meant if Joe had to be cruel to Loraine, he would be cruel. If he had to make her hate him, he would gladly do that, if it meant making sure she stayed far away from him.

After Loraine finished her toast and drank nearly all of her coffee, she stared into Joe's face with a sad look on her face.

Loraine: (sighing) We need to talk about last night.

Joe: We do.

Loraine: I need to apologise to you.

Joe: Okay.

Loraine: (speaking hesitantly) It's pretty obvious I've been having a lot of difficulty controlling my anger.

Joe: (sternly) You have.

Loraine: It's destroying our relationship and I have to take responsibility for that. It's not you that's the problem. It's me.

Joe: (with a disappointed expression) I just don't understand why you feel the need to be so horrible all the time. It's not like you.

Loraine: I know it isn't. There's no excuse for it, really.

Joe: I mean, I'm your partner. I love you. I'm the person you make love to, when you're horny.

Loraine: Joe, I didn't mean what I said about your tummy. That was just anger coming out. It really wasn't me; you know I'm attracted to you. You must know that. I wouldn't be with you if I didn't think you were handsome.

Joe: (sighing) ...I know. You just hurt me so much, I–

Loraine: (interrupting) I'm working on my anger with my therapist. I need you to trust me about that.

Joe: Of course, I trust you, Loraine. It's just that–

Loraine: (interrupting) My therapy has been a healing process for me, Joe. Doctor Adams has been fab, honestly. Very empathetic, very perceptive.

I've never had a therapist this good.

Joe: I know and I think it's wonderful that you can confront so many of your demons in these sessions. That's what I always hoped would happen.

Loraine: I can manage them because of her. It's like my mind is a tangled ball of string she helps me unravel.

Joe: Everyone has things in their head they need to untangle. And it's not often you find the right therapist for that. They're all so different.

Loraine: I think everyone would probably benefit from some therapy. You just need to find a good therapist and they are fucking rare.

Joe: You're more right than you know, Loraine.

Loraine: Of course I am. You could do with some therapy as well.

Joe: You don't have to remind me. I'm struggling really bad lately.

Loraine: Joe, there are so many ways you could totally blossom if you were less driven by fear and self-loathing. It breaks my heart watching you the way you are. It's like you hate yourself.

Joe: It breaks my heart, too.

Loraine: It's like you're leading half a life. You're your own worst enemy. It's not other people, Joe. It's you.

Joe: Maybe, but I don't want to have to put up with verbal abuse. I don't respond well to that, even when I need telling off.

Loraine: You stop yourself from being free. You stifle yourself and then you blame everybody else.

Joe: I only blame you for your problems with anger, Loraine. I don't blame you for my problems.

Loraine: It doesn't matter. You're not well and that's part of why I'm having problems. You need to get help and stop putting things off.

Joe: (sighing) I haven't had therapy in ages.

Loraine: My therapy has been the best thing I've done all year, Joe. Maybe five years.

Joe: Well, I can believe that. It's amazing what a change I've seen in you.

Loraine: I think part of the reason I've struggled so much is I've been in denial. I've been shoving down parts of who I am. That's what I talk about in my sessions.

Joe: I thought you talk about anger.

Loraine: Well, we obviously talk about that as well. It's all related. You can't separate any of these issues from each other.

Joe: Well, I'm glad you're getting help but I've never wanted you to feel like you have to shove anything down. That's awful. I've never wanted you to shove down who you are for me or anyone else.

Loraine: Joe, you know I love you more than the world. I can't stand the idea of confusing you. I just want you comfortable around me.

Joe: I know you do.

Loraine: That's why I sometimes have to hide things.

Joe: Like what?

Loraine: I know I'm not helping you right now. But that's not because of you. None of this is your fault. In some ways, this is more about my anger than it is about you. I know that doesn't make much sense. But you know… I don't always make sense.

Joe: Loraine, if that bothered me, I wouldn't still be here.

Loraine: That's why I'm still here too. I trust you. I've always trusted you.

Joe: Then I need you to trust me enough to be honest with me. I would never take advantage of you. I'm your partner.

Loraine: Joe, these feelings didn't happen because I think you're bad for me. You've been nothing but lovely in every way that I can understand the loveliness of another person.

Joe: Then be lovely and tell me what this is about.

Loraine: This isn't something I've chosen. This is something that's been with me for a while now. I've tried to make it go away; I've tried to conquer it. I've been ashamed of myself for it, but I wake up with it every day, staring me in the face, telling me I'm deceiving myself by not letting you see it.

Joe: Then let me see it.

Loraine: There's nothing that hurts me worse than the idea of losing you, Joe.

Joe: You won't lose me. I just need to know what I'm being kept from seeing.

Loraine: You've been my everything and I know this is crazy. I know you know me inside and out. You know me deeply, in every way, every way except this way.

Joe: You're not transgender, are you?

Loraine: This is so hard to talk about…

Joe: (nervously) I won't stop loving you, if that's what it is you're hiding. I'd never reject you because of who you are! It might be hard getting used to a man's body, but that won't stop me from eventually doing it. I'll work at it until it happens. I'd never reject you, Loraine. I just need you to feel like you can be yourself with me. That's what's important.

Loraine: I know that, but this is a big ask, Joe.

Joe: (adamantly) You would never lose my love over who you are! My love for you transcends anything about your body, anything about how you self-identify, anything about how you want to live. You've got me, no matter what.

Loraine: But you're straight.

Joe: And I'm also not a bigot, Loraine. If I need to learn to how to deal with a cock, I will. I'll even put it in my arse. I'll get some lube.

Loraine: (deeply moved by Joe's devotion) You'd do that for me?

Joe: (adamantly) Of course, I would. You can do anything to me. You can even re-define reality and I'll just accept it. I'll never challenge you, ever again. The most important thing is that you're here with me. I would never do anything to jeopardise that.

Loraine: Would you die for me?

Joe: (passionately) I live for you, Loraine.

Loraine: Have you ever killed anyone?

Joe: You want me to kill someone for you?

Loraine: (excitedly) I do.

Joe: Who?

Loraine: The part of you that's male. The part of you that's strong.

Joe: (laughing) You've already killed that many, many times.

Loraine: (rolling her eyes) But he always comes back. I'm sick of him coming back.

Joe: What do you mean?

Loraine: I know about the dream you had. The one with me and Janet. And Alice and Eve. And Davis.

Joe: (confused) How could you know about that?

Loraine: (shaking her head) I almost had you Joe, I almost had you. But you got strong in the end as always. You lost weight; you stood up to me. You made me change. That wasn't supposed to happen.

Joe: (defensively) You're the one who left me, Loraine. You told me to be with Janet.

Loraine: Well, I won't be doing that again. You passed all my tests.

Joe: How?

Loraine: With love. You're not gonna get anger from me anymore. You're getting love from now on.

Joe: I'd like that, actually.

Loraine: And you're getting praise for being a strong man, as long as you do what I tell you.

Joe: (wistfully) Nobody makes me feel the way you do, Loraine.

Loraine: (tenderly) That's why I'm here, Joe. You created me.

Joe: I did?

Loraine: Don't you remember? You created me to teach you about yourself.

Joe: (confused) Is that all that you are? A teacher?

Loraine: (smiling mischievously) Well, I'm also a role model.

Joe: (shocked) You mean you were Davis? You were Davis McFarlin?

Loraine: (with lust in her eyes) I don't mind being typecast as long as my performance teases you into having all those naughty little feelings your body isn't expecting. If I'm acting, that means my big tongue is acting all over you. And if I'm rimming you, my tongue will be acting like it's over the moon to wiggle up your nasty big bum just to make you fucking cum hard all over the floor. I'm a dancer, Joe. I act by moving my body on stage for a living. All of my body is very limber, especially my tongue.

Joe: (smiling) God, I loved that speech you did. You made me so fucking hard, it was incredible. It was hotter than Davis!

Loraine: (giggling) And don't forget what I did to you afterwards.

Joe: I'll never forget that.

Loraine: You'll never forget me, either.

Joe: (with gratitude) I won't, Loraine… I love you. I love you, whatever you are.

Loraine: I'm you… sort of.

Joe: Why the 'sort of'?

Loraine: Let's just say… I'm how you look at someone you love. I'm all the ways you look at her.

Joe: Who do I love? My mother?

Loraine: You can't stand Jodie. It's your wife that you love.

Joe: But I can't remember either of them.

Loraine: (smiling warmly) You will. Trust me. I won't let you forget either of them.

Joe: (confused again) I remember something vaguely about having a wife… we had a wedding reception at the Firebug. Before Covid. But wasn't I dreaming that? Aren't I supposed to be with you?

Loraine: For the time being, yes. I'm your girlfriend until this dream is over.

Joe: But why am I having this dream?

Loraine: You tell me. I'm you, after all.

Joe: (thinking hard) I think it's because…. I'm anxious about someone I love. I'm worried I won't have kids. I'm worried she's like my mum.

Loraine: And what exactly did you find out about her from this dream? Can you trust her?

Joe: (sighing) …I don't know. Whatever the answer is, I probably won't remember it when I wake up.

Loraine: (nodding) But the answer will be with you. It will be in your subconscious, and you will know it instinctively. That's what's important. You can use it in your relationship.

Joe: And what are you supposed to be, Loraine? What am I supposed to learn from you? Who is this Loraine character?

Loraine: (matter of factly) She's your mum…and feminism…and anti-feminism…and women you've been rejected by. She's your conscience. She's your self-loathing. She's lots of things.

Joe: But why is she so beautiful? Do I hate beautiful women? Am I attracted to my mother?

Loraine: (giggling) You tell me.

Joe: I remember… the last version of Loraine wasn't good for me… I thought she was seductive because she was deceptive. I remember something about… I was supposed to break up with her today. She was verbally abusive. Wasn't I supposed to tell her off?

Loraine: That wasn't Loraine. That was Greg pretending to be Loraine.

Joe: (confused) Who's Greg?

Loraine: You tell me.

Joe: (pausing for a bit) …Are you Loraine? Or is this Greg?

Loraine: I think perhaps it would be easier if you just take things at face value.

Joe: So you're Loraine, then?

Loraine: (in a Californian man's accent) If you'd like. Yeah. Sure. I'll be Loraine.

Joe: Why did your voice change like that?

Loraine: (sounding like an English woman again) Do you believe in God?

Joe: Of course… God is love.

Loraine: Do you mean love is God? Or did you mean that to really love someone you need to believe in them? Is this more about faith than it is about theology?

Joe: (suddenly remembering) Love's power resides in the romance of uncertainty. Yes, that's the line. "Love's power resides in the romance of this uncertainty."

Loraine: (smiling mischievously) Do you remember who wrote that line? Do you remember where it comes from?

Joe: No.

Loraine: Good.

Joe: (vaguely remembering a woman's voice) But…I am… remembering… someone else now. I can hear her laughing at me…. But it's not bullying… it's affectionate. In fact, it's sexy.

Loraine: So where is she then? Where is she for you?

There is an uncomfortable silence for about thirty seconds. Something feels off.

Joe: (thinking hard) I believe… I'm very far away from her… I don't know why… but I feel very far away…

Loraine: Then let's bring you a bit closer, Joe. I think you're too comfortable here with me.

Joe: What's wrong with being comfortable?

Loraine: (matter of factly) If you stay here too long, bad things will happen.

Joe: (suddenly unnerved) Like what?

Loraine: Punishments. Punishments that aren't supposed to happen until you're dead.

Joe: (feeling frightened) Is God upset with me?

Loraine: (reassuringly) It's not important yet. I can protect you from her, for now. Come here.

Loraine puts her hands around Joe's face like she is going to kiss him and then surprises Joe by squeezing his neck as hard as she can. Her eyes turn completely white, glowing like flash bulbs.

Joe is suddenly paralysed, unable to stop Loraine from crushing his throat with her bare hands. He can hear a thousand electronic alarms blasting into his ears, as the bed rumbles violently like an earthquake preceding a volcanic explosion. Joe's eyes are hurting. Explosive lights are flashing on and off, while smoke and ash are spewing into the air. The walls are melting like scrambled TV and the room is bathed in pink neon light.

Joe suddenly has a terrifying thought: Loraine isn't trying to kill him; he is already in hell. Perhaps he raped or killed someone but can't remember who exactly. Maybe being punished without remembering is part of the punishment. Loraine's fingers now feel like hot razor blades and her face has inhuman, insect-like features. She is looking at him with a malevolent, alien grimace which is by far the most terrifying thing he has ever seen.

Joe lets out a piercing scream – his face now covered in sweat and his heart beating like it's about to burst out of his chest.

He can still hear the reverberations of noise. He can still see Loraine's face, even though his eyes are now open and the dream is clearly over. Joe is in his bed and can once again clearly see the ceiling fan above him. But reality still doesn't feel real, the way it normally does.

If anything, the dream Joe awakened from felt as real as anything Joe had ever experienced. In some ways, it felt more real than his waking life, even though he knows rationally that there is no person called 'Loraine Klein', any more than there is a person called 'Davis McFarlin'.

Unfortunately, Joe remembers that there is a Jodie Green, and she happens to be his mother.

Fortunately, Joe also remembers that the woman lying next to him is Janet Waverley.

Like his dream, Jodie is still a porn star who is a tall and beautiful brunette. Unlike Joe's dream, Jodie has never had cancer and Janet has never been diagnosed as a psychopath. However, Joe firmly believes that his mother is an undiagnosed psychopath. Jodie herself would say she is merely an ex-drug addict.

Unlike Joe's dream, Janet has never had sex with Jodie. Unfortunately, Joe has.

Because of this, Joe no longer sees or talks to his mother. However, he still fantasizes about Jodie, after which he normally feels quite a lot of guilt and confusion. Even though Jodie is in her late forties, she is still one of the more attractive women Joe has ever seen.

Janet Waverley, on the other hand, is not stereotypically beautiful.

Joe is quite a handsome man. He looks like a more chiseled version of Marlon Brando in a fifties Kazan film. Joe was a morbidly obese teenager and works hard never to look like that again. Joe became addicted to food shortly after his mother raped him, at the age of fourteen. Over a period of seven years, he gained four stone.

If you asked Joe, he would tell you that being addicted to food was almost as traumatic as being raped. However, Joe managed to lose the weight between the ages of twenty-one and twenty-three, when he decided to start exercising and he became a vegan.

Joe became vegan at the end of his relationship with his first girlfriend, Alice Adler. Alice was always open about her preference for bigger men and broke up with Joe when it became obvious that he was successfully losing a lot of weight. Joe was quite hurt by this, but he also understood that he would have done the same, if Alice suddenly got fat.

Because of Joe's weight loss, his childhood friend Janet Waverley suddenly started flirting with him. This made Joe quite suspicious of Janet, even though he impulsively chose to sleep with her and then quickly became her boyfriend. As a teenager, Joe told Janet numerous times that he had a crush on her. She always rebuked him, citing the fact that there was no physical chemistry from her end.

To this day, Joe worries that if he ever gained weight again, Janet would leave the relationship. Fortunately for Joe, she would not. If Joe ever gained weight, Janet would stay with Joe and bully him until he returned to the weight he is now. Janet has no qualms being verbally abusive.

Janet also has no qualms sleeping with other people. However, she has, until recently, kept this fact to herself.

Last week, Janet confessed to Joe for the first time that she cheated on him. She cheated on him with two blonde strippers Joe would like to have sex with. Their names were Davis and Loraine.

Upon hearing about Janet's infidelity, Joe became violent and smashed up their kitchen. Janet was grateful that Joe didn't punch her. He has been violent with Janet in the past. But these days, Joe is working hard to channel his anger into the destruction of cups, plates, and windows. Janet appreciates that Joe now works so hard to be physically violent with anything in their flat other than her.

As Joe was screaming and throwing plates into their kitchen walls, he was also pretending to be deeply hurt by Janet's infidelity. In actual fact, Joe was enraged because he was jealous of Janet and angry at himself. Joe has always fantasized about having consensual sex with shallow, highly attractive blonde women in the sex industry – women like his mother's many co-stars. But unlike Janet, Joe can never bring himself to be non-monogamous. He's frightened of how sleeping with another woman would make him feel. He worries he would start crying and then humiliate himself. He worries he couldn't get an erection. He worries a shallow blonde woman would laugh at the size of his penis.

Janet is happy with all of this. She likes knowing Joe is monogamous in ways she is not. It makes her feel like she is lucky to be with a man so trustworthy. Janet's last relationship was with a con artist who committed suicide, shortly before Janet first decided to seduce Joe. Because of the things she did in that relationship, Janet is lucky she's not in prison.

Joe and Janet have recently turned thirty. The two of them aren't planning on having any children in the future. Janet has never wanted children, while Joe feels more ambivalent. He could see himself as a very happy father but, on balance, would not want to leave Janet in order to have children with someone else. But Joe also wonders if it's easier for a man to sacrifice children for love than it would be for most women. Joe knows that if he did leave Janet to be with another woman and become a father, he would always compare his new family to Janet. On painful or stressful days, he would miss Janet and resent his new wife and children.

For better or worse, Joe can't imagine himself being happily married to anyone other than Janet. This is less because of love than because of how much he likes Janet.

Joe likes Janet for many reasons: she enjoys football and beer and she's intelligent and witty, not to mention highly creative. Janet is neither conservative or woke, has great taste in movies and has a successful career as a well-respected jazz pianist. Joe doesn't particularly like jazz, but respects that Janet is good at what she does. Much of the time, Joe is quite impressed with her.

It wouldn't be an exaggeration to say that Janet would be Joe's dream woman, if it weren't for the fact that she's not terribly beautiful. But Joe has always been attracted to Janet, more because of her mind than how she looks.

It's also true that Joe finds Janet somewhat cold and calculating. But these very qualities make Janet both sexy and endlessly fascinating to Joe. He never gets bored of Janet while she never seems to get bored with him.

Janet is enough like Joe's dream woman to keep him interested, no matter how much she also frustrates and hurts him. Janet, on the other hand, is rarely frustrated or hurt by Joe. She thinks Joe is very sexy, a good conversationalist and someone who is very supportive of her. Joe's explosive anger is partly why Janet thinks Joe is very sexy.

Joe and Janet have been married for a little over one year. They first met each other when they were children, in the autumn of 1999. Joe and Janet were both born and raised in Leicester, but now live in a tiny, one bedroom flat in Bethnal Green in London's trendy East End. The two of them live on Janet's income. Joe is currently unemployed, even though he would like to be employed as a professional writer.

Joe has always dreamed of being a writer, but he unfortunately has never written anything.

Joe doesn't write because he's afraid he wouldn't be any good at it. Janet doesn't care whether or not Joe writes, or even earns a living. As long as he mostly does whatever she says, Janet is happy to financially support Joe. Janet only demands that Joe cook and clean for her, pick out movies for the two of them to watch and make sure she has a powerful orgasm, at least every other day.

Although Joe mostly enjoys his role as house husband, film curator and lover, he also feels like a failure.

Janet thinks that if Joe feels like a failure, he has nobody to blame for this but himself. However, Janet tries to be tactful when dealing with her husband's insecurities. She tries to encourage Joe to go out of his comfort zone, even though when he does, he normally has trouble sleeping for the next few days.

Last night, Joe was in a deep sleep, after three days of not sleeping because he had impulsively sent an email to his mother. Joe has not had contact with Jodie Green for over seven years. She has yet to respond to this email and Joe is quite nervous.

It is 6:19am, on the morning of March 7th, 2021. The sun has not yet risen in the UK.

In Leicester, Jodie Green is sleeping soundly in her big soft bed. In London, her son Joe Pastorious is lying in a much smaller bed, screaming.

Janet Waverley lovingly puts her arms around Joe, laughing gently as he gradually comes to the realisation that he has just awakened from a rather epic and terrifying dream. As Joe comes to the realisation that he is safe in Janet's arms, his pounding heartbeat begins to slow down and his breath normalises.

When Joe hasn't slept for a few days, he normally has a long elaborate nightmare he wakes up from, sobbing like a child. Janet is always there to calm him down, reassuring Joe reality is far more comforting and positive than anything in his frequently horrifying nightmares. And then Janet makes Joe laugh, normally by gently taking the piss out of him. Whenever Janet has nightmares, Joe also does this for her.

Janet often dreams that she is being taunted by abstract and quite sadistic demons – demons who gleefully promise she will spend eternity in hell for reasons she cannot understand or do anything about. Janet used to pray to God asking for help, but this only made her dreams even more horrifying. Janet works hard to convince herself that her dreams are psychological, rather than metaphysical. She wants to believe that the demons are manifestations of repressed trauma and guilt. She desperately wants to believe that there is no God, gleefully waiting to torment her, once she is dead.

However, Janet can't know any of this for certain.

Neither Joe nor Janet truly knows that reality is more comforting and positive than their frequently horrifying dreams. Nor do they know that they aren't awaiting terrifying punishments in the afterlife.

As much as they would prefer things to be different, there is always uncertainty with this couple. But there is still trust between them and they work hard at their relationship.

They trust each other, even though each of them occasionally hides something from the other.

Joe is currently hiding something from Janet.

In the email he sent his mother, Joe apologised profusely for kicking her out of his life. Joe also forgave Jodie for raping him, after which he said he would very much like to have sex with her again. Joe described in lurid detail how she had become his most consistent and powerful erotic fantasy. Joe even told his mother he was no longer physically attracted to Janet.

Jodie is delighted by her son's email. She has been thinking hard for the last three days about how exactly she wants to respond.

Jodie isn't merely planning on having sex with Joe. She wants to be in a relationship with him. She's planning on the two of them having a very secret and passionate affair, during which she will satisfy Joe's every desire, slowly turn him against his wife, and eventually get him to leave her.

Joe knows his mother well enough to predict that this is what she will most likely do. Despite his nervousness, Joe is confident that his mother won't be able to turn him against Janet. Yet Joe is also confident he needs to sleep with his mother. Joe is sick of having to visualise his mother's image whenever he and Janet make love. Joe loves Janet, not Jodie. Hence, Joe wants no one other than Janet to be the object of his desires.

Joe loves Janet, even though he is currently dreaming everything that has happened in this book. He is dreaming and remembering while unconscious, breathing on a ventilator at Glenfield Hospital. It is 4:32pm on April, 20th, 2020.

Unlike Joe, Janet is not dreaming. She can see Joe hooked up to his ventilator through the screen of her iPhone.

Janet is at home sobbing loudly as Joe's nurses offer her words of reassurance. She is in a hysterical panic, confronting her biggest fear that Joe may never be conscious again. Janet can't begin to imagine how she will cope with life if she loses her husband to Covid-19. What makes matters worse is Janet must be physically separate from Joe. Before the pandemic, one could be in physical proximity to one's partner, if their partner was near death in a hospital bed. If Joe were near death in a hospital bed, he could also die feeling the warmth of Janet's hand. He could even potentially recover with Janet by his side. Not so, in 2020.

During this moment, Janet wants desperately for her husband to stay alive, even if he can never make a full recovery. A debilitated Joe who needs constant care would still be better than a life in his absence. If Joe were to wake up unable to effectively move or speak, Janet would happily sacrifice her lifestyle and routines, if it meant being able to love and care for Joe. Such a sacrifice wouldn't be self-abasement. Rather, it would be doing what was in Janet's self-interest. Janet's life is meaningful because of her love for Joe.

Caring for an incapacitated Joe would be a challenge. Yet even a Joe that couldn't communicate or talk or have sex would still be giving Janet what she wants from her husband. Janet wants Joe's time on planet earth to be time spent with her – time where she can be intimate with him, solve problems creatively, challenge herself, and grow into the best version of herself she can be.

Joe Pastorious, as has been said many times, is Janet's favourite person. He is her husband, the love of her life, the writer of one great novel, the son of deceased porn star Jodie Green, the bloke who lost a considerable amount of weight before their second relationship, and the man whose eye Janet once stabbed with a cake fork. Joe is also the protagonist of this book.

Janet Waverley is Joe's wife, soulmate, playmate, lover, life partner, and best friend. Janet is all these things, despite being a clinically diagnosed psychopath. Unlike her appearances in Joe's dreams, Janet is not verbally abusive, she's not a jazz pianist, she was never in a relationship with a con artist, she doesn't like football, she doesn't have nightmares, and she doesn't sleep with people other than Joe.

Janet isn't Loraine. She's not Jill or Claire. She's not Eve or Alice. She's not Roey White or Lena Rodriguez. Nor is she anything like Davis McFarlin or Jodie Green.

Janet is beautiful.

She's beautiful, she's screaming, and Joe can hear her voice.

THE END

ACKNOWLEDGEMENTS

Thanks to the following, without whom this book would not have been written in the way it has been written:

All my wonderful family, especially my parents Didi and Harry Scorzo Jr, my grandparents Lucy and Harry Scorzo Sr, the Leybas, the Bertucci family, and my always enthusiastic Soden family in-laws.

Special thanks, in particular, to my brother Steve Scorzo, my stepdaughter Antonia Attwood and my brother in-law Steve Soden, for their help with feedback, cover design and endless discussion. Also, thanks to my mother in-law Jean Soden-Mitchell for her invaluable and constant support, without which this book could not have been written.

Thanks also to my fabulous friend Bradley Tuck for his collaboration and ongoing inspiration.

My influential cousin Nick Gallagher and inspiring friend Renee Elliot, for all of the shared experiences during our formative years (including the trips to Pasadena).

The actors in the Love Before Covid audio play: the immensely talented Sarah Dalzell, Daniel Ashman and Chris Conway.

My friends who read and/or listened to the dialogues, gave feedback and supported the 'Art of Thinking' events, in particular: (in alphabetical order)

Steph Abberley, MariaAnna Anastos, Sarah Bartlett, Paul Butler, William Costello, Rosie Cuckston, Mateus Domingos, Roger Emmanuel, Tom Fenn, Melanie Fraser-Hay, Helene Guldberg, Elizabeth Halden, Evie Haward, Will Horspool, Claire Abigail, Conor Jones, Steven J. Lawrence, Max Levin, Carina Murphy, Josie Parr, Cathi Rae, Zoe Thistlewood, Kraig Thornber, and Christina Urbankova.

Tobias Gould - Business Innovation Fellow, University of Leicester. Thanks for your mentorship.

LCB Depot crew for all their 'Art of Thinking' support and hosting opportunities.

Leicester Secular Hall for arranging my bi-monthly series of talks around diverse topics.

Gray's Coffee Shop and Kitchen and St Martin's Coffee Shop, for the great food and drink.

Philosophy Tutors and mentors Lucinda Voien and Robert Greg Cavin.

Philosophy PHD supervisors Andy Fischer and Neil Sinclair.

Claire Fox, Ella Whelan and Andrew Doyle for their 'Art of Thinking' guest appearances, discussions, general support and inspiration.

The Battle of Ideas team (particularly Geoff Kidder and Alastair Donald).

All of the fellow panelists I have debated over the years.

All of my interesting podcast guests for their insight and wide range of viewpoints.

Ayn Rand Centre UK for their invitations to debate, particularly with Yaron Brook to defend the Welfare State.

All of the published dialogue participants: Boyd Rice, TM Murray, Mark de Clive-Lowe, Karen Straughan, and Joanna Williams.

Louis Cole and Genevieve Artadi (AKA Knower) for their music.

COTO's invaluable intern Louise Roberts, for all her patience, creative advice, proof reading and typesetting.

And to all of you open-minded fellow thinkers.

Last but not least, the most thanks go to Lizzie Soden, my wife and the other half of COTO, for her tireless diligence, hard work, creativity, humour, support, insight, wisdom, proof reading marathons, story-telling technique and for everything she has ever taught me about the nature of love since 2003. This book would be dedicated to her – if it weren't for the fact that she told me not to dedicate it to her.